Mama's
Shoes

Mama's
Shoes

REBECCA D. ELSWICK

abbott press®
A DIVISION OF WRITER'S DIGEST

Mama's Shoes

Abbott Press books may be ordered through booksellers or by contacting:

Abbott Press
1663 Liberty Drive
Bloomington, IN 47403
www.abbottpress.com
Phone: 1-866-697-5310

Because of the dynamic nature of the Internet, any web addresses or links contained in this book may have changed since publication and may no longer be valid. The views expressed in this work are solely those of the author and do not necessarily reflect the views of the publisher, and the publisher hereby disclaims any responsibility for them.

Any people depicted in stock imagery provided by Thinkstock are models, and such images are being used for illustrative purposes only.

Certain stock imagery © Thinkstock.

ISBN: 978-1-4582-0066-2 (sc)
ISBN: 978-1-4582-0065-5 (e)
ISBN: 978-1-4582-0067-9 (hc)

Library of Congress Control Number: 2011916922

Printed in the United States of America

Abbott Press rev. date: 6/25/2012

For Daddy
Frank H. Davis
1924–2009
World War II Veteran

Acknowledgments

I am blessed to be surrounded by the love and support of my families. Without my Appalachian Writing Project family, especially Director Amy Clark, my stories would still be floating around in my head. AWP gave me the encouragement and direction I needed to put pen to paper.

To my Hindman family, I am thankful for the guidance I received at the forks of Troublesome Creek. The talented writers I have had the pleasure to learn from have enriched not only my writing, but also my life.

Thanks to my Grundy High School family, especially Leslie Horne, for being my biggest fan. To Zenobia Raines, my first reader, thank you for always laughing and crying in the right places. To Amanda Blankenship, my bosom friend, thank you for never doubting I could do it.

And to my blood kin, thank you for the love and support you gave me every step of the way. This is for my mama, Gladys Davis, who is the best beautician I've ever known. This is for my children, Katie, Ryan, and Ross. Thank you for being proud of your mama's stories. And to the love of my life—my husband, Hugh—thank you for your unfaltering love and support.

Many thanks to Writer's Digest and Abbott Press for your #Pitch2Win contest that made all of this possible.

"I am no bird; and no net ensnares me; I am a free human being with an independent will."
Charlotte Bronte, *Jane Eyre*

1940
Sylvia

I open the closet door and hang my wedding dress next to the dress I wore to my mama's funeral, and then my daddy's, not two weeks later. Its blue softness slips through my fingers. I count the tiny pearl buttons at the neckline, dyed to match the dress. There are ten. I pick up the box that holds my wedding shoes, my first high heels. I look down at my feet and wiggle my toes encased in saddle oxfords – a school girl's shoes.

I sit on my bed and place the shoebox beside me. My hand rests on the faded log cabin quilt and I remember it on Mama's bed. When she and Daddy died, I put the quilt on my bed, and sleeping under it comforts me. I open the box, lift a shoe out of the tissue paper, and hold it up to a spot of sunlight hovering over the bed. A giggle escapes my lips as I kick off my shoes and slip on my high heels. I sashay out of the room, admiring the *tap, tap, tap* rising off the floorboards.

"Sylvia, do you want to be a young man's slave or an old man's darling?" Gaines Richardson said when he proposed to me. I know everybody thinks he's too old for me and that I'm marrying him because I have no family left. But that's not true. I may just be sixteen, but life in these mountains has brought me up hard and fast. I could get on the bus tomorrow and head to Seattle, Washington and live with Aunt Hat, but I'm going to marry Gaines and live happily ever after—just like a fairy tale.

I am not like the women in Coal Valley, content to live in the hollers and raise a bunch of young'uns until life wears me out and I become old and wrinkled before I'm thirty. And Gaines is not like the men in Coal Valley—he has ambition.

Scratching out a living in the coalmines will not do for Gaines Richardson. Together, we are going to travel across the United States until we reach the ocean. Tonight I will sleep on Rock House Mountain for the last time. Tomorrow, I start my new life.

Summer, 1955

Sassy

Besides me, Mama loved two things best, shoes and bus drivers. Her shoes had to have high heels, and her favorite color was red. The bus drivers had to be handsome, single, and without baggage, and Mama wasn't talking about suitcases. As I recall, she kept her shoes longer than she did her bus drivers.

I guess you could say Mama had a different way of looking at things. She taught me that everything I needed to know about life could be summed up by shoes. "Sassy," she said, "living is just like buying a pair of shoes: if you choose the right ones, they'll take you where you want to go while keeping you comfortable. If you pick the wrong ones, they'll still take you, but every step will hurt."

What Mama didn't take in was that I learned a lot more from the things she done than the things she told me—just like what happened yesterday. It was my last day of sixth grade, and Mama said since school let out at noon, she'd take me out to lunch.

When the last bell rang, I headed over to the beauty shop where Mama worked. I was in high spirits. Summer rolled out before me like a gilded meadow. By the time I said hey to all the ladies in the shop, Mama was ready. I could tell she was in a good mood because she said after lunch, we'd walk over to the Family Shop and get me a pair of sneakers and some shorts since nothing I had from last summer fit.

It was court day, and town was crowded. Mama said the hollers emptied out twice a month when Coal Valley had court because the whole family showed up when one of their own had to go before the judge. She said she never understood why, but I figured it was because our town was so small and there was so little to do that court-watching was free entertainment.

The courthouse was Coal Valley's largest building and would've looked more impressive if it hadn't set flush against the mountainside.

It was made of gray stone and had three stories—four, if you counted the jail in the basement. It did have a tower with a clock that actually lit up at night and chimed with a loud *bong* to announce the hour—that is, when they could keep the pigeons from roosting in it. The last thing in the world I wanted to do was walk by that building on court day with Mama beside me.

Lunch was in full swing when we passed by. Families picnicked under the trees on the courthouse lawn, sitting on a hodgepodge of colorful quilts and blankets. Some feasted on fried chicken and potato salad, while others ate baloney sandwiches and cold biscuits stuffed with sausage or side meat. Old people ate out of mason jars filled with sweet milk and crumbled hunks of cornbread. Young mamas set cross-legged holding nursing babies, discreetly covered with a diaper or receiving blanket draped over them. Toddlers napped on the blankets. Older children chased each other or played with marbles in the dirt. Mama said it looked like a family reunion.

Other court onlookers walked over to get a sandwich at Matney's Drug Store's soda fountain, where me and Mama were headed, or on down to the Valley Diner since those were the only two eating places in town. But like always, there was a knot of men standing around the side door of the courthouse, and we had to walk right past them.

I kept my eyes on my shoes, but I could tell the minute they spotted Mama. The wolf whistles started first; then came the hollering. "Hey, **darling**! How 'bout a date?"

Please, Mama, please don't stop. I held my breath and crossed my fingers behind my back, but it didn't work. Mama slowed, cocked her head to the side like a bird that just spied a worm, and flashed her brightest smile. When the whistles and shouts got louder, she opened her eyes wide in mock surprise and threw up her right hand. I kept my eyes on the ground and wished I could disappear through the cracks in the sidewalk. At least this time she didn't stop to talk. She said she only spoke when she saw somebody she knew, but I suspected it was when she saw a man she thought was good-looking.

After passing the courthouse, we crossed over to Main Street, where the rest of Coal Valley spilled down the banks of the Coal River. Main

Street was nothing more than a long row of buildings stacked side by side, different colors and sizes like the shoeboxes in Mama's closet.

We were nearing the post office when Mama said, "Now, right there is a lesson about life."

I peered down the street and saw Nellie Rife and May Stacy standing in front of the post office doing some serious talking.

"What lesson?"

"Take a good look at them," Mama said, slowing her pace as we got closer. She straightened her back and threw back her shoulders like she did when she was going to say something important. "Look at how they're dressed."

I studied them. Both women wore what Mama called shirt-waisted dresses, a style that featured a button up front, belt at the waist, and full skirt. Mrs. Rife's dress was sky blue, and I could see the buttons straining to contain her generous bosom. Mrs. Stacy's was brown with a white collar and white belt.

"What do you think?" Mama asked.

"That they look nice?"

"Yes, now look at their shoes."

Mrs. Stacy wore sturdy black lace-up shoes like the old ladies wore to the beauty shop, but Mrs. Stacy was about the same age as Mama, who was just thirty. Mrs. Rife was older, and she had on pristine white heels with a little strap around the ankle. I wondered how she kept them so clean with all the coal dirt around here.

"Which one of those women has on lady's shoes?"

"Mrs. Rife's are prettier," I said.

"Yes, they are. But look closer. Both ladies have on their town dresses, but Mrs. Rife has on high heels like a lady should wear."

I stared at Mrs. Rife's shoes, then back at Mrs. Stacy's.

"What do Mrs. Rife's shoes tell me about her?" Without waiting for my answer, Mama continued. "It tells me she cares about more than how she *looks;* she cares about how she *feels.* She knows that when she puts on high heels, she'll stand and walk more graceful. And do you know why?" Mama plowed on. "Because when a woman puts on high heels, she feels like a lady. Mrs. Stacy's shoes will make her clomp like she's wearing horseshoes. You simply cannot feel like a lady in those shoes."

7

Mama smiled at me like she had just explained one of life's biggest mysteries. I looked down at my Mary Janes and wondered what my shoes said about me. But then, I figured the same lesson didn't apply when you were just twelve.

That evening, we carried our packages down the street to the CV Dry Goods Store, where we lived in the upstairs apartment. It was the last store building on Maple before the street gave way to residences— some of the oldest in town, like Doc Sutherland's white two-story that had his office on the first floor.

I looked up at our front room window, then back down at the old red brick building we called home. I could see the coal dust settled in between the bricks. With all the mines in Coal Valley, there was no escaping it. When the wind blew, it stung at your eyes and swirled with the dust on the street. It blackened patches of the river bank, dusted the trees and plants on the hillsides with black, and sank into every crack in the sidewalk. The only time Coal Valley was washed clean of its dullness was when it rained, and then the ditches ran black with it. But the rain always stopped and everything dried, and the coal dust returned with a vengeance. For that little bit of time when everything was clean and the air smelled fresh, Coal Valley was a right pretty place.

With the fan running, our apartment was comfortable in the evenings. I was anxious to get home so I could lie in front of it and read the McCall's magazine Mama bought me at the drug store. Inside its glossy pages were the Betsy McCall paper dolls I collected. I had a shoebox full of them under my bed.

Mama stopped on the sidewalk and turned to me. I already had my hand poised to open the door to our apartment's stairway. She looked at me and then down the street. I followed her gaze. Day was ending in Coal Valley. The sun was slipping behind the mountains that hugged our sleepy little town. People were heading home for supper and an evening of setting on the front porch. I thought today's lesson, prompted by Mrs. Rife and Mrs. Stacy's shoes, was over, but Mama said, "Remember, Sassy, people are just like shoes. They come in all colors, styles, and sizes, and some are worth what they cost and some are not."

I turned around to face her, prepared to listen to more, but she reached behind me, opened the door, and glided up the stairs in her smart high heels. I knew Mama wouldn't be caught hoeing corn in a pair of shoes like Mrs. Stacy wore. I also understood what she had been trying to explain to me: you can always tell a real lady by the shoes she wears—but then, nobody ever accused Mama of being a lady.

Mama was a beauty. Everybody said so. Even her name was beautiful—Sylvia Elizabeth Richardson. All the other girls' mamas had names like Gladys and Ethel, but my mama had a name and a face like a movie star.

I followed Mama upstairs to our apartment. She said it wasn't big enough to whip a cat in, but I liked it. We had a living room—Mama called the front room—just big enough for our old blue couch and chair, two end tables with ugly lamps, and a battered coffee table. The couch had a big red spot on the right arm from where I knocked over a bottle of nail polish when Mama was painting her toenails. She liked to remind me it happened because I was reading a book while I was walking instead of watching where I was going, and I liked to tell her it was too bad I didn't break those ugly lamps Aunt Hat gave her one Christmas.

I swear there were times when I was dusting that I was tempted to knock them over. The bases were made of dark blue glass and looked like upside down flower vases setting on blocks of wood. I could've lived with that if it hadn't been for the shades. They were a dirty gold color and had long fringes, but that wasn't the worst part. Peacocks and roses were painted all over them. I begged Mama to get rid of them, but she said it wasn't a good idea to bite the hand that feeds you.

We kept our apartment as neat as a pin. Every week, we dusted the furniture and swept the floors. I cleaned my room and Mama cleaned hers. Together, we did the bathroom and kitchen. Once a month, Mama scrubbed our old hardwood floors with a broom dipped in a bucket of ammonia and water. When the wood was good and dry, she got down on her knees with a rag and rubbed in a heavy coat of paste wax.

That summer I was twelve, I was convinced I was all grown up and didn't need a baby sitter. Mama wasn't so sure. It took me a whole lot of talking and a good bit of begging, but I finally won the sweet

9

ticket to freedom. Mama was going to let me stay home by myself. It didn't matter that I had to check in at the beauty shop throughout the day. It didn't matter that Mama had everybody on our street watching out for me. What mattered was that the bittersweet taste of childhood was about to be washed down with a chug of responsibility. I couldn't wait.

That first morning of freedom started like all the others, with me setting on the side of the cast iron tub watching Mama get ready for work. Mama stood in front of the big mirror above the sink in her nylons and underclothes. No matter how hot it got, she always wore nylons and a full slip under her uniform. All of her slips were silky and trimmed with lace that lay up against the tops of her breasts, like apple blossoms bursting open in springtime.

Her routine never varied. She washed and moisturized her face, and then opened the cabinet under the sink and took out the shoebox. She handed it to me, and I lifted the lid to reveal her beauty concoctions shimmering like lightening bugs at dark. I handed her the MAX Factor Pan-Stik, Mama's favorite foundation. She placed a dot of it on her forehead, cheeks, and chin; smoothed it over her face and neck; and then rummaged around in the box for the right color of rouge. She turned her head to the side and rubbed a spot of color over her cheekbones, blending toward her ear. Then she leaned over and rubbed the excess on mine. She stepped back and smiled.

"There. Just a little color makes all the difference in the world."

"Mama, when can I wear makeup?"

"When you get older."

"How many *years* older? I'm almost thir*teen!*"

Mama's laugh echoed off the old cast iron tub. "We'll talk about it when you get there. Now, hand me my powder."

When Mama opened the round container and pulled out the puff with its little pink bow, the fragrance filled the bathroom. I inhaled its sweet perfume while she dusted her face. Before putting the puff back and replacing the lid, she brushed it softly over my nose. That scent was my mother and the womanhood I desired.

The last step of her makeup ritual was the lipstick. Mama had about a dozen tubes in various shades of red. After choosing one, she applied a generous coat to her lips and then held out her hand. That meant it was my turn to deliver a scrap of tissue like a nurse handing a scalpel to a surgeon. While she blotted her lipstick, I put all of the make-up back in the box. When Mama was satisfied, she stepped back, took one last critical look in the mirror, and said, "There."

With her makeup finished, it was time to do her hair. Mama brushed it first, and then twisted it up on her head. I held the box of hair pins ready. With her right hand, she fished around in the box while holding her hair in place with her left. When she found a bobby pin, she opened it with her front teeth before sliding it into her hair. When it was all securely pinned, she pulled little tufts of short hair around her face, making what she called spit curls. Mama called this hairstyle a French twist. Now she was ready to slip on her freshly pressed uniform and high heels.

A swift kiss. She was gone. I stood at the front room window and watched her until she crossed the road and disappeared from view. I admired the way she swayed her hips just enough to make her skirt swish above her ankles. Sashaying, Mama called it. She even wore her high heels and carried her work shoes in a brown paper bag. Mama was of the opinion that "a lady does not wear her work shoes to town."

Mama's words were always bouncing around in my head. Just this morning, she said, "Sarah Jane," (she never called me Sarah Jane unless she was serious) "what did I tell you about the stove?"

"Don't touch it."

"That's right. And what did I tell you about the door?"

"Keep it locked."

"That's right. And what did I tell you to do if somebody knocks?"

"Holler, 'Who is it?' and don't open it if I don't know 'em."

"That's right. What do you do if you need anything?"

"Go downstairs to the dry goods store and ask Mr. or Mrs. Ashby."

"That's right. And what time do you come to the shop?"

"11:00, Mama."

"You better."

I looked at the clock on the stove. It said 8:35. I had dreamed of this moment—begged for it—and now it was mine.

I skipped into my room and saw splashes of lemony yellow sun warming the old pink bedspread on my bed. I rubbed my hand across it and thought of how dogs scratched at a slip of sunshine before curling up in it. I sat down and picked up the book *Jane Eyre*. I traced the gilded letters with my fingers, savoring the moment when I would open the book to reveal the world inside. This would be my first summer adventure.

I lay down on the bed and drew my knees up to my waist, keeping my body inside the gift of sunshine. Then I opened the book. I lifted it to my nose and breathed in the scent of its secrets. I thumbed through it, looking at the illustrations. I examined each one, my heart pounding as I got closer and closer to the story.

I closed the book and laid it on my chest. I felt uneasy, like something bad was going to happen. It was about Mama—I knew it. Her scent— make-up, White Shoulders perfume, and cigarettes—drifted through the apartment like a winged spirit. There were signs that I had been trying to put out of my mind—the strange man's voice I heard in the front room when I woke up last night and the way Mama went around humming that Hank Snow song she liked, "I Don't Hurt Anymore." But it was the new pair of high heels she showed me that could mean only one thing—Mama had a new boyfriend.

This was not how I wanted my summer to begin, worrying about Mama. When a new boyfriend came into the picture, it was like she lost her mind or something. I had heard it all before. It would begin with "he's just a friend" and end with "he's a no-good SOB." Somewhere in the middle of all that would be the words, "he's not like the others."

I sighed and opened my book to page one.

Mama may have given birth to me, but the Cut and Curl Beauty Shop gave me life. The perfume of cigarette smoke combined with beauty shop chemicals was the essence of my childhood. At exactly 11:00, I walked in the door and was greeted by a haze of smoke and a chorus of, "Hey, there, Sassy!"

I gave all the ladies a "Hey there!" while I surveyed the six beauty stations. All of them were full of women in various stages of hairstyling. I crossed the room to Mama's station, and the ladies called out questions.

"You enjoying your summer?"

"What book you reading now?"

"You wishing you was back in school?"

I don't think I ever saw Mama's chair empty. She used to laugh at the customers who wanted her saucy auburn hair color. More than once I heard Mama say, "Honey, this color don't come from a bottle."

The shop matriarch, Madge Dawson, stood center stage, barking orders, her helmet of dyed jet black hair teased high and sprayed as stiff as a week-old biscuit.

As soon as my feet were inside the door, she started giving me orders.

"Sassy girl! I need my ashtrays emptied. Know anybody who wants to earn a dime?"

"Yes, ma'am."

"Ruby! Miss Belcher needs her rollers took down." Madge hollered over her shoulder, a cigarette dangling at the corner of her orange mouth. Madge wore Harvest Moon lipstick that matched the dabs of orange rouge on her cheeks.

"Maryetta, check Mrs. Calhoun's dryer." Madge pointed in the direction of Minnie Calhoun, whose face looked like a teakettle about to boil. When Maryetta didn't rush to take care of her customer, Madge turned and glared at her. "Maryetta!"

I stopped emptying ashtrays and watched. The beauticians, Maryetta, Ruby, and Alice, had their heads together, whispering. They had no idea Madge was glowering at them. Since Madge shaved off her eyebrows and drew black half-moons to replace them, she had a perpetual look of surprise, so if it wasn't for the way her mouth stretched out in a grim orange line, you'd never know she was mad.

The whole time this was going on, Madge never stopped rolling Lanta Looney's hair, and Lanta never stopped talking.

"Did I ever tell you the story of how I got my name?" Lanta asked.

Madge made a sound that sounded like *"ump."*

Lanta plowed on. "My poor daddy, God rest his soul, named me and Sister after the city where we was born—Atlanta.

Madge grunted, "Uh-huh." She combed a section of hair straight up, held it with one hand, and reached over Lanta's shoulder for the hair roller she held ready.

Lanta continued, "Now, Mommy said that wouldn't do a'tall. She said he'd already named my sister Georgia, and that ought to be enough. She wanted to name me Alma, after Mamaw."

Madge grunted "Uh-huh" again and twirled Lanta's hair around the roller. She held it in place with one finger and reached over Lanta's shoulder for the little pink stick she was holding up. Magically, that little plastic stick held the roller in place. Madge stared at Maryetta, Ruby, and Alice while her hands flew over Lanta's hair.

Maryetta glanced up, saw Madge, and hopped back to her customer, but Ruby and Alice kept right on gossiping. I figured Mama had it about right when she said that Maryetta had more sense than Ruby and Alice put together.

Then Ruby laughed out loud, and Madge slammed down her comb. She grumbled over Lanta's head. "It's a good thing you and Georgie wasn't born in New York, New York." Then she strode across the room.

I watched Madge tap Ruby on the shoulder and smiled when she and Alice jumped apart like they'd been shot. To everyone else, Madge was a formidable woman, but to me, she was like a cream puff—hard on the outside but soft on the inside.

I finished emptying the ashtrays and waited while Madge put Lanta under the hairdryer. When she marched back to her station, I said, "I'm done, Miss Madge."

"Alright, Miss Sarah Jane. I guess I better pay up." Madge rummaged around in the top drawer of her station until she pulled out a shiny new dime. "I don't reckon you got time to fold towels for me," she said, pointing toward the back room where she stored supplies.

"Sure do," I said, heading for the back room. I parted the white curtains that covered the open doorway and pretended I was stepping inside a hidden chamber. The bottles of beauty shop products shimmered on the shelves. I gazed at them.

Magic.

Today, I pretended I was Cinderella, entering the castle for the dance. I walked past the shelves to the mirror that had a crack in the corner—a giant *z*—so Madge had hung it back here. When I asked her why she didn't just throw it away, she said we were all a little cracked, and if we learned not to look at the cracked parts, we'd do just fine.

I curtsied in front of the mirror like I was looking at Prince Charming and held out my hand. He took it, and we began to dance. He held my hand and twirled me around. While we danced, he told me I was the most beautiful princess in the world.

When the shop closed, Mama and I strolled home. It was just too hot to move any faster than was necessary. The evening sang with the heat it had stored during the day. There weren't even any bugs about, and the clouds in the sky were too lazy to move.

"Mama?" I hesitated, not sure how to ask her what was on my mind.

"Yes, Sassy."

"Why do women like Mrs. Calhoun come to the shop?"

"What do you mean 'like Mrs. Calhoun'?"

I felt my face turning red, but I trudged on. "Well, I guess I mean—old."

"*Old?*" I could hear the smile in Mama's voice.

"Yeah, I ain't—I mean—I'm not being disrespectful or anything, but she kept making Alice comb her bangs different ways until finally, Madge had to go over there and comb them herself. And I swear her hair looked exactly the same as when Alice combed it!"

Mama laughed. "Minnie Calhoun is a woman who's hard to please. She wants her hair done a certain way, and Madge is the only one who can suit her."

"But Mama, why does she act like her hair has to be perfect when the only place she ever goes is to church?"

"Well, I guess you could say that Minnie Calhoun is like a lot of the women around here. They've worked hard all their lives and getting their hair done every now and again is about the only thing they ever do for themselves."

We walked on in silence while I digested this.

Suddenly, Mama laughed. "Why, Sassy, every woman needs a little magic."

I grinned. "Even if she's not young?"

"Especially then."

"Mama? Do you like fixing hair?"

"I surely do."

"Even when you get women like Mrs. Calhoun who complain a lot?"

"Even then."

"What kind of job should I have when I grow up?"

"What kind of job do you want to have?"

"Something with books."

Out of the corner of my eye, I saw Mama smile. "Then you better study hard in school."

Just then, a pick-up truck drove by and stirred up the lazy dust. I didn't recognize the old man driving it, but he held up his hand in greeting just the same. The bed of his truck was full of bushel baskets of corn. We were almost home before Mama spoke again.

"Sassy," she said, "I want to tell you something important."

She looked off into the distance where the old pickup had gone. The dust was settling back on the road like a hen on her nest.

Mama said, "When you walk down the road with a man, don't always let him carry the torch so you can see. You got to know how to carry that torch too, because someday, you might want to find your way back alone."

And Mama knew better than anyone what it felt like to find her way back alone.

Mama only had one picture of my daddy. It rested alone on her bedside table in a plain silver frame that was always polished. He was wearing his Army dress uniform and holding me up for the camera, my face a solemn contrast to his big smile. I wasn't crying, but I wasn't far from it.

"You know, that picture was taken the day we started calling you Sassy," Mama said, her voice slipping over my shoulder like a cool breeze.

I wheeled around, clutching Daddy's picture to my chest. "You scared the daylights out of me!"

Mama smiled and took Daddy's picture from my hand. She wiped imaginary dust off of it with the heel of her hand. "You were fussing for your bottle, but nothing would do your Daddy but to get your picture taken." Still holding the picture, she put one hand on her hip and said in a sing-song voice, "'Now listen here, you sassy girl, we'll have none of that.' From that day on, we called you Sassy."

"Mama, why weren't you in the picture?"

"Because I was the one helping Mr. Goins take your picture. I remember waving my arms and talking a blue streak, trying to get you to stop fussing long enough for him to take it."

"But couldn't my daddy have done that too so you could take a picture with me?"

Mama frowned. "Law, Sassy, what a peculiar question." She set Daddy's picture back on the table and started to walk off.

Shoot, I messed up again! Every time I tried to get Mama to talk about Daddy, I said something stupid, and she'd quit talking. But this time, she turned back like she'd heard my thoughts. She even stroked my cheek with the back of her hand while she talked. "Sassy, your daddy loved me, and I loved him. It never mattered that he was ten years older than me. We had something special."

Her voice trailed off, and I held my breath as her face gently transformed like the sky at dawn. Mama picked up the picture and studied it. "Your daddy was the only man who ever made me feel like a real lady. I loved him, but I didn't love him then like I do now."

I watched Mama pore over Daddy's picture. All I knew about love came from the books I read, but somehow I sensed the love my mama and daddy shared was rare. I had heard Mama and Madge talk about the women of Coal Valley who lived hard lives. They had spoken of women who married men they didn't love because they needed someone to take care of them—or worse, because it was expected of them. Madge said some women "jumped from the frying pan into the fire" when they ran off and married to get away from a daddy who drank and beat on them and then ended up with a husband who was just as bad or worse.

"Mama, tell me about Daddy. Please."

Mama sat down and slipped off her shoes, still holding his picture. She patted the bed next to her. She waited for me to sit down before she continued. "You know, I was only sixteen when we married, and World War II was fixing to start—even if we didn't know it." She paused, set the picture back on the nightstand, and looked off into the past.

My heart raced. Maybe just this once, she would tell me something about my daddy—something real I could hold on to and take out in the middle of the night when I couldn't sleep and study it.

Mama drew herself up and threw back her shoulders. She said, "Your daddy was born and raised in Pinewood, Kentucky. His daddy died when he was seventeen, leaving him on his own. His Mama ran off when he was little, and he didn't even remember her. I don't think he even knew what she looked like. He had some people on his daddy's side living in Pinewood, but he never said much about them. He came to Coal Valley looking for work in the mines. After working underground awhile, he quit and went to work for the Black and White Transit Bus Company when they started running buses here."

"And that's how you met?"

"Yes." She smiled and set Daddy's picture back on the bedside table. She took a strand of my hair, letting it slide between her first two fingers and thumb. "You know that part. We met when I started riding the bus to Pinewood Beauty School."

"Why were you going to beauty school?"

"My mama and daddy were getting old, and I knowed I had to do something so I could take care of myself. The last thing I wanted was to marry some coal miner and move up in a holler and have a bunch of young'uns. I wanted more out of life. You see, that's one of the things that attracted me to your daddy. He was a dreamer, like me."

She cupped my chin in her hand. "Did I ever tell you he sang to me?"

"He did?"

"When I rode your daddy's bus, I used to get sick on those curvy roads, so he always reserved the front seat—right behind him—for me. When I started feeling sick, he would sing to me, and it took my mind off of it."

"Could he sing good?"

Mama took a deep breath and let it out with a soft *puff* sound. She closed her eyes. "Your daddy had a deep, bottomless voice that could charm a snake. When he sang, his blue eyes would turn the deep sapphire of a songbird." She opened her eyes and tilted my chin up so she could look in my eyes. "Lord, Sassy, I see so much of your daddy in you."

"But I thought Madge said I look just like you."

Mama smiled. "There's more ways a person can favor another than just looks."

She took my hand and traced over it with her index finger. She turned it over and studied my palm like she was fixing to tell my fortune. "Besides, you may not look like him in the face, but you have his hands.

"I do?"

"You surely do."

She turned my hand back over and brushed her hand over mine, lingering at my fingers. I looked down at her hand; the nails were long, rounded, and polished a dark red—a sharp contrast to my short, stubby nails.

Mama said, "You have your daddy's long, slender fingers. His hands didn't look like a working man's hands. They looked like he ought to be playing the fiddle or painting pictures."

20

I was afraid to move or speak and break the spell, so I sat still and waited. Mama was still holding my hand when she said the thing that made my daddy real to me. No longer would he be a shadow in a silver frame.

Mama said, "Sassy, you are just like your daddy—a thinker. He always had his face stuck in a book, just like you. Lord, that man loved to read ever bit as much as you do."

My heart was pounding so hard, I knew Mama could hear it. I never knew my daddy loved to sing, or that I had his hands, but books—my daddy loved books. I asked, "What kind of books did he read?"

"All kinds. I guess his favorite was history stories. He liked to read about the Civil War and the Indian Wars. And people. I used to kid him that he was only interested in reading about dead people. He used to stop the bus at the library in Pinewood and tote in a load of books and come out carrying another load. He was all the time telling me stuff that had happened a long time ago."

"Like what?"

Mama slipped on her high heels, signaling that our conversation was over. She walked to the door, but stopped at the threshold. With her back to me, she said, "I suspect he knew a good bit more than I ever will."

Then she turned back around and leaned against the door facing like she needed it to hold her up. She said, "Sassy, do you know how many times you find a pair of shoes that are perfect in every way? They are the right color and style. They fit like kid gloves. They can last for as long as you want to wear them and can take you wherever you want to go. Now just how many times do you think you'll find that?"

I stayed quiet, knowing I wasn't supposed to answer and that Mama wasn't talking about shoes.

She stood up straight and put one hand on the door facing and one hand on her hip. She said, "If you're damn lucky, once. Once in your life."

She paused and dropped her voice so low I had to hold my breath to hear her.

"I used to think I could have anything I wanted just because I wanted it. Then I lost your daddy. It was hard, but for a while, I still believed in second chances." She broke off and dropped her head. "Then I learned there are people like me who don't get second chances."

She looked up and registered the shock on my face. She smiled but her lips trembled. "Sassy," she said, "we've done alright for ourselves, haven't we?"

I nodded.

"We got a roof over our heads, plenty to eat, and a dollar in our pocket. That's a whole lot more than some people's got."

Then she was gone. I took one last look at Daddy's picture before going to my room. My thoughts swirled around, making me dizzy. I lay back on the bed and held my hands up to the afternoon light hovering over my bed. I stared at them like I had never seen my hands before— hands like Daddy. Mama had just told me more about my daddy than she ever had before.

I had much to think about. I lowered my hands and sat up. Mama hadn't just talked about Daddy; she'd talked about herself. And that was something she never did. I wanted to think over all the things I learned about my Daddy, but her words, *people like me don't get second chances,* kept whispering in my ear.

"Do you know what today is?" Mama asked, stepping into her uniform and sliding her arms in the sleeves. I could see the shimmer of talcum powder between her breasts. Mama said it helped her to stay cool. I watched the tiny rosebuds that bordered the top of her slip disappear as she buttoned up the front of her uniform.

She walked by me, and I caught a whiff of starch. On Saturdays, after Mama did the laundry, she got out the blue box of Argo starch and poured some in her starch pot, added water, and put it on the stove. After it boiled, she let it cool a few minutes, dipped her freshly washed uniforms in it, and wrung them out in the sink. She hung them up to dry on the clothesline she strung in the bathroom.

On Monday nights, she drug out the ironing board and iron. I got the empty pop bottle and filled it with water, fitting the mushroom-shaped sprinkler on top. I'd learned to push the cork-end securely on the bottle top, so it didn't come off and pour water all over the clothes.

When everything was ready, Mama would spread out her beautician's uniform, let me sprinkle water on it, and start ironing. I watched the iron glide forward over the crumpled material, the smell of hot starch rising off it and burning my nose. Then Mama pulled the iron back and a path of smooth, wrinkle-free cloth appeared. To me, there was nothing in the world like that smell of clean—like a brand new snowfall.

"I *said,* do you know what today is?" Mama stared at me with her hands on her hips. "Looks to me like somebody needs to go back to bed."

"Sorry. It's Friday, ain't it?"

"Yes, it's Friday, and don't say ain't."

"Sorry, Mama."

"What I was asking is," Mama continued, smoothing down her skirt and slipping on her high heels, "do you know who's coming one week from today?"

I yawned and looked up at Mama. She had her eyes fixed on me. I was still rubbing sleep from my eyes, having read far into the night finishing *Jane Eyre*. I felt her gaze roll over me like a black cloud. Not only was I suddenly awake, I was wide awake. I said, "Aunt Hat."

My great-aunt, Hattie Mae Mason, turned our world upside down every summer when she came to visit. Only this summer was different. I felt like a grown-up, getting to stay home by myself, and what was Aunt Hat going to say about it? If there was one thing you could bet your last nickel on, it was that Aunt Hat had an opinion about everything, and she didn't hesitate to voice it.

With only three days left before Aunt Hat's arrival, Mama and I sat in the kitchen, eating fried baloney and tomato sandwiches and enjoying a cool breeze wafting through the window. A sudden storm had passed through, settling the coal dust. On the radio, Tennessee Ernie Ford sang *Sixteen Tons*.

"Mama," I said, "maybe Aunt Hat won't come this summer."

"Uh-huh. You dreaming with your eyes open again?"

"Well, maybe she won't stay so long this time."

Mama got up from the table and opened the refrigerator. She took out a bottle of Pabst beer. She opened it before setting back down at the table. She took a sip and studied me for a moment.

"Sassy, let me explain something to you. We're all the family Aunt Hat's got. This visit is the best part of her year."

Mama took a long drink of beer and set the bottle down on the table. She threw back her head and laughed. "That don't mean we have to like it."

Surprised, I looked up and crashed into her beauty. I smiled. "Well, then, what does it mean?"

Mama picked up her beer. "It just means we have to understand it."

"But Aunt Hat acts like she don't even like us."

"It's not that, Sassy; it's more like she don't understand us. People like Aunt Hat don't understand people who don't think like them."

I tried to comprehend this, but all I could see in my mind was Aunt Hat's sour face. "Do you understand her?" I asked.

"God knows, I try."

The only blessing of the situation was that the size of our apartment made it impossible for Aunt Hat to stay with us, so she took a room in town at the Coal Valley Hotel, where Mama said she'd hold court. Shelby Compton, who ran the hotel, hated Aunt Hat's visits worse than we did. Every year, she tore the place apart, cleaning and painting just before Aunt Hat's arrival. She swore it was just her yearly cleaning, but Mama and I knew better.

On Friday, June 17, 1955, Aunt Hat came in on the Black and White Transit bus, the last leg of her journey from Seattle, Washington. All that day, I dreaded her arrival worse than a trip to Doc. Doc Sutherland treated my every ailment with a shot of penicillin—and you can guess where he put it. The truth was, I hated going to the bus station. It was a place of sad faces—either the people leaving on the bus or the ones left behind. The ones left behind were the saddest. I could tell Mama didn't like it either. She never went into the waiting room, where there were benches to sit on, but stood outside, smoking one cigarette after another.

The bus finally rolled in the station, belching diesel smoke, a few minutes after 3:00. Mama and I stood there, all dressed up like we were expecting the Queen of England. The hissing of the air brakes signaled that the door was about to open and Aunt Hat was going to appear.

The driver emerged first and held out his hand to help the first passenger. Slowly but surely, Aunt Hat rolled off the steps and onto the pavement. I looked her over. Everything about Aunt Hat was round, even her gold-rimmed glasses. She wore her navy blue traveling dress, a matching hat with a little veil, and white gloves. *All* of Aunt Hat's dresses were the same—ugly. Making them look even more dreadful was the way she always cinched a narrow belt at her waist—only Aunt Hat didn't have a waist, so the belt squeezed her short, plump body into two round halves.

I steeled myself for what was surely to come out of her mouth, and she didn't disappoint me.

"Aunt Hat, it's good to see you," Mama said, briefly hugging her and kissing her cheek.

"Sylvia," Aunt Hat said, moving her head from side-to-side while she strained to see me. "You're looking well."

Cowering behind Mama, I winced at the sound of Aunt Hat's voice—sandpaper rubbing stone. Stepping back, Mama pulled me in front of her. She said, "Sassy, say hello to your Aunt Hattie Mae."

"Hello, Aunt Hat," I mumbled, bracing myself for her embrace and kiss. Abruptly, she pillowed me in her soft bosom. I came up gulping for air, trying to escape her old-person smell—mothballs and Ivory soap. Then she pushed me back and scrutinized me with a look of utter disapproval.

"Sarah Jane, when are you going to grow? You're as scrawny as that chicken they served on the train yesterday. Just look at you. You're the spitting image of your Mama when she was your age, and that's the *God's* truth." Aunt Hat always punctuated her estimation of the truth with *God*.

Aunt Hat started for the bus station to retrieve her luggage with Mama and me trailing behind her. I watched her walk. Her legs were so skinny, they looked like they couldn't possibly support her girth, and her feet, shod in black leather lace-up shoes with pointed toes and little square heels, made her lean forward, so she looked like she was rolling instead of walking. I smiled, because it occurred to me that Aunt Hat looked like a jelly doughnut someone had tied a string around—right down to her crop of powdered sugar curls. Then my smile faded. Aunt Hat's likeness to a doughnut stopped dead when you got to the filling. Nothing was sweet or squishy about Aunt Hat.

It took us the rest of the evening to help Aunt Hat get settled in at the hotel. You could hardly call it a hotel, anyway. The two-story clapboard structure stood at the end of Main Street and housed the Valley Diner on the first floor and the hotel—all three rooms of it—upstairs. Aunt Hat's room was freshly painted, white with dark green trim around the windows and doors. Shelby Compton had handmade the curtains and matching bedspread from green and white dotted Swiss.

"Ugh, I hate green," Mama said in a voice only I could hear.

Boy, did I know that. Mama wouldn't even let me have a pair of green socks, and there was nothing green in our apartment—not even a plant.

A round braided rug covered the pine floors that Shelby had scrubbed with river sand until they were almost white. The old iron bed set dead center in the room, flanked on either side by a small sofa and a chiffarobe. On a table by the window was a radio. Shelby knew Aunt Hat never missed The Grand Ole Opry on WSM Friday and Saturday nights. Next to it set an oversized rocking chair that looked like it had rocked many miles. I wondered what stories it would tell if it could talk.

"How nice your room looks," Mama said, bustling around, helping Aunt Hat unpack. When I say helping, I mean Aunt Hat was sitting in the rocker, directing Mama where to put everything. "Why, what's this?" Mama said. She acted surprised as she pulled a fat package wrapped in tissue paper and tied with string from Aunt Hat's trunk.

"Sarah Jane," Aunt Hat said, pointing to the package. "Help your Mama open that."

The way Mama held the package reminded me of how the preacher gripped his Bible with both hands and held it out to the congregation saying, "Brethren, believe the Word of God."

I tore the paper off, revealing a pair of black and white saddle oxfords, a jumper, four blouses, and two skirts—and one was a beautiful powder blue poodle skirt. On the bottom of the stack were socks, hair ribbons, petticoats, and a shiny red purse.

"Those are for school, Sara Jane. That's what all the girls your age in Seattle are wearing to school."

I ran to Aunt Hat and hugged her.

She chuckled and whispered in my ear, "Look in the left side of my trunk for another package wrapped in brown paper."

I ran back to the trunk and reached my hand under the pile of clothes to find the promised package. I knew the minute I pulled the heavy square out that it could only be one thing—books. I ripped off the paper and in my hands were *Alice in Wonderland, Little Women, My Friend*

Flicka, Anne of Green Gables, Huckleberry Finn, and *Rebecca of Sunnybrook Farm.* I was afraid if I took my eyes off them, they'd vanish.

Mama laughed. "Sassy, aren't you going to thank Aunt Hat?"

All I could do was nod my head.

Mama laughed again. "Sassy?"

Aunt Hat threw up her hand like a stop sign. "She's already thanked me. Now Sylvia, I believe there's a package in there for you."

While Mama opened her package, I sat down on the couch, and one by one, touched the pages of my new books. I couldn't wait to get back to our apartment so I could start reading. Maybe, I thought, Aunt Hat wasn't so bad after all.

Then, before my newfound veneration could take hold, Aunt Hat said, "Sylvia, I thought you could use a decent dress. It's time you stopped dressing like a teenager. You must set an example for Sarah Jane."

I looked up at Mama, who was staring at an ugly green dress. She opened her mouth, closed it, and then looked up at me. I must have been holding my breath, because when she hopped up and planted a swift kiss on Aunt Hat's cheek, a puff of air escaped from my lips.

"Thank you, Aunt Hat," Mama said, as sincere as a preacher.

Aunt Hat couldn't let it go there. She said, "Sarah Jane is a young lady now, and she needs proper guidance."

"Yes, Aunt Hat." Mama stood behind Aunt Hat's chair so she couldn't see Mama wink at me.

What Aunt Hat didn't realize was that Mama had just taught me a valuable lesson—how to deal with hateful, old, know-it-all aunts.

Mama flopped down in a chair. "I swear, Madge, I may as well be living in a dry town! I ain't had a beer since she's been here, and right now, I sure could use one."

Madge grinned and started sweeping up the hair that had accumulated on the floor. Closing time. There was something reassuring about seeing everything put to rights for tomorrow. This particular evening, I had come to the beauty shop to walk with Mama over to the hotel diner. Shelby Compton had chicken and dumplings on the menu, and Mama and me were having supper with Aunt Hat.

Mama groaned. "She ain't even been here a week, and it seems like a month."

"I don't understand why you let her get you in such a tiz. She ain't even been over to your place, has she?" Madge asked.

"No, not yet. But she'll show up just like she always does for her yearly snoop. First, she has to gather enough tittle-tattle from those cackling hens she's setting with. They gather ever afternoon at the diner to eat pie and gossip. Then she'll come at me with her, 'Is this the kind of life you want for your daughter?' talk." Mama swiveled around in her chair and caught a glimpse of me in the mirror. Her startled look told me she'd forgotten I was there. For a second, we froze, eye to eye, and then with a skip, I bounded across the room and into Mama's lap so the chair would start spinning. Laughing helplessly, we finally came to a stop facing the mirror.

Mama gathered my hair in her hands and started fashioning a pony tail. "We better get this hair slicked up before we leave," she said. With one hand, she reached over and plucked a rubber band off her station, and holding it with her teeth, started brushing my hair up toward the crown of my head. "And speaking of slicked up," she said, snapping the rubber band around my hair, "Madge, you get *your* inspection before I do this visit. She's coming in tomorrow morning to get her hair done."

When Mama and I got to the diner, supper time was in full swing. Aunt Hat sat in the back, her table by the rear window. A delicate breeze wafted off Coal River and into the diner, getting lost in the smells of the place—food cooking, coffee perking, and bodies pressed close together. We crossed the crowded room, the old, warped floorboards moving under our feet. I'd been reading *Treasure Island,* and I imagined this was what it felt like walking across the deck of a ship rolling on the ocean. When we reached Aunt Hat, she tilted her face to receive my kiss on her cheek before saying, "Sylvia. You're late."

"Mama had a late customer," I said, surprising myself at how easily the lie slipped out. I looked down at my lap, afraid to catch Mama's eye.

Mama leaned back in her chair and crossed her legs. Aunt Hat cleared her throat and seemed about to speak, but she thought better of it. I thought she was going to give Mama a break until I looked up and saw Shelby Compton coming toward us with her order pad in her hand. The minute she was gone, Aunt Hat lit in on Mama.

"I can't believe I've been here five days and this is the first time you've broke bread with me."

"I've been real busy at the shop."

"Too busy to visit with your only living aunt? You know I'm getting old. I might not be able to travel next summer."

Mama spent the next five minutes trying to tease her out of her bad mood, but all Aunt Hat did was grunt. Giving up, Mama said, "Now Hattie Mae Mason, you know you are as spry as a woman half your age. You'll be traveling as long as you have a mind to."

Lucky for Mama, Shelby appeared with our food. We fell on our plates and concentrated on the business of eating, happy to have something we could all agree on. Too bad it didn't last long. I saw it coming, because me and Aunt Hat faced toward the front of the diner, but Mama had her back to the room, so she had no idea she was about to be bushwhacked.

The diner was shaped like a long hallway, so I saw him come in. He made his way toward the counter, looking for an empty spot.

Unfortunately for Mama, the crowded counter made him keep going toward the rear of the restaurant, and that's when he saw us—or saw Mama. She was sitting sideways in her chair, legs crossed, swinging her foot up and down. She had on her new high heels—white with little bows across the toes. She didn't have to turn around for him to recognize her. I could tell by the smile that flashed across his face, he knew it was her. I could also see this was Mama's new boyfriend.

I tried to warn Mama, but I was frozen. She looked up, saw the panic in my eyes, and glanced over her shoulder just as he made it to our table. His deep bass voice boomed out, "Why, Sylvie, I thought that was you!"

"Hello, John," Mama said, her voice as calm as Coal River in the middle of summer. She gestured toward us. "This is my Aunt Hattie Mae Mason. She's visiting us from Seattle, Washington. And this is my daughter, Sarah Jane."

John glanced at Aunt Hat, who fixed her sour stare on him. You could see her eyes rake over his bus driver's uniform—a white dress shirt with his name stitched on the breast pocket, black slacks that were shiny from days sitting in the same seat, and a black captain's hat with the words *Black and White Transit* emblazoned across it. At least he had the good sense to take off his hat before speaking to Aunt Hat.

"How do, ma'am," he said.

I held my breath. For a second, I thought he was going to turn around and head back through the diner; instead, he picked up the chair next to Mama and whipped it around. Then he straddled the seat and sat down, laying his arm across the back and smiling like he'd been invited. I had to hand it to Mama—she didn't bat an eye.

"Aunt Hat came in last week on the bus from the train station in Bluefield. She'll be here for another three weeks visiting us," she said.

John nodded. "Well, ma'am, I hope the Black and White Transit Bus Company made your trip a pleasant one."

"Seeing as how you people are the only transportation in and out of these mountains, I suppose it had to do." Aunt Hat glared at him.

A laugh rushed up my throat, but I choked it back. Laughing right now would be like laughing in the middle of church. John stood, flipped the chair back around, and said to Aunt Hat, "Well, ma'am, I hope you have a nice visit."

I noticed that even though his words were for Aunt Hat, his eyes were for Mama. He started to walk away, but thought better of it. He turned back to Mama and, putting his hand on the back of her chair, leaned down and said, "I don't reckon you'll be playing cards Saturday night?"

"No," Mama answered with her eyes on my face.

"Well, next time, then." He tipped his hat to Aunt Hat and made his way back through the diner and out the front door.

No one had taken a bite since John had disappeared. Mama was the first to react. She took a biscuit from the bread basket and started spreading butter on it. I picked up my fork and stabbed a dumpling. Aunt Hat didn't move. She sat looking toward the door where John had just left. The air fairly crackled around us. I closed my eyes to pray, but I didn't know if I should pray for something to happen or for something *not* to happen. I opened them and saw Shelby standing over us with the coffee pot in her hand. "Can I get y'all some pie?"

Mama was right in the middle of one of her lessons about life, and I hadn't seen her worked up like this in a long time. She paced back and forth in our little kitchen, puffing on a cigarette and slinging ashes all over the place. She was supposed to be getting ready for work, and she did have her makeup on and her hair fixed, but she was still running around in her slip. I stared at the red lipstick on the rim of her empty coffee cup and the overflowing ashtray and thought, *It's too early for this.*

"Some things should be kept private," Mama said. "Personal things should not be drug out in the light of day for everybody to see. A *lady* does not talk about personal things like . . . like family."

Growing up in a beauty shop, Mama taught me early on to keep my ears open and my mouth shut. Gossip seemed to migrate to the Cut and Curl Beauty Shop like a flock of stool pigeons coming home to roost. I guess you could say I was brought up on gossip.

Mama stubbed her cigarette out and grabbed another one. When she lit it, I noticed her hands were shaking. She threw her match in the sink and took off again. "There's nothing in this town but a bunch of nosey old biddies that have nothing better to do than stick their noses in everybody's business!"

I stifled a yawn and kept my eyes on the table. Everything in Coal Valley was news, no matter how humdrum. Not only did we know each other, but a good bit of us were also related, and that just made it worse—like being kin was a license to snoop and talk trash about each other. Gossip vined around our family trees, and each person it passed added more poison to it. But God help them if the person being talked about found out. Like Mama.

It happened every summer when Aunt Hat came to visit, because she snooped around, trying to find out what Mama had been up to, and got everybody to talking. But this summer, they really did have something to talk about—Mama had a new boyfriend.

At the shop, Mama acted like nothing bothered her. It was when she got home that she walked the floor and carried on about it. I knew she didn't want me to hear what people were saying about her. I also knew that when she said she didn't give a damn what they said about her, she meant it.

"A lady does not gossip," Mama said. "And a lady does not listen to gossip, because there are three sides to everything: mine, yours, and the truth."

She looked down at her wristwatch and stopped dead in her tracks. "Shit fire! I'm late. Sassy, get me my uniform."

I jumped up and helped her finish dressing. When Mama breezed out the door, I could hear a trail of "how dare hers" all the way down the stairs. I hated to see her upset, but this was just a repeat of what happened every summer when Aunt Hat came to town. No matter what Aunt Hat said or how mad Mama got, it didn't change anything. Mama didn't change her ways—not for Aunt Hat or for anybody.

I didn't want to think about Aunt Hat or Mama. I was wrapped up in my own feelings. The sweet taste of independence was blooming on my tongue like the wild daisies and rosebushes on the hillside next to our apartment. I had my own daily routine that revolved around my passion—books.

This morning, I hurried through the dishes so I could get back to *My Friend Flicka*. I had no more than settled on the couch when I heard somebody coming up the stairs, and I could tell by the steady *thump, thump, thump* that it wasn't Mama. I jumped off the couch and went to stand by the door. I pressed my book to my chest and my ear to the door. The footfalls stopped, and there was a long pause before someone knocked. Following Mama's rules, I yelled out, "Who is it?"

"Sarah Jane, this is Aunt Hat!"

I froze. My heart started pounding.

"Sassy! Open this door! It's your Aunt Hat!"

I unlocked the door, and Aunt Hat pushed past me, huffing and puffing. "I swear. You're slower than fog rising off cow manure."

"Sorry," I mumbled.

Aunt Hat marched over to the couch and plunked down. She parked her enormous pocketbook on the end table, where it overflowed the top and sagged off the sides. She proceeded to reach up her sleeve, extract a lace edged handkerchief, and mop her face.

"Sarah Jane, where are your manners? Can't you offer your poor old aunt a drink of water?"

I ran into the kitchen, dropping my book on the table. When I returned, she was stuffing her handkerchief back up her sleeve. I gave her the water, and she patted the couch next to her.

"Well, stop standing there gawking. Sit down."

I perched on the edge of the couch, knowing without a doubt that Mama didn't know she was here. I also knew why. Aunt Hat wanted to say something she didn't want Mama to hear. I wasn't fooled when she asked me to tell her about the book I was reading like we didn't have anything else to talk about. I decided to play along and launched into a rundown of *My Friend Flicka*. Aunt Hat gave me an encouraging nod now and again until I slowed down like a clock that needed winding.

Aunt Hat turned in her seat so she could fix me in an unwavering glare. "So, what do you do besides sit here and read all day?"

I knew it wasn't really a question. On the contrary, as far as Aunt Hat was concerned, she *knew* what I did. I thought for a minute before replying. I knew it wouldn't matter what I said. It would be the wrong answer, so I took the middle road. I said, "I do lots of things."

"Like what?"

"Well, I do chores and help out at the shop."

"So you hang around that beauty shop."

"Well, no, I—I mean, *yes*. Mama makes me check in with her."

"Thank the good Lord for that!" Aunt Hat crossed her arms and puffed out her chest like a chicken ruffling its feathers. "At least she's keeping up with you."

Anger flashed through me. I raised my chin and looked directly into her eyes. "I am not a baby. I am almost thirteen years old, and I don't need a babysitter!"

Shocked, she stared at me, and for an electric moment, I stared back. I half expected her to box my jaws—or at the very least, give me a tongue lashing. Instead, she clutched her bosom and laughed.

"Well, well, Sarah Jane, you do have the Mason blood running through your veins, and that's the *God's* truth. You are the spitting image of your Mama—*including* her mouth."

I dropped my eyes, took a deep breath, and tried to think of what to do next. I attempted to change the subject. "I wish I did look like Mama."

"Why, you look exactly like your Mama when she was your age. I ought to know—I saw her every day until I left for Seattle."

"How old was Mama when you left?"

"Fourteen going on twenty-one, I reckon. Your Mama always did look and act older than she was. I guess that's why now she thinks she has to make up for it and act like a young'un. I remember when I come back here when my poor dear sister—your granny—died. God rest her soul. I couldn't believe what Sylvia had done to her hair!"

"What did she do?"

"Ruined it. That's what she done. Ruined it with that red hair dye."

Confused, I touched my hair like the secrets of mama's youth were hiding there. "I don't understand. Mama has beautiful auburn hair."

"Lord, Sarah Jane. Your Mama's hair is no more red than mine is. It's dishwater blonde just like yours!"

Dumbfounded, I stared at her. I knew I wasn't supposed to argue with adults, but I couldn't help it. "But Aunt Hat, Mama has *natural* red hair. It's not like my hair at all."

Aunt Hat's laugh hooted like an owl. "Your Mama has dyed her hair since she was sixteen years old, and that's the *God's* truth."

I opened my mouth to argue but nothing came out. How many times had I heard Mama tell her customers that her hair color "don't come from a bottle"? And now here was Aunt Hat telling me that Mama dyed her hair! I tried to speak, but it didn't matter anyway, because Aunt Hat had commenced to talking about school.

My head was spinning. This was supposed to be my perfect summer, and now it was falling apart. I had intended to spend my time reading and getting lost in new worlds. Now Aunt Hat had yanked me back from the McLaughlin's Wyoming ranch in *My Friend Flicka*. One minute, Ken and I were arguing with his father that the beautiful golden colt should be his, and the next, Aunt Hat was telling me things about my mother that I didn't know—that I didn't want to know.

I had to get away from her to digest it; more than that, I had to stop her from telling me anything else. I decided to tell her it was time for me to check in at the beauty shop when her words floated into my consciousness. "You know that you would have every advantage."

"What? What are you talking about?" I was thoroughly confused.

"I'm talking about you going to school in Tacoma, Washington. Haven't you heard a word I've said?"

"But I go to school here. Why would I want to go to school in—where did you say?"

"I said, Sarah Jane, there's a school for young ladies in Tacoma, Washington, which is near Seattle. It would be perfect for you. It offers classes in things like botany, mythology, and European history, and it has a huge library." Aunt Hat stopped and waited for this to sink in.

"But Mama and I live here," I foolishly pointed out.

"Listen to me." Aunt Hat put her hand on top of mine, which were clasped in my lap. "This would still be your home. You'd just be living in Tacoma while you were in school. That's why they call it a boarding school—because you live *there*."

I looked down at Aunt Hat's hand on top of mine and saw a steel strap closing on me. I wanted to run and yell that I would never leave Mama to go to her stupid school. Instead, I sat mute while Aunt Hat stared at me. She let go of my hand and reached for her pocketbook. She dug through it until she pulled out a large, thick envelope. "Here, Sarah Jane, read this. It's about the school. We can talk about it later. Right now, I've got to get down to the beauty shop."

She rose from the couch and laid the envelope on the table. She lumbered to the door and opened it, saying, "Now, come over here, and lock this door behind me."

I obeyed, mumbling good-bye. I listened to her stomping down the stairs before I walked to the kitchen to retrieve my book. I refused to acknowledge the envelope that lay on the table by the couch. Seeking solace in my room, I lay on my bed, staring at the ceiling. *Boarding school,*

I thought, *girls like me don't go to boarding school.* Out loud, I said, "Mama will be so mad when I tell her! She'll . . ."

I jumped from my bed and darted into the living room. I grabbed the envelope, ran back to my room, and slipped it under my mattress. I opened my book and started reading, but I couldn't get back into the story. Just like the fairy tale, *The Princess and the Pea,* I felt the envelope under my mattress, stabbing me in the back. I tossed and turned, trying to get comfortable, but I could still feel it. With a yowl, I jumped up and threw my book on the floor. I knew this was not going to end like the fairy tale, because there was more than a pea under my mattress, and I sure wasn't no princess.

"I done told you I ain't going," said Madge. "You can take my car, but I ain't going."

It was Saturday afternoon, and Madge had just put the "Closed" sign on the door of the shop. Mama was cleaning up around her beauty station, and I was supposed to be in the back room folding towels, but instead I had one wrapped around my head and another one around my shoulders. Last week, Mama and I had seen the movie *Ali Baba and the Forty Thieves,* and I was pretending to be Ali Baba when he finds the cave.

"Open, Sesame!" I said as I flung back the curtains and stepped through the doorway into the shop.

"That better not be one of my clean towels on your head," Madge said.

"No, ma'am," I said, whirling around and jumping back through the curtains.

"I'd go with you," Mama said.

"Uh-huh, but I ain't going with you."

I peeked through the gap in the curtains. This was more interesting than playing Ali Baba; besides, I had a feeling Mama was going to lose this fight. She had tried all day to talk Madge into going with us to take Aunt Hat to the old home place, and Madge hadn't budged.

"Here's my key. The car's out front," Madge said, sliding it across the table.

"Are you really going to make me go by myself?"

"You ain't going by yourself. Sassy's going."

"You know what I mean."

Madge sat down at her station and lit a cigarette. She examined the tip like she'd never seen a cigarette before, then put it between her lips, took a long draw, and blew smoke out her nose. She laid it in the ashtray and then looked at Mama. "Sylvie, just go on and get it over with. You know she ain't going to hush till you take her. Besides, how many years has it been since you been there? And Sassy ain't never been, has she?"

"No, and I ain't been there since I left after Mommy and Daddy died."

I stepped through the curtains and went over to one of the hairdryers. I sat down and looked up to find Madge studying me. Without taking her eyes off my face, she said, "Sylvie, I know I ain't one to talk, but it won't hurt you to tell Sassy about her family."

"Yeah, and sometimes you're better off to leave the dead buried."

An hour later, we picked up Aunt Hat at the hotel. She was dressed in a long-sleeved dress and carried an enormous straw hat with a veil gathered on top of it. "Mosquitoes," she said when she saw me looking at it. This made Mama laugh, and Aunt Hat set her mouth in that grim line that usually meant trouble.

Today marked the end of the second week of Aunt Hat's month-long visit, and Mama and I were secretly celebrating the halfway mark. That eased some of the aggravation Mama felt from having to take her to see the home place. I didn't dare tell Mama I considered this a first-class adventure, but as we followed the road out of town and headed up the mountain toward Little Creek, I couldn't stop smiling.

"It's as hot as the devil's breath!" Aunt Hat said, pulling a Davis Brothers Funeral Home fan out of her gigantic pocketbook. She began fanning her face.

"Well, no wonder! You got enough clothes on to walk through a snowstorm." Mama tried not to laugh but she couldn't help it.

Fanning furiously, Aunt Hat said, "I don't plan to get eat up by bugs."

We drove for a while in silence. The road narrowed and became like a rope of *S's* strung together. Setting in the back of Madge's old Ford, I felt like I was being swirled around in a jug. We were now deep in the woods, and the air sweetened as we climbed. There wasn't a trace of coal dust anywhere. We rounded a bend where the trees were so dense, they formed a green canopy over our heads. Tiny flashes of sunlight danced in front of the car. Mama slowed down.

"Now take the left-hand fork," Aunt Hat said.

"I remember the way."

Ignoring Mama, Aunt Hat launched into a description of the area. "Now, the right-hand fork turns into a old sled road that goes to the top a Rock House Mountain. The Watkins family owned from the fork all the way to the top of the mountain. I reckon they still do. This left-hand fork is called Little Creek, and the Mason family home place is up here a ways."

"What's a sled road?" I asked, sitting up straight and leaning forward so I could see. I glanced over at Mama and was surprised by her stony face. Her eyes focused hard on the windshield, and she frowned like she expected something to come at us any minute.

"Now, a sled road is what loggers used. They cut down the trees, and the men would come with their mules, pulling wagons that had big runners like a sled instead of wheels."

"Why didn't they just use regular wagons?" I asked.

"Because they cut down the trees in the summer time, but they didn't haul them out until late winter or early spring, when the dirt roads were snow-covered—or more likely, ice-covered. They had to get the logs out of the mountains and down to the river so that when the snow melted and the rains came, they could float them down the river."

I watched Aunt Hat while she talked. Her face was flushed, and her hands fluttered up and down as she pointed and talked about the holler. Just then, the road topped out, and a clearing appeared. Nestled inside of it was a little brown log house.

Aunt Hat sat up straight and pointed out the window. "Lord-a-mercy, Mommy's flower bed's still there! Looky!"

Mama pulled off the road, and Aunt Hat jumped out of the car. Mama stretched her right arm across the back of the seat, turned her head, and smiled at me. She said, "She was out of here faster than shit through a goose. I didn't know she could move that fast. Did you?"

I grinned.

"Well, what do you think?"

41

"I think it looks like a storybook place."

"Lord, Sassy, that sounds like something your daddy would've said. The first time he come here, he said he expected the old mountain witch to meet him at the door."

I laughed with Mama as we climbed out of the car. We could see Aunt Hat up ahead, walking around through the weeds in the front of the house. For a while, we just stood, looking around. I didn't know who I should watch, Mama or Aunt Hat. Both of them looked like they'd stepped back through time into a world I couldn't enter. The funny thing was that Aunt Hat looked like she was greeting old friends, and Mama looked like she was seeing ghosts.

We walked up the slight incline to the well that stood just off to the right of the house. Made of creek rocks that had been cemented together, the well was a circular structure about three feet high. The rusted pump set on top like an ornate hat. Mama leaned up against it and lit a cigarette. "Go on and look around," she said. "Just don't wander off too far."

I walked around the house, taking it all in. My Mama was born and raised here by my grandparents, who I'd only seen in my mind's eye. I looked back at Mama in her pink sundress and white high heels. How could she be the same person who had pumped water from that well or slept in that little log house? She leaned against the well, one slim ankle crossed over the other, smoking a cigarette. She made smoking look so elegant and ladylike, I wanted to smoke just so I could look like her. Funny, she'd never said a word to me about smoking or not smoking. Aunt Hat, on the other hand, said smoking caused corruption. But she never said whether it was inside corruption or outside corruption.

Up ahead, Aunt Hat stood, hands on hips, looking at the trees that tiptoed up the mountainside. I made my way over to stand with her under a giant Silver Maple waving its hoary fingers in the evening breeze.

"Ain't this the most beautiful place on God's earth?" Aunt Hat asked. "When I was a little girl—after I done my chores—I'd get my doll, Polly, and head for the woods." Her voice trailed off into the past. "Lord, how I loved that old rag doll."

"What's a rag doll?"

Aunt Hat turned and looked at me. "You don't know nothing about how your Mommy was raised, do you?"

I shrugged. "What's a rag doll?"

Aunt Hat bent and picked up a twig that had three leaves attached. The leaves were still green and looked like they'd just been plucked. I looked up, expecting to see a bare spot where it had been; instead, the bough swayed, full and lush.

Looking down at the leaves, Aunt Hat said, "One Christmas, when I was about five, Mommy took some rags and scraps of material she saved for quilts and sewed me a doll out of them. She used blue buttons for the eyes and a scrap of red yarn for the mouth. She made her dress from the scraps of a feed sack she'd used to make me a dress."

"She made your dress out of a feed sack?"

Aunt Hat laughed. It sounded rusty, like it had been a long time since she used her voice to make that sound. She said, "Mommy made all our dresses and just about everything else from feed sacks. She washed them until the words faded off. They made the prettiest dresses and curtains you ever seen."

She walked on a few steps until she could touch the trunk of the silver maple. The wind picked up, and the leaves danced around like they were trying to hide from the sunlight. "Times was hard. We farmed, had a cow for milk, kept chickens, and Daddy hunted for deer and other game. Even during the depression, we always had food on the table. I was the oldest of nine young'uns, you know."

"Nine!"

"Let's see—there was me and your Granny, Mary Jane, and two other girls, Ruby Jo and Betsy. Betsy only lived a few weeks, and Ruby Jo died of the typhoid when she was three. It took Noah, Jr. too. He was the oldest of five boys—Roy, Willard, Jack, and the baby one, Danny Ray. Roy and Willard went off to the Great War and never come back. They're buried somewhere in France, just like your daddy. Jack and Danny Ray are gone too. They're all gone now—except me."

"Did all of you live in that little house?" I turned around and shaded my eyes so I could see it.

"I reckon so." Aunt Hat dropped the twig and turned around so she could see the house too. "It used to be a lot smaller than it is now.

It started out as a two-room cabin. It weren't till I was about ten that Daddy took the old lean-to on the back of the house and made us two more rooms."

"What's a lean-to?" I tried to picture the little log house smaller than it was already.

"It's a room that Daddy made by adding three walls to the outside wall and putting a roof over it. One wall had a small window, and one had a door so you could get in and out, because you couldn't get into it from inside the house. We used it to store all our canned goods, seed taters, and things like that. My brothers slept in there."

"Wouldn't it be cold in the wintertime?"

Aunt Hat laughed. "It was colder than a well-digger's be-hind! But they'd come in and sleep in the front room by the fireplace when it got too cold for them."

"Can we go in the house?"

"I reckon so, but first let's walk over to where Daddy shoed the horses and mules."

We walked back down the hill and headed to the backyard of the little house. As we walked, the yard sloped downward, and Aunt Hat pointed to where my grandmother had planted her vegetable garden. Aunt Hat said, "Mommy was so proud of her garden patch. She raised some of the prettiest cabbage, squash, and tomatoes you ever seen. Daddy was a right good farmer too. Up on the ridge, he farmed acres of corn, beans, taters, and just about any other vegetable you can name. But even Daddy said when it come to growing things, Mommy had a green thumb."

"A green thumb?"

"It weren't really green. That's just what people say when you have a talent for growing things. And Mommy could coax just about anything from this poor, hard ground—and that's the God's truth."

We stopped in front of a pit in the ground that still held the spirit of hundreds of fires. An open shed stood, looking like it was stitched together with kudzu vines. Aunt Hat said, "My Pappy could shoe a horse better than just about anybody. He'd build a fire in that pit and make the horseshoes by beating the hot iron with a sledge hammer on the anvil that used to stand there." She pointed near the pit. "He shoed his mules and plow horses—and just about everybody else's on this holler."

I looked around at the weeds and vines and tried to see it as it must have been with the early morning dew sprinkled like sugar on the grass. I closed my eyes and saw the mists rising on top of the ridge like steam off hot coffee, and there was my Mama—a girl like me—walking across the yard to the vegetable patch, carrying a big dishpan. She wandered through the rows of vegetables, stopping here and there to pick something. I listened for her girlish laughter, but it didn't come. I opened my eyes and realized that somewhere in this place was a part of Mama that she'd hidden from me. I wondered if she'd hidden it from herself.

Aunt Hat turned and walked toward the house, talking and gesturing all the while. She stopped near the house, got down on her knees, and started pulling weeds. "Now, Mommy loved flowers, and so did your granny," she said, pulling handfuls of weeds and tossing them aside. "Mommy'd dry some of the blooms and save the seeds to trade with the women folk. That's how she got this flowerbed started. Would you looky here!"

I knelt down next to Aunt Hat, and there—disguised by the profusion of weeds—were flowers. "Oh, look," I said and started pulling weeds too, careful not to pull up the flowers.

Aunt Hat's words tumbled over one another like water splashing on rocks. "Over yonder is yarrow, bleeding heart, butterfly weed, milkweed, and a patch of bluestars. I can't believe they're still here! Mary Jane, your granny pampered these flowers, 'cause she knew our Mommy had planted them."

"What was my great-grandmother's name?"

"Pricy Horn Mason. Lord, help me," she said, leaning back on her heels, laughing. "I remember when I was a little girl, Mamaw Mason would set me down between her legs and comb my hair with a fine tooth comb. She'd about pull me bald-headed trying to get the tangles out."

I looked up at Aunt Hat's cap of tight gray curls and tried to imagine my great-grandmother combing her hair.

We pulled weeds side by side, and the flowers emerged like a rainbow sprouting from the ground. We were so engrossed in our work that we didn't hear Mama come up behind us. "Well, well, would you look at you two? What in the Sam Hill are you doing down in the dirt?"

Aunt Hat kept weeding, so I answered, "We're finding all the flowers that are under these weeds. Aunt Hat says my granny and great-grandma planted these a long time ago."

"Is that a fact? Well, when you two get through with your . . ." She hesitated. ". . . walk down memory lane, I'll be in the car."

"Don't you want to go inside the house with us?"

Mama turned her back and started around the house, her voice a bridal train floating behind her. "I don't need to—some things you never forget."

I turned to see Aunt Hat's eyes on me. She waited until Mama was out of earshot before she said, "Your Mama never wanted to live way up here in this holler. When I left to go to Seattle with your Uncle Danny Ray, your granny and papaw moved out of the coal camp and up here to the home place. Your Mama was about your age, and I know it was awful lonesome up here for her. I come back the next summer and stayed with them, and when I left to go back to Seattle, she cried to go with me." She paused and dusted off her hands. "I reckon we found enough flowers to make a fine bouquet to take to the graveyard."

I looked around, puzzled. "Where's the graveyard?"

"At the church on up the holler a little ways."

Together, we started picking flowers, and in no time, we had a big bouquet. I pulled the red ribbon off my ponytail and handed it to Aunt Hat. She tied the flowers together. "Now, that looks right nice." She held out her arm so I could help her up. "I reckon we better get a move on before it gets dark."

We walked around the house to the sagging front porch, where Aunt Hat had left her pocketbook. She dug through it until she found a big, rusty key. After some coaxing, the door creaked open. It took a minute for our eyes to adjust to the dimness. I don't know what I expected to see, but it looked like an ordinary, dusty old building. I stood in front of a window and watched the dust moats pirouette in the sunlight. Aunt Hat's memories echoed alongside her footsteps.

Bit by bit, the scents came to me. Traces of wood smoke, thousands of meals, the sweat of hard work, and the aroma of fresh-turned earth wrapped around me. All those smells were still alive in this house. They were more real to me than any of Aunt Hat's stories about the living that took place here. I carried those smells off the mountain that day and kept them tucked away. I never caught a whiff of fried cabbage that I didn't see that little log house resting up against the mountainside of Little Creek Holler.

When we got to the car, Mama was lounging against the driver's door, smoking a cigarette. She saw the flowers but made no comment. She dropped her cigarette and ground it out with the toe of her high heel. We got in the car, and she backed up and pulled out on the road. Mama drove on up the holler with Aunt Hat pointing out houses and telling me all about who lived there. All of the houses had gardens, and most had barns with cows milling about.

We soon came to a little white church with a sign that said "Little Creek Old Regular Baptist Church." Mama stopped the car but made no move to get out. Aunt Hat glanced over at her but didn't say anything. I hesitated, with my hand on the door handle. Mama said, "Y'all go ahead. I'll be there in a minute."

We could see the graveyard on the hill behind the church. Aunt Hat led me right to the Mason family plots. She showed me the graves of my grandparents, great-grandparents, and several cousins. At my grandmother's grave, she knelt and put the flowers next to the headstone.

"These come from your own flowerbed, Mary Jane. I know you'd be right proud if you could see your granddaughter, Sarah Jane. She helped me pick these for you."

I heard Mama coming up the hill and walked down to meet her. "It's a right nice little graveyard," she said, putting her arm around my shoulder. "Real peaceful."

I nodded my head and leaned into Mama. Together, we walked around, looking at the graves, with Mama commenting every now and again about the people she'd known. We made our way over to my grandparent's graves, and Mama kneeled down and brushed away some leaves. She straightened the flowers, stood, and smiled. "Flowers from Mama's own flowerbed—she'd be so proud. She loved flowers better than anything." Her voice trailed off, and for a second, I thought I saw tears in her eyes. She turned away. "Let's head back to the car. I want to show you something."

When we got back to the church, Mama started around the side of the building and motioned for me to follow. She stopped and pointed. There in the wall, about ten feet apart, were two identical red doors. The puzzled look on my face made Mama laugh. Finally, she said, "You don't know why they have two doors, do you?"

"No, I don't."

"At this church, the women use this door, and that's the *only* door they use, and that's the side of the church they sit on. The men use the other door and sit on the other side of the church."

I looked at Mama like she had lost her mind. "Do you mean they did that back in the old days?"

Mama laughed. "No, Sassy. They still do that today. At least, at this church they do."

I stared at the two doors. *Who in the world would have thought of a thing like that?* I wondered.

"Do you know why they painted the doors red?" Mama said.

"No, I reckon I don't know that either."

"My daddy said that the red doors meant sanctuary for all people—the red stood for the blood of Christ that had been shed for us, so that all who came to him could be saved. He said that anyone—even the worst sinner—was safe as long as they stayed behind those red doors."

"Safe from what?"

"Why, the devil, of course."

I shook my head. "Well, at least that makes sense."

"Be careful what you wish for. You just might get it."

"Aw, Mama!" I felt my face flame. I hadn't heard her come up behind me. I was gazing in the bathroom mirror, my pajama top stretched over my chest, looking for signs that my breasts were finally growing.

"It's too hot for anything to grow," Mama said. "Even boobs."

Mama was right. July had stomped in with the humidity of high summer clinging to its shoes. The cool evenings had disappeared, and the heat of the day lingered far into the night. I dropped my hands but continued to stare at myself in the mirror.

Mama said, "Are you going to stand there primping all day? I got to get ready for work."

"Sorry, Mama." I grabbed her around her slender waist on my way out the door. She surprised me by wrapping her arms around me and hanging on a bit longer than she usually did. I looked up at her face, but she wouldn't make eye contact with me.

"Well," she said. She pulled herself away from me and headed into the bathroom. "Some of us have to go to work around here."

I smiled. Just like that, Mama was back to being Mama. She was a lot of things, but sentimental wasn't one of them. That didn't mean she didn't show me affection—she did—but Mama wasn't one for hugging and kissing, and she sure wasn't one for crying.

I was sitting on the couch, deep in my book, when Mama came in, ready for work. I felt her stare on me, so I looked up. She stood with her hands on her hips, elbows cocked. She smiled. "You forgot what today is, didn't you?"

I had to pull myself back from my favorite book, *Anne of Green Gables,* which I was reading for the third time. The main character, Anne Shirley, had grown up in an orphanage, and every time she was

49

taken in by a family, they ended up sending her back to the orphanage. I knew one of the reasons I loved the book was because I was a half-orphan. After all, I didn't have a daddy. But to be sent away because nobody wanted me—I'd just die!

I smiled up at Mama. I said, "Happy Fourth of July!"

"I thought so. You forgot whose birthday is today."

My smile melted.

Mama laughed. "If you ask me, it's perfect. Aunt Hat is an old firecracker! What better day for her birthday?"

That afternoon, I pulled my hair back into a pony tail and tied a red ribbon around it. I put on my new red and white polka-dot dress with the wide circle-tail and my new white patent leather shoes with the half-inch heels. I set off for the beauty shop feeling like Cinderella going to the ball. When I opened the door, I found Mama and Madge cleaning up. When Madge saw me, she let go a wolf whistle. "Look at you, Sassy! Ain't you as pretty as a doll baby!"

I twirled, letting my skirt whirl around me.

"You're growing up, Sassy," Madge said, looking over at Mama, who just nodded. "Sylvia, give me that broom, and I'll finish up here. Go change your clothes. You two have a party to get to over at the Valley Diner."

Mama and I sashayed in our high heels—well, I *pretended* I was wearing them—over to The Valley Hotel. The streets were crowded, and there was a carnival festiveness in the air. Everybody was waiting for dark, when the fireworks would be shot off on the cliff across the river. The courthouse square was already crowded, and a group of men had gathered with their guitars, mandolins, and banjos. They were setting up on a platform that had been erected yesterday. I recognized Lanta and Georgia Looney's husbands, Millard and Roby, tuning their banjos.

There wasn't a parking place left on the street, and a man was selling watermelons out of the back of his pick-up truck. He was giving a piece to anybody who wanted one. The Methodist Church Ladies Auxiliary was having a bake sale, and the Baptists Women's Mission Union was selling bags of popcorn, peanuts, and cotton candy.

We stopped by the Mic or Mac Market and picked up the birthday cake Mama had ordered for Aunt Hat. I carried a bottle of Evening in Paris perfume wrapped in white tissue paper and tied with a pink bow. In honor of Aunt Hat's birthday, Shelby and Brenda Sue were fixing us a dinner of chicken and dumplings and bringing it up to Aunt Hat's room.

The diner was crowded when we entered. Shelby and Brenda Sue had strung red, white, and blue crepe paper streamers all around, and the ceiling fans made them dance. We made our way through the maze of tables to the back stairs and up to Aunt Hat's room, saying "Happy Fourth!" to everyone we passed. We found Aunt Hat sitting in her rocking chair, listening to the radio. I took a deep breath and used my happy voice. "Happy birthday, Aunt Hat!" I handed her the present.

Mama joined in. "Happy birthday, Aunt Hat!" She planted a swift kiss on her cheek.

"Why, thank you, my dears."

Mama set the cake in the center of the table that held our dinner.

"Sarah Jane, don't you look pretty all gussied up."

I laughed and twirled so my full skirt fanned out around me. Mama laughed and shook her head at me. Aunt Hat looked Mama up and down. "Sylvia, that's a pretty dress," she said. Then before Mama could say "Thank you," she continued, "A bit too tight, isn't it?"

My eyes flew to Mama's face. She looked beautiful in a white dress with red polka dots. A navy scarf tied around her waist completed the holiday look. Her red lipstick and fingernail polished matched the dots on her dress. I was afraid Aunt Hat had hurt her feelings, but she smiled and winked at me.

"Open your present," I said.

Aunt Hat tore the tissue paper off of the box that held her favorite perfume. She looked genuinely pleased. "Why, thank you! This is just what I need. I'm almost out. Now, we better get to the table. Those dumplings is getting cold. Nothing tastes worse than a cold dumpling. Sylvia, would you go down and get us a pitcher of tea? I'm powerful thirsty, and this little glass won't do me."

"Sure, I'll be right back."

The minute Mama was out of the room, Aunt Hat started in on me. "Have you read the information I brought you about the boarding school in Tacoma?"

"Yes, ma'am."

"What do you think?"

I felt the sweat pop out on my forehead. I looked down at my hands and realized I was sitting at the table, even though I couldn't remember doing it. "I . . ."

"Well?"

"I think it's a nice place, but I don't want to go to school there."

"I see." She stared at me like I was some strange bug she'd never seen before but was going to squash anyway. "And why is that?"

I knew she was expecting me to say I didn't want to leave Mama, but that wasn't the reason. The truth was, I was scared. I had never been out of these mountains, and I didn't know if I could leave. I couldn't explain this to Aunt Hat, so I shook my head and refused to look at her. All I could manage was a miserable, "I don't know."

"There's still time. You don't have to decide right now. I'm leaving next week, but you can write me if you change your mind."

Just then, I heard Mama's footsteps on the stairs. "Here's your tea!" Her voice rang out as she stepped into the room. When she set the pitcher on the table, I jumped.

"What's the matter, Sassy girl?"

"Nothing, Mama. I guess I was thinking about eating that cake."

As soon as we got home, I went to bed. Aunt Hat and her stupid boarding school talk had ruined the fireworks for me. Mama had already asked me ten times why I was so quiet. When she felt my forehead and told me to stick out my tongue, I decided to go to my room. I couldn't tell her what was eating away at me—that I was so confused I didn't know what to do. Part of me wanted to stay in Coal Valley, just like I'd told Aunt Hat, but part of me wanted to go to boarding school in Tacoma.

The next morning, I went into the kitchen, expecting to find Mama getting ready for work. Instead, her bedroom door was closed, and the apartment was quiet. The clock in the kitchen said 8:35, and

I knew Mama was usually ready for work by now. Puzzled, I went over and listened at her door. When I didn't hear anything, I decided to make her some coffee. It had just started smelling good when her door opened.

I saw right away that something was wrong. Mama looked like she hadn't slept a bit. Her eyes were all swollen and red, and she kept rubbing her hand through her hair.

"Is that coffee I smell?"

"You okay, Mama? It's almost 9:00."

"Shit fire!" Mama headed for the bathroom, calling over her shoulder, "Fix me a cup, will you, Sassy?"

I took Mama her coffee—black, no cream, two teaspoons of sugar—and stood in the door of the bathroom, watching her put on her makeup. "Are you all right?"

"I'm fine! I just overslept."

"Are you sure you feel okay?"

"I done told you! I just had trouble going to sleep last night. Too much excitement with the fireworks and Aunt Hat."

I watched her twisting her hair on top of her head. "Mama?"

"Hmmm."

"Did you ever go to Seattle with Aunt Hat?"

Mama's hands froze. She lowered them, her hair forgotten, and turned to me. "I took you there for a visit when you were a baby. Why—did Aunt Hat say something?"

"No, I was wondering what it was like there."

"Best I remember, there was a whole lot of rain."

Mama went back to fixing her hair. For a moment, I thought she was going to stop there, but she looked at me in the mirror.

She said, "You know, that I was just sixteen, when in a week's time, first my mama, and then my daddy died from the influenza. I sent Aunt Hat a telegram telling her they'd died, and she set out for here to 'take in her poor, little, motherless niece.'" Mama snorted and reached for her lipstick. "Well, I'm here to tell you, I was having none of it. By the time she got here . . ." Mama capped her lipstick, reached for the tissue I held out to her, and blotted her lipstick. "I'd buried my dead and married your daddy."

I followed Mama to her room, where she grabbed a uniform out of the closet and started putting on her nylons.

"Sassy, put my work shoes in a bag for me."

I went to the kitchen to get a bag, and when I came back, Mama was almost ready. I put her shoes in the bag and handed it to her. Mama pulled on her high heels and looked at me like she was seeing me for the first time. She took a deep breath. "When my mama and daddy died, Gaines Richardson was the first one to come to me. He stood quietly in the background while I said my good-byes, and when it was all over, he looked at me and said, 'Sylvie, do you want to be a young man's slave or an old man's darling?'"

Mama stood with her hand on the doorknob, looking past me to the long-ago. She smiled. "I thought there for a while that Gaines and me had the world by the tail. But the war changed all that." She dropped her hand from the doorknob and put it on my shoulder. With her other hand, she lifted my chin so she could look me in the eye. "Sassy, war is hell on earth. It grabbed your daddy away from me so fast, there were days I couldn't remember what he looked like." Then she was out the door, her heels echoing down the stairs.

I closed the door and leaned against it. Bits and pieces—that's all I ever learned about my daddy, but I did find out something about Mama. Aunt Hat told me Mama had cried to go to Seattle with her, but then she'd got married at sixteen to keep from going there. There was only one thing that could have changed her mind. And that must have been my daddy.

Aunt Hat's annual visit to Coal Valley was duly noted as an important occasion by all the elderly women in town. All summer, she had entertained a steady stream of little old ladies at the hotel diner. Shelby Compton and her sister, Brenda Sue, had a hard time keeping enough pies baked to feed Aunt Hat's company. Just about every afternoon, they met after the lunch crowd for coffee and pie. They showed up wearing their Sunday dresses and white gloves. The smell of Evening in Paris perfume was so strong that it almost drowned out the aroma of Shelby's fresh pies.

I liked to stop by to get a piece of pecan pie. Of course, they stopped talking about people when I got there, but if I sat real still and kept quiet, sometimes they started gossiping again. Since Aunt Hat's visit was almost over and the ladies were used to me being there, I figured that's why they started talking about Madge right in front of me.

I was setting in the corner booth, eating a piece of pecan pie and reading a McCall's magazine, when they got my attention.

"Did you hear," Frieda Mays said, leaning toward the ladies. She wore her long, curly hair swept up on top of her head in what Madge called a beehive hairdo. It looked so heavy, I expected it to slide off her head every time she nodded. Mama said it was no wonder she bobbed her head all the time—with all that hair, it was seven wonders she could hold her head up at all.

She glanced at me and dropped her voice. "Buster Dawson showed up at Madge's door and expected her to let him in?"

"You a lie!" Ida Wade said, spitting coffee all down the front of her dress.

I grabbed my napkin and ducked behind it. Mrs. Wade was famous for her exclamations, but this one caught me off guard. I managed to keep from laughing, even though my eyes smarted something awful.

55

"No, it's true! Mr. Stiltner seen him go by the store late Friday evening," Myrtle Stiltner said.

"Was he drunk?" asked Mrs. Wade.

Mrs. Stiltner snorted. "I'll say! Mr. Stiltner said he was as wobbly as a rooster's socks."

I smiled at the "Mr. Stiltner." Myrtle Stiltner always called her husband *Mr. Stiltner,* even at the grocery store when she was speaking right to him. One time, I overheard Madge tell Mama, "I bet Myrtle calls him Mr. Stiltner in the bedroom."

I asked Mama what Madge meant by that, but she just laughed and told me to forget it—so of course, I've always remembered it.

"I ain't seen Buster Dawson in so long, I don't know if I'd recognize him," said Lanta Looney.

"Sister, there are some people you never forget," Georgia Looney said.

Georgia was Lanta Looney's baby sister. She never called her sister by name, but rather addressed her as Sister, only she pronounced it *sis-tah*. By the same token, Lanta called Georgia Baby Doll, pronounced *babe-dol*. Madge said no wonder they didn't call each other by their given names after what their crazy daddy done. She said it was alright to like a place—even *love* a place—but it was just plain crazy to name your young'uns after it. Besides their names, Lanta and Georgia were known for marrying brothers, and that made their children double first cousins.

"You are so right," Ida Wade said.

"Uh-huh, that's so true," Frieda Mays agreed, her head bobbing up and down like a big boat riding rough waves.

"Mr. Stiltner said he looked a sight," said Myrtle. "Said he was gray-headed and walked all bent over like an old man. You ask me, he never was much to look at anyway." She folded her arms under her bosom, making it rise like a loaf of bread baking in the oven.

"How many years has it been since he last come sneaking back?" Aunt Hat asked.

"It's bound to be going on five," said Mrs. Mays.

"Five, you say?" Mrs. Wade waved her hand, sloshing coffee onto the clean white tablecloth.

"Five or more," said Mrs. Stiltner. As usual, she decided the issue. "You know what happened the last time he showed up."

"Hoooo, boy!" Mrs. Wade fairly shouted. Coffee and pecans spewed from her mouth in all directions. Lanta Looney, who was sitting across from Mrs. Wade, ducked just in time. Mrs. Wade kept talking like nothing happened. "How could we forget? He just about burnt the town down."

The ladies make clucking sounds and shifted in their seats.

Aunt Hat said, "I swear, somebody ought to have locked him up that time instead of just running him off. A bad penny always turns up."

"Did they ever divorce?" asked Mrs. Looney.

I held my breath and waited. I never knew Madge *had* a husband, let alone divorced one. I kept my eyes on my magazine and turned the page like I was engrossed in the story.

"I reckon so," Aunt Hat said. "She ought to of knowed better than to marry a Dawson, and that's the *God's* truth."

Just then, Brenda Sue came out of the kitchen with a fresh pot of coffee, and the conversation turned back to boring stuff like planning the church homecoming at the Old Regular Baptist Church. I finished my milk while they discussed how much chicken to fry. Mrs. Stiltner said they ran out of legs last year, so they ought to do more. "Everybody knows," she said, "chicken's the Baptist bird."

Mama and I stood at the curb, watching the Black and White transit bus roll away with Aunt Hat parked in the front seat. Mama closed her eyes and took a deep breath. She opened them and said, "Smell that, Sarah Jane?"

"What is it?"

"That there is the sweet smell of freedom."

We looked at each other and burst out laughing. After a long month of jumping through Aunt Hat's hoops, she was gone.

"Let's go to the drugstore for lunch," Mama said.

"Home fries!" I jumped up and down. "Let's go!"

As much as I liked to eat at the Valley Diner, the lunch counter at Matney's Drug Store was my favorite place. You could get an ice cold cherry Coke or just about any kind of milkshake you could think of. Sometimes I got a peanut butter milkshake that was so thick I had to eat it with a spoon. They also served sandwiches, hotdogs, hamburgers, and home fries—my favorite.

Mama and I entered Matney's and stood for a moment, letting our eyes adjust to the dimness. I breathed in the music—voices and laughter, food frying, the cash register ringing, and feet shuffling across the old wooden floors—the medley of life in Coal Valley.

Mama led the way to the lunch counter, throwing out "Hey there" to the crowd. She knew I loved to spin around on the stools, so she found us two side by side. The once red seats were faded to a deep rose, with tape covering the holes worn into the padding by thousands of people like us setting on them. We settled in, and I looked into the mirror that covered the wall behind the counter. Reflected in it was a row of booths where people were eating, and beyond that, the aisles that contained remedies for what ails you.

I spun around on my stool while Mama placed our order. When I saw Mavis reach into the bucket of sliced potatoes she kept soaking in cold water, I leaned over the counter and watched her drop a big handful in the hot grease of the deep fryer. I peered into the grease well at the basket of potatoes sizzling in the hot grease and watched them turn golden brown. When Mavis handed me a plate, I took the red squirt bottle of catsup and lathered my fries. Mama laughed and helped herself to one. I smiled at her, realizing I hadn't heard that carefree laugh since Aunt Hat rolled into town.

When Mavis brought Mama her ham salad sandwich, Mama said, "Mavis, I believe these two hungry ladies would like chocolate milkshakes."

"Coming right up."

I spun around on my stool, and Mama laughed again. *Yep,* I thought, *our lives are definitely back on track.* Through the crowd, I spied John, the bus driver, coming toward us. The last time I seen him was at the diner the night Aunt Hat insulted the Black and White Transit Co. He sat down on the empty stool next to Mama, and in no time, they were talking and laughing while we finished our lunch and polished off our milkshakes.

He walked out of the drugstore with us, and I saw him lean down and whisper something in Mama's ear. She laughed and told him good-bye. We walked in the opposite direction to the beauty shop.

I blurted out, "Mama, is John your boyfriend?"

She laughed. "Lord, no! We're just going to play cards with some people Saturday night."

We walked on. Mama swung her purse back and forth and hummed a song we heard on the radio last night, "That's All Right, Mama," by Elvis Presley. We'd almost reached the door to the shop when I said, "It's okay, you know. To have a boyfriend, I mean."

Mama turned to me and smiled. "I reckon you really are growing up."

We entered the shop, and the next round of customers soon followed. It was so hot that I just wanted to go home, fill the bathtub with cool water, and sit in it all afternoon reading *Little Women.* I had fallen in love with the March sisters in the book, and even though Amy and I were the same age, it was Jo—fifteen and feisty—who stole my heart. Just like me, she loved to read books, and I couldn't believe she had to be a companion to her Aunt March, who reminded me too much of Aunt Hat. Thanks to Madge, instead of following what the March sisters were up to, I was in the back room, putting up supplies.

I heard Mama say, "I been paroled, Madge! I put her on the bus myself."

Madge laughed. "'Bout time!" she said. "Now you can let that red hair down! When's John coming 'round?"

"Now, Madge. John's just a friend. We like to play cards is all."

Minnie Calhoun decided to chime in. "I don't think there's nothing wrong with playing cards, mind you, but some people think it's a sin—gambling, you know. When I was coming up, me and my sisters would play cards after we did the supper dishes and cleaned up the kitchen. There wasn't nothing else to do on the farm."

There was a chorus of, "*Um-hum,* that's right."

I peeked through the curtains and saw Madge at the shampoo bowl, washing Iris Albans's hair. Mama was taking Mrs. Calhoun's rollers down. I wondered how many times she'd comb Mrs. Calhoun's bangs before they suited her. I stepped out from behind the curtains and said, "I'm done putting up the stuff, Mrs. Madge."

"Good girl!" she hollered over her shoulder. "Now, you empty these ashtrays for me."

"Yes, ma'am." It didn't look like I was going get back to *Little Women* any time soon. Madge had a list of stuff for me to do as long as her arm, so I worked my way around the shop, emptying ashtrays and listening.

When Madge raised Mrs. Albans up out of the shampoo bowl, she commenced to put her two cents in about playing cards. "Now, I don't think there's nothing wrong with playing cards either. The problem is when money and drink get involved."

"Lord, Iris," said Madge. "Any time money and drink get mixed up with *anything,* there's trouble."

"Ain't that the truth," Minnie Calhoun said.

It never failed—when a woman got her hair shampooed, her scalp wasn't the only thing that relaxed. That went double for the women under the hairdryers. The heat and the noise gave them a false sense of privacy. They thought that if they couldn't hear you, you couldn't hear them, so when they tried to talk to the person next to them, they were practically yelling.

Madge handed her box to Iris Albans. All of the beauticians had a box where they kept their hair rollers, bobby pins, and hair clips. As Madge combed and worked her magic, Mrs. Albans handed her the right size curler and bobby pin without Madge even asking for it. Their fluid movements syncopated their conversation until it was like watching a couple dancing who'd been together for years.

I finished emptying the ashtrays, picked up the broom, and started sweeping up hair around Madge's station. I heard Mrs. Albans say, "You know that a game of poker is how Ed Bowman wound up dead."

"Is that a fact?" Madge asked.

I swept a path a little closer to Madge's station. I could tell by the look on her face, this was going to be a good one.

Madge said, "I thought him and Shorty was fighting over Ed's old woman."

"Mavis! Lord, no, she left Ed long before he and Shorty got into it."

I couldn't believe it, but it had to be! They had to be talking about Mavis Bowman, who worked at the lunch counter at Matney's Drug Store.

Madge said, "I knowed she left Ed, but I thought he said he'd kill the man he caught her with—and her too."

"I'm sure he did, but Ed was just blowing up a onion sack." Mrs. Albans paused to polish her big ruby ring on her sleeve. She held it out so she could admire it before she continued. "And Shorty wasn't the only man Mavis was running around with."

"Yeah, that's the truth."

They laughed, and for a moment, I thought their conversation was over. I got the dustpan and started sweeping the pile of hair into it when Mrs. Albans said, "If they hadn't got into shine that night, Ed might still be around."

Madge said, "God knows neither one of them had no sense to begin with, but when they got liquored up, something bad was bound to happen. Daddy said they bought that moonshine off old man Coot Justus. Said he'd run it too fast, and it was a mean batch. Hell, Daddy said Coot didn't make but two kinds of moonshine—the fighting kind and the crying kind."

"Ain't that the truth? Lucille was the one who told me about it."

"Lucille?"

"You know Lucille, Mavis's baby sister. She said that bunch of men was playing poker and drinking shine. Shorty accused Ed of cheating, and Ed pulled a knife on him. The only trouble was, Shorty had a pistol and shot Ed straight through the heart."

Madge shook her head. "It was just like Ed to bring a knife to a gun fight."

I gathered up my broom and dustpan and headed for the trashcan in the back. Madge was putting the hairnet over Mrs. Ablans's rollers, and that meant she was going under the dryer and that would be the end of the story—at least for the moment.

I learned more at that beauty shop about life than anywhere else. My teachers were the mothers, wives, and daughters of coal miners. I watched them labor to carve a home from the mountains as surely as their men toiled to extract coal from underneath them. I listened to them talk about the gardens they raised and the food they preserved. I heard about the chickens, cows, and hogs they kept, and how from them, they made their own feather pillows, butter, and sausage. I saw them come to the beauty shop and get their hair fixed when the mines were working and stay away when they weren't.

That evening, I helped Mama and Madge get the shop ready for the next day. I came out of the back room carrying a stack of towels and found them sitting with their shoes off, smoking cigarettes. "One of these days," I said, stacking the towels in the cabinet under Madge's station, "I'm going to have a big, fancy ring like Mrs. Albans. I watched her rub her ring on her sleeve a hundred times today."

"Lord," Madge said, pausing to take a drag off her cigarette, "that ring ain't nothing but a hunk of glass! Iris Albans ain't got a pot to piss in."

I stared at Madge, her mouth forming a puckered orange ring around her cigarette. I saw Mama was nodding in agreement. "But she lives in that big old house and wears fancy clothes," I argued.

"Sassy, Honey! You got to learn that people ain't always what they look like on the outside."

Mama nodded again.

"What do you mean?"

"I mean," said Madge, tapping her cigarette on the side of the ashtray, "that people like Iris Albans may act like they got money, when really, they are just like the rest of us."

"The rest of us?"

"Yeah, the rest of us—living from day to day." Madge balanced her cigarette on the edge of the ashtray. "Now, at one time, the Albans's had money. That's why she's got that big old house. But take a good look at it. It's just a few steps away from falling down, and all her fine clothes is as old as I am. She goes on about her *style* when the truth is, that's all she's got. Those clothes were her mama's clothes, bought back when they had money. That old house and them old clothes is all her mama and daddy left her when they died."

Madge smiled, and I noticed how the deep lines etched at the corners of her eyes intersected with the dark shadows underneath them.

"Sassy, just remember that we all have things about us that we don't want people to know. And some people, like Iris Albans, live their lives believing they've got people fooled."

I looked at Mama, expecting a comment, but she was looking off into the distance. I said, "You mean that everybody has something to hide, like secrets?"

Madge said, "Maybe not everybody, but most people's got a secret or two. Some just ain't as secret as they want them to be."

August moved in, and the heat cranked up to high. It soon baked Coal Valley to a well done brown. Our little apartment absorbed the day's heat like a bowl of cornbread soaked up buttermilk. Mama bought another fan, but all it did was move the hot air around. The days were punishing enough, but at night, the heat was so heavy it was palpable. I couldn't sleep, so I read far into the night. I often heard Mama up and moving around. She was down in the mouth since John left, saying he was going out west, and the heat just made her feel worse.

Life in Coal Valley slowed down to a crawl. Mama said every customer at the shop wanted an early appointment before it got too hot, and many of them just canceled. The only thing people were talking about was the heat. When I stopped at the post office, Myrtle Stiltner was telling Lanta Looney that Mr. Stiltner said it was dog days, and according to the signs, it was supposed to break soon. She said that people had to watch out during dog days, because "snakes was blind" and "people went crazy." (I decided to ask Mama about that.) As I walked back to the apartment, I looked through the envelopes, and there was one addressed to me from Aunt Hat. Just when I thought things couldn't get any hotter, I was proved wrong.

I sat on my bed, looking at the letter, knowing what it said before I opened it. I slid it under my pillow and went to the kitchen for some water. Mama and I kept a pitcher in the refrigerator. I had just sat down with *Little Women* in front of the fan when I heard someone coming up the stairs. I stood and listened to the footsteps until they stopped. When the knock sounded, I jumped like I wasn't expecting it. I waited until the second knock before calling, "Who is it?"

"Hello? This is Jean Wallace, Assistant Principal at R. F. Harmon Elementary School. Is Mrs. Richardson at home?"

Shocked, I just stood there. A million thoughts—most of them focusing on everything I'd ever done at school that I wasn't supposed to—ran through my head. I put my hand out to unlock the door, but it refused to obey me.

"Hello, Sarah Jane, is that you? It's Mrs. Wallace from school. May I come in?"

I unlocked the door, and there she stood, holding a large, official-looking notebook. I managed a weak, "Hello, Mrs. Wallace."

"How are you, Sarah? May I come in for a minute?"

I stepped back and swept my arm toward the living room. "My mama's still at work."

Mrs. Wallace looked around and smiled when she saw my book lying face-down on the couch. "I see you're reading *Little Women*. How do you like it?"

"I love it!" My enthusiasm momentarily made me forget that the assistant principal of my school was standing in front of me, wanting to speak to my mother.

"It's one of my favorites. Have you read *Little Men* and *Jo's Boys*? Those are also by Louisa May Alcott."

I shook my head.

"Well, if you like *Little Women,* then you should read those too." She paused and shifted her notebook to her other arm. "I guess you're wondering why I'm here."

I nodded.

"Do you remember the standardized test you took before school went out?"

"Yes, ma'am." I finally seemed to find my voice. "Did I do bad on it?"

"Heavens, no!" Mrs. Wallace said. "As a matter of fact, you did very well. That's why I want to talk to your mother."

Relief flooded my face, and I smiled at her. "Would you like to sit down? It's about time for Mama to come home."

"Yes, thank you."

For the next twenty minutes, we talked about books. I couldn't believe that Mrs. Wallace liked the same books I did—*Jane Eyre, Anne of Green Gables,* and *Little Women*. I got so excited when she told me there were more books about Anne Shirley, besides *Green Gables,* that I fairly bounced in my seat. I completely forgot we were waiting for Mama, so I was surprised when Mrs. Wallace said, "I think I hear your mother coming up the stairs."

I jumped up and met Mama at the door. She bent over to kiss my cheek and didn't see Mrs. Wallace until she straightened up. I said, "Mama, this is Mrs. Wallace. She's the assistant principal at my school."

Mrs. Wallace stood and held out her hand. "It's nice to meet you, Mrs. Richardson."

Mama and Mrs. Wallace shook hands. Mama opened her mouth, but nothing came out. She looked from me to Mrs. Wallace.

"I'm sorry to barge in on you like this," Mrs. Wallace said, "but I want to talk to you about a test that Sarah Jane took last spring."

"Oh, this is about a test?"

"Yes, a test she did very well on."

Mama looked at me and smiled. She turned back to Mrs. Wallace. "If you don't mind waiting a few more minutes, I'd like to change clothes."

"Of course."

Mama soon returned in a red sleeveless top and white pedal pushers. She went to the refrigerator, started to reach for a beer, but pulled out three Cokes instead. She got the bottle opener and popped off the tops before handing one to me and offering one to Mrs. Wallace.

She said, "Thank you," and we all set down at the kitchen table. Mrs. Wallace opened her notebook and handed Mama some papers. She explained they were my scores on a standardized test that had been given to all fifth-, sixth-, and seventh-graders last spring. The test measured reading, writing, and mathematical achievement. Mama studied the paper and looked over at me. "This says reading level—college, writing level—college, and mathematics level—high school."

"That's why I'm here. Sarah Jane's scores are, well—incredible for a student who was just finishing the sixth grade."

Mama straightened up in her chair and laid the papers down on the table. "Sassy does love school and is always reading a book."

Mrs. Wallace looked over at me and smiled. "Mrs. Richardson, based on her test scores and her achievement at school, her teachers and I feel that Sarah should skip seventh grade and start high school in the fall."

Stunned, I gasped, and Mama grabbed on to the table edge like it was moving. "What did you say?"

"It's obvious that Sarah—ah, Sassy—wasn't challenged by sixth grade, and she won't be challenged by seventh grade. If she were to go on to the high school, she would have an opportunity to take other classes that might be more challenging."

Mama turned to me. "What do you think about this?"

"I don't know."

"Take some time to talk about it," Mrs. Richardson said. "Just get back to me before school starts. You can reach me at the school if either of you want to talk about this."

We all stood, and Mrs. Wallace shook hands again with Mama. They walked to the door, and since my legs were having trouble holding me up, I sat back down in my chair. I could hear Mama and Mrs. Wallace talking in hushed voices at the door. When the door closed, I looked at Mama. She was grinning from ear to ear.

"Well, don't you just beat all?"

The day the heat finally broke was the day I got the courage to open Aunt Hat's letter. Instead of a long epistle about why I should go to boarding school, there was only a short note and another smaller envelope with my name on it in unfamiliar handwriting.

Sarah Jane,

I have enclosed a letter from Amelia Hall. She is your age and comes often to visit her grandmother, who is a friend of mine. I asked her where she went to school, and she said Tacoma Ladies Academy. I told her I had a niece in Virginia, and I was trying to get her to come here and go to school at the Academy. She said she wanted to write you a letter and tell you all about it. I have enclosed her letter.

Love,

Aunt Hat

My hand trembled as I opened the pink envelope. This was my first letter from anybody but Aunt Hat. It didn't matter that I had no intention of going to that silly old school. I still wanted to know what this Amelia person said about it. I unfolded the pale pink stationary.

Amelia Hall
Orchard Grove Estate
Seattle, Washington
August 5, 1955

Dear Sarah Jane,

My name is Amelia Hall and I am twelve years old. When I come to Seattle to visit my grandmother, I often see your aunt, who is her friend. When she discovered I attended Tacoma Ladies Academy, she told me she was trying to persuade you to go to school there, and asked if I would write and tell you about the school.

Last year was the first time I went to the Academy and I had a wonderful year. The teachers made us work hard but they were very nice, especially Miss Malory the piano teacher. She plays and sings beautifully! The headmistress, Miss Calloway is very strict and wants us to always act like proper ladies! We even have to attend seminars on manners and etiquette.

All of the buildings on campus are big, old stone buildings. I lived in a dormitory called Langley-Simpson Hall and my roommate was Rebecca Anderson. She was from Montana. Our room was very comfortable. We each had a bed, closet, dresser and desk. We had to share a bathroom with the other girls living on our floor. Our hall mistress was Miss Weisman and she checked to make sure we were keeping our rooms tidy.

We ate our meals in the dining hall and had our classes in the academic building. Last year I studied French, Grammar, Literature, Botany, Piano, European History, and Arithmetic. Your aunt said I should tell you about our library because you love to read. Our library is in a building by itself. It has thousands of books and other things like maps and magazines. We are free to borrow as many books as we like.

I hope this tells you what the Academy is like. Please write to me if you have any questions. I have a question for you. I was wondering if everyone down south has two names like you and your aunt? She mentioned that your grandmother's name was Mary Jane, and you and your aunt have two names, so I was just wondering.

Yours Truly,
Amelia

I read the letter over and over, soaking up the words like the dry ground after a good rain. Finally, I folded it and slid it back in the envelope. I reached under my mattress and pulled out the big packet that Aunt Hat had given me about *that* school. I slipped Amelia's letter inside the stack of papers and put it back under my mattress.

All at once, I couldn't breathe. I grabbed my book and fled like the room was on fire. I didn't want to be anywhere near that letter. I had made up my mind—I wasn't going to that stupid school—and now, Amelia's letter made it sound like a place in a fairy tale. I didn't want to imagine this place where they had a building full of books, but I could see it in my mind, and I was there!

I made myself sit down on the living room couch, took a deep breath, and closed my eyes. *I will not think about that Amelia girl and her letter.* I opened my eyes and picked up my book, *Little Women.* After two pages, I realized I couldn't remember one word, so I read them again.

I jumped up and slammed the book shut. It was too hot to read. It was too hot to do anything. I went into the kitchen and looked out the window. Clouds. There were actually clouds gathering in the sky. The air was still hot, but it felt different. I wondered how hot it was in Tacoma. I wondered if Amelia was reading a book right now or looking out the window like me. There was something in the air besides the heat—something electric. I could feel it. Maybe I *was* going to that school. Maybe it would finally rain. Whatever it was, something was going to happen.

At 3:00, I took the list Madge had given me that morning and walked to the Mic or Mac Market. Madge called it the jot-'em-down store, because Mr. Stiltner wrote down what you bought, and you paid the bill later. When I entered the store, Mr. Stiltner was standing behind the counter in his starched white shirt and bow tie. I couldn't believe he was all trussed up, as hot as it was. His bald head gleamed in the overhead lights.

"Hello there, Sassy."

"Hello, Mr. Stiltner."

"Is there something I can help you with?"

"No sir, I just have a few things to pick up for Mrs. Madge."

"If you need any help finding anything, just holler."

I walked down the first aisle, feeling the floor slope down and then up again. The old wooden floors were stained almost black from years of coal dust being ground into the wood. In sharp contrast, the shelves were painted white and gleamed in the overhead light. It didn't take me long to collect the five pounds of coffee, one pound of sugar, two cans of cream, box of saltine crackers, bottle of Jergen's lotion, and jar of Vaseline that Madge wanted. While I waited for Mr. Stiltner to finish writing the ticket, I looked at all the signs he had nailed to the walls. Behind the cash register was a giant bottle of Coca-Cola with the words "Drink Coca-Cola" and a Winston cigarette sign that promised, "Tastes Good." An enormous blue box of Argo Starch and cup of steaming coffee with the words "Maxwell House" were tacked up over the door. I turned around to look at the signs on the wall behind me when I spied Mrs. Stiltner coming out of the back room. I whipped back around to face Mr. Stiltner, hoping she hadn't seen me, but there was no such luck.

"Sassy, what are you up to today?" she said, hurrying up to the front of the store.

"I'm just picking up a few things for Mrs. Madge."

"How are you and your mama making it through this terrible heat?"

"We've been just fine. There's a lot more clouds in the sky today. Maybe it'll rain."

Mrs. Stiltner turned to her husband. "Mr. Stiltner, isn't the heat supposed to break this week?"

"That's right, Myrtle. I wouldn't doubt it if we don't have rain this evening. Dog days is over."

I gathered up the bag of groceries and inched toward the door, with Mrs. Stiltner following right on my heels.

"Do you need some help carrying that?"

"No, ma'am. It's not heavy."

"By the way, Sassy," Mrs. Stiltner said, like she just remembered to ask me something instead of chomping at the bit the minute she saw me. "I was in the dry goods store yesterday, and Mrs. Ashby said Jean Wallace, from the school, had been up to your place."

She paused and narrowed her eyes at me, waiting for a reaction. Out of the corner of my eye, I saw Mr. Stiltner pick up a broom and start sweeping the floor. Without answering, I moved toward the door. Mrs. Stiltner matched me step for step. I had to admit, she didn't give up easy.

She continued, "Mrs. Ashby said Miss Wallace stayed a good while."

"Yes, ma'am."

Mrs. Stiltner folded her arms and pursed her lips like she was sucking on a lemon. Her stance said she wasn't moving until she got

71

out of me what she wanted to know. I kept inching toward the door. When I was able to put my hand on the doorknob, I decided to make a run for it.

Mrs. Stiltner tried one more time. "Well, I hope everything is all right."

"Oh, yes ma'am, just some school stuff." I opened the door and saw that the clouds had gotten thicker and blocked out the ruthless sun. "Oh, look! It's clouded up like it's going to rain. I better go before I get wet. Thank you!"

Before she could reply, I was hurrying down the street for the shop. *Nosey ol' biddy! She's always sticking her big nose into other people's business.* By the time I got to the shop, the wind had picked up. Inside, the place was humming. "Hey there, Sassy!" everyone called as I made my way over to Mama's station.

Mama stamped my cheek with her red lips. "Where you been, Sassy girl?"

"I went to Mic or Mac for Mrs. Madge."

About that time, Madge came out of the back room, carrying an armful of towels. "Sassy! Did you get my groceries?"

I held up the bag.

"Good girl. Can you put those things up in the back and fold the rest of them towels back there?" She strode across the room, yelling at Maryetta, who sat at her station smoking a cigarette. "Mrs. Belcher's dryer's gone off. If you set there, I'm sure her rollers will jump right off her head, and her hair will comb itself!"

Out of the corner of my eye, I saw Maryetta hop up and head for Mrs. Belcher. I smiled and went through the curtains.

I was putting the lotion and Vaseline in the cabinet when it thundered, low and mean. I looked up at the ceiling, expecting to see it shake. I went back to folding the towels and it thundered again, more brutal than before. I heard Madge holler, "Ladies, the devil's beating his wife."

I giggled. I could hear the keyed-up voices of the women in the other room. It had been so hot and dry for so long that everyone welcomed the coming storm. I thought it was going to be a typical thunderstorm—a welcome relief from the heat and coal dust—but that storm was an epiphany that changed me from the little girl I was into the young woman I thought I wanted to be.

With a crash of thunder, the rain pounded like angry fists on the roof. I carried a stack of towels into the main room and put some in each beautician's station. Just about everybody was crowded around one of the room's two windows, watching the storm. I went in the back to get more towels, and that's when I heard the door open and the storm come rushing in. I glanced through the gap in the curtains and saw a woman I didn't recognize drenched from head to toe.

Alice was the closest person to the door, so she went over and tried to give her a towel, but the woman just stood there, dripping all over the floor. Curious, I walked closer to the curtain so I could watch her. She just stood there, her chest heaving up and down like she'd been running.

Madge took a step toward her. "Can I help you, honey?"

She turned in the direction of Madge's voice, but didn't answer. Instead, her eyes darted around the shop, searching. I almost turned away and went back to stacking towels when I heard her say, "I'm looking for Sylvia Richardson."

"I'm Sylvia," said Mama, stepping forward from her station, where she was combing Ruth Watkins's hair.

"I want to show you something," the mystery lady said. She opened the pocketbook she had clutched under her arm and took out what looked like a picture. Striding across the room, she handed it to Mama.

Mama looked down at the picture and froze. The woman stared at Mama like she was a dog that was going to perform some amazing trick. I saw the blood drain from Mama's face. She tried to give the picture back to the woman, but she made no effort to take it.

"I don't think you looked at it good enough," said the woman, her voice rising to a shout. "Look at it again!"

But Mama just stood there with her arm outstretched, the picture shaking in her hand.

"In case you don't recognize that man, it's *my husband,* John Stapleton, and those two little boys setting on his lap are his twins."

The air fairly crackled around them. The storm outside could not measure up to what was happening right in front of me. I was still standing behind the curtain, where I had a bird's eye view of the whole thing. I didn't want to see any more, but my legs had turned to lead.

The woman snatched the picture out of Mama's hand and clasped it to her breast. "You stay the hell away from *my* husband."

Mama was shaking her head and trying to say, "I didn't know—" but the woman wouldn't let her.

"I *know* what kind of woman you are. Sniffing around other woman's husbands like a stray dog. Breaking up their homes. Leaving young'uns without a daddy."

"Now, hold on just a minute!" Madge stepped forward, brandishing a comb like a weapon.

Mama glanced at Madge and held up her hand like a stop sign. She straightened her back, threw back her head, and said, "I didn't know John was married."

The woman stared at Mama. All my life, I was haunted by her eyes. I saw the pain of a thousand lost chances, dead ends, forgotten wishes, and dashed hopes. She clenched her fists and spat out the words, "The *hell* you didn't. You knew. You didn't give a damn. You're nothing but a cheap whore!"

Madge headed for her. "Get the hell out of my shop!"

The woman turned and stalked toward the door. She jerked it open. The force of the wind grabbed it out of her hand, crashing it into the wall. She turned around in the doorway and faced the shop. The wind picked up her long hair and blew it straight out on either side of her head, making her look like she was going to lift up into the air. No one moved. She fixed her eyes on my mama. "I'm going. I said what I come here to say."

The door slammed, shutting out the storm.

Mama's eyes shifted from the door to the curtains. I was still behind them, but she could see my face through the gap. We locked eyes. She took a step toward me. I spun around and spied her coffee mug—unmistakably hers, with blood red lipstick stamped on the rim. I grabbed it, reared back, and hurled it at the mirror with the big, cracked *z* on my way out the back door.

I ran toward the river, my feet slipping and sliding down the rocky bank. The rain's angry fists pushed me toward the river's edge, my cries swallowed by the storm. I stopped when I reached the water and doubled over in pain. This was the first time in my life I wanted to die from pure shame.

I raised my face to the sky and tried to open my eyes, but the storm's fury blinded me. The cold rain felt like needles against my skin. I turned and ran away from town, following the river bank. Thunder crashed over my head, and lightening spears split the sky apart before landing right in front of me. I screamed and slipped on the rocks, skidding forward on my hands and knees. I landed with my face in the mud at the river's edge. Its rotten egg smell made my stomach churn.

I got up and kept running. Rivulets of blood ran down my legs. I balled my hands into tight fists to keep the blood from dripping off my fingers. The pain helped keep me going. I just didn't know where.

When I was safely out of town, I slowed, and so did the rain. Like me, the storm seemed too tired to continue but not ready to stop. I saw a place up ahead where I could climb up the riverbank to the road. It was covered with ferns and vines that slapped at my face as I climbed. I tried to grip them with my fingers so they wouldn't touch the cuts on the palms of my hands. The rain had beaten the smell of honeysuckle into the air. It tasted raw in my throat.

I made it to the top of the bank, raised my face, and opened my mouth. The rain cooled my tongue. I felt my heartbeat match the steady pulse of the rain. I looked up and down the empty road. *What do I do now? I can't go back. I won't.*

I followed the road that led away from town. The rain had slowed to a fine mist, but not before scrubbing everything clean. The air tasted so fresh, I stopped and tilted my face to the sky to drink it in. Ahead was a little white church on the hillside. In the gloaming, it looked like someone had hung it amongst the trees like a birdhouse. I heard a truck coming, so I ran across the road and hid in the trees. When it passed, I started running again. This time, I had a destination.

The door was heavy, taking the last of my strength to open it. Inside the sanctuary, I stood still, letting my eyes adjust to the dimness. The silence filled every nook and cranny. I took deep breaths. My lungs felt like they were filled with fire. I leaned forward and put one hand on my knee and one over my chest, pressing down to still my galloping heart.

I don't know how long I stayed like that before I looked around at the sparse furnishings. Straight-back pews lined the aisles like wooden soldiers standing at attention. A pulpit set in the middle of a stage that rose about two feet above the polished wood floor. In front of it was a table with the words "In Remembrance" crudely carved across the front. I walked up the center aisle, looking for what I thought should be in a church—piano, hymn books, candles placed in polished candlesticks, cushions on the benches, even Bibles. But there was nothing. I stopped halfway up the aisle and turned in a slow circle. The windows were small, with milky white glass making it impossible to see in or out. I thought how there would be no looking out the windows to distract you from the preaching in this church. The only decoration, if you could call it that, was a simple wooden cross on the front of the pulpit.

I approached the stage and saw a curtain behind the pulpit—a dark burgundy red. I hesitated, but my curiosity convinced me to look behind it. I discovered a large concrete rectangle filled with water. Aunt Hat called it a baptistery. I couldn't tell how deep it was, but I knew it was deep enough to totally immerse the person being baptized. I noticed there was a door in the wall on either side of the baptistery, so a person could come out and walk down steps leading into the water. I stepped back and dropped the curtain. There was also a door in the wall on either side of the stage. I chose the left one and turned the knob. It opened.

There were no windows, so I couldn't see what was in this room. I stepped through the doorway and rubbed my fingers up and down the wall until I felt a light switch. I clicked it on, and a single, bare light bulb threw a pastel veil over the room. It looked like a small dressing room, with half a dozen white robes hanging from pegs on the wall. I went in and shut the door. There were only two chairs in the room, and one of them held a stack of white towels. I peeled off my wet clothes, wrapped my hair in one towel, and dried myself with another, being careful with the painful scrapes on my hands and knees. I pulled one of the robes over my head, sat down, and examined the cuts on the palms of my hands. Unbelievable weariness washed over me. I pulled the stack of towels down in the floor, took all the robes, and made myself a bed in the corner of the room. I lay down and let the tears scald my face. *What am I going to do?*

I writhed and twisted while the pain closed like a giant fist around me. I rolled over on my back, and the tears ran into my ears. I admitted things about my mother that I never had before—she smoked, drank beer, loved to dance, and played cards. She blasted music on the radio and dyed her hair. She had pierced ears, for God's sake. She wore high heels *everywhere* and never left the house unless her hair and makeup were perfect.

The tears fell faster. I remembered the time Mama's Hank Williams album was playing "I'm so Lonesome I Could Cry" and got stuck on the word *cry*. That's how I felt right now—*cry, cry, cry, cry, cry*—like I was never going to stop. Cry for the way I saw men look at my mama, and cry for the way I saw her look at them. Cry for the way she laughed and smiled when men flirted with her. Cry for the men like John who swore they'd never leave her, and most of all, cry for her when they did.

I cried myself to sleep. Then I dreamed. I was walking through a dark forest. Thunder crashed over my head, and lightening flashed, revealing a hideous monster with long talons and bright red eyes coming toward me. I turned around and ran back the way I came. The fiend clawed at my back as I stayed just one step ahead of it.

I woke, flailing my arms around, certain the monster had grabbed me. I sat up. My heart pounded and the blood rushed to my head, making the room spin. *Where am I?* I looked at the stark white walls and eerie light above my head. Then it all came rushing back. That woman called my mother a cheap whore.

I stood. The pain in my knees brought tears to my eyes. The scrapes and cuts had scabbed over, stretching the skin so tight that every time I moved my legs, it felt like the skin was ripping from my knees. I hobbled over and opened the door to the sanctuary. The darkness told me it must be the middle of the night—the time for sleep and sweet dreams.

I left the door open so I could see to walk into the sanctuary. I sat down in the first pew. "Are you here, God?" The voice didn't sound like mine, but rather that of a little girl. "This is a church, so you're here, right?" I waited, but nothing happened. There was no sign that

God heard me—no music, no bright light, no sudden feeling of peace. I bowed my head, but no words came to me.

The tears slid down my face.

I sat with my head bowed. I tried to recall how the preacher prayed when Aunt Hat took me to church, but all I could remember was, "Our most precious heavenly Father." After that, I didn't know what to say.

I was afraid to say the wrong thing. Aunt Hat said God answers prayers, so what if I asked for the wrong thing and he made it happen? What if I asked him to make my mother change and she did? Did I really want a mother who wore long skirts and a beehive and went to church every time the door opened? Should I ask God to send my mother a boyfriend that wasn't married and would be good to her? I didn't even know if I could ask God for something like that.

Finally, I got up and went to the pulpit. I put my hands on the cross that had been nailed on the front of it. I ran my fingertips across the rough wood.

"Please, God, tell me. What do I do now?"

A cool breeze drifted past my bedroom window and nudged me awake. I looked at the clock—10:35. The only time I ever slept this late was when I was sick. I sat up, and pain shot through me. Peeling back the sheet, I winced at the sight of my legs—skinned from knees to ankles. I turned my hands over and examined the cuts, flexing my fingers. They were stiff, but I could write.

I limped into the kitchen and saw the note on the table—*Gone to work, Love, Mama.*

I snatched it and crumpled it in my fist. My eyes watered from the pain that shot through my hand. Last night, I had hid in the shadows and watched Mama pacing up and down the street in front of our apartment. Every time she passed under the street light, I could see her smoking a cigarette and stopping periodically to peer down the street—waiting for me.

I had stood there for almost an hour, letting Mama suffer. When the court house clock struck 4:00, I gave up and stepped into the light. Mama came running, but she didn't cry and apologize all over me. She just hugged me and whispered, "I'm sorry."

When we got to the apartment, she sat me down and doctored on my cuts and scratches, helped me into my pajamas, and left me alone. By that time it must have been going on 5:00, and Mama had still managed to get up and go to work.

I went back to my room and found the box of stationary Aunt Hat gave me last Christmas. I remember how she said that now I had no excuse for not writing her. I wonder what she would say about what happened yesterday. Mama better be thankful she was already gone.

I took the box and a pen to the kitchen and sat down at the table.

Sarah Jane Richardson
#12 Maple Street
Coal Valley, VA
August 30, 1955

Dear Amelia,

Thank you for the interesting letter about your school. It was nice of you to write to me. Yes, my Aunt Hat wants me to go to school at Tacoma Ladies Academy, but I told her I didn't want to go to school so far away from home. But lately some things have happened to change my mind. I am now very interested in coming to your school.

I am supposed to be in the seventh grade this fall, but the assistant principal came to see my mother and said the school thinks I should skip seventh grade and go to eighth grade because of a test I took last year. That means I would have to go to the high school which is a much bigger building and has a lot more students than the school I am used to. I guess what I'm thinking is, if I have to change schools anyway, maybe going to your school would be a good idea after all.

Your school sounds very nice, especially the library. I have never been to Seattle, or to any city for that matter, so I can't imagine what it must look like. I do love to read and right now I'm finishing Little Women. *It's one of my favorites! Have you read it?* Anne of Green Gables *is my absolute favorite book. Have you read it?*

You asked me if everyone here has two names like me. I expect most people in Seattle have a first and middle name just like they do here, but I also suppose it's true that a lot of people here say your first and middle names when speaking to you. I don't know why. I never really thought of it before. At the beauty shop where my mama works there's Alice Mae, Ruby Sue, and Maryetta, which is spelled as one name but sounds like two. But then there's Madge, who owns the shop, and my mother whose name is Sylvia Elizabeth, but she just goes by Sylvia. Oh, and most people don't call me Sarah Jane anyway. They call me Sassy. That is everyone but Aunt Hat, of course. She doesn't like to call me Sassy, but you've met her so you can probably tell why.

Your Friend,
Sassy

I read the letter a second time, folded it, and slid it into an envelope. I wrote Amelia's address on it and took it to my room. I reached under my bed and pulled out the packet from Tacoma Ladies Academy. For what must have been the hundredth time, I read the information, pausing long enough to dream I was sitting in the library surrounded by shelves of books reaching from ceiling to floor. I sighed and placed my dream alongside the glossy pictures and eloquent descriptions of Tacoma Ladies Academy, included the letter I'd just written, and slid them all into the big envelope and hid it under my mattress.

I went to the bathroom and filled the old claw foot bathtub with warm water. Inch by inch, I eased my legs down, fighting the tears that sprang into my eyes when the raw skin touched the water. I gritted my teeth, and gradually the stinging stopped and the warm water began to feel good. I lay my head back against the tub's edge and thought about everything that had happened since yesterday. In twenty-four hours, my life had changed. The summer heat had exploded like a falling star, leaving the air clean and cool. No doubt, all of Coal Valley had heard about the woman who called my mama a whore. My face burned with shame. Would I ever feel the same about my mama? Or would it be like the cuts on my legs when they touched the water—excruciating but not unbearable?

I blinked back the tears. How could my mother be the kind of woman the stranger said she was? I knew Mama hadn't tried to take that woman's husband, but then—in my heart, I knew my mother wasn't like other mothers. Her beauty made her different. Everywhere she went, people stared at her. And it wasn't going to change. It was just a matter of time before a new boyfriend came along who was a no-good deadbeat—or worse, married—and I'd want to run away again. I knew there was only one way I could leave Mama and her boyfriend problems, and that was with Aunt Hat's help.

I was lying on my bed, reading *Little Women,* when I heard Mama come in from work. When she came to my room and looked in, I pretended to be asleep. I couldn't face her, and I didn't want to talk about yesterday. She closed my door, and I relaxed. I read a few more pages, closed my book, and drifted off to sleep. When I woke, it was dark outside, and my stomach was rumbling. I hadn't eaten since sometime yesterday, and I was famished. I went into the kitchen, and there was a note on the table. *Chicken and dumplings on the stove. Gone to bed. Love, Mama.* I looked up at the clock and saw it was just past 9:00.

I took my bowl of dumplings and a Coca-Cola and went back to my room. I sat Indian-style on my bed and ate. I watched the curtains quiver at the window like they were chilled by the coolness of the breeze. I thought of how easy it would be to write to Aunt Hat and tell her I wanted to go to that school in Washington, and then I thought of my mother, who was asleep in her room. I took my empty bowl to the kitchen and turned off the light. I stood at the kitchen window and finished my Coke. A myriad of stars danced before me. I searched the sky to see if one would fall so I could make a wish. I turned away, knowing that if one did fall, I didn't know what to wish for.

Summer, 1955

Sylvia

"'No, *my* little Pearl!'" said her mother. "'Thou must gather thine own sunshine. I have none to give thee!" Nathaniel Hawthorne, *The Scarlet Letter*

The storm changed everything. It broke the heat's brutal grasp and washed the coal dust from the valley. And it broke something in Sassy. I could feel it when I hugged her to me and she wilted like a flower in my arms. I wanted to swear I had no idea John was married, but I couldn't—the truth was, I never asked. The whole truth was that I didn't care.

When Sassy went to bed, I set up waiting—no, hoping—she'd come out of her room and talk to me. It hurt my heart to see all those cuts and scrapes on her hands and knees. I tried to fuss over her, but she shuffled away, bent over like an old woman. Why didn't she yell and scream at me? Hell, why didn't she cuss me or at least slam the door in my face?

But she just walked away.

I went to my room and got the cedar chest that held Gaines's letters.

August 8, 1943
PFC Gaines Richardson
33647746
7th Infantry 3rd Division

My Dearest Sylvia,

I know it's been awhile since you got a letter from me. I hate to worry you but there was nothing I could do about it. We were in transport to Sicily and finally landed in a town called Licata July 10. I am only allowed to write you about my personal experiences in battle, nothing else.

The day we landed, I got my first baptism by fire. Shells were falling all around us, and one hit about 20 feet from me. Since then I've marched what seems like hundreds of miles in the heat. I thought Georgia was hot, but I can't believe hell could be any hotter than this place. We fought our way to Palermo where we stopped to let General Patton's tanks go through the city first. We saw some hard fighting especially at night.

When I'm not marching, I'm driving General Patton around. The other night we were going up this road and shells started falling about a hundred yards up the road. Patton never even flinched. There was nothing to do but keep moving and pray. I just kept thinking about you and Sassy and that got me through it.

I must close because we are getting ready to move out. We are pushing up the coast of Sicily to Messina. Sylvie always know, wherever this war takes me next, knowing you are there waiting for me is what keeps me going. Give my baby girl a kiss. I will write again as soon as I can. Try not to worry.

I love you and miss you more every day.

Gaines

Oh, Gaines—I sure as hell have made a mess out of my life, I thought. *And Sassy . . . I'm so afraid I'm going to mess up her life too.*

I walked to the window and pushed back the curtains. A whisper of a breeze touched my face, and I let the tears escape. *What now?*

The sun was coming up on a world washed clean by yesterday's storm. I thought, *it's just like my life. I think I've got it figured out, and my future looks as fresh as the world out that window, and then the coal dust covers everything with layers of black again, and me and Sassy are back to sloughing through life as best we can.*

I eased open my bedroom door and went into the kitchen. In a chair by the window, I watched the clouds riding on angel's wings over the mountains. I whispered, "What do I do now, Gaines? How do I fix this?"

I studied the clouds, looking for a sign that Gaines had heard me. It had been years since I looked for him in the clouds. After he died, I spent hours staring at the sky. I thought if I could see the shape of his face or his hands in the clouds that somehow it would make losing him easier—like a guarantee that he was in heaven. Then one day, I stopped looking up—and that was the biggest mistake of my life.

After a few cool days, the heat was back with a vengeance. Sleeping was next to impossible. By Friday, I was so exhausted, I fell asleep only to wake bathed in sweat. The clock claimed it was just after 2:00 a.m. I got up and went to the bathroom, splashed cold water on my face, and then wet a washcloth. I sat down on the side of the bathtub and rubbed it over my arms and around my neck. Three more times, I wet it with cold water and rubbed it over my body, trying to cool the fire in my skin.

I went into the kitchen, took a beer out of the refrigerator, and drank it, staring at the purpled darkness. The full moon hung in iridescent silence. There was nothing in the heavens but empty promises of heat lightening.

I finished my beer and went back to my bedroom. I switched on the lamp and turned on the record player. Hank Williams's "I'm so Lonesome I Could Cry" wafted across the room. The cedar chest that held Gaines's letters was in the top drawer of my dresser, and at times like this they were the only comfort I could find. I spilled them on the bed, crawling in among them. I propped my pillows up against the headboard, sat back, and picked up a letter.

October 28, 1942
U.S. Army 7th Infantry, 3rd Division
Fort Wheeler, GA

My Dearest Sylvia,

You will never know how good it was to hold you in my arms. You are more beautiful now than you were before you had Sassy. Being a Mama sure agrees with you! I keep looking at the picture of you two and I can't believe you're mine. I keep it with me everywhere I go. And ain't she a pretty little thing! Sylvie she looks just like you. And I ain't ever seen a baby like her. She hardly cries and smiles all the time. I wish I could have had more time with you but the army seems to be in a hurry to make a real soldier out of me. Word is we ship out soon. Can you see me, an old mountain man, traveling across the world?

Sylvia, I know this war has changed everything we planned. We no more got our life together started than I had to leave you. I know when I married you I promised I would take care of you and now I've left you with a baby to take care of by yourself. When I lay here at night missing you I try to think of this war as just a detour. God knows when I drove a bus I took many a detour but

I always got to where I was going. Knowing that you are there waiting for me is going to get me through this. So don't worry too much about me. Just take care of yourself and my baby girl. She's a sassy little thing that's for sure! And you mark my words, she's a smart one! She'll make us proud.

I'll write more as soon as I get a chance. I love you more ever day.
Gaines

I read the letter again. *Gaines, you were right! Sassy is a smart one! I wish you could of heard what that principal at the school said about her.* I took Gaines's picture off the bedside table, touched his face, and closed my eyes, remembering. *That was the last time you ever got to hold your daughter. That was the last time I ever saw you.*

I opened the drawer of the bedside table and pulled out a soft rag. With the picture cradled close to my chest, I started polishing the silver frame. "Well, Gaines," I said as if he were sitting right next to me, "do I let Sassy go to high school? Part of me thinks it's a good idea, and part of me thinks she's too young." I turned my head to one side like I was listening to his reply.

I set the picture back on the table and laid the rag in the drawer alongside the life I could never have. I picked up Gaines's letter, folded it, and slid it back in its envelope. The softness of the pillows reminded me of Gaines's last embrace, and fell asleep holding his letter.

I dreamed I was lying under a brilliant white light that vibrated with voices. My eyes tried to open, but the light was too heavy; its brightness paralyzed me. My head threatened to explode. Pain lay on top of my body like a thick coat of ice. All I could manage was a moan.

"She's trying to wake up."

"Child, can you hear me? Are you in pain?"

A light shined in my eyes. I wanted to scream, "Turn it off! Please!" But nothing came out of my mouth. Then someone took my hand. "Child, can you squeeze my hand? Can you hear me? Squeeze my hand."

Then the voice faded, and the blackness swallowed me.

The pounding in my head was so brutal I couldn't bear it. I got up and tried to walk to the bathroom but staggered and fell against the wall. Down on all fours, I crawled the rest of the way. Somehow,

I managed to get the aspirin out of the cabinet and swallowed five, gulping water from my cupped hand. Then I lay down on the floor in front of the bathtub and prayed for the throbbing to go away.

When the pain eased, I managed to sit up and wet a washcloth with cold water. I held it to my forehead. I hadn't had one of these headaches in almost two years. The doctors had warned me that as I got older, the headaches would probably get worse. Now here I was, thirty years old, and the headaches were coming back.

God help me.

"Wake up, sleepy head!" I opened Sassy's bedroom door and leaned myself against the doorframe. She pulled the covers up over her head, making me laugh. I had the radio in the kitchen turned up so I could hear my favorite singer, Hank Snow, crooning "I Don't Hurt Anymore."

"You better get up or I'm going to start singing," I said. "Madge is picking us up in thirty minutes. We're heading over to Bluefield to do some school shopping."

The covers flew off her head, and Sassy sat up. I said, "That's more like it."

Several weeks had passed since the incident at the shop, and Sassy hadn't said a word about it. She also hadn't said a word about school, even though it started next week.

"Now get ready. Breakfast is in the kitchen, and there's a package for you."

"A what?"

"Hurry and get ready, and you'll see."

I set two plates of fried baloney, eggs, and toast on the table, turned around, and there was Sassy, dressed and eyeing the box on the table.

"Your principal, Mrs. Wallace, came in the shop for a haircut yesterday and asked me to give that to you."

"What is it?"

I laughed. "I don't know. Open it and find out."

Sassy tore open the box and there were the books: *Anne of Avonlea, Anne of the Island, Anne's House of Dreams, Little Men,* and *Jo's Boys.*

"Oh, Mama, look!"

I sipped my coffee and smiled. Sassy spread the books out on the table, grabbing *Anne of Avonlea* and clasping it to her chest.

Sassy said, "These are the books Mrs. Wallace told me about when she was here that day."

"It was nice of her to send them to you." I set down my coffee cup and picked up my fork. While I ate, I watched Sassy look through her books. As casual as if I was asking about the weather, I said, "Mrs. Wallace wanted to know what you decided about school. I told her you hadn't said."

Sassy placed *Anne of Avonlea* back in the box and sat down. She stared at her plate, the color draining from her face. I ate in silence, waiting for her to make the first move. I finished eating and put my plate in the sink. Sassy was still staring at hers. "It's time to decide," I said, sitting down at the table.

Sassy took a sip of orange juice and refused to look at me. "What do you think I should do?"

"Mrs. Wallace seems to think you are more than ready for high school. But I don't know . . ." I leaned over and lay my hand on top of hers. It was the first time I touched her since the incident at the shop, and I half expected her to push my hand away. She glanced down at my hand and her back went rigid. I said, "Sassy, I know you can do the work at high school. That's not what's bothering me. I just don't want you to be thrown in with a bunch of kids who are all a lot older than you."

"Are you saying I'm too *young* to go to high school?"

"No. Well, yes, I guess that's part of it. It's just, there's more to school than learning. There's friends . . ."

Sassy exploded, her face turning as red as the devil's horns. "You think I'm a *baby,* so I need to stay at elementary school?"

"Now, hold on just a minute. I'm not saying you're a baby. I just want you to realize that you will be the youngest student there, and *somebody's* bound to say *something* about it. Are you ready for that?"

"I . . . yes, I'm ready."

I leaned back and nodded like it was settled. "All right, then. I'll just ask you one more thing, and then I'll hush about it. Do you realize that once you start at the high school, you won't be able to go back?"

Sassy nodded, but I could see the indecision in her eyes.

"Well, I'm glad we got that settled." I stood and put my coffee cup in the sink. "Now, hurry up and eat. It's time for Madge."

As if on cue, I heard Madge coming up the stairs. She breezed in wearing a blue dress with a field of little yellow flowers on it. I rarely saw her in anything but her uniform, so I couldn't help but stare. Right away, I noticed the little yellow bows she had clipped in her hair—one over each ear. I wondered how in the world she managed to get them through all that hairspray. She poured herself a cup of coffee and sat down at the table. She gave me a knowing look and inclined her head toward the bathroom. I said, "I need to put on some lipstick. I'll be back in a minute."

I hurried off to the bathroom, but I left the door cracked so I could hear them. Sassy was setting with her back to me, but I could see Madge through the small opening. She picked up one of Sassy's books and said, "What you got there, Sassy?"

"Some books Mrs. Wallace sent me."

"Well, wasn't that nice." Madge laid the book on the table and took a sip of coffee. She asked, "Have you decided what you're going to do about school?"

Sassy didn't hesitate. She said, "I'm going to high school."

To my surprise, Madge said, "Good for you, honey."

I watched Sassy straighten her back. She said, "Do you think I should?"

I pressed my ear to the opening so I wouldn't miss it.

Madge said, "Yes, ma'am, I do. I wish I'd paid more attention to my schooling. There's one thing I learned, though, I'll never forget. It's Latin—*carpe diem*—means 'seize the day.' And Sassy, that's what *you've* got to do. Get everything out of school while you can. There's a great big world outside of these here mountains, and you've got what it takes to make it out there. *Carpe diem*."

I didn't have to see Sassy's face to know she was thinking it over. *Carpe diem? Where the hell did Madge get this stuff?*

Sassy stood up and put her plate in the sink. She said, "I'm going to get my shoes."

"Wait a minute, hon."

Finally, I thought, Madge was going to get to the point. She hadn't mentioned what had happened at the shop, even though that's what she was supposed to talk to Sassy about.

I saw Madge point to the scars on Sassy's legs. She asked, "So, how are you feeling?"

Sassy shrugged and said, "I'm fine."

"That's it," Madge said, crossing her arms. "You're fine."

I saw Sassy raise her face and stick out her chin. She said, "Yes, ma'am."

"You know your mama feels real bad about what happened," Madge said.

It's about damn time.

"And you know what that woman said isn't true," she continued. "Sylvia believed John when he said he wasn't married. She'd never go out with a married man."

Sassy gripped the back of a chair. I could see her profile, and she looked frozen. I held my breath.

Madge said, "Well, I guess we won't need to talk about that nonsense again, will we?"

In a voice barely above a whisper, Sassy said, "No, ma'am. I guess we won't."

And we never did.

When I came back in the kitchen, Madge had her pocketbook looped over her arm, and Sassy was putting her dishes in the sink. I said, "Well, girls, where do you want to shop first?"

Madge led the way down the stairs. She said, "That depends on what we're looking for."

We climbed in the car. I said, "I need me a new pair of red heels. I think that's just what the doctor ordered. Don't you girls?"

In spite of herself, Sassy's laugh spilled out of the car window. I turned and watched it shimmer in the morning sun as we sped out of Coal Valley.

"What did Doc say?"

"Jesus, Madge, let me get in the door first." I brushed past Madge and went into the back room to change into my work shoes. When I came back, Madge was setting in the chair at her station, smoking a cigarette and tapping her foot. "You know what Doc said. I told you yesterday."

"And I know you didn't tell me all of it."

I walked over to my station and pretended to arrange the bottles of shampoo and crème rinse that were already in perfect order. With my back to Madge, I said, "He said my headaches were probably from the accident . . ." I broke off to light a cigarette.

Madge left the room and came back with two cups of coffee. We were so in tune with each other that we could pick up in the middle of a conversation—even in the middle of a sentence.

Madge handed me a cup. She said, "And what?"

"And," I said, pausing to take a sip of my coffee, "he said I needed to see a head doctor."

"Head doctor?"

"A neurologist."

"Did he say why after all these years, you've started having headaches again?"

"No, he just said for me to see this neurologist in Bristol. He's going to get me an appointment."

"Let me know when it is, and I'll take you."

"You don't have to do that. I can take the bus."

"I know you can." Madge set her coffee cup down and picked up her cigarette from the edge of the ashtray. "And I also know that if I take you, then you'll *go*."

I set my cup down and glanced at myself in the mirror. "I'll go; don't you worry. I can't stand many more headaches like the last one. I'd rather have a hangover from bad moonshine than another headache like that."

With my cup of coffee, I set down in the chair in front of my station, cradling it in my hands like I was trying to absorb the warmth. I could feel Madge's eyes on me, but I wouldn't look at her. "Madge," I said, "there's one thing I want you to promise me."

"What?"

"Promise me you won't tell Sassy I'm going to see a neurologist. It'll scare her. She's already fretting over me. I try to hide it from her, but sometimes when I get a bad one, I have to go lay down, and she worries. And Madge, if something was to happen to me . . ." The tears I felt stinging my eyes spilled over.

Madge hopped off her chair and came to me. She took my cup, set it down, and patted me on the back. "Sylvie, honey, this ain't nothing to worry about. The doctor will fix you up."

I started to sob.

"Sylvie, what in the world is it?"

I put my head in my hands and let the tears come. Madge went over to her station and got me a tissue. Then she hovered over me, waiting for me to calm down and dry my eyes.

She said, "Honey, tell me, what is it?"

"It's time, Madge. Time for me to pay up."

Madge didn't even pretend she didn't know what I was talking about. "Sylvie," she said, "you've paid dearly for that already."

"No. I ain't come close. But I'll pay—and keep on paying—as long as Sassy don't find out."

Madge put her hand on my shoulder. "Have you ever thought about telling Sassy what happened?"

I was too shocked to reply. All I could do was shake my head.

Madge continued. "Think about it. If you told her about the accident and everything that happened, then you wouldn't have to carry that burden around inside of you. If you ask me, that's what's causing your headaches—worry and guilt."

"But Sassy would never forgive me. She'd hate me."

"How do you know that? You don't give her enough credit. She's a smart girl. Look how she's going to skip a grade and go to high school. And she loves you. You could make her understand."

"Jesus, you sound like Aunt Hat!"

"I'm just saying that you can't keep worrying all the time. Worry will kill you."

"Then let it. I can't take a chance on losing her. This will go with me to my grave."

Autumn, 1955

Sassy

"I'm not a bit changed—not really. I'm only just pruned down and branched out. The real *me*—back here—is just the same." Lucy Maud Montgomery, *Anne of Green Gables*

The first day of high school, I refused to let Mama walk with me to the hanging bridge that connected our part of town with Muddy Bottom, where Coal Valley High School set next to R. F. Harmon Elementary School. Technically, an open field separated the two schools, and that's where the kids played at recess and the football team practiced after school. With so many feet on it every day, grass had as much a chance of growing there as hair did on Mr. Stiltner's bald head.

I wouldn't have been nearly as brave as I walked up that front walk if Mrs. Wallace hadn't met me and Mama there a few days ago and gave me a tour of the building. The whole place shined like a new penny, and I loved the way it smelled—Pine-Sol and beeswax. The building was newer than the elementary school, having been built right after WWII. The classrooms were large and bright. Sunlight poured through the polished windows like ice-cold lemonade splashing into a glass.

That first morning, I was determined to look like the other high school girls. I wore my new black and white skirt with the wide black patent leather belt and a white button-up blouse. Mama put my hair in a high pony tail and tied a black and white scarf around it. I even talked her into letting me put on lipstick. But I was proudest of my new shoes—black and white saddle oxfords, complimented with white bobby socks rolled down around my ankles. Even though my shoes were brand-new, Mama had polished them.

The first day went by in a blur of books thumping, lockers slamming, bells ringing, and voices bouncing around like rubber balls. None of the students spoke to me. No one even looked my way. I floated past them like a shadow. But as soon as school was out, I headed to the beauty shop to tell Mama and Madge what a wonderful day I had. I breezed through the door, my stack of books balanced in front of me, expecting to see

Mama's eager face, but she was nowhere to be seen. "Where's Mama?" I said to no one in particular.

Madge stepped through the curtains in the back room doorway. "Honey, she went home early with a headache."

My heart started beating faster. As far as I could remember, Mama had never left work before because of a headache or any other ailment. I turned on my heel and headed for the door. "I'll go home and see about her."

When I got home, the apartment was quiet. Mama's bedroom door was open just enough so I could see in. She was asleep on her side, facing the door. Her arm was thrown over her forehead as if she was protecting her head from the outside world. I started to ease the door closed when I glimpsed a glass of water and a packet of pills on the nightstand. I stepped inside the room and waited for my eyes to adjust to the darkness. When I was sick, Mama took me to see Doc Sutherland, and he always gave me pills in a little white paper envelope. I picked up the packet and took it over to the door so I could see it better. It was full of big white pills, and on the envelope, written in Doc's spidery hand, were the words *1 every 4 to 6 hours for headache.*

I returned the pills to the nightstand and went to the kitchen. It was one thing to find out she'd left work, but to go to the doctor—Mama *never* went to the doctor. I sat down at the table and tried to remember if Mama had acted unusual this morning. I had been so nervous about school that I couldn't conjure up her face. I remember asking her why she wasn't dressed for work, but she'd said her first appointment wasn't until 10:00. I should have realized that Mama always left for work by 8:30, whether she had an appointment or not.

At 5:00, I looked in on Mama and saw that she was stirring around like she was going to wake up, so I went to the kitchen and heated up two cans of chicken noodle soup. I heard Mama come out of her room just as I was pouring the soup into bowls. I'd already set the table and poured two glasses of milk.

"Would you look at this." Mama came up behind me and hugged me.

"Set down. It's ready. How's your headache?"

Mama eased into her chair and took a sip of milk. I pretended to be busy opening a pack of crackers and getting napkins, but I was really studying her.

"It's almost gone."

The dark shadows under her eyes told me a different story. She sat hunched over her bowl like she was trying to get warm from the steam rising from the soup.

"Eat a bite. It'll make you feel better."

Mama picked up her spoon but just looked at the bowl. "Tell me about your first day at the big school."

I began with entering the building and talked my way through the whole day. In no time, I had Mama laughing. She even took a few sips of soup. I went to my room and returned with my books. I showed them to her and told her all about my teachers. She knew most of them, except Mr. Hess, who was the new history teacher from West Virginia.

"Is that all?"

I thought a minute. "Yes, that's pretty much it."

"Well, you've left out the most important thing of all."

"What's that?"

"The boys!" Mama smiled and leaned back in her chair. She took a pack of cigarettes out of the pocket of her robe. I noticed that her hands shook when she took one out and held the match to it.

"Aw, Mama, I didn't notice the boys."

"Un-huh, is that right?" She took a draw on her cigarette and fixed her eyes on me. "Well, if that's true, I can guarantee it won't be long before you start noticing."

I went to take a bath, and when I came out, Mama was lying on the couch, listening to the radio, and looking at a *Life* Magazine. She started singing along with Frank Sinatra: "Don't you know that it's worth every treasure on earth/ To be young at heart/ For as rich as you are its much better by far/ To be young at heart."

"Well, you *are* feeling better." I joined in and sang with her. She gave me her hand, and I pulled her up and off the couch.

She kissed me on the cheek. "I believe I'll go to bed now."

"Are you going to go to work tomorrow?"

"Lord, yes! It was just a sick headache. Your granny used to get them, and Aunt Hat gets them too. Doc Sutherland calls them migraine headaches, but your granny always called them sick headaches."

"What causes them?"

"Meanness, I guess. Since most of the Mason women seem to get them." She kissed me on the top of my head and went off to bed singing, "Don't you know that it's worth every treasure on earth . . ."

That night, I lay awake worrying about Mama. She was having headaches a lot lately, and they always left her looking pale with dark circles under her eyes. She looked like she'd lost weight, too. Sometimes I woke up and heard her moving around the apartment. The other night, I got up to go to the bathroom and found her sitting in the dark kitchen drinking a beer. She said she couldn't sleep, but I wonder now if it was a headache.

I turned over and listened to the night song outside my window. The moon glittered under the sky. Fall was coming, and I was in high school. In a little more than two weeks, I would be thirteen. I shivered and pulled the blanket up to my chin. I could be in Seattle, Washington right now in a fancy boarding school instead of here in my room. Did I make the right decision? Aunt Hat said I could transfer anytime if I wanted to.

"Ladies, I got me a teenager!" Mama shouted and pointed at me as I stepped inside the shop.

Everyone called out, "Happy birthday, Sassy!"

I was pleased, but I felt my face flush. I laughed and twirled around, my ponytail whipping across my cheek and my new poodle skirt, Mama's gift, swishing around me. The ladies in the shop clapped their hands and laughed. I skipped over to Mama's station just as Madge came through the curtains that separated the shop from the back room.

Madge said, "Lord-a-mercy! If it ain't the birthday girl!"

She came over, and I held my arms straight out and hugged Madge and Mama at the same time. Madge leaned over and whispered in my ear, "I believe you're filling out that sweater pretty good for a teenager."

I blushed, and Mama smiled. "I better get back to work so we can go celebrate later."

Mama was giving Mavis Bowman a haircut. Mavis said, "Come on down to the lunch counter, and I'll fix you a big plate of home fries—no charge—for your birthday."

"Why, thank you, Miss Mavis," I said. Mavis had beautiful blue eyes, but she hid them behind black cat's eye glasses that had rhinestones on the corners.

I followed Madge back to her station. I said, "Miss Madge, got any towels that need folding?"

"Why, Sassy, I don't expect you to work on your birthday."

"I don't mind."

"Well, all right, then. I just got one more head to do, and I'm through for the day. Frieda Mays should be here in a minute."

I went through the curtains and started folding the pile of towels in the laundry basket. When I finished the towels, I grabbed the broom and started sweeping up so we could leave as soon as Mama and Madge finished with their last customers. They were taking me to the diner for supper and then to the movies to see "East of Eden" with James Dean. He was so handsome; I couldn't wait to see it.

The bell rang over the shop, and I glanced up as Frieda Mays ambled in. She had a black scarf tied around what looked like a hundred hair rollers resting on top of her head. While I swept, I watched Madge. As each roller was removed, a strip of gun metal gray hair fell to Mrs. May's waist. Even though she was well into her seventies, her hair was kept long and uncut in the custom of the Pentecostal faith. As was also their tradition, it was twisted into elaborate curls that were pinned up on top of her head, producing the beehive hairdo. Mrs. Mays always came to the shop with her hair already washed, dried, and rolled, but it still took Madge close to an hour to create her beehive.

"Now Frieda, you ain't going to die," Madge said. "You're a whole lot spryer than I am!"

I smiled at Madge, who winked at me. I knew exactly what Madge was talking about. She said every time Frieda stumped her toe, she thought she was going to die.

"Now, Madge," Mrs. Mays said, "you promised you'd do my hair for my laying out."

"Yes, Frieda, don't you worry. But you ain't going to need my services any time soon."

Mrs. Mays continued, "And don't forget, I done paid you."

"I won't forget, Frieda; you tell me every week."

I stopped sweeping and glanced at Madge. She smiled at me. I knew all about how Mrs. Mays had already paid Madge—one whole dollar—which was exactly what she paid her every week to comb her hair into that elaborate hairdo. Madge said Frieda was too tight to pay for the whole shampoo and set, so ten years ago, Madge charged her a dollar to comb it, and now she was still only paying her a dollar.

"A woman's hair is her glory," said Mrs. Mays. "Now, promise me, Madge, you'll do my hair just like this."

"Yes, Frieda. I done told you."

By the time I finished sweeping, the shop had emptied. Madge disappeared into the back room and came back with a box wrapped in white tissue paper and tied with a yellow ribbon. She handed me the gift and shouted, "Happy birthday, Sassy!"

"Oh, Miss Madge, thank you!" I hugged her, and the familiar smell of cigarette smoke and beauty shop chemicals hugged me back. I looked over at Mama, who watched us, smiling.

"Well," Madge asked, "what are you waiting for?"

"Open it!" Mama chimed in.

I set the box down on the table next to an array of beauty supplies and half-empty coffee cups. I was careful how I untied the bow so I could keep the ribbon. Mama came to stand next to me so she could see what Madge had cooked up this year. I lifted the lid and peeled away more tissue paper to reveal the most beautiful pink nightgown and robe I ever saw. I held it up to my face and said, "Oh, Mama, look." Then I couldn't manage to say another word. All I could do was run my hands over the soft material.

"Take it out and get a good look at it," Madge said. She was so proud of herself, she was as puffed up as a balloon.

I lifted it out, and the gown rippled through my hands like a pool of still water moves when you toss a pebble into it. I held it up against me and looked in the mirror. I could see Mama and Madge smiling behind me. I wheeled around and hugged Madge. "Thank you, thank you! I love it!" I said, gathering folds of pink softness to my face.

"You're growing up, Sassy," Madge said, looking over at Mama, who nodded. "Now, ladies, I believe we have a birthday dinner to get to."

We strolled down the street to the diner, the scent of wood smoke wandering through the air. The mountains were trading their green coat for a riot of colors. I stuck out my tongue, and Madge laughed.

"What in the world are you doing?" Mama asked.

"I'm tasting autumn on my tongue."

Madge and Mama both stuck out their tongues. *"Mmmm,"* Madge said.

We were still laughing when we got to the diner. Brenda Sue and Shelby met us at the door. They hugged me and told me happy birthday, then led me to the back of the diner to a table covered with a white tablecloth. In the center of it was a chocolate cake decorated with yellow roses and thirteen yellow candles.

We devoured a dinner of fried chicken, mashed potatoes and gravy, and hot buttered biscuits. Then Mama lit the candles, and Brenda Sue and Shelby joined Mama and Madge to sing "Happy Birthday" to me. We were eating the cake when, without knowing it, Madge ruined my birthday.

"So, Sassy," Madge said, "tell me about your friends at school."

"Friends?" I felt my heart start racing.

Madge laughed. "Yes, friends. Who you hanging around with these days?"

"Oh, that." I managed a weak laugh. I took a big bite of cake and chewed slowly, stalling. I had no idea what to say. How could I tell them I had no friends?

Mama looked down at her watch. "We better get or we're going to miss the start of the movie."

I jumped up and practically ran from the room, throwing the words "I better use the restroom before we go" over my shoulder. I only went around the corner and stood against the wall, waiting for my heart to quit thumping. I heard Madge say, "What was that all about?"

Mama said, "I guess she really had to go."

"Maybe."

"What do you mean, 'maybe'?"

"I mean, it looks to me like she don't want to talk about school."

Mama laughed. "Lord no, Sassy loves school."

"Maybe."

I came into the room and grabbed Mama by the hand. "We better go or we're going to miss the start of the movie! I don't want to miss one minute of James Dean!" We took off through the diner. I glanced back at Madge, and she was still standing there with a funny look on her face.

"Sassy, I'm going out tonight." Mama stuck her head in my room. "You okay with that?"

"Sure, Mama." I was wrapped up in the book *Jo's Boys* and didn't even look up. It was Friday evening, and all day, I couldn't wait for school to be out so I could get home and read. It had been a rough week. I had had an algebra test, a history test, a quiz in science, and a theme to write for English. Now I could finally kick back and read what *I* wanted to read instead of what was assigned to me.

"Chuck is picking me up at 5:00. We're going over to Princeton to some fancy club for dinner, so I'll probably be back real late."

"Okay, Mama. Have a good time."

"You want me to fix you something to eat before I go?"

I looked up from my book. "No, I'll fix something later. I'm not hungry." I went back to my book but felt Mama's eyes on me. I looked up, and she was still standing in the doorway, looking at me. "What is it?"

"Sassy, are you feeling all right?"

"Sure, Mama, I'm fine. I'm just tired. It's been a long week."

"Are you sure there's not something bothering you?"

"I'm sure. Everything's fine. Now go on, or you're not going to be ready on time."

Right at 5:00, I heard a horn blow down on the street. I looked out my window and saw Chuck's shiny black Cadillac. I went into the living room and ran into Mama coming out of her bedroom. She looked stunning in a simple off-the-shoulder black dress that fit tight at the waist and flared out over her hips. She wore black patent leather high heels and carried a small black clutch. Her hair was swept up in her usual French twist, and she wore the opal earrings Chuck gave her. A strand of pearls lay against her throat. When she walked, the stiff skirt of her dress whispered like she was walking through dry leaves. "Mama, you look beautiful!"

"Thank you, sweetie." Mama breezed past me and grabbed her coat. "Don't forget to keep this door locked."

I listened to her heels clicking down the stairs while I breathed in the traces of her perfume; then I ran to the window and watched her get into the car. Just as I thought, Chuck didn't even bother to get out and open her door.

I didn't like Chuck. I didn't like his looks. I didn't like his actions, and I sure didn't like the way he treated Mama. I was used to men falling all over her and following her around all moon-eyed. But not Chuck. He acted like he was some kind of blonde haired, blue-eyed gift that Mama should be thankful for. Maybe that's why she seemed so taken by him. He didn't even bother to walk upstairs and knock on our door. He just drove up and honked the horn, and Mama went running. Ever since her birthday, she'd been talking about being old, and then she started dating Chuck. Whatever the reason, I was uneasy about the way she was acting.

He said he was a *salesman,* and that was why he carried his clothes around in the back of his car. When I asked him what *kind* of salesman, he said he was into mercantile goods (whatever that means). All I knew was that sometimes he disappeared for weeks, and just when I thought he was gone for good, he turned up, a fancy suit draped on his tall, lanky frame, flashing money around like it grew on trees.

I couldn't believe the way Mama acted when he gave her a pair of opal and diamond earrings. I just knew she was going to refuse them; instead, she acted like a little kid at Christmas. When she showed them to Madge, I could tell by the look on her face that she didn't like it either.

I fell asleep reading. When I woke up, I was shivering with cold. I'd gone to sleep with my window slightly ajar, and the October nights were getting cold. I got up and shut the window and started to crawl back into bed, but something told me not to, so I grabbed a sweatshirt and pulled it on over my nightgown. I went into the kitchen. The clock over the stove said 4:45.

I turned on a lamp in the front room and saw that Mama's bedroom door was open. I glanced inside. The bed was still made up. I went back into my room and sank down on my bed. I said, "Mama, where are you?"

I found the book I had been reading before I fell asleep, pulled a blanket off the bed, and back went to the front room. I parked myself on the couch that just so happened to face the door. I wrapped up in my blanket and settled down to read and wait. The grayness of first light was filling the sky when I heard Mama's heels on the stairs. She eased through the door and slipped off her heels before she looked up and saw me. She clutched her chest. "Jesus Christ, Sassy, you like to gave me a heart attack."

I just looked at her and made no reply. She took off her coat and hung it on the coat rack by the door. She came over to the couch and sank down beside me with a rustle of contentment. She smelled faintly of cigarette smoke, whisky, and White Shoulders perfume. She clasped her hands over her stomach, and I saw her perfect white hands with perfect red nails. Every night, she coated her hands with a special cream and wore white cotton gloves while she slept. She spent hours on her nails too, keeping them polished, even though her hands spent so much time in the water washing hair.

She said, "What are you doing up so . . ."

She broke off, and I finished for her. "Early? Late? Take your pick."

Mama stood up and stared down at me. "And what's that supposed to mean?"

I looked her straight in the eye. "That means, where were you? You stayed out all night."

Mama turned on her heel and started for her bedroom. "I don't want to hear this. I'm going to bed."

"But Mama, it's time to get up." I bolted from the couch, my book crashing to the floor. "I know—let's clean the apartment or do the laundry! Then we can pack a picnic and go for a walk in the woods. We've got the whole day ahead of us!" I flung my arms out and wheeled around in a circle.

Mama whirled around. "What in the hell is wrong with you?"

"*Me?* What's wrong with *me?*" I pointed to myself and then pointed at her. "What's wrong with *you?*"

Mama stood her ground, hands on her hips. "I don't know what you mean! I just went out on a date and got home a little late."

"A little late! A little late!" My voice rose to a shout. "You stayed out all night again with that man!"

Mama stared at me like she'd never seen me before. "This isn't about me being out late; it's about Chuck, isn't it?"

"Mama, there's something *wrong* with that man."

"Wrong? There's nothing *wrong* with him."

We glared at each other, chests heaving. I had a sudden urge to run to Mama and shake her. Instead, I took a deep breath, and in a calm voice, said, "Mama, what do you *really* know about Chuck? Who is he? Where did he come from? Where the heck does he live?" I could tell my sudden change in voice had thrown her. She wasn't expecting me to back down and act reasonable. I could also tell she didn't know how to answer my questions. So she did what she always does when she didn't want to talk about something—she avoided it.

"Sassy, honey," she said in a small voice. "I'm tired and sleepy, and we can talk about this later. I promise you, Chuck is just a good friend. That's all. There's nothing for you to worry about." And she disappeared into her bedroom and closed the door.

I stomped off to my room and dropped down on the bed. Why couldn't Mama see Chuck like I did? Why couldn't she see anything like I did? I got out my stationary and started a letter.

October 6, 1955
Sarah Jane Richardson
#12 Maple Street
Coal Valley, VA

Dear Amelia,

I received your letter and was happy to hear that you are excited about getting ready for school. As I told you, I decided to skip seventh grade at the elementary school and go to the eighth grade at Coal Valley High School. This is my fourth week of school, and I'm doing well in my classes. My algebra teacher,

Mr. Noland, is very strict and gives way too much homework. He calls all of us Miss *and* Mr. *and he loves to refer to himself in third person. Mr. Noland isn't happy with your quiz grades . . . .*

My favorite class is English. I love writing compositions and reading in my literature book. Right now we are reading Romeo and Juliet. *Everybody complains but I love it! Can't you just imagine what it was like to live in Shakespeare's day? We'd spend our days wandering around in beautiful gardens wearing magnificent gowns reciting poetry and playing the lute while handsome gentlemen tried to win our hand. Of course, they did have the Bubonic Plague, but hey, we could just move to another palace.*

The hardest part of school is the other students. Everybody ignores me like I don't even exist. I've never really had a lot of friends, but it would be nice to have someone to talk to. I heard a boy whisper to his girlfriend that I was that "freak" they sent over from the elementary school who was supposed to be smart. And if that wasn't bad enough, I was coming into the girls' bathroom when a group of girls were leaving. I recognized them from my English class, so I thought if I smiled a bright smile they might speak to me or at least smile back. Instead, they walked right past me like I wasn't even there. As the door closed I heard one of them say, "Just how old is she anyway? She doesn't even have any boobs." And then they all laughed. I stayed in the bathroom and cried instead of going to class. I was afraid everyone heard what those girls said and they'd laugh at me.

I'm starting to think I should have taken Aunt Hat up on her offer and come to Tacoma Ladies Academy. But I can't leave my mother. She's been having migraine headaches and not acting like herself. She's also dating this man who I really don't like. I just have a bad feeling about him and I don't feel like I can leave her right now.

Be sure to write to me about everything that happens at the Academy! How's your new roommate? I wish it was me.

Your friend,
Sassy

I addressed the envelope and laid it with the letter on my nightstand. Sleep wrapped its warm arms around me, so I lay down and pulled the covers up to my chin. I wondered what my life would be like if I was at Tacoma Ladies' Academy. What would it be like at a private girls' school? What would life be like without Mama? As I drifted off to sleep, my lips mouthed the words of a poem I'd memorized in English class, "The Road Not Taken," by Robert Frost.

> I shall be telling this with a sigh
> Somewhere ages and ages hence:
> Two roads diverged in a wood, and I—
> I took the one less traveled by,
> And that has made all the difference.

"This calls for a celebration, Sassy girl!" Mama grabbed my hand and twirled me around like we were dancing.

"Thanks, Mama." I smiled. I was proud of the grades on my report card. The lowest grade I had was a 95, and that was in algebra. "Wait till Madge sees this."

"Wait till Madge sees what?" Madge strode across the shop carrying a big bottle of crème rinse. It was Friday evening, and Mama and Madge were the only ones in the shop.

"Look at my report card." I handed it to Madge. She took it over to her station and pulled her glasses out of the drawer. She set down in her chair and studied it, her face expressionless.

I stood still, waiting for her to say something. Finally, she peered over her glasses at me. "Not bad."

"Not bad!" I sputtered like a rusty faucet.

She laughed, and Mama joined in. "Had you going there, didn't I?"

"Aw, Madge." I took my report card and slipped it inside my history book.

"I tell you what," said Madge. "Let's have us a girls' night out."

"A what?"

Mama repeated it. "A girls' night out. Yeah, I like that idea. What did you have in mind?"

Madge took off her glasses and spun herself around in her chair. "Let's see, we could start with dinner over to the diner, and then I believe there's a new movie on at the Alamo."

I looked at Mama, who was smiling with such pride in her eyes that I almost cried. Chuck hadn't been around the last two weeks, and Mama was acting like her old self. "Let's do it," she said, heading for the back room to get her things together.

I gathered my books and sailed out of the shop. I called to Madge as I left. "Tell Mama I'm going on home so I can get the bathroom first."

A gust of cold air pushed Mama and me into the diner. Madge was sitting in a booth by the door, sipping coffee. "Who you two running from?" she asked.

We laughed and peeled off our coats. "It's cold out there! Feel my hands." Mama laid her hands of the back of Madge's bare neck.

"Jesus, you're froze!"

We settled into the booth just as Brenda Sue appeared carrying a tray laden with food. She started handing out plates piled with salmon cakes, fried potatoes, and mustard greens. In the center of the table, she set down a basket covered with a towel. I didn't have to look under it to know it covered a mound of hot cornbread. The smell was making my stomach growl. Next, she handed each of us a bowl of pinto beans and a tall frosted glass of sweet milk. "Can I get you anything else?"

Madge said, "No, that'll do it. Thanks."

When Brenda Sue was gone, Madge looked at Mama and me, grinning at us across the table. "Well, I knew you two'd be late, and I was hungry."

We laughed and picked up our forks. We dug in and ate until we couldn't swallow another bite. Then we bundled up and headed down the street to the Alamo Theatre. "Can you believe it's this cold and it's not even Halloween?" Madge asked.

"I swear, it feels like it's going to snow." Mama buried her hands in her pockets. "You all walk a little faster."

We made it just in time for the start of the movie *Seven Brides for Seven Brothers*. I sat between Mama and Madge and laughed more at them than I did at the picture show. When we left the theatre, Mama and Madge sang, "Bless your beautiful hide/Where ever you may be. We ain't met yet but I'm willin to bet/You're the gal for me" all the way up the street to the beauty shop, where Madge had left her car. We piled into the car, and Madge dropped us off in front of our apartment.

"Good night, ladies," she said. "I believe our ladies' night out was a success." And with a wave, she drove off.

On Saturday morning, I heard Mama calling me from the kitchen. "Sassy, I need you to run down to Mic or Mac for me."

I stuck my head out of my room. I was already dressed and holding a book with my finger stuck inside to hold my place. "What do you need?"

"A can of Folgers," Mama said, rubbing her forehead. "There's no way I can make it today without my coffee."

"Okay, let me get my shoes."

"Tell Mr. Stiltner to put it on my tab."

I left Mama setting at the kitchen table, rubbing her forehead.

Autumn, 1955

Sylvia

"I may be strong-minded, but no one can say I'm out of my sphere now, for woman's special mission is supposed to be drying tears and bearing burdens." Louisa May Alcott, *Little Women*

I stumbled into the kitchen, took the bottle of aspirin out of the cabinet, dry-swallowed two pills, and lit a cigarette. I set down at the table and smoked, wishing for a cup of strong black coffee. The pain between my eyes was a steady hum. I stubbed out my cigarette and got up. I said, "May as well get up from here and do something."

I went into Sassy's room and peeled back the bedspread, yanked off the sheets, and went around to the side of the bed that was so close to the wall I had to inch in sideways. I smiled at the books spilled on the floor. I looked at the titles as I made a neat stack that grew until it was even with the top of the mattress. Next, I picked up the pillow and started pulling off the pillowcase—and that's when it happened.

The pillow slipped out of my hand. I grabbed for it and stepped into the tower of books. They went sliding under the bed, scattering dust bunnies in their wake. "Shit fire!" I said, getting down on my knees to restack the books. I laid my head on the mattress and blind-fished with my left hand under the bed. I raked out books, stacked them, and reached back under the bed again. This time I raked out more than Sassy's books.

In my hand was a large, heavy envelope. I turned it over, but there was no writing on either side. I sat down on the bed, opened it, and pulled out a stack of papers. The heading leaped off the page: *Tacoma Academy for Young Ladies.* I scanned down the page until I saw the words *boarding school.* Forgetting all about the sheets, I took the envelope into the kitchen and spread its contents on the table, sat down, and began to read. *Situated close to Seattle and Mt. Rainier, Tacoma Ladies' Academy has a long history of educating young women who want to reach higher standards and place importance on their future place in society . . .* I read about the *diverse* classes in botany, sketching, and music appreciation. I read about the *quality* of the student resources, such as the dormitories, athletic complex, theater facilities, music conservatory, and library.

I put my hand to my chest, trying to stop the hammer pounding away at my heart. It was easy to see the papers had been read again and again, the creases worn deep into the page. From the stack, I pulled out a letter that began, *Dear Hattie Mae Mason, Thank you for requesting information about Tacoma Ladies Academy.* "Son of a bitch!" I shouted. *I should have known this was her doing.*

I was putting the papers back in the envelope when I saw there were two letters in the bottom of the packet. I pulled them out, expecting them to be from Aunt Hat, but they were from Amelia Hall, Seattle, Washington. My hands shook as I opened the first envelope and unfolded the letter.

September 9, 1955
Amelia Hall
Orchard Grove
Seattle, Washington

Dear Sassy,

It was so good to hear from you. I am getting ready to start the fall term at the Academy and I am so excited. I would love it if you decided to come to school here, and I'm sure you would love it here too. We would be such good friends, I just know it! I am so glad your Aunt asked me to write to you.

I adore the books you mentioned, especially Little Women. *I have read it three times and I've also read* Jo's Boys *and* Little Men. *If you loved* Little Women, *you will love them too. I think* Anne of Green Gables *is such a wonderful book! I just know if you come to the Academy with me, we will be best friends just like Anne and Diana!*

I understand how you feel about leaving your mother because I miss my father when I am away at school. My mother died when I was five, so it's just me and my father, and of course, my grandmother, who is a friend of your Aunt. Why don't you talk to your mother about coming to the Academy? You might be surprised at what she thinks if you are honest with her and tell her how you feel. Just tell her what you told me, and I feel sure that you would be much happier at the Academy.

Take care and write back soon,
Amelia

Just tell her what you told me . . . I felt like someone had just doused me with ice water. I stared at the words until they blurred on the page. What had Sassy told this girl? Did something happen I didn't know about? Was it because of what happened when John's wife showed up at the shop? I picked up the second envelope.

Amelia Hall
Tacoma Ladies Academy
Tacoma, Washington
October 19, 1955

Dear Sassy,

How are you? I am back at school so from now on when you write to me, please use my school address. My roommate is Emily Ann Johnson and she is from Wyoming. She has beautiful long blonde hair that falls in perfect curls down her back. She reminds me of Amy in Little Women! *She is very nice, but she snores! It's been very hard to get to sleep because she falls asleep before I do and starts snoring right away. I hope that she will either stop snoring or I will get used to it. I wish you were my roommate and I wouldn't mind if you did snore!*

I am so glad you are doing well in your classes and I know how you feel about algebra! I am definitely like you; I love to read and write stories and I don't even mind history, but algebra is horrible. My favorite class is art history. Mademoiselle Bouvier, our teacher, is a wonderful artist. She is from Paris, France and speaks with a French accent. When she gets excited you can't understand a word she says! Last night we had a concert in the conservatory. I love music and wish I could play the violin but my fingers are too fat.

I can't believe the students at your school treat you that way. Did you tell your mother how they act? Perhaps if things change with your mother and her boyfriend, you could come to the Academy after Christmas when we begin the second semester. That would be so lovely! I must close now and put this letter in the mail basket. I look forward to hearing from you again soon!

Your Friend,
Amelia

I read it again stopping at the words *I can't believe the students at your school treat you that way.*

Oh, God, I thought, *how do they treat her?* I put the letter and everything else back in the packet just like I found it. Then I took it to Sassy's room and put it back under the bed. I made up the bed, being careful to put her book back face down on the bed like she had it.

I thought back to a conversation I had with Madge, just last week. She asked me why Sassy never brought any friends around, or why she never mentioned having any friends. I had laughed it off, saying if anything was amiss, surely Sassy would've told me.

Only she hadn't.

I heard Sassy come in and set the coffee on the counter. She called out, "Mama, here's your coffee. Mama?" She knocked on my bedroom door.

"Come in."

Sassy opened the door just enough to peek in. I had the shade at my window closed, blocking out the morning sunshine. I lay on my side, facing the wall.

"Mama?"

"I got a headache. I'm going to lay here awhile."

"Can I get you anything?"

"No."

"I got your coffee. Want me to make you some?"

"No, thank you. Maybe later."

Sassy closed the door, and I sat up. I pulled out the drawer of my bedside table and got out the bottle of pills the neurologist had given me. I had seen him last week, but I told Sassy that Madge and me had gone to see a beauty show.

I opened the bottle and took a pill. Sometimes it helped, and sometimes it didn't. All that doctor could tell me was my headaches were from head trauma I got from the accident, and there wasn't much he could do about it. He said stress and worry could bring them on and make them worse.

I told that doctor to tell me something I didn't already know. And now, I had one more thing to worry about. Sassy could make straight one hundreds at high school—it wasn't the classes that were the problem. She had no friends. And according to that letter, the kids were mean to her, and it was clear this Amelia girl was just the kind of friend Sassy needed.

By the first of November, the mountains of Coal Valley were ablaze with the colors of fire. The first frost had come and gone, and the wooly worm was promising a bad winter. I stood in the front room window and watched Sassy walk down the sidewalk to school, her ponytail a blonde blur disappearing around the corner. I wanted to see a spring in her step, like she was eager to get to school, but all I saw was a little girl trying to look grown up.

Since discovering Amelia's letters, I realized Sassy had never really *told* me about school. She *talked* about her classes, homework, teachers, even the lunch in the cafeteria—anything but the other kids. No matter how many jokes I made about the good-looking boys or the silly girls, Sassy never offered anything specific about anybody. She told me how Sam Akers always gave the wrong answer in history class and how Nancy Carol Waters was the most popular girl in school, but she never recounted a single conversation or even a "hi, how are you" from another kid.

What I hadn't realized was that sometimes it's what people don't say that speaks the loudest, just like it's easier *not* to ask questions when you don't want to know the answers in the first place.

In the kitchen, I set down with paper and a pen. It had been a mistake. I should've never agreed to let Sassy skip a grade. Now I had to fix it. I got up and poured a cup of coffee, added sugar, and took a sip. With both hands, I hugged its warmth and worried. When I went to take another sip, I realized the cup was empty. I opened the cabinet and got out a pack of cigarettes and a box of matches.

Back at the table, I set down and stamped the box of cigarettes against the heel of my hand, before drawing one from the pack. The match flared and I took a hard draw on the cigarette. While I smoked, I stared at the blank page. In the quiet, the clock ticking over the stove sounded like a steady drum beat. I put down my cigarette and picked up my pen. *Tick. Tick. Tick.* The rhythm of the clock kept perfect time with my heartbeat.

Sylvia Richardson
#12 Maple Street
Coal Valley, VA
November 5, 1955

Dear Aunt Hat,
    I know about the boarding school in Tacoma and . . .

I slammed my fist down on the table, knocking my cigarette out of the ashtray and shedding hot ashes across the table. *Damn it!* I jumped up and knocked over my chair, but I managed to grab my cigarette and a wet dishrag out of the sink. I put the cigarette back in the ashtray and wiped up the ashes. For a moment, I stood staring into the sink; then I righted my chair, set down, and continued.

I know about the boarding school in Tacoma and I think it's a good idea for Sassy to go to school there. Can she still go this year? Could she start in January? If she can, can you come to Coal Valley and get her? I can't bring myself to send her all that way by herself.
    Why don't you plan to spend Christmas with us? We can tell her about it then. For now, let's keep this quiet and not mention it to Sassy. She has enough on her mind without us worrying her about it.
    I will wait for your reply.
    Love,
    Sylvia

I folded the letter without reading it a second time because I was afraid if I did, I would tear it up. Instead, I grabbed an envelope, stuffed it inside, and wrote Aunt Hat's address on the front. Then I picked up the bag with my work shoes in it, put on my coat, stuffed the letter in my pocket, and left for work.

"You and Sassy coming with me to Mommy's for Thanksgiving, ain't you?" Madge asked. She was busy laying out the permanent wave rods and solutions for her first appointment.

"We won't be able to come this year," I said. I wouldn't look at Madge; instead, I turned on the water in my shampoo bowl, took all of the combs out of the disinfectant, and dropped them into the bowl.

"Why not?" Madge stopped counting rods and turned around to stare at me.

I knew this moment was coming, and I had been dreading it. For the past three years, me and Sassy had gone with Madge to have Thanksgiving dinner with her mommy and Aunt Bertie in West Virginia. I said, "I reckon we'll eat at the diner this year."

"You might as well tell me."

"Tell you what?"

"Why you're washing combs that's already clean, and why you've been as nervous as a long-tailed cat in a room full of rocking chairs."

I turned off the water, picked up a towel, and set down in the chair at my station.

"Here." Madge handed me a cigarette. "You look like you need one."

"Thanks." I lit the cigarette, took a long drag off it, and leaned back in my chair. "Aunt Hat is coming for Thanksgiving."

"Well, no wonder you're so down in the mouth. When she's coming?"

"Next Wednesday on the noon bus."

"How long's she staying?"

"I'm not sure."

Madge laughed. "You told Sassy?"

"Not yet."

"Well, you better hurry. You just got a week."

I woke and moved my head to see if the pain had subsided. The clock said it was after 10:00. I'd slept almost eight hours. Bit by bit, I stood up. Lately, I was dizzy after one of my headaches—sometimes for a couple days. I made it to the bathroom and washed my face. I stared at the dark circles under my eyes. "Jesus," I said, "I look like hell."

This one had caught me by surprise. I usually knew when a headache was coming on—flashes of light and a cloud of light around objects. But this time, I was working on Ava Lou's hair when the pain hit me in the back of the head, almost knocking me to my knees. I had to get Madge to finish Ava Lou so I could go home.

I went into the living room. Sassy had left one of the lamps on. I went over to her room and listened at her door. I eased it open and saw she was asleep with a book next to her. I smiled. Wherever there was Sassy, there was a book.

I went into the kitchen. Even though the doctor told me not to mix those pain pills with alcohol, I figured it had been long enough since I took one to have a beer. I took it back to my room and closed the door. I put Hank Snow on the record player and "I Don't Hurt Anymore" drifted into the room. "All my teardrops are dried . . ."

I got out the cedar chest that held Gaines's letters and spread them on the bed. I set cross-legged and sipped my beer while looking through them. I took one out and started to read.

November 1, 1942
PFC Gaines Richardson
33647746
7th Infantry, 3rd Division

My Dearest Sylvia,

We've had a break in the fighting so I can sit down and write. As long as I keep going I'm alright, but when we stop I get so tired I don't think I can go on. That's when I think of you and my baby girl and the reason I'm here in the first place. I can't lose sight of that Sylvie. We have to save the world from evil like the Nazis. You know how your old man likes to read those big books and spout words at you. Well, a lot of those words have helped keep me going. I keep thinking about these lines by my favorite poet Walt Whitman. "The question, O me! so sad, recurring—What good amid these, O me, O life? Answer. That you are here. That life exists."

We're still moving through Italy and it's rained for a solid week. I thought the heat was bad, but the constant rain is worse. What I'd give for a dry pair of socks! I was thinking about you and Sassy and how the mountains at home must be beautiful with all the colors of fall. There's nothing even remotely pretty about this place.

I won't even write where I am because it will get marked out by the sensors. But I can tell you that the Italians hate the Jerries as much as we do. For one thing, they've taken everything here whether they needed it or not. The Italians say "Tedeschi robatti tutti" (the Germans have taken everything).

Keep me in your prayers and try not to worry. I love you and miss you more every day.

Gaines

I lit a cigarette and put the letter back in its envelope. *Well, Gaines, Thanksgiving is almost here, and I wish I had something to be thankful for. But all I have is Aunt Hat coming to take our baby away.*

It was time to tell Sassy that Aunt Hat was coming for Thanksgiving. I knew Sassy thought we were going with Madge to her mommy's like always, and I hated to disappoint her. Aunt Hat wasn't supposed to come until Christmas, but her letter said she'd be here for Thanksgiving. Her excuse was we needed time to get Sassy's stuff together for school. I didn't have any more excuses. It was time to tell Sassy what I'd done.

Autumn, 1955

Sassy

"Five minutes ago I was so miserable I was wishing I'd never been born and now I wouldn't change places with an angel." Lucy Maud Montgomery, *Anne of Green Gables*

The air was so cold, it made my eyes sting and my nose run, but I slowed my pace as I passed the houses on Maple Street. Wisps of blue smoke curled from the chimneys, and lamps cast a lazy glow through the windows. Someone was baking an apple pie, and the sweet aroma hung in the air, making me long for Thanksgiving Day. I couldn't wait to curl up with a book in front of the fireplace at Granny Bess's house after feasting on turkey with all the trimmings. I had two books, *The Scarlet Letter* and *The House of Seven Gables,* in my book bag, and I couldn't wait to read them. I knew it was going to be hard to save them until next week, but with all of the algebra homework I had, I didn't have time to read anyway.

I was looking forward to Thanksgiving dinner with Madge and her family. I called Madge's Mama Granny Bess and her sister Aunt Bertie. If you lined them up, they looked like the same person in different sizes. Granny Bess was the tall, skinny version; Madge the middle-sized version; and Aunt Bertie the short, round version.

Nobody in the world could make pumpkin pie like Granny Bess. She had her own pumpkin patch behind her house. She grew sugar pumpkins that she swore were the best kind for pies. They were smaller than the big pumpkins that made good jack-o-lanterns. Granny Bess said the secret to growing good pumpkins was to keep the slugs and snails away from the new plants. She surrounded each mound of dirt with pieces of cardboard she saved from boxes. She also said she never watered the leaves of the plant because they'd mildew. She must've known what she was doing, because her pumpkins were beautiful, and her pies were scrumptious.

Last year, I asked her what she put in her pumpkin pie to make it taste so good. Aunt Bertie and Madge laughed when Granny Bess wouldn't tell me. Granny Bess said it was a secret recipe and she never told anybody. According to Madge, she had more than one secret recipe she wouldn't give out. Living up on top of Bradshaw Mountain, I don't know who she thought was going to steal her recipes. Mama said some people are like that—they ain't got much, but they want to hang on to what they got, even if it's just a recipe.

I thought back to last year and how we all laughed and ate and laughed some more. When the dishes were done, I piled up in front of the fireplace with a book while Mama, Madge, Aunt Bertie, and Granny Bess played cards. Listening to their banter, I felt like I was at the center of a huge, loving family. There were times I yearned for a family—wished I could look at someone and think, "I have her hair color. Her nose is shaped just like mine. His eyes are the same color as mine."

Sometimes, I longed for the security of having a place where I belonged, surrounded by people who loved me. Being with Madge and her family, I learned that family doesn't have to mean relatives, or blood kin, as Mama called it. Family means the people you care about and that care about you. It means the people you can depend on—the ones you can go to when you're down and out. It also means the people you celebrate all of life's blessings with, and in my life, those people were the women who laughed and joked over a silly game of cards and kept secrets about making pies.

Still thinking about pumpkin pie, I entered room 104 of Coal Valley High School. I was, as usual, the first person in the room. This was where I spent the first fifteen minutes of every school day—the dreaded homeroom period. I dreaded it because I sat in a room full of kids who were chatting with each other, but none of them ever spoke to me. I usually busied myself with checking over my homework or reading—anything to pretend I didn't care.

This morning, Mr. Sanderson entered the room right after I did. Since he usually came in on the heels of the students when the last bell rang, I looked up. A girl I didn't recognize followed him into the room. She had that unmistakable "new student" look—somewhere between dazed and bewildered. Mr. Sanderson was in the middle of explaining her schedule to her when he looked over and saw me.

"Ah, Sarah Jane, this is—" He hesitated, looking down at the schedule he held in his hand. "Katherine Martin. She is a transfer student. Would you mind showing her around?"

I stood and smiled. "Sure, Mr. Sanderson, I'd be happy to."

The girl turned to me, relief flooding her face. Mr. Sanderson handed me her schedule and left the room. For an awkward moment, we stood looking down at our feet. Then she said, "Hi, I'm Kitty Martin. Thank you for rescuing me from Mr. Sanderson. He smells like rotten fish."

Startled, my eyes went wide, and then I started to laugh. She joined in, and soon we were wiping tears out of the corners of our eyes. "Come on, Sarah, you better show me how to get to my first class."

"Call me Sassy." We walked off down the hall together.

I couldn't wait to tell Mama about Kitty. She was from Allentown, Pennsylvania and was an only child like me, but she did have a daddy. He was the reason they moved to Coal Valley; he was a mining engineer, and his company back in Pennsylvania sent him to work with the engineers at Coal Valley Mining Co. Kitty and I had three of the same classes together and the same lunch period. For the first time all year, I had someone to talk to during lunch. For the first time all year, I had someone to talk to *period*.

I expected the house to be empty when I got home, so I was surprised to see Mama's shoes lying on the floor and her coat hanging by the door. It was unusual for her to be home before 5:00; worry doused me like a sudden spray of cold water that interrupts a hot shower. I put my things away and tiptoed over to her bedroom door. Afraid to knock and wake her, I eased open the door and saw Mama asleep, curled on her side. A glass of water and the packet of pills from Doc Sutherland were on the table next to her bed—another headache.

It was cold in the apartment, so I changed into pants and a sweater. I made myself a sandwich and sat down on the couch with it and my homework. I kept glancing over my shoulder at Mama's bedroom door. Her headaches were getting more often, and sometimes she was sick for days after them. Thanksgiving was only a week away, and I didn't want Mama to feel bad over the holiday.

I finished my homework, packed up my books, and went to my room to get the diary Aunt Hat sent me for my birthday. The bed looked so inviting that I sat down cross-legged in the middle of it and began to write.

Dear Diary,

Do I dare say I finally have a friend? Kitty Martin just dropped into my life this morning and I'm afraid that when I get to school tomorrow, she'll have disappeared, a figment of my imagination. Or what if she is real, but she meets some of the other girls and they tell her I'm that little freak from elementary school and that they don't have anything to do with me? Will she speak to me then? Will she walk by me like I'm not even there? Like they do. Or worse, will she whisper about me and laugh like they do?

Diary, I am going to ask God to answer my prayer and let me have this friend. He answered my last prayer; Chuck hasn't come around anymore in his fancy black Cadillac.

Sincerely,

Sassy

I woke to snow flurries wandering by my window like lazy white butterflies. I lay for a while and drifted with them, dreading getting up and going to school when it felt so good to burrow under the covers like a groundhog. I don't know why they were having school anyway—it was two days before Thanksgiving, and I still burned because Aunt Hat was ruining our holiday. Heck, she was ruining two, if she made good on her threat and stayed for Christmas.

I found Mama in the kitchen cooking oatmeal. "I figured you'd need something warm this morning. Have you looked outside?"

"Yeah. Maybe it'll start up good and keep Aunt Hat's bus from making it."

"Oh, Sassy, don't be like that."

Instead of replying, I hurried to get dressed. After school, Kitty and I were spending the afternoon together. I planned to take her to the beauty shop and introduce her to Mama and Madge. I couldn't wait to see their faces when they saw I had a friend. I don't know why I hadn't told Mama about her. For one thing, I was pouting at her for not telling

Aunt Hat to stay in Seattle. But the real reason was I liked keeping Kitty all to myself because it made me feel like she belonged to me.

By 1:00, when the last bell rang, the snow had stopped, and the sky sang clear as a bell. Coats buttoned up to our chins, arms locked together, heads bent against the cold, Kitty and I flew out of Coal Valley High and headed across the bridge to town. "What do you want to do first?" I asked.

"Let's go to your house."

Surprised, I stopped and looked at her. "Really—I thought you'd want to go to the drugstore for a cherry Coke, or something."

Kitty laughed. "Don't you have stuff to drink at your house?"

"Why, sure, let's go."

We locked arms again and turned down Maple Street toward our apartment. We only had until 5:00, when her father was picking her up in front of the post office. Kitty said they were leaving early in the morning going to their house in Allentown, Pennsylvania to spend Thanksgiving with her grandparents.

I wrapped my scarf tighter around my face so that my nose was covered. It was freezing, and my hot breath felt good bouncing back on my cold nose. By the time we made it to the apartment, we were both out of breath. I led the way up the stairs and put my key into the lock, only the doorknob turned all by itself, and the door swung open.

There stood Aunt Hat. Clad in solid gray, she looked like a giant boulder lodged in the doorway. I froze. Kitty bumped into me from behind, no doubt wondering why I stopped. My first thought was to slam the door and run. Instead, in one swift movement, Aunt Hat grabbed me and hauled me over the threshold and into a bear hug.

"Well, looky here," Aunt Hat shouted, almost knocking me backward. "And who's this?"

Kitty had stepped in behind me and stood gazing open-mouthed at Aunt Hat. I couldn't find my voice, but Kitty stepped forward and held out her hand. "I'm Katherine Martin. It's nice to meet you."

"Hattie Mae Mason." Aunt Hat shook hands with Kitty. "What you girls doing out of school early?"

"We got out early today for the Thanksgiving holiday." I found my voice, which sounded far away and foreign to my ears.

"You young'uns must be hungry. Go put your stuff up, and I'll fix up something to eat—that is, if Sylvia's got anything in that kitchen."

And she was off to the kitchen. I motioned for Kitty to follow me. We ducked into my bedroom and closed the door. I turned to Kitty, ready to babble apologies, when she started to giggle. I collapsed backward across my bed. Kitty plopped down next to me. "I'm sorry, Kitty. I had no idea she was going to be here. She's supposed to be at the Valley Hotel."

"Don't worry about it! I love old people!"

This was not turning out like I imagined it. We were supposed to be having fun doing girl stuff. Instead, Aunt Hat had ruined it—just like she'd ruined my Thanksgiving, and it hadn't even happened yet.

I woke up in a haze of fever, my throat so sore I could barely swallow. Mama felt my head and announced that I was staying home from school. "But Mama, I have a history test today."

I pushed myself up on my elbows and then fell back against my pillow. I hated to go to Doc Sutherland, because that meant a shot. Doc's wife would put me in a little room where I had to sit and stare at the silver syringes lined up on a white towel. When Doc came in, he made me stick out my tongue and say *ahhh,* and then he held down my tongue with a big wooden stick that always gagged me. The nurse would get me a little white envelope of penicillin pills while Doc picked up one of those syringes and filled it from a little rubber-topped bottle. When he gave me the shot, he made me stand on one leg and stick out my tongue just like I was a little girl.

Mama said, "Sassy, you're sick, and you're staying in bed. I swear— you're bound to be the only kid in Coal Valley who argues to *go* to school." She left the room and came back with two aspirin and a glass of water. "Here, take this, and try to go back to sleep. I'll be back after lunch to take you to Doc's."

When I woke up, a beam of sunlight had escaped from the corner of my window shade and was dancing on the wall. I lay watching it, dreading getting up and admitting that I felt terrible. I heard the front door close and realized Mama must be going to make good on her threat to take me to see Doc. I sat up, and that's when I heard the voices. Mama was home, and she was talking to somebody. It was hard to tell who the other voice belonged to, because my swollen throat reached into my ears.

I eased open the door and peeked out. The unmistakable girth of Aunt Hat sat in the living room, and Mama stood in front of her with her hands on her hips. Neither of them saw me as I slipped out of my room and stood at the threshold of the living room.

"I know we need to tell her, but she's sick. Let's wait a few days." Mama said.

Aunt Hat said, "Sylvia, it's the fifth of December. We will be leaving here in exactly one month."

I started to say something to let them know I was there, until I heard *we will be leaving here.* I stepped back from the doorway, where they couldn't see me, and listened.

"I know that," Mama said. "A few more days won't make any difference."

"I don't understand you. You told me Sassy wanted to go. What is it? You afraid I'll cut your money off?

"I can't believe you said that!"

Aunt Hat snorted. "Cause if that's it, you needn't worry."

"It's nothing like that," Mama said. "I just worry this isn't the right thing to do."

"The right thing to do—the right thing to do? When did you ever worry about doing the right thing? With Sarah Jane gone, you can come and go as you please, stay out all hours of the night, run around with any man you please."

"Stop it!" Mama said. "Please, just stop."

I held my breath. For a moment, no one spoke, but I could feel Mama and Aunt Hat glaring at each other.

Then Aunt Hat spoke in her "let's be reasonable and do it my way" voice. "Sylvia, remember, you wrote to me. You said this is what Sarah Jane wanted."

I stepped into the room and said, "*What* exactly did I say I wanted?"

Mama spun around, stunned. Her hands flew up and landed on her heart. For an agonizing moment, no one spoke. Then Aunt Hat took charge. "Sarah Jane, come over here and sit down, dear." She pointed to the couch. "How're you feeling?"

I stood still and said, "What are you two talking about?"

Mama took a step toward me and reached out like she was going to feel my forehead. I dodged her hand and went over and sat down on the couch. Aunt Hat leaned forward in her chair and said, "Now we can talk. Sylvia, sit down next to Sarah Jane."

Mama sat down, and this time, when she touched my forehead, I didn't move away. "You're still a little warm; let me get you some aspirin."

"Mama, I'm fine. I want to know what this is about."

Aunt Hat said, "Your mother and I have a surprise for you."

I looked from Mama to Aunt Hat. All at once, dread went tumbling past me like a ball of yarn unraveling across the floor. When neither of them spoke, I asked again, "What's the surprise? Are we going on a trip?"

"No, darling," said Mama. "I know it's been hard for you." She hesitated, her eyes falling on her pack of cigarettes. "Going on to high school, I mean. And I'm real proud of how good you've done."

She paused and put her hand on my knee. I looked down at her perfectly manicured nails and then up at her face. There was something there I had never seen before—fear. Mama was afraid. Fear hung around her like a shroud. But I saw something else too. Whatever it was that Mama was afraid of, she had the courage to look me in the eye.

She said, "I found out that you wanted to go to that boarding school in Tacoma, and, well . . ."

"You're going to start in January," interrupted Aunt Hat. "Ain't that wonderful?

1942–1944

"'God gave me the child!' cried she. 'He gave her in requital of all things else which ye had taken from me. She is my happiness—she is my torture, none the less! Pearl keeps me here in life! Pearl punishes me, too!'" Nathaniel Hawthorne, *The Scarlet Letter*

Sylvia

The only thing missing were the bars on the windows. I lit another cigarette. The flash of the match and the smell of sulfur hypnotized me until the fire singed my fingers. I dropped the match in the sink and looked down at my hands—chapped, the nails short and uneven, the cuticles torn. My hands had never looked like this before.

I took a draw on my cigarette and raised the window just enough to let the smoke out. The cold rushed in and wrapped an icy shawl around me. Blue cold—the kind of cold that made your chest burn and your nose run; the kind of cold you never take a baby out in.

Trapped.

I crouched on the floor beneath the bathroom window, sneaking a cigarette like a prisoner hiding from the guards. My whole body vibrated with fear. Fear set close to me, tapping me on the shoulder, whispering in my ear. Fear said, "It's just you and Sassy. You're all alone."

Except for the two weeks that Gaines was home on leave, I was never without Aunt Hat or Madge. And when Gaines was here, I didn't need them. He took care of Sassy ten times better than I could. Two weeks—that's all the happiness I ever got with this baby. For two sweet weeks, I had it all.

Then Gaines went overseas, and Uncle Danny Ray died, and Aunt Hat went back to Seattle to bury him. She promised to come back as soon as possible, but it was taking longer than she thought, and now the bad weather had set in and it was hard to tell when she'd get back. On top of that, Madge was sick and afraid to stay with me because she didn't want to bring her cold in on the baby.

I went to my bedroom to check on Sassy, but she was still fast asleep. I lay down on the bed and reached for Gaines's latest letter. I held it up to the light coming in from the open door so I could read it for what must have been the hundredth time.

November 1, 1942
PFC Gaines Richardson
33647746
7th Infantry, 3rd Division

My Dearest Sylvia,

We've had a break in the fighting so I can sit down and write. As long as I keep going I'm alright, but when we stop I get so tired I don't think I can go on. That's when I think of you and my baby girl and the reason I'm here in the first place. I can't lose sight of that Sylvie. We have to save the world from evil like the Nazis. You know how your old man likes to read those big books and spout words at you. Well, a lot of those words have helped keep me going. I keep thinking about these lines by my favorite poet Walt Whitman. "The question, O me! so sad, recurring—What good amid these, O me, O life? Answer. That you are here. That life exists."

We're still moving through Italy and it's rained for a solid week. I thought the heat was bad, but the rain is worse. What I'd give for a dry pair of socks! I been thinking about you and Sassy and how the mountains at home must be beautiful with all the colors of fall. There's nothing even remotely pretty about this place.

I won't even write where I am because it will get marked out by the sensors. But I can tell you that the Italians hate the Jerries as much as we do. For one thing, they've taken everything here whether they needed it or not. The Italians say "Tedeschi robatti tutti" (the Germans have taken everything).

Keep me in your prayers and try not to worry. I love you and miss you more ever day.

Gaines

144

I sat up and smoothed the letter against my chest before folding it and putting it in the little cedar chest I bought for Gaines's letters. Lately, I slept with it on my bedside table or sometimes in the bed next to me, like in some way the letters made Gaines closer. Sleeping was something I didn't do much. Sleep brought dreams of what could've been—or worse, nightmares of what could come.

I swung my legs over the side of the bed and buried my face in my hands. What would Gaines say if he knew the baby girl he loved with all his heart was nothing more to me than worry in a diaper. What would he think of a mother who believed all that "bundle of joy" shit was just that – shit.

The tears stung at my eyes. Nothing had gone right this live long day, and it wasn't the baby's fault. It was mine. I didn't have enough fingers to count my worries – her bottle was too hot or too cold; the diaper pin was sticking her; she was cold and needed a blanket; she was hot and had too much cover on her; I didn't feed her enough; I fed her too much; when she cried I worried something was wrong; when she hushed, I worried harder. But more than anything, when I looked into her dark blue eyes, I worried would the love I desperately wanted to feel, ever come?

I got up and went to stand by the baby bed. I looked down at my daughter and knew that if she woke up and saw me, she wouldn't smile. Sassy liked everybody better than me. When Madge talked to her, she smiled and cooed. When Aunt Hat was here, Sassy turned her head toward the sound of her voice. Yesterday, when Mr. and Mrs. Ashby from the dry goods store came upstairs to see her, she smiled all over them. Then they handed her to me, and she studied me with those big solemn eyes like she couldn't figure out who I was.

I crept from the room and gathered all the dirty clothes. Thank the good Lord that Mr. and Mrs. Ashby let me use the washer and dryer in the back room of their store. I peeked in and made sure Sassy was still asleep, then got the diaper pail and dragged it to the door. By the time I wrestled it down the stairs, I was close to tears. I was loading the washing machine when the light caught the slim gold band on my left hand. "Eighteen," I whispered, staring at it. "Eighteen. A wife and a mother. And I'm alone."

I was hurrying back upstairs when the tears surprised me like a kiss in the dark. I stumbled and went down on my hands and knees. The tears ran down my face and dripped on the stairs. I rolled over and set back, my sobs bouncing around the empty stairwell. I cursed and stomped my feet. *Why did Aunt Hat and Madge leave me alone?* I wailed and beat my fists on the wall. *Why is my husband fighting a war halfway around the world? Why does everybody I love leave me?*

I wrapped my arms around myself, but I couldn't stop my body from shaking. I leaned forward, then rocked back and forth. *Oh God, what if something happens?* If the Ashby's were in the store, I wouldn't have felt so scared. But it was Saturday evening, and they were closed until Monday. There was nobody in the building but us.

I don't know how long I set there before I come back to myself, but when I was able to make it up the stairs, Sassy was still asleep. I looked at the clock. She should have been awake, so I debated whether to warm her bottle or wait until she woke up. *What should I do?* If I waited until she woke up, she'd more than likely start crying before I got it ready. If I warmed it right away, she'd stay asleep, and I'd have to throw it away. If Madge or Aunt Hat were here, they'd know what to do, but there I stood like a jackass.

For the next five minutes, I watched the clock and walked back and forth to the bedroom. I went into the kitchen and got her bottle out of the refrigerator. I filled the pot with water and put it on the stove to boil. Before the water got hot, I turned off the stove and put the bottle back in the refrigerator. I paced back and forth for another five minutes before looking in the bedroom, but she was still asleep.

I went into the bathroom and lit a cigarette. While I smoked, I argued with myself whether or not to warm that damn bottle. I laid my cigarette on the sink, went back to the bedroom, and looked in again. I eased into the room and waited for my eyes to adjust to the dark. I bent over her crib so I could make sure she was still breathing. I laid my hand lightly on her back. Then I took one finger and touched her cheek. Its warm softness caressed my fingertip. She didn't move, so I left again and went back to the bathroom to finish my cigarette.

It was a relief when I heard Sassy fussing. For the next two hours, I was busy feeding and changing her, then running up and down the stairs with her on my shoulder to the washer and dryer. By the time I finished the washing, it was the edge of dark. I lay Sassy down on her stomach on a pallet on the floor. I paced back and forth while she kicked her legs and waved her arms like she was swimming.

At 9:00, I stopped dreading it. Madge and Aunt Hat both told me to wait until bedtime to bath her and she would sleep longer, but the real reason I waited was because I knew she was going to cry. She did every time I bathed her, and this time was no different. I tried—I really tried. I did everything Madge and Aunt Hat showed me, and she still balled up her fists, puffed out her cheeks, and squalled. Her face turned red, and she cried so hard, the sweat popped out on her forehead. I cried too—hot tears of frustration. When I finally set down and gave her a bottle, both of us were exhausted.

Shortly after 10:00, I put Sassy in her crib. I made sure she was asleep before I went to the bathroom to smoke. This time, I took paper and pen with me. I settled down on the floor with my cigarette and began a letter.

December 10, 1942
Sylvia Richardson
#12 Maple Street
Coal Valley, VA

Dear Gaines,

It was so good to get your letter and know you are safe. I think about you every minute of every day. Thanksgiving without you was hard. Me and Sassy went with Madge to her Mommy and Daddy's. Bessie and Roy are fine people. They live just over the West Virginia line on State Line Ridge. Would you believe, we had a big turkey Roy shot sitting on the front porch! He was sure proud of that turkey and must have told the story about how he shot it from the front porch at least ten times that day. Madge said her daddy wasn't doing too good and hadn't been able to get out in the woods and hunt like he used to, so she was tickled to death he had a "turkey tale." Madge said he'd worked in the mines since he was sixteen, and now his lungs is about to give out.

Sassy sure is growing. She's eating like a little pig and is finally getting some hair. It's so blonde that she still looks bald headed! Her eyes are still blue but they are starting to get darker. I think they're going to turn brown like mine. If they do, it'll be the only thing she has that looks like me! Everybody says she looks just like her daddy.

It's been too cold here to take Sassy out much. The day after Thanksgiving we had one little skiff of snow. I guess it's saving up for a big one. I can't imagine what the weather is like where you are. I worry if you're too hot or is it cold there?

Gaines, I beg you to take care of yourself. Know that I love you and am praying for you to come back to us. I hope that in the New Year, things will change and bring peace to all of us. I pray that the New Year will bring you back to me and Sassy. I give her a special kiss every day just for you.

My husband, stay safe. I love you more ever day.

Love,

Sylvia

Madge

Monday morning, Sylvia opened the door and practically threw the baby into my arms. She was wearing the same clothes she had on Friday, and her hair was a mess. She was as pale as a ghost, with big black circles under her eyes. Her hands shook. What scared me most was her eyes.

I seen eyes like that once before when I was a little girl.

In the woods behind our house, there was a creek that had a lot of beaver, and Daddy would put out traps for them. I begged and begged him to take me with him to check his traps, and one day, he finally let me. We was going along the creek when I heard Daddy cuss under his breath. He told me to stay right there and wait for him, but of course, I sneaked up on him so I could see what he didn't want me to see. Laying on her side, her leg caught in one of Daddy's traps, was a doe. Her eyes have haunted me to this day. This morning, when Sylvia opened the door, it was like looking into the eyes of that doe.

I followed Sylvia into the apartment. I'd made myself stay away because I didn't want to give Sassy this cold. I even tried to convince myself I was doing a good thing, that it was time for Sylvia to learn how to take care of her baby by herself. Sassy was almost three months old and somebody had been with Sylvia every night since she birthed her. But looking into her eyes, I could see how wrong I was.

The place was a shambles. The kitchen was a mess of dirty bottles and coffee cups, and the whole apartment reeked of dirty diapers. There was a pile of clean clothes thrown on the couch, and the baby's blankets and things were scattered everywhere.

I looked down at Sassy, relieved to see she was clean, dry, and sleeping like an angel. "Sylvia, honey, set down over there and calm down. I'll put Sassy in her bed and be right—"

"No!" Sylvia flew at me, grabbing for the baby. "You can't lay her down."

I stopped in my tracks and turned back to Sylvia. She looked for all the world like a crazy woman. "Why? What's wrong with her? She looks fine."

"You can't lay her down," Sylvia pleaded.

"Okay, honey, we'll just set down and talk about this." I went over to the couch, pushed the clothes out of the way, and set down. Sylvia stood over us, wringing her hands. Finally, she set down on the edge of the couch.

"What is it, honey? Did something happen?"

"You can't lay her down. You have to hold her."

"Why, honey? Why can't I lay her down?"

Sylvia looked down at her hands and whispered, "Because she will die."

"Oh, Sylvie, honey, she ain't going to die. Look at her." I held her out so she could see her. "She's just fine."

Sylvia kept her eyes on her hands. When she spoke, her voice was flat, like it took all her energy to speak. "I had a dream. I knew I shouldn't have gone to sleep."

I was relieved when she said it was a dream. At least that made some sense why she was acting like this. I tried again. "Sylvie, it was just a dream. Honey, Sassy is fine. Look at her." Again, I held her out to Sylvia.

"You don't understand. If I lay her down, she will die." Sylvia finally looked at Sassy but made no move to touch her.

I stared at her and thought about what I should say. Never in my life had I seen a woman have the birthing blues as bad as Sylvie. When we went over to my Mommy's for Thanksgiving, Mommy said Sylvia acted like she was scared of her baby, and that I had to stop staying with them and let Sylvia learn how to tend to her baby by herself. Mommy said every woman goes through this, and you got to suck it up and put your shoulder to the plow. I figured Mommy knowed better than most, having birthed nine young'uns, but what would she say if she could see Sylvie right now?

I asked, "When was the last time you had any sleep or anything to eat?"

"I went to sleep Friday night after I put Sassy down. I was so tired . . ." The tears started coursing down her face. "And I had that dream."

I shifted Sassy to my shoulder so I could put my other arm around Sylvia. She melted into me, her body shuddering with sobs. It felt like I was holding a bird whose wings beat frantically against my chest. Guilt washed over me. I should've never left her alone with Sassy. I spoke into her hair. "Honey, it was just a dream. It's all right."

Sylvia's voice rose until it was a wail. She pulled away from me. "I can't do this, Madge. I just can't!"

I stood and made my voice calm but firm. "Now, I'm going to put this baby in her bed so she can rest, and you are going to go into that bathroom and take a bath." I pointed in the direction of the bathroom. "Go on, Sylvie." I walked on to the bedroom without looking back.

I laid Sassy in the crib and grabbed hold of the rails with both hands. I had to admit that Sylvia was in trouble and had been since the day Sassy was born. In my mind's eye, I seen Sylvia laying in the hospital bed after Sassy was born, telling the nurse to give the baby to me. I had tried to show Sylvia how to feed her. I even put Sassy on her shoulder, to show her how to burp her, with Sylvia saying the whole time, she couldn't do it. It wasn't until Sassy fell asleep, that I got Sylvia to hold her, but she kept her arms stiff and away from her body like she was afraid to let the baby touch her.

I leaned over the crib and rubbed Sassy's back. I whispered, "Sassy, I'm so sorry. I thought your mama would get over the blues by now." I straightened up and tucked the blanket around her. I took a deep breath and started out of the room. I had to help Sylvia, but how? Why do people think a woman is supposed to just *know* what to do with a baby? We ain't born knowing how to tend to them. Most times, a woman learns how to take care of a baby from her mommy and from coming up with babies around her. When you don't have that, it's hard on a woman to be handed a baby and told, "Here you go; now take care of it." No wonder Sylvia is so blue. Since the war snatched Gaines away, she ain't got nobody but me. I hope nothing don't happen to him. If it does, God help Sylvie.

I went to the bathroom and stood outside the door until I heard the water stop running. "You all right?"

"Yeah."

In the kitchen, I attacked the mess. When Sylvia came out of the bathroom, I had a bowl of oatmeal ready. I pointed to the table and poured her a glass of milk. Sylvia sat down and stared at the bowl. I sat down across from her and took her hand. "Honey, I'm worried about you. You can't go on like this."

Sylvia looked at me but said nothing. "The first thing you're going to do is eat," I said, getting up from the table. To her credit, Sylvia picked up the spoon and took a bite. While she ate, I folded the clean laundry, put it away, and got the diaper pail. "I'm going to go downstairs and put these diapers in the wash. You eat every bite and drink all that milk."

I hauled the diaper pail downstairs. While I loaded the washing machine, I fretted about Sylvia. When I brought them home from the hospital, I thought I would stay with Sylvia a few days and help her until she got on her feet. But those few days turned into a week, and that week turned into two, then three. Then Gaines come home on leave, and I thought surely she'd be all right by herself when he went back, but it didn't matter no way, because Hattie Mae come to stay the winter with them. Maybe things would've been alright if Hattie Mae hadn't had to leave. But that ain't neither here nor there now. People don't pick their time to die, and Hattie Mae had no choice but to go back to Seattle and take care of her brother's funeral.

When I got back upstairs, Sylvia was in the bathroom, brushing her hair. I went to the door and watched her. The brush glided through her hair like a silk stocking sliding up a shapely leg. She was painfully thin, and the dark circles framing her big, brown eyes made her look like a dying invalid instead of an eighteen-year-old.

"Honey, you feeling better?"

Before answering, she carefully laid her brush on the side of the sink. "Yes, thank you, Madge."

"Oh, honey, you don't have to thank me."

She placed her hands on either side of the sink and bowed her head. "My mama would be so ashamed of me."

I stepped inside the bathroom and placed my hand on her shoulder. I turned her around, and she gently laid her head on my shoulder. I patted her on the back and felt her sharp bones through the softness of her robe. "Sylvie, honey, your mama would not be ashamed of you. She'd understand how you feel."

"How?" Sylvia whispered against my shoulder. "I don't understand it myself."

I patted Sylvia's back. "Now, I know I ain't never had no baby, but I know plenty of women who have. And you've got what they call the birthing blues. A lot of women get them. Some gets over it easy. Some don't. Listen to me." I pushed her back and cupped her chin in my hand. "I'm going to the shop, and I'll be back directly. You come out here and lay down on this couch."

I had a blanket and pillow ready. Sylvia curled up on the couch, and pulled the blanket up to her chin. "I'm going in to check on Sassy, and then I'm going to the shop. I got the door open so you can hear her if she wakes up. I'll be back before you know I'm gone."

Sylvia reached up and took my hand. "Thank you, Madge."

I patted her hand. It hurt me to see it so chapped and red when I knew how soft and beautiful her hands used to be. I said, "Honey, you don't have to thank me."

By the time I came out of the bedroom, Sylvia was asleep. I stood for a minute, watching her. With all the worry lines smoothed out of her face, she looked like a little girl. *God, she needs your help. Please help her.*

I let myself out of the apartment and headed down the stairs to the street. It had just come to me, and I knew what I needed to do.

Sylvia

It was the smell that woke me. There is no smell on earth like chicken and dumplings cooking. I laid there with my eyes closed, letting the smell take me back home to my mama's kitchen. My eyes fluttered open, and I sat up. I got off the couch and went into the kitchen. Sure enough, there stood Madge at the stove, stirring a big pot of chicken and dumplings with one hand and holding Sassy on her shoulder with the other. Her little head bobbed up and down, looking around. When she saw me, she gurgled and waved her fist in the air. Madge turned around.

"Well, looky here, it's Mama. She's just in time. Supper's almost ready."

"Supper? What time is it?"

Madge laid her spoon down, walked over, and handed Sassy to me. I took her and laid her on my shoulder.

"It's almost 6:00. You hungry?"

"6:00!" I glanced at the window and saw that it was pitch dark. I looked at Madge, who was grinning like I'd just handed her a hundred-dollar bill. "I can't believe I slept all day! Who took care of Sassy?" I shifted her to the crook of my arm so I could look at her.

Madge leaned down and spoke to Sassy. "We had us a good day, didn't we, baby girl?"

Sassy waved her fists and smiled at Madge. Madge laughed and took the lid off the pot. She ladled chicken and dumplings into two bowls,

154

set them on the table, and then she took a pan of biscuits out of the oven. "Let's eat!"

Madge took Sassy into the living room and laid her on her pallet with a rattle. I set down and the fragrant steam from the bowl stroked my face. I closed my eyes and saw my mama standing in the kitchen of our little log house. She was dropping dumplings into the big iron pot she always used for cooking chicken and dumplings. I could see the old rolling pin lying on the table next to the floured board where she rolled out her dough. She turned around and smiled at me, and there were smudges of flour on her face. *Oh, Mama, I need you.*

"Let's see if we can find us some music on . . ." Madge stopped her hand on the radio. "What's wrong?"

My eyes flew open. I felt like I'd been dreaming and woke up before the best part of the dream. "I was just thinking about Mama. I loved to come home from school and find her making chicken and dumplings."

"Mrs. Mary Jane sure was a good cook, and that's a fact." Madge turned on the radio and found a station playing Tommy Dorsey. She started snapping her fingers and swaying her hips. She grabbed a dish rag and started waving it in circles over her head.

I laughed in spite of myself. "You can dance all you want to, but I'm going to eat these dumplings."

While we ate, Madge talked non-stop about the shop and the latest gossip. Myra Justus, whose husband was in the army, was running around with a good-for-nothing from Convict Holler. I half-listened, nodding my head now and then. When we finished eating, I jumped up and started doing the dishes because I heard Sassy fussing. I knew if I cleaned the kitchen, Madge would bath Sassy and get her ready for bed.

Madge came out of the bedroom and handed Sassy to me. I held her to my nose and inhaled the scent of new life. She was dressed in her pink sleeper with the bunny embroidered on it and wrapped in her pink blanket. She looked and smelled like a bouquet of pink flowers. I sat down in the rocking chair and started rocking. She stared up at me so intently that I felt like she was trying to send me a message. "What is it, darling?" I whispered. She just stared at me with rapt concentration. "What do you want to tell me?"

Madge came out of the kitchen with Sassy's bottle. I turned her around so that she was sitting up against my chest, facing Madge. I could feel her little body start to tremble with excitement. She waved her fists and started to coo.

"Lord, looky here at this pretty girl." Madge laughed and squatted down so she was eye level with her. "Ain't you the sweetest little girl I ever saw!"

I watched Madge widen her eyes and exaggerate her smile. Her voice came out high-pitched and sing-song, and she bobbed her head up and down. The more animated Madge got, the more excited Sassy got. I could feel her squirming like she wanted to get a hold of Madge.

"How do you know what to do?"

"Do what?" Madge stood up, and in one fine swoop, picked up Sassy and settled her in the crook of her arm. Without looking, she popped the bottle into Sassy's waiting mouth.

"That." I pointed at Sassy, nestled like a baby chick under the mama hen's wing. "How do you know the way to talk to her? How to feed her? And hold her just right?" I could feel tears pooling in my eyes.

"Sylvia, honey, I don't know how to answer you. I just know it, that's all." Madge stepped toward me like she was going to hand Sassy to me. I backed up, my arms stretched out in front of me, the palms of my hands facing Madge. "Why don't I know how? I want to know how," I whimpered. "I want to know what to do! I want to do it like you." Angry tears wet my face. "It's not fair!"

"Honey, listen to me. We'll figure this out." Madge started toward the bedroom. "Let me get Sassy down, and we'll talk."

When Madge came out of the bedroom, she found me sitting in the kitchen, smoking a cigarette. She picked up the coffee pot, filled it with water, added coffee, and set it on the stove. I envied her fluid movements and how she made everything look easy.

She sat down at the table and covered my hand with hers. "Now, listen to me. I know you're having a hard time, but I think I've figured out something to help you."

"Help me how?"

156

"Help you go back to work."

I was expecting anything but that. I inhaled and sat up straight. "Work?"

"I found somebody to tend to Sassy so you can go back to work."

For the first time in weeks, I felt like someone had extended a hand to pull me out of this dark pit that was my world. I watched the coffee perk on the stove.

"Sylvie, did you hear me?"

"Back to work? When?"

"Whenever you want—even tomorrow."

"Tomorrow!"

"When I left here this morning, I stopped and talked to Loretta Wilson, and she said she'd come over here and keep Sassy."

"Here? You mean I wouldn't have to take her out?"

"No, Loretta said she'd come to the apartment and help you clean and do the wash."

"But Aunt Hat said I shouldn't work—that I was supposed to take care of my baby myself."

Madge got up and poured two cups of coffee. She started to add sugar but put it back. "I know they're going to start rationing sugar, so I best learn how to drink coffee without it." She placed the steaming cups on the table, set down, and wrapped her hands around her cup before she continued. "Sylvie, there ain't nothing wrong with you working. Sassy will be just fine with Loretta, and I think it'll help you get over these baby blues that's smothering you. And besides," she paused to take a sip of coffee, "what the hell does Hattie Mae Mason know about children? She ain't got none of her own, so who is she to tell you what to do?"

Madge leaned forward in the chair. For the second time, she placed her hand on top of mine. "Sylvie, I know this is what Gaines would want you to do, and you know it too."

I grasped Madge's hand. "Can I do it, Madge? Can I work and give my baby what she needs? I just feel so . . . so lost."

"I know, honey. I wouldn't tell you to do this if I didn't think it would help you." Madge took her other hand and held mine between

157

both of hers. "Look, just try it. You don't have to work ever day. You can start with a day or two and see how it goes."

My stomach tied itself into a hundred knots. I knew Madge was right, but I felt like I was going against what a good mother should do by even thinking about leaving Sassy with someone else. I also knew that if I didn't get out of the apartment, I was going to go plain crazy. I took a gulp of coffee. "How does Friday sound?"

I heard the knock at the door but stayed out of sight in the bedroom. I was finally dressed after trying on every uniform in my closet. It had been almost a year since I worked, and all of the uniforms were so big, they swallowed me.

The bedroom door was ajar, so I could hear Madge and Loretta talking. Madge was showing her where everything was—something I should have been doing. Instead, I sat poised on the edge of my bed, watching my baby sleep. She looked exactly like a baby doll little girls play with—right down to the pink blankets and bald head—exactly like those baby dolls I never wanted.

Madge stuck her head in the door and motioned for me to come out. I couldn't wait any longer. All those emotions I was supposed to feel weren't going to come. In fact, the guilt I felt was not for leaving her, but for *wanting* to leave her.

With a last look at the sleeping bundle, I slipped into the living room. Madge was already buttoning up her coat. Loretta had a blanket over her shoulder and was folding diapers with the deftness of an expert. She smiled, and I saw in her eyes how sorry she felt for me because I was leaving my baby. *If she only knew.*

"Now, don't you fret none," Loretta said. "Me and Sassy will be just fine."

Madge whisked me into my coat and out the door before I could barely say "thank you."

It was like coming home after a long journey. The shop looked new and unfamiliar, but my feet led me straight to my station, and my hands knew where to find everything. It had been so long since I worked, I was afraid none of the customers would want me to do their hair, but by 9:00, I had Josephine Byrd in my chair and Lanta Looney waiting. I was just starting to relax when Josephine said, "Ain't you going to show us a picture of that baby?"

"Uh-huh," Lanta chimed in, "I want to see one."

I went into the backroom and got Sassy's picture out of my pocketbook. I studied it. She looked just like Gaines, but there was a faint shadow of me there—it was her eyes. I thought back to the day I had the picture taken. I remembered Mr. Goins saying, "You'll smile for your mama," so I tried to get Sassy to smile because I was going to send the picture to Gaines. But she wouldn't. She just stared at me until Mr. Goins gave up and took the picture.

I stepped back into the main room. Lanta was the first one to look at the picture, and then it got passed around. I was proud to hear the women going on about how pretty she was. Then Josephine got her hands on it. "Lord, what a pretty little doll! How in the world did you go off and leave her this morning?"

I froze. Her words slapped me right across the face. But she wasn't finished with me just yet. "I never left my young'uns in anybody else's hands. No, sir."

I dropped my comb and ran to the back room, wishing the floor would open up and swallow me. When Madge reached me, I was putting on my coat. "Where the hell do you think you're going?" She grabbed me by the shoulders and forced me to look at her.

"I should of never come back. I knew it was wrong." I shook her off and grabbed my purse.

I didn't get two steps before Madge grabbed me again and wheeled me around. "Now you listen to me. Set down over there and get yourself together. You ain't going to let Josephine Byrd run you off. Everybody knows she's crazier than a run-over dog. I'm going out there to finish her hair and get her the hell out of here."

Madge disappeared. For the first time that day, I wondered how Sassy was doing. Did she even know I was gone?

I hung up my coat and stopped to look at myself in the mirror. I traced the *z*-shaped crack with my finger. Like a fool, I laughed at Myrtle Stiltner the day it fell off the wall and she said I was going to have seven years bad luck.

I had only been working a few weeks, and I don't know why I was messing with the mirror in the first place. I thought it was a little crooked, even though Madge swore it was hanging straight. I meant to ease it over an inch or two, and it just slipped out of my hands. It didn't shatter, but a chunk broke off the corner.

The way Myrtle Stiltner had took on, you'd-a thought somebody died. All of the women in the shop that day had acted just like her. Then Madge got mad the way they was carrying on and took the mirror into the backroom. I thought she throwed it away, but the next time I worked, it was hanging on the wall in the backroom.

I asked Madge why she didn't just throw it away. "Why?" She asked. "It's not broke—just cracked. You can still see yourself just fine as long as you don't look at the cracked part."

Maybe that was my problem. Maybe I was looking too hard at the cracks. I turned my face so the cracked corner wasn't visible. There. I raised my chin and took a deep breath. Maybe if I tried harder, I could see past the cracks.

I had to admit that in the three years since I broke that mirror, my mama and daddy died, the war had snatched away my husband, and I had a baby that I couldn't love. And God help me, I had four more years to go.

I threw back my shoulders and marched through the curtains straight over to my station. I saw Madge glance at me and grin. She handed over the comb, and I picked right up where I left off. I knew two things—every eye in the shop was on me, and Josephine wasn't going to say another word.

I waited until I finished combing her hair before I spoke. Then, holding the can of hairspray up like a sword, I said, "You know, Mrs. Byrd, we live in different times than when you was bringing up your children. War is hell on earth."

She muttered, "Sure is," closed her eyes, and put her hands up to shield her face so I could spray her hair.

When she left, it was like somebody threw a switch, and everybody started talking at once. I figured most of the women in the shop felt like Josephine—I should be home with my child instead of working. But I could guarantee that after that day, they'd keep their thoughts to themselves. After all, I fooled them anyway. They thought I was working for the money because my husband was overseas, but instead, I was working for my peace of mind.

Before I knew it, the last customer said good-bye, and Madge and I were sweeping up. "You tired?" she asked.

"A little." I stopped sweeping and leaned on my broom. "Can I tell you something?"

Madge stopped sweeping. "Sure, honey."

"You were right. It felt good to be back to work, even if Josephine Byrd did run her mouth."

"Sylvie, just take it one day at a time."

I was in the back room, getting my coat, when I heard the bell ring on the shop door. *Who in the world could that be?* I stuck my head through the break in the curtains that hung in the doorway. Buster Dawson and a man I didn't recognize were talking to Madge. Buster was shifting his weight from foot to foot. His hands were in his pockets, like he was afraid to touch anything in this world of feminine gadgets. I went back to gathering my things. I knew Buster was sweet on Madge, but Madge wouldn't give him the time of day. I guessed he was trying again to get a date with her. I had to give it to him—he wouldn't give up.

I stepped through the curtain, and the man with Buster turned around. He smiled and took a step toward me. I hesitated. His smile radiated through me like I just knocked back a shot of whiskey. I looked past him and said, "Hello, Buster."

"Sylvie, I didn't know you was here," Buster said.

Madge spoke up. "Today's her first day back, and we was about to leave."

I buttoned up my coat and pulled my gloves out of my pockets. "I'm going to head on home now," I said.

"Well, hold on a minute, and let me get my coat." Madge disappeared into the back room.

The stranger took another step forward. "I don't believe we've met." His voice sounded like pure golden honey pouring over a hot biscuit.

Buster said, "This here's a buddy of mine."

"Hello," I said. "I'm Sylvia Richardson."

"Hello, Sylvia. I'm Francis Howard. My friends call me Fancy."

In spite of myself, I smiled—Fancy—it just fit. He pushed a lock of blonde hair out of eyes as green as spring's first blade of grass. I noticed he wore a wide silver band with odd etchings on the middle finger of his right hand, but nothing on his left.

Buster spoke up. "Fancy here's from Pennsylvania. He's doing some work up at the mines for his daddy's steel company."

"Well, it's nice to meet you, Mr. Howard. Good to see you, Buster." I took a step toward the door.

"Please, call me Fancy." He stepped in front of me like he was going to open the door for me, but instead, he put his hand on the doorknob and leaned his shoulder against the door frame.

"All right, it's nice to meet you, Fancy. Now, if you will excuse me, I need to get home to my baby."

Madge came up behind me and swept us all out the door. Without looking back at Buster and Fancy, we started up the street at a fast pace. I tried to disappear inside my coat to hide from the brutal cold.

"Hey, ladies, wait a minute," Fancy called, jogging to catch up with us. "My car's right up there. It's too cold to be out walking. Let me drive you."

Madge stopped walking and let Fancy catch up. She started to refuse, but changed her mind when she looked over at me. I had my hands buried in my pockets and the collar of my coat turned up, but I was so cold my teeth were chattering.

"All right," she said. "Let's go."

My first thought when I slipped across those leather seats was that his car cost more than most of the buildings in Coal Valley. I'd never seen such an expensive car, let alone rode in one. He flipped a switch, and the heat poured out, warming me instantly.

"How you like this ride?" Buster asked. "Ain't it smooth?"

From the back seat, I heard Madge snort.

"I do a lot of traveling for work," Fancy said, like he was apologizing for the pricey vehicle.

"Turn right up there at the stop sign," Madge directed.

"What kind of work do you do?" I asked.

"I'm an engineer."

"Fancy here works for his daddy's steel mill," Buster interrupted. "They're making steel for the war. And making steel takes a lot of coal, and we damn sure got a lot of coal around here."

Madge said, "Stop in front of that dry goods store."

Fancy pulled over, and I turned to face him. "Thank you for the ride. And thank you for making steel for the war. I'm sure my husband would thank you if he could."

Before I opened my door, Madge was already on the sidewalk and heading for the door to the stairway that led to my apartment. Buster got out to move to the front seat and called out, "Hey, Madge, why don't you change your mind and let me buy you dinner? We're heading over to the diner. Hey, Madge?"

But Madge opened the door and disappeared up the stairs without even a backward glance. Behind me, Buster muttered, "Damn stubborn woman."

C.D

Sylvia

December 20, 1942
Sylvia Richardson
#12 Maple Street
Coal Valley, VA

Dear Gaines,

It finally snowed today. It's been so cold you couldn't put your nose out the door without freezing it off, but we haven't had any snow. For the longest time, I set in the kitchen with Sassy on my lap so we could watch it snow. We just set and listened to the radio and watched it snow. Every time "White Christmas" played I ached for you and all the soldiers who are missing Christmas with their loved ones.

I couldn't take my eyes off of Coal Valley covered in snow. Even if it'll just last for a few hours, it's nice to see everything clean and white. I wish you could've seen it. It was the most beautiful right at the edge of dark. I could see the lights shining through the windows of the Methodist church. It was so beautiful it took my breath away. I said a prayer for you and all the men over there fighting to keep the world safe for all of us.

Madge came over yesterday with a little pine tree we put in the front room. We strung lights and put decorations on it that my Mama had made with her own two hands. I remember how every Christmas she'd crochet little angels, stars, bells, and trees, with fine white thread, then starch them until they were stiff and hang them on the tree. Lord that made me so homesick for her and Daddy. Sassy loves to look at the lights! She fell asleep in my arms watching them. I

put the baby doll you wanted me to get under the tree with a tag that says "to
Sassy from Daddy."

I worked for Madge two days last week. I got Loretta Wilson to come to the
apartment and keep Sassy. She and Sassy took right to each other. I know that
you told me to go back to work if I wanted to, but it was hard to leave Sassy.
Madge said I could work a day or two a week or as much as I felt like. I'm going
to work tomorrow and half a day on Christmas Eve to help Madge get out of
there early.

Me and Sassy are going to spend Christmas with Madge at her Mommy's
so don't worry about us being by ourselves on Christmas. I know your love will
be with us, just as I am sending mine and Sassy's to you. Gaines, take care of
yourself. I pray every night for your safe return. I love you with all my heart and
will be waiting here for you when you come back.

Love,
Sylvia

I read the letter again. My eyes lingered on the line *it was hard to
leave Sassy.* Would Gaines know that was a lie? Would he know that in
my heart of hearts I couldn't wait for tomorrow because I was going
to work? I could never explain to him how helpless I felt with Sassy.
At least at the shop, I knew what I was doing—knew I was in control.
When I was with Sassy, I second-guessed everything I did, from how
to feed her to whether she needed one blanket or two. When I saw her
with Madge or Loretta, I knew she'd be better off with someone who
knew how to take care of her—someone who was strong. Someone
who could teach her how to be strong. Anybody but me.

Would the truth mock me one day? Would Gaines come home from
the war and see what a failure I was as a mother? Would Sassy grow up
with some defect in her character because I didn't know how to be a
mother? *God help me.* Would she know that I didn't want her?

"Stop it, Sylvia!" I cried. I got up and went to the cabinet where I
kept the envelopes and addressed one to Gaines. I folded the letter and
went to my room to get the Chantilly perfume Gaines had bought for
me. I sprayed some on the letter and tucked it into the envelope. Then
I scooped Sassy out of her crib, changed her diaper, and bundled her
up. "Let's go mail Daddy a letter," I said.

After our trip to the post office, we stopped at the dry goods store to visit with the Ashbys and wait for Madge. I'd taken to going downstairs when Madge was at the shop so I wouldn't have to be alone with Sassy. I was sitting in a chair at the back of the store with Mrs. Ashby when it happened.

The door opened to let in a customer. At first, I paid no attention. I'm sure Mr. Ashby said his usual "Can I help you with something?" but I was watching Sassy laugh at Mrs. Ashby and didn't hear him. But I did hear, "I need a pair of gloves. I seem to have lost one of mine."

There was no mistaking that voice. It had a clipped spice that was so far removed from the slow drawl of our mountain voices, there may as well have had a sign around its owner's neck that said, "I'm a Yankee." I heard something else too. I heard the voice of a college-educated man. It was Fancy Howard.

I looked up and saw the tall, lean body and the blonde tousled hair that looked like it had been washed with sunlight. His face was flushed from the cold, and he was holding out a glove for Mr. Ashby to examine.

"I believe I have just the thing you're looking for," Mr. Ashby said, handing the glove back to Fancy. "The gloves are back here." He started toward the back of the store—right where we were sitting.

There was no escape. I sat still, and for the first time in days, worried about how bad my hair looked—and why in the *hell* had I gone out without putting on lipstick?

Fancy was walking behind Mr. Ashby, so he didn't notice me at first. This gave me a chance to take a good look at him. He looked younger than I had first thought. The way his hair fell into one eye gave him a boyish look. He was dressed in a brown leather jacket that showed off his broad shoulders and slim waist. They stopped about six feet from where we were sitting, and Mr. Ashby took a box of gloves off the shelf and set it on a table. Sassy picked that moment to let out a squeal.

The men turned around, and Mr. Ashby laughed. Sassy had seen him coming toward her and thought he was coming to pick her up. She waved her arms and squealed with delight. Mr. Ashby turned back to Fancy and said, "Excuse me, I seem to be needed."

Fancy's smile followed Mr. Ashby as he walked toward Sassy; then it collided with mine. He dropped the gloves and came toward me. I felt my heart start racing and my mouth go dry. "Hello, Mrs. Richardson. Do you remember me?"

"Why, yes, I do. Hello, Mr. Howard." I turned to the Ashbys and introduced him as Francis Howard. I expected him to say "call me Fancy," but he didn't.

"Is this your little girl?" Fancy asked.

Before I could answer, Mr. Ashby said, "This here is Miss Sarah Jane Richardson, the prettiest little girl in Coal Valley. And she likes her friends to call her Sassy."

Fancy held out his hand in a mock handshake. "Hello there, Sassy. It's nice to meet you."

Sassy had been studying Fancy intently while chewing on a toy. All of a sudden, she dropped it and leaned toward Fancy.

I leapt from my seat and started to protest, but Fancy swept Sassy into his arms. "Well, how do you do, Miss Sassy?"

"She doesn't do well with strangers. I don't want her to cry on you." I started to reach for her when all at once, she smiled up at Fancy, raised her little arms, and patted his face with her hands.

"Would you look at that," Mrs. Ashby said. "I ain't never seen her take to a stranger like that before."

Fancy swayed from side to side, and Sassy laughed out loud. "I guess I have the magic touch. Don't I, Sassy?"

Just then, the door opened, and Madge strode into the store. "There you are. I figured you two was down here." She walked straight to Fancy and plucked Sassy from his arms like an apple from a tree. She turned on her heel and set off for the door, chattering to Sassy.

I hugged Mrs. Ashby. "Thanks for letting me visit." She patted my back, and Mr. Ashby said, "Come back any time."

I had to walk by Fancy on my way out. I only glanced up at him and said in passing, "Well, Mr. Howard, it's nice to see you again." Then I followed the path Madge had just taken through the store. I could feel Fancy's eyes on me.

"You have a beautiful little girl," he called after me.

When I got to the door, I turned toward him and smiled.

Sylvia

The day my life ended began as any other day. It was January 29, 1943—a Friday. I got up, changed Sassy's diaper, and gave her a bottle. Madge went to open the shop while I got ready for my third week back at work. Madge and I had settled on Thursdays, Fridays, and every other Saturday. I hated myself for it, but from Sunday to Wednesday, I counted the days. God help me—I couldn't wait to walk out of that apartment.

I wanted to wake up one morning and feel different. I kept waiting—hoping—that being away from Sassy would make me miss her—make me love her. Instead, I counted the minutes until I could hand her to somebody else.

When Loretta arrived, I bundled up and stepped out into the weak sunshine. Each step that brought me closer to the shop took me further away from the darkness coiled at my feet like a rattlesnake ready to strike. I had a purpose again.

I was bent over the shampoo bowl, washing the crème rinse out of Shelby Compton's hair, when the bell over the shop door jingled. I didn't bother to look up to see who came in or went out. For that matter, I wasn't even aware that the door had opened. I was so used to the bell I seldom paid any attention to it. It's like living near the railroad tracks and hearing the trains all the time. After a while, your brain learns how to turn off the clacking of the empty cars and the singing of the wheels, or you'd go plain crazy.

What finally got through to me was how the prattle of voices gradually stopped, like one by one, they'd been switched off. I wrapped a towel around Shelby's hair and stepped back so she could sit up. Her gasp made me wheel around. Madge was approaching two men who were standing just inside the door. I heard two things— Shelby whispered "Jarvis," and Minnie Calhoun started saying the Lord's Prayer. I looked down at Shelby, who was fingering a gold heart she wore around her neck, then up at the clock on the wall. It was 2:03.

It wasn't until Shelby reached up and grasped my hand that I realized what was happening. Preacher Stephens from the Methodist church and Delbert McCoy, the Western Union boy, were talking to Madge. The hum of the hairdryers disappeared as one by one, the customers turned them off. Delbert held a telegram in his hand, and there was only one reason he brought a preacher with him—a soldier was dead or missing in action. My eyes swept over the shop. Shelby's husband, Jarvis, was overseas like Gaines, and everyone was trying not to look at us.

I knew. Before they walked toward us—before I saw the pain on Madge's face—I knew. It had happened again. Death had taken another person who loved me.

Western Union

SA2-59 GOVT=VXX UR Washington, DC 2611A January 27 AM 3:00

Mrs. Gaines Richardson

#12 Maple St. Coal Valley, Va.

The secretary of war deeply regrets to inform you that your husband P.F.C. Gaines Richardson, 7th Infantry, 3rd Division was killed in action in the performance of his duty and in the service of his country. The department extends to you its sincerest sympathy in your great loss.

On account of existing conditions the body if recovered cannot be returned at present. If further details are received you will be informed. Letter follows.

Lt. General George S. Patton

Madge

If the good Lord lets me live to be an old woman, I'll still be haunted by what happened that day. I was in the middle of combing Minnie Calhoun's hair when Preacher Stephens and Delbert Justus walked into my shop. The Justus boy had a telegram in his hand, and there was only one reason he stopped and got Preacher Stephens—somebody was getting bad news. At first, I didn't think of Gaines. I looked around the shop and saw Sylvie washing Shelby Compton's hair. Her husband, Jarvis, was in the Army like Gaines, so my first thought was that something had happened to Jarvis.

I walked over to the men, who were standing just inside the door. They looked like they'd rather be hoeing corn in the July sun than delivering that telegram. Preacher Stephens spoke barely above a whisper, "I'm sorry. It's from the Army. It's for Sylvia."

My mouth formed the word *no*. Preacher Stephens put his hands out, like he was going to catch me if I fainted. I think that's when I said, "Are you sure?"

He repeated, "I'm sorry." It was the sudden silence in the shop that made the hair on the back of my neck stand up. The shop was full that day, but the talking stopped like somebody drew a curtain across the sound.

Delbert glanced past me and shuffled his feet. I said, "Let me do it." He handed me the telegram, and I turned around. I saw fear dart around the room, touching every woman. It was the worst kind of fear—fear of death. I hesitated. It didn't help when Minnie Calhoun started praying out loud, "The Lord is my shepherd; I shall not want."

That was the shortest and longest walk of my life. Sylvia never took her eyes off me as I made my way across the shop. Before I could say a word, she took the telegram out of my hand. I think I said, "I'm sorry, honey." I know I tried. I know my mouth formed the words. I saw Shelby drop Sylvia's hand. She let out a sob of pure relief. And Sylvie—her hands shook so bad I thought she would never get it open; then she stared at the words for the longest time before she looked up at me with such pain in her eyes, my heart wrenched. Then she swayed and fell to her knees.

I grabbed for her, but she fought me off like she couldn't stand to be touched. A sound rose up out of her—a sound like I never heard from a human in my life, and I pray to God I don't ever hear it again. It started deep in her soul and rose up until it gushed out of her like water from a busted pipe. It made the hair on my scalp raise up. I saw Ida Wade close her eyes and cover her ears. The only thing I knew to do was fall to my knees and cry with her.

The women in the room advanced toward us but stopped before they got too close, like Sylvia's grief drew a line they couldn't or wouldn't cross. It was Preacher Stephens who roused me to action when he got down over Sylvia and started praying.

"Maryetta!" I yelled. "Go in the back room and get my coat and pocketbook, and get Sylvia's too." I got up off the floor and grabbed Preacher Stephens by the shoulder. "You got a car? We need to get Sylvie home."

He jumped up. "I'll go get it."

Maryetta came back with our things. "Here, Madge." She knelt down with our coats. "What else can I do?"

"Help me get Sylvia into her coat. I've got to get her home. Can you get everybody finished up and close the shop?"

"Yes."

"I'll help her," said Shelby, getting out of her chair.

I turned back to Sylvia. "Honey, you got to get up. Come on. We're going home." She looked at me, but the light had gone out of her eyes. They looked dead—like they did that time she stayed the weekend alone with Sassy. "Sylvie, honey, do you hear me?"

Shelby got down on her knees and took Sylvia's face in her hands. "Sylvia, it's Shelby. You have to get up now."

Sylvia let Shelby help her up, then stood as docile as a lamb while we put her in her coat and helped her to the door. Preacher Stephens came back with his car. When we got to the apartment, she surprised me by getting out of the car by herself. She still hadn't said a word; she just stared off like she was in a trance. She wouldn't turn loose of that telegram, either. She had it clutched in her hand. By the time I got up the stairs, Sylvia had walked right past Loretta and Sassy and crawled in the bed with her coat and shoes on.

I managed to get Sylvie into her nightgown. She never spoke a word, and she wouldn't turn loose of that telegram. I got her in the bed and went to tell Loretta what happened. We decided it would be a good idea if she took Sassy home with her.

I helped Loretta get Sassy's things together. I was kissing that baby good-bye when I broke down. "Loretta, what are we going to do? Sylvie was just now starting to come out of the baby blues, and knowing Gaines was coming back is what kept her going."

Loretta put her arms around me. "When you hit rock bottom, the Lord is the only one who can lift you up. There's prayer meeting at the church tonight. I'll go and start a prayer chain for Sylvia."

Now the good Lord knows I ain't a church-goer like I should be, but I was raised in the old regular Baptist faith, and I believe in the power of prayer. And I prayed more that day and the days to come than I ever have in my life.

Sylvie had just finished beauty school and started working for me when her mommy and daddy died. I could already tell she was going to make a real beautician. Lord, I hated to see that girl have to go through that—I remember how hard she took their passing. She was just sixteen, but anybody who knew her would've swore she was older—not because of the way she looked, but the way she acted. Sylvie never did act like a teenager. Her soul was old. A hard life had already left its mark on her by the time I knew her.

They say the Lord won't put more on you than you can stand. For Sylvie's sake, I prayed that was true.

Sylvia

If I lay here and let the darkness swallow me, will I know what Gaines felt when he died? Will I ever feel one-tenth of the pain he felt? Oh, God, did he know he was dying? Did he call my name?

Dear Mrs. Richardson,

It is with regret that I am writing to confirm the recent telegram informing you of the death of your husband, PFC Gaines Richardson, 33647746, US Army, 7th Infantry, 3rd Division who was killed in action on January 27, 1943 in Anzio, Italy.

What if he hadn't been in the path of that bullet? What if he'd stepped left instead of right or right instead of left? What if he'd moved faster or slower? Would the bullet have missed him? What if he was standing where some other man was supposed to be?

I fully understand your desire to know as much as possible concerning the circumstances surrounding his death and I wish I had more information to give you. Unfortunately, reports of this nature only give us the briefest of details since they are prepared under battle conditions and the means of transmission are limited.

What if they are wrong? What if it's a mistake and Gaines is not dead? He said he was coming back to me and Sassy. He promised! How am I supposed to take care of Sassy by myself? Oh God, I can't raise her alone.

I know there is little I can say to alleviate your grief, but I hope you will derive some consolation in the knowledge that Gaines Richardson served with honor in the United States Army and died with the best traditions of the service.

I want to see his body. I have to see his face! I want to have a grave to go to, so I can put flowers on it and look at his headstone. If there was a grave then at least I could look at his name. I could take Sassy there and tell her about her daddy.

Before they were laid to rest, a Protestant funeral service was held for Gaines and the other heroes killed in this campaign. He was interred in the American Cemetery in Anzio, Italy in grave # 15, row # 9, plot #2, on 3 February, 1943. You have the deepest sympathy of the officers and men of this organization. He was a splendid soldier and outstanding character. His loss will be deeply felt by his many friends.

My daddy, my mama, and now Gaines. Why? God, why did you have to take Gaines? What did he ever do to anybody? He was a good man. He never had much of a life until we got married. He danced a jig when I told him I was going to have a baby. He had so many plans for us. We were going to have a real home. Now what am I supposed to do? How can I go on alone? I've got nobody—nobody but this baby who I can't even take care of.

Oh God, please. Let me die too.

In closing, I wish to extend my own personal sympathy to you and his family.

Sincerely yours,
George C. Marshall
Chief of Staff

Madge

February came and went and Sylvia didn't stir past the front door. Most of the time, she laid in her bed facing the wall, holding that letter from the Army. She didn't even fight me no more. When I told her to eat, she ate. When I told her to drink, she drank. When I told her to take a bath, she set in the bathtub until the water got cold; then I had to tell her to get out. The only response I got at all was when I brought Sassy to her, but that didn't last long, because she ended up crying and saying, "Poor baby won't ever know her daddy."

When I can get her to take the pills Doc Sutherland gave her, she sleeps a little. I wish I knew what she sees—or thinks she's going to find—in that letter. Gaines is gone; and someway, somehow, she's got to learn to go on with her life.

That first week, I was so afraid she'd do something to hurt herself, I stayed with her day and night. Then I got Loretta to come and take care of Sassy and watch over her so I could go back to the shop. There was no way I would leave that baby alone with her. I sent Hattie Mae a telegram telling her what happened and got one back saying she'd come as soon as she could, but the weather there was so bad it was going to be at least a month—maybe more—before she could get here. I decided I had to get her out of that apartment. I never thought I'd ask Buster Dawson for help, but I got him coming over tonight with Fancy's car. I still can't believe it was Buster's idea to get the car and take her over to the diner. Maybe his head's not as thick as I thought it was.

When I got home, Sylvia was setting at the kitchen table with a cup of coffee and a cigarette. I stared at her, surprised she could look so beautiful after everything that had happened to her. Her haunted eyes and pale skin glowed in the evening light. I realized she didn't look like a teenager anymore. The permanent stamp of sadness was on her face. It couldn't erase her beauty, but it had extinguished her youth like a bucket of water doused out a fire.

"Sylvie, honey, you're looking better!" I tried to sound sincere and encouraging. "I got a surprise for you."

Sylvia stubbed out her cigarette. "That's the last thing I want. I've had enough surprises to last me a lifetime."

I managed a short laugh. "Well, this is a good one. Me and you are going over to eat supper at the diner." There it was—just a faint spark in her eyes.

"Thank you, Madge. I really do appreciate it, but do you really want to walk over to the diner in this cold?"

"Well, that's part of the surprise. We're going to ride. Buster's got Fancy's car, and he's picking us up." There it was again—that spark. I was sure I saw it flicker in her eyes.

"I can't take Sassy out in this cold." She got up from the table and put her cup in the sink.

"I took care of that too. Loretta's staying until we get back, and then Buster will drive her home." I waited while Sylvia wrestled with it. She was still at the sink with her back to me, but I knew she was struggling over what to do. Without turning around, she said, "All right, then."

Sylvia was in the bathroom when I heard Buster coming up the stairs. As the sound got closer, I realized Buster wasn't alone. I opened the door, and there he stood, grinning like an undertaker at a deathbed. He said, "Look who I got to come with me."

I stepped back, and Buster walked in, followed by Fancy Howard. I gave Buster a dirty look and turned around to see Sylvia staring at us. There it was again. The light was dim, but it definitely flickered in her eyes. Sylvia said, "When do we eat?"

Damn Buster Dawson to hell! I should've knowed not to listen to him. He told me Fancy would be *good* for Sylvia—that he was a real gentleman. Well, maybe he is and maybe he ain't, but even a *real* gentleman can break your heart.

I saw right away that Sylvia had perked up after that dinner, and I was glad. But what's going to happen to her when he up and goes back to Pennsylvania to his daddy's big steel mill—and no doubt, his daddy's big money? I like to have fell over when I came in from work the other day and there he set like he owned the place. Sylvia was all flustered, running around making coffee that *he* brought with a five-pound bag of sugar! Said he knew she liked sugar in her coffee! Well, big deal! I do too, but with the food rationing going on, sugar is scarce. I guess Mr. Big Shot with all his money don't have to go by the same rules as everybody else.

Then he gets up to leave and pulls that little white stuffed dog out of his pocket—says to give it to Sassy when she wakes up from her nap. For the first time in months, Sylvie's smile lit up the room. When he left, she took that toy dog and disappeared into her room.

Sylvia

I dreamed last night about Gaines. It was so real, I could smell the sweetness of his skin—all wood smoke and tobacco—all comfort and love. We walked through a forest with the early morning mist purring around our ankles. We held hands, our fingers locked together, and I could feel the warmth of his skin. We walked for what felt like miles, and neither of us spoke until we came to a clearing covered with a carpet of violets. Then Gaines kissed me and said, "The letter." And I woke up.

I lay still and tried to go back to sleep, praying to fall back into my dream, but sleep was gone. I got up and went to make coffee. I set by the kitchen window, sipping coffee, and watched the sun come up. My dream was still fresh with the bittersweet taste of Gaines on my lips. I raised the window a couple of inches and inhaled the morning. The pretense of spring was in the air, but I knew it was a charade. Winter would be back.

It was going to be a warm day, so I promised Madge I would take Sassy out for a walk in her buggy. I knew she wanted me to bring her by the shop, but I couldn't stand the pitying eyes of the old women who were sure to be there.

Madge thought if she could get me in the shop, I would want to come back to work. But I just can't—I'm paralyzed. I can't move forward, and time won't let me go back, so I set and wait. Even though I have no idea what I'm waiting for, I have to believe this can't be all there is. *Dear Lord, please, there has to be more.*

I went to check on Sassy and found her still asleep with her knees drawn up under her like she was going to crawl in her sleep. I got the cedar chest that held Gaines's letters and went to the front room. In my dream, Gaines had said "the letter." But what letter? I read them all again, but I couldn't find a clue. What was Gaines trying to tell me?

After lunch, I settled Sassy in her buggy, and we started off down the street. There were a lot of people stirring today, taking advantage of the warm spell. I was walking away from town toward the school when Fancy's car pulled up to the curb. He got out and fell into step beside me.

"It's a nice day for a walk," he said.

"Yes, it is."

"Mind if I join you?"

I laughed. "Looks to me like you already have."

He laughed and put his hands in his pockets. For a while, we walked in silence. We passed the new walking bridge that crossed the creek to Muddy Bottom, where the new high school was going to be built. The path hugged the mountainside, and even though the temperature was near sixty, long, knobby fingers of ice crept down the side of the cliff. It was eerily quiet here. The rocks jutted out from the mountain, absorbing everything. The sweet aroma of wet soil and moss hung in the air. "You know," I said, "no matter how far from here I might go or how long I might stay away, I would never forget this smell."

Fancy stopped walking and stared up at the mountain—craggy stone faces of old men with icicle beards. "Would you look at that? That's incredible." He waved his arm in an arch across the mountainside. "It must be sixty degrees, and those icicles haven't even started to melt."

I watched his green eyes darken in concentration. He swept the hair back from his forehead and spoke as if he were talking to himself. "The sun can't reach the north side of the mountain—not this time of year."

I looked at the icicles and shivered. Fancy looked down at me like he just remembered I was there. He said, "You know what else today is?"

"What?"

"It's a nice day for a drive."

I laughed. "Don't you have to work or something?"

"As a matter of fact, I need to run over to Bluefield and pick up something for the mines. Why don't you and Sassy come with me?"

"Are you serious?"

"Of course. I wouldn't have asked you if I wasn't."

He smiled, and the same strand of hair he'd just swept out of his eyes fell forward. My eyes were drawn to the silver ring on his right hand. "I've never taken Sassy that far from home before. I don't know how she'd do in a car." I hoped he didn't see that the idea terrified me.

"Well, then, don't you think it's about time you found out?"

I put my hands on my hips. "You don't know much about babies, do you?"

He leaned over Sassy's buggy and tickled her chin. "You might be surprised." She rewarded him with a grin.

"Babies have to have diapers and bottles and blankets and . . ."

Fancy put his hand on my arm. "Look, I have five older sisters and a bunch of nieces and nephews." He paused to let that sink in. "So I know a thing or two about babies."

"Are you serious?"

Fancy laughed deep in his throat. "You've already asked me that. Now, let's go get all that stuff babies need and take off."

Madge,
Sassy and I have ridden over to Bluefield with Fancy. Be back later.

Sylvia

Sylvia

The snow was drifting in front of me like white cotton sheets drying on the clothesline. I knew those warm days wouldn't last, but the sudden snowstorm had startled me. I started to turn back, but I was almost to the post office, and it had been awhile since I got the mail. When I ran into Myrtle Stiltner, I was thankful for the snow. Instead of her poking and prodding me with her nosy questions, she was in a hurry to get back to the store. She only stopped long enough to tell me how Mr. Stiltner had predicted the storm. "Sylvia! What are you doing out in this weather? Mr. Stiltner says this is going to be a big one!"

"I'm just getting the mail, Mrs. Stiltner, and then I'm going right home."

"Now you know Mr. Stiltner is always right about the weather." And she disappeared into the blizzard, the rest of her words swallowed by the snow.

Like I expected, the mailbox was full, so I didn't notice the letter. There was one from Aunt Hat on the top of the stack, so I stuffed everything in my pockets and hurried home. When I got there, Sassy was asleep, so I sent Loretta home, got a cup of coffee, and settled down on the couch to read the mail. I sifted through the stack, laying Aunt Hat's letter to the side. Then I saw it. The letter was addressed to me, but the handwriting was unfamiliar. One thing was clear, though—it was from overseas. *Gaines. It has to be about Gaines! Maybe there was a mistake.*

My heart pounded so hard that the blood rushed into my ears, making me dizzy. I ripped open the envelope. There was one sheet of folded paper and another envelope holding another letter. There was nothing written on the second envelope. I took a deep breath and unfolded the paper.

February 1, 1943
PFC Thomas McClellen
76593302
7th Infantry, 3rd Division

Dear Mrs. Richardson,

My name is Tom McClellen and I was a friend of your husband Gaines. I don't know any easy way to say this so I will just write down what happened. I was with Gaines when he died and I promised him that I'd write to you and see that you got this letter. He had written it but never got a chance to mail it. He also asked me to tell you that he loved you and his daughter and that his last thoughts on this earth were of you.

I want you to know that your husband was a fine man and a good friend. I trusted him with my life. He was a good soldier and fought bravely for his country. I know there is nothing I can say except I'm sorry. May God bless you and your daughter during this terrible time.

My deepest sympathy,
Tom McClellen

I don't know how long I stared at Gaines's letter before opening it. I turned it over and over in my hands, tracing my fingers over the envelope. I held it to my nose and inhaled deeply, trying to find a hint of his scent. Then I slipped my thumbnail under the flap and eased it opened. It was when I slipped the letter from its cover that I remembered my dream. In it, the only thing Gaines had said to me was *the letter*. This must be it! This had to be the letter in my dream.

When I saw his handwriting, all the pain I felt because of his death came rushing back. I had wished for another day with him—for another chance to tell him how much I loved him. One more letter was not something I had wished for, but I was thankful.

December 27, 1942
PFC Gaines Richardson
33647746
7th Infantry, 3rd Division

My Dearest Sylvia,

We are constantly on the move and the fighting goes on all day and all night. I spent Christmas in Italy. There was a brief break in the fighting that day. I thought of you and Sassy and how I'd love to have seen her face when she saw her baby doll.

The nights are the worst. Sleep is impossible with shells exploding all around us. Sylvia, I have seen things I wish I never had, and I know I will never forget them. When I do get to close my eyes I think about you and my baby girl. I keep the last picture you sent me in my pocket. I know I must take it out and look at it a hundred times a day. Can you feel me thinking about you?

Sylvia, I must face the fact that something could happen to me and I won't make it back. It's hard for me to write these words and I know you don't want to read this, but there are some things I want to say in case something does happen. First, I love you. I know God gave me a special gift the day you said you'd be mine. I never told you much about my past. For one thing, I don't like to think about it. You know that my mommy disappeared when I was two and my daddy tried, he really did, but he was never a man easy to get close to. My granny was there, but she was so old and sick she couldn't do much. She did hold me on her lap that I do remember. I was always so starved for love. Until I met you I never knew what it was to be loved. So you see, having you and Sassy is more than I ever hoped for, and if God lets me come home I'll never want for another thing the rest of my life.

But Sylvia, if something does happen and I don't make it back, then you go on with your life. Find you a good man to marry who will take care of you and Sassy. Sylvie I only ask two things first, please let it be somebody who will treat you and Sassy right. Don't ever let no man mistreat you and Sassy. And the other thing is please make sure Sassy grows up in a home with love. That's all I ask.

Now enough of this old sad talk. I wish I could have been there for Christmas to see her play with her baby doll. Does she have a tooth yet? Keep giving her kisses from her Daddy.

I love you and Sassy more ever day.

Gaines

Madge

It was like Gaines died all over again. When I got home from the shop, I found Sylvia in the bed, facing the wall. Sassy was awake in her crib and fussing to get out. At first, I thought Sylvia was asleep, so I got Sassy and started out of the room.

"Madge?" Sylvia raised her head off the pillow.

"Yeah, honey. Are you all right?"

Her answer was a sob.

I wheeled around and went back into the room. "Honey, what's wrong? Are you sick?" The only answer I got were sobs that racked her body. I set down on the edge of the bed, scared to death of what she was going to say. I put my hand out and lightly touched her back, and she turned over to face me. That's when I saw she was holding a letter. At first I thought it was the one from the army, and I couldn't understand why she was so upset. Then I got up and turned on the bedside lamp so I could get a better look. That's when I saw the handwriting, and I knew it was from Gaines.

"Sylvia, honey, what is it?"

She sat up, reached behind her to the bedside table, and handed me a piece of paper. I held it up to the light and began to read. When I got to the part that said *I was with him when he died,* I knew why she was holding a letter. I said, "Oh, God, no wonder you're so tore up."

Sassy started to fuss and reached for the letter, so I handed it back to Sylvia. "Honey, I'm going to change Sassy and feed her. Can I get you anything?"

She shook her head and laid back down, facing the wall. When I started out of the room, she said, "It's true, Madge. He's really gone."

"I know, honey. I'm so sorry. Can I do *anything* for you?"

"Turn off the light."

When I came back in to check on her, she was asleep. I pulled the blanket over her and pried the letter out of her hand. I stared down at her, wishing I could take all the hurt away. *God, what are we going to do now? I don't know if she can make it through this.*

I was folding diapers when I heard someone coming up the stairs. *Now what?* I jerked open the door before anyone knocked, and there stood Fancy Howard. "Hello, Madge. Is Sylvia home?"

"She's asleep."

Fancy looked down at his watch. "At 7:00?"

"Yeah."

"Is anything wrong?"

"No."

He shifted his weight from side to side but made no move to leave. I could see he was thinking about what to say next. I said, "I'll tell her you were here," and started to shut the door.

"Madge, wait." He held up his hand. "Let me leave something for her." He unzipped his jacket a ways and reached inside. He pulled out a big envelope and a little teddy bear.

"What's that for?"

"It's something for Sassy. It's for . . . well, no reason."

I snatched it out of his hand and barked, "I'll give it to her."

"Thank you. Are you *sure* Sylvia is all right?"

"I done told you she's fine."

I watched him digest this and brood over what to say next, finally deciding to let it go. Before he could say anything else, I closed the door in his face.

When the third day dawned and Sylvia still wouldn't get out of bed, I sent for Doc Sutherland. He stayed with Sylvia a long time before coming out looking grave. "I gave her a shot full of vitamins, but she's got to get up out of that bed, or . . ." He broke off and looked at me.

"Or what?"

Doc ran his hand through his thinning hair. "Have you heard from Hattie Mae? Is she coming?"

"Wait a minute." I turned around and went to find the stack of mail Sylvia had left on the couch. I remembered putting it on the coffee table. Doc came up behind me just as I was going through the envelopes. "Here it is. I knew I saw a letter from Hattie Mae." We both stared at the letter. Then I said, "Do you think we should open it?"

"I think we have to. Sylvia needs help. What we do will depend on whether or not Hattie Mae is coming."

I ripped open the envelope and pulled out the letter. I handed it to Doc. He read it and handed it back to me. "She's not leaving Seattle for another two weeks. I don't think we have any choice but to put Sylvia in the hospital."

"Hospital!"

"She needs fluids and help that I cannot give her."

My mind started racing. I needed to get Loretta to take care of Sassy, pack Sylvia a bag, and see about the shop. I said, "If you can help me get her in the car, I reckon we can get her up there."

Doc put his hand on my arm. "I'm not talking about the hospital here. She needs more help than they can help her."

I froze. Doc frowned, and the worry lines deepened. I said, "Doc, what are you talking about?"

"I think Sylvia needs to go to the state mental hospital. I'm afraid of what might happen to her if she doesn't."

"The crazy hospital! You want to put Sylvia in the crazy hospital! Doc, Sylvie's not crazy!"

"Of course she's not crazy, but she has severe melancholy. She's had a hard time since the baby was born. I know that if it hadn't been for you, she couldn't have taken care of her, and since Gaines died, I've been worried she was going to hurt herself. We've got to do something before that happens."

"But Doc, she'll never forgive me if I take her there."

"Madge, I'm afraid you'll never forgive yourself if you don't."

My knees buckled, and I sat down on the couch. I covered my face with my hands.

Doc sat down next to me and patted me on the back. "I'll take care of it. I was hoping Hattie Mae was on her way, and she could—but she's not, and we dare not wait much longer."

I knew Fancy would come to see Sylvia, and I was ready for him. He said, "Why can't I see her?"

"I done told you she's sick."

Fancy leaned against the door frame, his eyes concentrating on the room behind me like he thought he might see Sylvia hiding behind the couch.

"She's asleep, and Doc says no visitors."

"What exactly is wrong with her?"

"Doc says it's the influenza."

Fancy thought that over. He stood up straight and put his hands in his pockets, but didn't act like he was going to leave. He said, "You told me on Sunday she was sick."

"That's right."

"Then, when I came by on Tuesday, you said the same thing."

"Glory be hallelujah! It looks like you're finally catching on."

He frowned and folded his arms across his chest. "Today's Thursday, and she's still sick. Don't you think she needs to be in the hospital?"

"Look, here, Doc comes to see her ever day and if he thinks she needs to go to the hospital, then we'll take her." *He'd die if he knew where we were taking her tomorrow.*

"We have really good doctors in Pittsburgh. I would be happy to take her and…"

"Hold on, Mr. Big Shot!" I put my hand, palm up, in his face. "She don't need your big shot doctors, and she don't need you to take her nowhere."

"I'm just trying to help."

"Tell me something, Fancy Howard, just what is it you want from Sylvia?"

He frowned. "I don't understand what you mean. I don't want anything from her. I just offered to help because she's a friend."

"A friend, huh? Well, just remember this—she's eighteen and a widow with a baby. She's got more on her plate right now than she can carry, and she sure don't need you hanging around for *whatever* reason."

Fancy gathered up his full six foot height and nodded. "Please tell Sylvia I stopped by to see how she was feeling." He turned and headed down the stairs. I shut the door and leaned my head against it. I should've know he'd come back.

I set down on the couch and lit a cigarette. That's when I realized my hands were shaking. I know Sylvia wouldn't want him to know what bad shape she's in, but God help me, what if he could take her to some high-priced doctor who would help her?

Sylvia

I pulled the darkness up to my chin and melted into its softness. I finally found the place I wanted to be. Madge kept calling me back, but I wasn't ready. *Just let me sleep. I'm so tired of living, so tired of hurting. So tired.*

I woke up in the back of a car. Blankets were wrapped around me like poison ivy around a tree trunk. Madge kept telling me they were taking me to the hospital. I tried to tell them I wasn't sick—I just needed sleep—but my voice wouldn't work. I tried to sit up and show them there was a mistake, but I couldn't move. The last thing I remember before I fell asleep was hearing Doc's voice and seeing Madge's face looking down at me.

It was the light that woke me. I tried to open my eyes, but it was so bright I thought I was looking into the face of the sun. When my eyes focused, I was afloat in a sea of green—green walls, green floors, even the people were wearing green. Somebody kept talking to me. *Mrs. Richardson. Mrs. Richardson, Sylvia . . .* on and on. Why didn't they shut up and turn off the lights? I needed to rest. If they would have just let me sleep . . . I needed sleep.

"Sylvie, honey, can you hear me?"

I opened my eyes, and there was Madge. She stroked my forehead. Her fingertips spread comfort like a cooling salve. "Madge." I lifted my hand, and she grasped it between hers.

"Sylvie, honey, you're going to be all right."

191

"Where am I?"

"You're in the hospital."

"Hospital?"

Madge smoothed my pillow. I tried to raise my head, but the room started spinning, so I closed my eyes and lay back. Madge jumped up and got me a cup of water. I took a sip and looked around.

"Where am I?" My voice came out like a whisper.

"Do you remember anything?"

"I remember . . ." I stopped and looked up at the bottle hanging on a pole by my bed. My eyes watched the fluids dripping into the tube that ran down to my arm. "Can I have another sip of water?" Madge held the cup to my lips. I drank and lay back. "I remember Doc holding my hand, and voices. And lights."

Madge started talking a blue streak. "Now, I don't want you to worry about Sassy. She's with Loretta. She's just fine."

"Why am I here? Where's Doc?"

I looked around at the green walls. The small window was up toward the ceiling, and I could barely tell it was daylight. "Help me set up."

"Are you sure?"

I gave Madge my hand, and she helped me sit up. She put pillows behind my back and gave me another drink of water.

"Where am I?"

Madge sat down on the side of the bed and took my hand. "Sylvie, you know I wouldn't do nothing in this world that was going to hurt you. I only want to help you. But you scared me so bad, I didn't know what to do."

Tears blurred my vision. "I'm so sorry."

Just then, the door opened, and a strange doctor walked in. "Well, Mrs. Richardson," he said in a voice that put me in a mind of a preacher greeting worshippers at the church door. "It's good to see you're awake." He strode across the room and held out his hand. "I'm Doctor Chaney, your psychiatrist."

"My *what?*"

"I'm your psychiatrist. How are you feeling?"

"*Where* am I?"

"You are in the Southwest Virginia Mental Health Hospital."

"Oh, God." I started to cry. Madge jumped off the bed and put her arm around my shoulders. I leaned against her and said, "What happened?"

"You were brought here two days ago," said the doctor, looking down at a clipboard he whipped out from under his arm.

"Two days!" I closed my eyes and tried to remember.

"Your doctor was concerned for your safety and wanted us to take care of you."

"When can I go home?"

He slid the clipboard back under his arm. "I'm sure you'll be ready to go home soon, but let's not worry about that right now. Let's just worry about helping you feel better. I'm here to talk about what's bothering you and—"

"Bothering me! I'll tell you what's bothering me!" I held up my right hand, balled into a fist. I unfurled my fingers one by one. "One, my husband is dead. Two, my mama is dead. Three, my daddy is dead. And four, I have a baby to raise. Do I need to keep going?"

The doctor pulled a chair up to the side of the bed and set down. He still hadn't acknowledged Madge. When he leaned toward me, I could see his Adam's apple bobbing up and down in his neck like a log rolling and pitching as it traveled down the river.

"I can certainly understand why you've been feeling so melancholy," he said. "That's why I'm here to help you. Tomorrow we will begin your treatment."

"*What* treatment?"

"It's called electroconvulsive therapy. We will give your brain an electric shock that will trigger a seizure. This will help to relieve your depression."

"My depression?"

"Yes, your depression—your melancholy. That's what we call your feelings of sadness."

Fear tapped me on the shoulder. I pressed my body down into the mattress in an effort to get as far away from him as possible. "You can't do that to me."

He reached over and patted my hand. His Adam's apple protruded so far from his neck that in spite of my panic, I wondered how he could swallow.

"I assure you we are only trying to help you. You may experience some temporary memory loss and confusion and some muscle soreness, but that will only be temporary."

"If you do this—this therapy—will I get to go home?"

"We'll worry about that when we see how you respond to the treatment. It usually takes six to twelve treatments before you feel better."

I looked at Madge and saw the fear on her face. She tried to smile and squeezed my shoulder. For the first time, the doctor looked at her. "Miss Hagerman, may I speak to you in the hall? I think it's time for Mrs. Richardson's lunch to be served."

Madge stood up, and panic seized me. "Don't leave me!" I grabbed for her as she stepped away from the bed. "Please, don't leave me!"

Madge looked at the doctor and then back at me. She took a step toward him and then turned around. "Sylvie, I'll be right outside the door. I *promise* I'll be right back." The doctor stood by the door, staring at me like he was afraid I was going to leap from the bed and run. He opened the door for Madge and followed her into the hall. Before the door could close, a nurse came in, carrying a tray. She didn't speak, just placed the tray on a small table and wheeled it over to my bed. She unrolled the napkin that held only a spoon and opened the cover on the plate. The smell of grease that had fried too many potatoes escaped. I closed my eyes and tried not to gag.

"Mrs. Richardson, it's time for lunch," she said.

"I'll eat it in a minute."

She stared at me for a moment like she was trying to memorize my face. Then she said, "You have to eat, Mrs. Richardson. Doctor's orders."

"I will. My friend. She's talking to the doctor. She'll help me."

She pursued her lips. "All right, then." She put the cover back on the food.

I couldn't remember my address, I didn't know my shoe size, and God help me, I couldn't remember what my husband looked like, but I will never forget the pain—pain that twisted and squeezed the life out of my body until I felt like a wet rag that had been wrung out and shook hard before being hung up to dry.

I couldn't focus my mind on anything. I tried, but it hurt too much to concentrate. It was better to drift around inside my head and stay away from remembering, but it came for me in the night. It surrounded me. I was in a green room, strapped down on a table with wires attached to my head and a block of wood in my mouth. I feel death ooze through my body while I watch it shake and convulse, desperate to get away. That's when I know how Gaines felt when he died.

Doc Sutherland rescued me. He and Madge came to see me right after I had one of those "treatments." I can't remember that doctor's name, but I'll never forget how his Adam's apple looked like a fist trying to poke through his neck. He kept saying I needed to complete my treatments, but Madge took to crying—then Doc took to swearing. That doctor stood over me like a dog guarding a bone and said he wanted to do three more treatments. Doc swore again and said I couldn't stand it. Next thing I knew, we were in Doc's car, and I was going home.

"What day is it?" I asked Doc.

"Monday."

"What's the date?"

"April 1."

"How many days was I there?"

"Ten."

I was half-sitting, half-laying in the backseat, propped up in the corner so I could see where we were going. Madge had so many quilts piled on me, I could barely move—which was good, because my body hurt like somebody had beat me. She kept turning around in her seat and looking at me. She prattled on about the late snowstorm we had while I stared out the window at the pastures with patches of snow here and there like fallen Christmas ornaments left lying under the trees.

"It'll be all right," Madge said.

I tried to smile. "I know."

When I woke up, we were pulling in front of the dry goods store. Madge said, "We're home, honey. I know you can't wait to see your baby girl."

I sat up too fast, and my head started swimming. *My baby?* I rubbed my forehead and tried to conjure her face. Was I supposed to feel something? I couldn't even remember what she looked like.

Doc and Madge got out of the car and walked around to the trunk. I could tell by the nervous way Madge kept glancing at me that they were talking, and she didn't want me to hear it. Thank God the dry goods store was closed. I rubbed my forehead, trying to remember who worked there. I could picture an old man and woman, but I couldn't recollect their names.

Madge jerked open the door and started yanking quilts off me and rolling them into a huge ball. Doc helped me out of the car; I was surprised it wasn't as cold as I thought it would be.

Madge said, "Let's hurry, honey, before you freeze to death."

"I'm fine, Madge." I looked up. Night spread across the sky—a fresh bruise on pale skin. I looked down the street, where I could see the clock glowing faintly on the courthouse tower. Winter still held Coal Valley in its dirty fist. I shivered. *Will I ever get out of this town?*

Doc stepped up to take my arm. He and Madge helped me up the stairs to my apartment, Madge jabbering the whole time like she does when she's nervous. The door swung open before we made it to the top, and there stood Loretta, beaming at me with Sassy in her arms. "Welcome home!" she said.

I looked at my beautiful baby covered in pink ruffles from head to toe, and I laughed. I actually laughed out loud, surprising everyone—me most of all. Then it happened. Sassy smiled—not at Madge, not at Doc—at *me*. I held out my hands and wiggled my fingers at her. "Come to Mama, baby!" And she reached for me.

We settled around the kitchen table that was so full of food you couldn't see the new checkered tablecloth under it. Loretta bustled around, pouring tea and cups of coffee. "Lordy, Loretta," I said, "you must of cooked all day."

She beamed and gave me a brief hug. "I just wanted to cook you a welcome home dinner."

Madge ate with Sassy on her lap, feeding her tiny bites of mashed potatoes and dumplings. Sassy was the life of the party, smiling and banging her rattle on the table. Even Doc stayed to eat with us. When he left, he patted my hand and said he'd be back to check on me tomorrow.

I said, "Tomorrow sounds good."

On Sunday, a warm breeze lured me outdoors. Madge and I put Sassy in her buggy and started off for the post office. I could feel the sun seeping into my skin, warming away the soreness. After a few minutes of Madge throwing sidelong glances at me, I stopped and said, "Out with it."

"With what?" Madge stopped but wouldn't look at me.

"If those looks you been shooting at me out of the corner of your eyes was bullets, I'd be dead by now," I said.

"I don't know what you're talking about."

I put my hand on Madge's arm and stared at her until she looked at me. "I'm tired of you walking on eggshells around me. Since I got home, all you've done is watch me."

"No, I ain't!"

"Damn it, Madge, stop it. You know it's the truth."

"I'm just worried about you. That's all."

She turned around and started fussing with Sassy's blanket. I stood my ground with my hands on my hips and waited. When she finally turned around, there were tears in her eyes.

My righteous anger melted. "I'm going to be all right. You don't have to watch me."

"I know that," Madge said. "That's not it." She dug in the pocket of her jacket until she came up with a handkerchief and blew her nose.

"Then what is it?"

"I figure you hate me for letting them put you in that place. But I can hold my right hand to God and swear I didn't know what they was going to do to you!"

"Madge, honey—"

She grabbed me by the shoulders and crushed me to her. "I'm so sorry; please forgive me." She broke down and sobbed.

I hugged her and rubbed her back, murmuring, "Honey, it's okay. I don't hate you."

With her head on my shoulder, Madge said, "When me and Doc come in your room and you was laying there looking like a corpse, I—" She started wailing. "God in heaven knows I never would have left you there if I knowed what they was going to do to you."

"Oh, Madge. I know you wouldn't. It's all over now." Then I lied. "I don't hardly remember it, anyway."

Madge straightened up and looked in my eyes. I smiled at her. Sassy picked that moment to start fussing for us to get moving. Madge mopped her face. We started back up the road, and for a while, no one spoke. We got the mail at the post office and turned back toward home. "Madge," I said, "me, you, Doc, and Loretta are the only ones that know I was in the crazy hospital. Right?"

"Yeah—but—"

"No, listen to me. I'm going to say this, and then we won't never talk about it again."

Madge nodded and pursued her lips.

"I'm going to go on living," I said. "It's what Gaines wanted. He wrote me that letter. He told me to go on with my life if something happened to him, and that's what I'm going to do.

Madge

I knew Sylvie told me she didn't blame me for putting her in the crazy hospital, but I couldn't help but blame myself. I should've never left her alone that weekend with Sassy. I knowed she was deep in the baby blues, but I thought going back to work would do the trick. I still wonder if she would've pulled out of it if she hadn't got Gaines's last letter—but that's neither here nor there now.

Sylvia was barely home from the hospital when Fancy showed up. I kept my mouth shut when she started going out with him. I didn't know if she told him the truth about where she'd been, but I doubted it. I told the nosey busybodies at the shop that she took the pneumonia on top of the flu and had to spend ten days in Mattie Williams hospital in Richlands. Keeping a secret in this town was near impossible, but nobody knew but me, Doc, and Loretta, and we ain't talking. There was plenty of talk anyway, with ever old biddy at the shop talking about her running around with Fancy. For two weeks, she didn't do nothing but ride all over in that pricey car of his. I tried to get her to come back to work, but she said she wasn't ready. That was all right; Hattie Mae would be there any day, and she'd clean house right quick.

When I got to the apartment, Sylvie was gone, but Loretta was there with Sassy. "Where is she this time?"

"Sylvie and Fancy Howard are gone to Princeton. Said they was going out to dinner and would be back late."

"Again? They went there a few days ago."

"Fancy said Sylvie loved to eat at that place, and he was trying to fatten her up. He begged to take Sassy, but Sylvia said she's taking a cold and needed to stay in."

"What's wrong with Sassy?"

"Not a thing, as far as I can tell."

I went to change out of my uniform and peeked in on Sassy. She was sleeping with her knees up under her like she was fixing to crawl. I smiled. She was seven months old and would soon be crawling all over the apartment. It wouldn't be long before she was walking. I run my hand over her forehead and slipped it under her shirt so I could feel her back—cool as a cucumber. I leaned down so I could listen to her breathe; her nose was clear. Sylvia knowed there wasn't anything wrong with the baby.

I left the room and found Loretta putting on her coat. She hesitated at the door like she wanted to say something, but couldn't manage it. God knows I didn't want to hear anything that would cause me more worry, but I knew if Loretta had something on her mind, I better hear what it was.

"You don't have to run off, do you? I was fixing to make some coffee. Why don't you stay and drink a cup with me?"

Loretta slipped off her coat and hung it up. While I made coffee, she set a plate of cookies on the table. Thanks to Fancy, we always had sugar around, even though with the war, it was being rationed. Loretta set quiet at the table while I fixed the coffee pot and put it on the stove. I set down across from her and lit a cigarette. She had her hands clasped in front of her on the table.

"Is ever thing alright?"

"Honest to God, Madge. I don't know."

I put my cigarette in an ashtray and leaned across the table. "Well, tell me what you think."

Loretta fidgeted in her chair. Her eyes glanced from me to the coffeepot to her hands, where they stayed. I took another drag on my cigarette.

"When is Hattie Mae coming?"

So that's it, I thought. Loretta was worrying about Hattie Mae coming and her not getting to baby sit. I knowed how bad she needed the six dollars a week I paid her. Her husband had hurt his back in the mines and was still out of work. I said, "The last I heard, she planned to be here by the end of the month, but with the war and the bad weather, it's hard to get the train she needs. We're supposed to get a telegram when she's coming in on the bus. But you know Sylvie is still going to need you to help with Sassy."

"That's not it. I'm worried about Sylvia. She's still—she *looks* better, but she still ain't herself."

I jumped up and took the coffeepot off the stove. I got two cups out of the cabinet and filled them. The whole time, Loretta didn't say another word. When I turned around, she looked like she was going to cry. I set the cups down and clutched the corner of the table with both hands. "It's that damn Fancy! He won't leave her alone. He's filling her head with his rich man's bullshit, throwing money around left and right. Sylvie ain't never had anything in her life, and here he is, taking her out to restaurants and buying her pearl necklaces." I leaned down in Loretta's face. "And what about all them toys and things he buys for Sassy? I guess that's supposed to make up for taking Sylvia away from that baby!"

Loretta leaned toward me and put her hand on my arm. "Sit down, Madge."

I realized tears were running down my face, so I grabbed a dishrag off the sink and fell back in the chair. I wiped my eyes and took a deep breath. "Loretta, Sylvie is like my own flesh and blood. I *know* what a hard life she's had, and *damn it to hell,* I can't stand to see nobody take advantage of her."

"Now Madge, I've knowed Sylvia all her life. You know she's Earl's kin. His grandma was a sister to her grandma. They're both from the left-hand fork of Rock House Mountain, and I know how hard the whole bunch of them was raised. I also know that you don't like Fancy. But I swear to you, Madge, I don't think Fancy is doing her wrong."

My eyes about popped out of my head. I opened my mouth to protest, but Loretta held up her hand.

"Now hold on a minute. That man is a fool over Sylvia *and* that baby. You've seen how Sassy acts when she sees him, and I swear he's as bad as she is. If he had his way, he'd take that baby everywhere they go." She looked down at the table, and her voice dropped to a whisper. "It's Sylvia who don't want to have nothing to do with her."

This time, the tears were from Loretta. She wiped her eyes with the back of her hand. We both stared at our untouched coffee. "You know I love Sylvia and that baby. And I wouldn't say this if I didn't believe it in my heart. Fancy Howard loves that little girl like she's his own. If he had his way, he'd pack her around ever where he goes. It's Sylvia that makes excuses to leave her here."

We sat unmoving, thinking about what we'd said and what we'd left unsaid. Since Sylvia had gotten out of the hospital, we'd both seen how she acted around Sassy, and God knows we was both worried about it.

I heard Sassy fussing, and we jumped up at the same time and looked toward the door. Loretta hadn't said a word about me still having Sassy's crib in my bedroom. It was supposed to be put back in Sylvia's room after she got back on her feet, but a month had gone by, and Sylvia hadn't mentioned moving her back in her room. "I'll get her," I said. "I know you need to go home and get Earl's supper."

Loretta nodded, picked up her coffee cup, and put it in the sink. As I left the kitchen, I looked back and said, "Hattie Mae's coming. She'll straighten things out."

Sylvia

When I got out of the hospital, Fancy treated me like a fine piece of china. He never asked me any questions—just told me he was happy I recovered. Last night, we were setting in the diner, drinking coffee, when he said it was nice to know he could knock on my door and I was the one who answered. I warned him Aunt Hat was going to be there in a few days and things would change, but he just laughed and said that nobody could be as bad as Madge. I didn't say anything, but I thought to myself, *That's what you think.*

2:00 in the morning, I threw back the blankets and got out of bed. *God, I need a cigarette.* I crept out of my bedroom, careful not to wake Madge or Sassy. I didn't feel like hiding in the bathroom. If I smoked anywhere else in the apartment, Madge would smell it and know I wasn't sleeping again, so I slipped on my shoes, grabbed my coat, and eased out the door. I tiptoed down the stairs. When I got to the bottom, I set down and lit my cigarette.

While I smoked, I thought about Gaines. I knew I would never know love again. Nobody gets to be loved like that twice in one life. Most people don't even find it once, but I was only eighteen, and the mountains were closing in on me; I couldn't even see the damn sky without stretching my neck! Fancy was my only chance to get out of there. I couldn't do it alone with a baby hanging on to me. I had to get out of Coal Valley.

I lit another cigarette off the fire from my first one. When Fancy left, he'd said he had to go to Pittsburgh for a few days—said he had to make a report to the board of his daddy's company about the coal mines. *What if he don't come back? What if this is just an excuse to get away from me?* I jumped up, dropping my cigarette. I could see the fire and ash spilling down the front of my coat. "Shit!" I brushed my hands up and down so I wouldn't set my fool self on fire. I stubbed out the cigarette with my shoe and picked up both butts so Madge wouldn't find them. I crept back upstairs to my room. *Well, by God, if Fancy is going to Pittsburgh, then I'm going with him.*

It was so easy. It was the edge of dark and so warm we had the windows rolled down; even the icicles were losing their grip on the north side of the mountains. The radio was on, and the Andrew Sisters were singing "Don't Sit Under the Apple Tree with Anyone Else but Me." I asked, "When you leaving for home?"

"Day after tomorrow."

I stayed quiet. Fancy pulled over in front of the apartment and cut the engine. I set still, looking out the window. I could feel his eyes caressing me like the warmth of a fire.

"Are you going to miss me?"

I turned the full force of my smile on him. "No."

His face fell, and I saw what he must have looked like when he was a little boy.

"No." I brushed the hair out of his eyes. "I'm not going to miss you, cause I'm going with you."

That time, I kissed him. When he opened his eyes, it was slow and deliberate, like he was waking from a dream he didn't want to end. His green eyes deepened, and the amber flecks in them smoldered like flames. He cupped my chin in his hand and ran his thumb across my cheek.

"Sylvia," he said, "will you go to Pittsburg with me?"

Two days later, we left just ahead of the storm. Spring had disappeared overnight, and the temperature slipped below freezing. I could tell Fancy was worrying about the weather, so I tried to distract him. "Can I ask you a question?"

He glanced sideways at me. "Sure."

"What do those marks on your ring mean?"

He twisted the ring around with his thumb. I loved to watch his hands. He had long, slender fingers and short, rounded nails that were always clean—almost feminine. He was the only man I'd ever seen who wore a ring that wasn't a wedding band, and he for sure was the only man I knew who wore one on his middle finger.

"These are Celtic etchings," he said. "My family is Irish, and the Celts were ancient tribes of people who lived in Ireland, Scotland, and Wales. This is the Celtic trinity. It symbolized the mother earth, heavens, and the underworld and the past, present, and future."

I mulled this over. I said, "Most people in these mountains can claim Scotch-Irish heritage. My mama always said our family was Welsh."

"That's true. The difference in my descendants and yours is likely religion."

"What do you mean?"

"The majority of the Scotch-Irish and Welsh who settled in these mountains were Protestants, and most were—in the beginning, at least—Presbyterians. My family settled in Pennsylvania, and they are Catholic."

"Catholic!"

Fancy chuckled. "Afraid so."

"Are *you* a, a . . .?"

"You can say it, you know. I don't think God will strike you dead if you say *Catholic*. And yes, I *am* a Catholic."

I stared straight ahead, trying to digest it. I'd never known a Catholic before. *Hell fire,* I wasn't even sure what a Catholic was! I was raised in the Old Regular Baptist church, and according to them, Catholics had devil horns and carried pitchforks. My silence filled the car. We drove for a while; a fine, misty rain was falling. Fancy's voice jarred me loose from my thoughts.

"I may as well tell you all of it."

"There's more?"

"Much more. My brother's a priest."

"Shit fire!"

Fancy laughed and covered my hand with his; the ring that had started all this was cold against my skin. "He was the one who gave me this ring. He got it in Ireland."

"Ireland?"

"Yes."

"He went to *Ireland?*"

"Actually, he and I went together."

I whistled low and stared at him. "What else, Fancy Howard? What else do I need to know about you?"

"How about that I'm a hard-working, decent fellow? It doesn't matter that I'm Catholic, or that I've been to Europe, or college, or anywhere else. I'm just a man who loves chocolate cake, the smell of fresh-cut grass, and big, shaggy dogs. I'm just a man who wants to settle down and raise a bunch of kids with a woman I love."

"A bunch of kids, huh?" *Sweet Jesus, why didn't he say he was just a man who wanted to get married and travel all over the world with his wife? Does he really want to settle down and have "a bunch" of kids, or does he think that's what most women want to hear? Hasn't he figured out yet I'm not like most women?*

Fancy laughed. "Is that all you got out of what I said?"

As if on cue, we heard Sassy waking up. I glanced behind me. The basket Fancy had rigged up as a bed took up almost all of the backseat. *God, why didn't he let me leave her with Madge?* I tried, but there was no stopping him from bringing her with us. I said, "I need to get her out and change her. She'll soon be ready for supper."

"I have all the places mapped out where we can stop. It's not far."

And he wasn't kidding—he actually made a written a list of places we could stop from Coal Valley all the way to Pittsburgh. What he hadn't planned on was the change in the weather. It was getting dark, and the rain kept coming down. That morning, I thought he'd change his mind about taking Sassy when he saw how cold it was, but instead he acted like a kid on Christmas. Even a tongue-lashing from Madge hadn't done any good.

After dinner, I dozed. It had started raining harder right after dark, and the windshield wipers hypnotized me into sleep. Finally, I stretched and sat up straight.

"I know I sound like a young'un, but how much further is it?"

"We're almost to the Pennsylvania state line. I'm going to stop soon and get some gas. I need a cup of coffee. How about you?"

"Coffee sounds good."

We drove for a while in silence. The *swish* of the wipers whispered secrets I would never know. "Fancy?"

"Hum?"

"I know I've already asked you this, but are you sure you're parents are okay with you coming home with a woman and a *baby?*"

"I'm sure," Fancy said. "Mother has everything ready, including a room with a baby bed."

"You're kidding." I turned in my seat and stared at him.

He laughed. "I told you there are a lot of children in my family."

"And how many is a lot?" I remembered hearing somewhere that Catholics had a lot of kids—but then, so did mountain folk.

"I'm the youngest of eight," Fancy said. "Five girls and three boys. How about you?"

"I'm the only one my mama had that lived—born when she was past forty, long after she gave up on having any. Aunt Hat says Mama bargained with the devil to get me. Says I have the devil's mark." I touched the small, perfectly round birthmark no more than an inch from the corner of my right eye.

"Ah, the infamous Aunt who is coming from . . . where is it?"

"Seattle."

"And what makes her think you have the devil's mark?"

"According to Aunt Hat, when Mama discovered she was going to have me, she went up on Rock House Mountain—that's where her people were from—to find the Granny woman, who at the full of the moon, was seen walking up the mountain with the devil. At the time, Daddy was working in the mines, and they were living in the coal camp that had a doctor. But Mama refused to see this doctor, because every baby of hers he birthed had died. Before her time come, she moved up on the mountain to her family home place, where Aunt Hat and Uncle Danny Ray were living, so she'd be near this woman they called Granny Zee. Granny Zee would come to the house and rub Mama's belly, whispering spells, and give her a potion that she drank from every day. When Mama's time come, Aunt Hat said Granny Zee just appeared at the door before Uncle Danny Ray could fetch her.

"Aunt Hat said that when I was born, I wasn't breathing. She swears I was as blue as the sky. She said Granny Zee rubbed her hands over my body, chanting spells, and then opened my mouth and blew into it—and I breathed. Aunt Hat said at the exact moment I took my first breath, this mark appeared on my face."

I paused to see if Fancy would say anything, but he was staring ahead at the rain. When a minute passed without a comment, I laughed and broke the spell.

He smiled. "So, I'm assuming there is some punishment element in this story—the old 'pay for your sins' component."

"Oh, yes."

"So, what did your mother have to pay?"

"That's just it—Mama didn't have to pay anything herself. 'The sins of the fathers,' Aunt Hat called it. I can hear her reciting the Bible verse—Exodus 34:7: 'Keeping mercy for thousands, forgiving iniquity and transgression and sin, and that will by no means clear the guilty; visiting the iniquity of the fathers upon the children, and upon the children's children, unto the third and to the fourth generation.'"

Fancy flinched like a fist was coming at his face.

"So you see," I said, "it's me who has to pay."

"You? How?"

"According to Aunt Hat, no one can ever possess me, because I belong to the devil. When Gaines died, she said any man who ever loved me would die."

"Horse malarkey!" Fancy thumped the steering wheel with his hand.

"Horse what?" I looked at Fancy, expecting to see him laugh, but even in the dark, I could see his anger.

"Malarkey! A load of crap—that's what it is! How could anybody believe that?"

"You don't know Aunt Hat." *In truth, sometimes I believe it myself.* We drove for a while in silence. "Could we talk about something besides me?"

Fancy chuckled. "Okay, what would you like to talk about?"

"How about your family?"

"Okay, back to my family. The oldest is Thomas, Jr.; he's in business with my father. Then there's Mary Catherine, Elizabeth, Teresa, Beatrice, Patrick, and Angela. All of them are married, except me—and Patrick, of course. All of them have kids. My sister Beatrice has a little girl Sassy's age named Katherine. She had a twin sister who died shortly after birth, but Katherine's thriving. Another of my sisters, Angie, just had her fourth."

"Fourth?"

"Yes, fourth—little John Thomas was born on Christmas Eve."

"So he's named after your father?"

"Yes, and his father—*and* St. John of God, who is the patron saint of the sick, and St. Thomas, patron saint of architects."

I was glad it was dark and Fancy couldn't see my face, because I know I must have looked at him like he'd lost his mind. I didn't even know what to say. I'd heard of a saint before, but a *patron* saint—what the hell was that? I could feel him waiting for me to say something, so I said, "So, Catholics name their kids after saints?"

"Some do—not all. My parents named all of us after patron saints."

"What exactly is that? A patron saint."

"A patron saint is a special guardian especially for a group of people. Francis, my patron saint, is the guardian of merchants or businessmen."

While I was digesting this, hail began to pelt the windshield. "Know any weather saints? Cause we sure could use one right now."

By the time Fancy stopped for gas, the hail had stopped, but the rain kept coming down. Across the road was a diner, so we got coffee and let Sassy out of her basket for a while. The lady who served us said to watch out for black ice and that if we needed a place to spend the night, there was a motel not far up the road.

When we got back in the car, Fancy strapped Sassy into her basket and climbed under the wheel. He turned to me, and out of the blue, kissed me long and sweet.

"What was that for?" I asked.

"Sylvia Richardson, I'm falling in love with you."

Sylvia

They say the last sense you lose before you leave this world is your hearing. When my Mama passed on to heaven, I held her hand and talked to her. It comforts me that my voice was the last earthly sound she ever knew. But there is another reason why I know this to be true. Once in my life, I stood between this world and the next.

All I remember is the cold. Cold bit and tore at my flesh. I tried to scream, but death clasped its hand over my mouth. I tried to struggle, but the cold held me down. It flowed into my eyes and blinded me. My head throbbed in rhythm with my heartbeat, but I could hear. Sassy cried—loud and strong. Then I stepped into the next world.

Gaines and I set under an enormous silver maple. A soft carpet of grass spread before us. I lay back and put my head in his lap. With one hand, he stroked my hair while I watched the leaves shimmer and dance. In his other hand, he held a small book with a battered cover. His fingers sank into the leather like they belonged there. He opened the book, and in a rich, bottomless voice, read, "Weep not, child/Weep not, my darling/With these kisses let me remove your tears/The ravening clouds shall not long be victorious."

I closed my eyes and let the words float around me. I felt his fingers stroke my forehead. When I opened my eyes, Gaines was gone, and Fancy was smiling down at me. He was wearing a plaid flannel shirt that belonged to my daddy. The leaves pranced their shadows across his face. "I'm sorry," he said. "Can you forgive me?"

"Forgive you?" I laughed and touched the soft fabric of Daddy's shirt. It felt like home. "For what?"

"I promised to take care of you."

I laughed again and touched his face. He turned his head, and I saw it—the whole side of his face was gone. Blood poured from the wound and splashed onto my face. I screamed—and opened my eyes.

"Child, can you hear me? Are you in pain?"

A dazzling cloud of light swirled before me, faster and faster, until a face emerged. It was a face the years had softened into a maze of lines. It came closer until I could see gray eyes so pale they were almost colorless. They were filled with concern. At first, I thought she was an angel, but angels are only found in heaven, and this pain couldn't follow me there.

"You were in an accident. You are in the hospital." She took my hand in hers. "Child, can you squeeze my hand?"

I concentrated all my strength into my hand. Her smile told me I had done it.

"That's good. Can you move your legs? Try for me."

She lifted the sheet and watched while I tried to move. I was able to move my feet, but the effort made my head throb. I moaned. She replaced the sheet and took my hand again. "Rest now, child."

The room was dark when next I opened my eyes. I knew she was there. Her scent was like the mustiness that escapes from a book that's long been forgotten. I couldn't judge how much time had passed, but whenever I woke, she was there. Her touch was kindness and comfort. She called me "child" and said prayers for me when she thought I was sleeping. When she prayed, her fingers flew up and down a strand of beads that hung from her belt. She never prayed out loud, but her lips moved, and she always ended the prayer by kissing the beads. Sister Marie was her name. She wore an enormous cross on a chain around her neck, and sometimes when she leaned over my bed, it clanged against the metal rails, sounding like an iron skillet hitting a stove.

There were other nuns and a doctor who took care of me. They called him Father. He asked my name, and at first, I didn't know, but

211

Sister Marie brought Sassy to me, and when I touched the softness of her skin, I remembered. "She's Sarah Jane. I am Sylvia Richardson."

The man frowned. "Richardson? Your name is Richardson? Do you remember the accident?"

I tried, but I couldn't recall anything. My head throbbed, but I managed to raise my hand and touch the thick bandages that surrounded my head. The man leaned over my bed. His starched white collar peeked above his black shirt. I realized he was a priest.

"My name is Father Michaels," he said. "I am a doctor. You are in Mercy Hospital in Somerset, Pennsylvania. A tractor trailer slid on the ice and hit your car head-on. Your head hit the dashboard. You have a severe concussion and were in a coma for three weeks."

"Fancy?"

He looked at Sister Marie. She took my hand.

"I'm sorry," he said. "Francis Howard didn't make it. He was thrown from the car and died instantly. Is there someone we can contact for you?"

A lone tear traveled down my cheek. "No."

"Surely there is someone we can contact for you."

"No. All my family is dead."

"What about the child's father?"

"He died. In the war."

"What about his family?"

"We didn't have nobody but each other."

The doctor and Sister Marie walked across the room and talked. Sister Marie came back alone and set in the chair next to my bed. I closed my eyes and drifted off. When I woke up, she was still there, reading from a small book. It looked old and worn, like the pages had been turned every day for many years. She closed it and smiled at me. I pointed to her book, and she held it up for me to see. "This is my prayer book."

"Say one for me."

I began to notice the difference in day and night. When I could sit up, the sisters spooned broth and warm tea into my mouth. Before long, I could stand and feed myself. Sister Marie put me in a wheelchair and took me outside to sit in the sun. It was summer. I was surprised the world had moved forward while I was lost somewhere in time.

Each day, I gained strength from the sun. Outside, I was surrounded by color—a welcome contrast to the stark black and white of the hospital. I basked in the sun and the warmth of its yellow. I feasted on the blue of the sky and the green of the grass. It satisfied me more than the food I ate.

The headaches became less severe, and I knew it was time. I made my decision. All I ever wanted was to be loved, and all I ever got was pain and suffering. There was no place left in my heart for love. It had turned to stone. Maybe Aunt Hat was right—maybe I did belong to the devil. But there's one thing I did know—if I let love in my life again, it would destroy me. I was not fit to love or be loved.

Sister Marie told me I must pray—I must search my heart. She said God answers prayers. What she didn't understand was that I'd searched my heart every day since Sassy was born for the love I was supposed to feel. I had prayed a million times for God to let me love her—to unwrap the shroud from around my heart—but each day, it squeezed me tighter and tighter. Since she was born, I'd tried to run away from her. I'd lived in fear that something bad would happen because I didn't know how to take care of her. Many's the night I'd laid awake and worried about what I was going to do. The only thing that kept me hanging on was knowing Gaines was coming back. He would have changed everything—he could've loved Sassy enough for both of us.

Sassy knew—I could see it in her eyes. They bore into me and saw what I tried to hide in my black heart. Living was my punishment. There was only one thing I could do for her. She didn't deserve a mother like me. I was going to give her to a woman who *wanted* a baby and knew how to love her. When Sister Marie brought her to me, I told her to take her away—I was meant to be alone. Maybe one day I could ask God to forgive me.

I was sitting in the garden, watching a gentle wind ruffle the grass, proud I made it to the courtyard on my own two legs. It was early, so there weren't any visitors cluttering the benches. I saw Sister Marie and a woman approaching. The woman stopped when she saw me looking at them, and Sister Marie came to me alone.

"You have a visitor," she said.

"Visitor?" I turned and looked at the woman. I didn't recognize her, so I looked around to see if there was anyone else.

Sister Marie said, "Her name is Mary Howard." She paused.

"Howard?"

"Yes, she is Francis Howard's mother."

The resemblance was unmistakable—the same green eyes and blonde hair, even though it was streaked with gray. We sat together in silence; neither of us wanted to cross the chasm of grief between us.

At last, I offered, "I'm sorry about Fancy."

"Thank you."

The breeze picked up, and I shivered. "Why did you want to see me?"

"I have something to ask you."

I waited. I could feel how painful this was, so I decided to make it easy for her. "Look, Mrs. Howard. I don't blame Fancy for what happened. It was an accident. I wasn't planning on contacting his family for—for anything." I stood and grabbed the back of the bench to steady myself.

"Please, don't go." She turned in her seat and reached for my hand, stopping short of touching me. "Fancy was bringing you home to meet us. He'd never done that before."

I was sure if my eyes met hers, she'd see me for what I was. I had used Fancy—made him fall in love with me—and he was gone. The tears came then, making me look like the innocent, injured woman I was not.

"I want to show you something," she said. She pulled a folded piece of yellow paper out of her pocket. There was no mistaking that yellow paper—it was a telegram. The last one I saw told me Gaines was dead. She unfolded the paper and handed it to me. I wiped my eyes and read, *Be home Monday night/stop. Bringing the woman I love and baby/stop. Will explain when I see you/stop. Love, Fancy*

214

Sylvia

Father Michaels put his elbows on the desk and clasped his hands. He rested his chin on his hands, pondering what to say next. I sat with my hands folded in my lap, waiting for him to finish questioning me so I could go.

"Mrs. Richardson, I know you said there was no one we could contact for you." He paused.

I stared at him until he dropped his eyes and sighed. He opened the top drawer of his desk and pulled out an envelope. He placed it in the exact center of the empty desk.

"Here's the train ticket you asked for and some money. Are you sure there's nothing else we can do?"

I stood and extended my hand. "Thank you, Father; you've done enough. I reckon I'll have to do the rest."

I hurried toward the corridor that would lead me away from the people who had cared for and protected me. I turned the corner, and there stood Sister Marie. Without a moment's hesitation, I let her fold me into her arms. Unlike Father Michaels, who wanted to solve all of my problems, Sister Marie just let me cry. When I straightened up, she released me and pulled a handkerchief from the folds of her dress.

"Go with God, child."

I knew it was just a matter of time before the news of the accident made its way back to Coal Valley—it was that kind of place. So before I got on the train, I sent Madge a telegram. *Am leaving Philadelphia today/ stop. Going to Seattle/stop. Be back in the fall/stop. Love, Sylvia.*

The first thing I did on the train was buy a pack of cigarettes. The second was plan out what I was going to tell Aunt Hat. For days, I watched the world float by my window. At night, I climbed into the tiny bunk and felt the sway of the train—*Sas-sy, Sas-sy, Sas-sy.* I wished I could stay on that train and ride until it reached the end of the world, but the day came when I had nowhere else to go.

I stepped from the train into a sea of soldiers—Goliath green turtles—their duffle bags like giant shells secured on their backs. I watched them hug and kiss the women they were leaving—mothers, wives, sisters. They shook hands and slapped the men on the back. A few succumbed and hugged their fathers and sons, but most maintained the soldiers' stance. They were stoics who believed that this was their destiny—to endure the adversities of war without complaint. Moving through them was like swimming against a strong current. The last time I saw soldiers boarding the train, Gaines had been one of them, and he was coming back. Now, Lord help me. I searched their faces. In spite of everything that had happened, hope had not died in me.

A porter offered to help me find the right trolley. He asked for the address, and I panicked; I couldn't remember. Since the shock treatments, I had holes in my memory, and now with the accident, there were whole stretches of time I couldn't remember. The doctors said most of my memory would return, but I might never remember the accident. I prayed they were right.

The porter saw my confusion and ushered me into the office. He gave me a cup of coffee and went about his work, but he kept an eye on me. No doubt, he thought I was one of the wives who'd just kissed her soldier husband good-bye and was overcome by the farewell. Through the open doorway, I watched people buying tickets. A middle-aged lady carrying an enormous pocketbook came to the window. She had round glasses perched on the end of her nose, her hair a mass of graying curls. She reminded me of Aunt Hat, and all of a sudden, I remembered her address.

I got off the trolley at Capitol Hill and stood looking down at the bay, hypnotized by the smell of salt water. The sun was shining, and the clear blue of the sky melted into the similitude of the water. I realized that never in my life had I been to a place where the purity of the sky matched the land. Thanks to the coal dust, Coal Valley was a world of grays and black. For the first time, I saw the world without a veil of coal dirt in front of me.

A row of modest houses sat on lush green lawns like they'd sprouted with the grass. At the end of the street, I found Aunt Hat's box-like house. It looked brighter and whiter than the rest. A profusion of red and white impatiens nestled against the porch and spilled down the front walk. I knocked on the door, but Aunt Hat wasn't home, so I settled down in one of the two rocking chairs on the porch—but not before running my hand over the seat. *Clean.* In Coal Valley, you never set down on anything outside without first checking for coal dust.

The sun was slipping away when the trolley stopped in front of the house and Aunt Hat emerged. She carried an enormous pocketbook slung over one arm and an umbrella hooked over the other. She trudged up the walk and paused to examine her flower beds, muttering about snails. She looked so much like my mama that it added yet another ache to my heart. She turned back toward the porch and still didn't see me, so I spoke.

"Hello, Aunt Hat."

Her purse and umbrella fell, clattering on the walk. "Good heavens! Sylvia, is that you?"

I stepped forward out of the shadows. "Yes, it's me."

She left her things on the sidewalk and rushed up on the porch. I thought she was going to hug me, but she passed me up before stopping and wheeling around. She demanded, "Where's the baby?"

It didn't take long for Aunt Hat to recover and set to feeding me. The small kitchen table filled with steaming dishes of fried pork chops and gravy, creamed potatoes, and peas as if by magic. Aunt Hat belonged to that group of Appalachian women who believed when someone showed up at your door, you had to feed them. It was as much a part of her as church twice on Sunday and making quilts out of old clothes. The fact that she hadn't lived in the South for many years didn't matter; there are some things so ingrained in your being that they will not change no matter where you go.

I watched Aunt Hat cook while lie after lie slipped out of my mouth between sips of coffee. Yes, I'd been to Pittsburg. Yes, there was an accident, and Fancy was dead. No, Sassy was not with us. She was with Madge. It was easier than I thought.

When we set down to eat, Aunt Hat didn't waste any time telling me what a fool I was. She started with, "When are you going to learn to stop running off with every man who asks you?"

I held on and tried to keep from losing my temper. I didn't want to say something that would make my carefully crafted ball of lies unravel, but when she started in on "that man," I had to stop her. "*Please,* Aunt Hat, you don't know anything about Fancy. He was good to me and Sassy." Something in my voice must have gotten through to her, because she stopped in mid-sentence. That's when I realized I was crying.

"Now, there's no need to cry." Aunt Hat jumped up and bumped the table, making the dishes rattle. "You need some rest. Just look at you. You've aged ten years since I last seen you!"

Aunt Hat whisked me into her guest room, and within minutes, I was in one of her old flannel nightgowns that smelled like the wild lilac bushes that grew on Rock House Mountain. That part of my life had died with Mama and Daddy, and I could no more go back there than I could bring back Gaines or Fancy—no more than I could be a good mama to Sassy.

I slid under the log cabin quilt. It was just like the one my mama had made that covered my bed in Coal Valley. I hadn't slept on a featherbed since I left home, and for the first time in weeks, I felt an easy sleepiness settle over me. I fell asleep promising myself that as soon as I was stronger, I would tell Aunt Hat the truth.

Madge

Am leaving Philadelphia today/stop. Going to Seattle/stop. Be back in the fall/stop. Love, Sylvia.

"Has that girl lost her mind? Something's up. She wouldn't go to Hattie Mae's without a good reason." I folded the telegram and put it in my pocket.

The bell rang over the shop door, and Buster Dawson stepped inside. He glanced around to make sure I was alone before he spoke. "You ready?"

"Do I look like I'm ready?" I grabbed the broom and waved it in his face. "Set down over there." I pointed at a chair with the broom handle. "I just got a telegram from Sylvie that makes no damn sense. It says she's gone to Seattle to stay with Hattie Mae."

Buster shifted in his seat and looked down at his hands. I knew right away he was hiding something. I set the broom in the corner and said, "What is it?"

He looked at me, opened his mouth, and then snapped it shut. I said, "You got any idea why she'd leave here with Fancy going to Pittsburg and end up with Hattie Mae in Seattle?"

"Yeah, I just heard they was in a car wreck, and—"

"Car wreck!"

Buster ran his hand through his hair. "Madge, come over here and set down and let me tell it."

I set down next to him. When I was still, he said, "One of the big bosses was over at the mines this morning, and he said they was in a car wreck the night after they left here. They had just crossed into Pennsylvania when a tractor-trailer slid on ice and hit them head-on."

"Oh, God. Why didn't she tell me? What about Sassy—dear Lord—if something happened to that baby!"

Buster took my hand. "Listen to me, Madge. Sassy's fine. Sylvie was hurt pretty bad, but she's all right now. It's Fancy. Fancy's dead."

My mind was racing. I couldn't imagine what Sylvia must be going through. *Why in the world hadn't she come home instead of going all the way to Seattle?* I looked at Buster and realized he was upset about Fancy. It hadn't occurred to me how much Buster had thought of him. On impulse, I took his face in my hands and kissed him. We stood and wrapped our arms around each other. "Oh, Madge, he was such a fine feller. He was good to all the men at the mines."

"God knows I gave him a hard time, but I knowed he was crazy about Sylvia and that baby. I never wanted for nothing to happen to him."

I pulled away from Buster and went to the back room for my pocketbook. I locked up the shop, and we headed for the diner. Lightening bugs chased the night, and moths clung to the streetlights, but the beauty of the summer evening was lost on us. When we got to the diner, we found a booth along the back wall. Neither of us ate much; we just sipped coffee and talked. I kept saying, "It don't make no sense."

Buster said, "Wonder why she didn't have somebody get a hold of you when she was in the hospital?"

"I can't figure it out," I said. "I would of caught the next bus up there and got Sassy. Why didn't she want me?" I saw Shelby Compton coming toward us with the coffee pot, so I hushed. When she walked away, I spotted Myrtle Stiltner striding toward us, practically dragging her husband, Luther, with her. "Oh, shit, here comes Myrtle Stiltner."

"Why, Madge, I thought that was you with Buster," Myrtle said. Her voice was barely below a shout. "I told Mr. Stiltner I thought that was Buster Dawson with Madge, now didn't I, Mr. Stiltner?"

Luther nodded his head so fast his bowtie bobbed up and down. He said, "You sure did, Myrtle. How are you, Madge? Buster?"

Buster stuck out his hand and shook with Luther while Myrtle zeroed in on me. "I'm right as rain," I said.

"We just heard the news about Sylvia's terrible accident. And that poor young man, Francis Howard. What a tragedy! I hope that beautiful baby is all right. When are they coming home?" Myrtle asked without pausing for a single breath.

Buster looked at me and raised his eyebrows like, *Well, here we go.* I said, "Thank you for your *concern* for Sylvia and Sassy. They are both fine and have gone to visit Hattie Mae in Seattle."

"So that's where they are," she said. "I told Mr. Stiltner I bet they was in Seattle. Didn't I say they was with Hattie Mae?"

Luther nodded his head, giving the bowtie another workout. He looked at Myrtle. "You certainly did. You said they was with Hattie Mae."

"Sylvie said they was going to stay awhile," I said, sipping my coffee. I could tell Myrtle wasn't satisfied with my answer, but I wasn't giving her nothing else. She tried, though—I was ready for her. When she saw she wasn't getting nowhere, she grabbed Luther's arm and left.

Buster waited until I signaled him they were out of earshot before he spoke. "Good job, Madge."

I said, "I'll be damned if the likes of Myrtle Stiltner is going to know Sylvie's business. Her mouth's big enough for two sets of teeth."

Buster nodded and took a sip of coffee.

"Something's wrong, Buster. Sylvie wasn't herself when she left here with Fancy."

"She's had a hell of a time, that's for sure. Losing Gaines like that."

"It's more than that. Sylvie ain't been herself since Sassy was born. She never took to mothering."

Buster frowned. "I know you stayed with her all the time. I thought she was just sickly. I knowed she was in the hospital a while back."

I wanted to tell Buster about having to put Sylvie in the mental hospital, but I was afraid to. I knowed he wouldn't do nothing to hurt Sylvie, but I also knowed he was bad to throw a drunk, and no matter how much he promised he wouldn't drink no more, I couldn't risk it. I'd seen Buster drunk, and his tongue was loose at both ends. I said, "Maybe that's it. Maybe it's just been too much. She's been through more than a body can take."

Buster laid his hand on top of mine. I looked up, surprised. It wasn't like Buster to show his feelings. He smiled, and I smiled back. He said, "Don't worry. Sylvie will come home when she's ready.

Sylvia

I woke to the smell of coffee perking and bacon frying. I found Aunt Hat cooking breakfast and getting things ready for work. Her enormous pocketbook set in the center of the table, open like the expectant mouth of a baby bird. Every time she walked past it, she threw something in. She turned to toss in a handful of clothespins and saw me.

"Sylvia, you're up. Coffee's ready." She gestured toward the coffee pot.

I helped myself to a cup and set down at the table.

"How did you sleep?" she demanded, turning from the stove with two plates heaped with bacon and scrambled eggs. She set the plates on the table and grabbed her pocketbook, snapping it shut before carrying it into the front room. She came back and fetched a plate of biscuits that she placed at my elbow. Before sitting down, she got a jar of homemade apple butter and a dish of butter from the refrigerator.

"I slept just fine," I said. I dug into my plate, grabbing a biscuit and biting into it without pausing to add butter. I couldn't remember the last time food had tasted this good. I looked up at Aunt Hat, who was actually smiling at me.

She pushed the butter dish toward me and said, "Mary Jane may have made the best dumplings, but she always said nobody could beat my biscuits, and that's the God's truth."

Aunt Hat attacked her plate, and together we polished off the plate of biscuits. When we had eaten every scrap, she took our plates to the sink and poured us another cup of coffee. With one eye on the clock over the stove, she took a sip. "Sylvie, I wouldn't go off to work and leave you here, but I've got to. I've been having a time trying to get the store in shape since Danny Ray died."

Relieved I wasn't going to have Aunt Hat lobbing questions at me all day, I tried to act nonchalant. "Don't worry about me. I'm just going to rest up from my trip."

"Well, then, I guess I better get ready. The trolley will be by here soon," Aunt Hat said, but she didn't move from her seat.

I tried to remember how to flash my brightest smile. "Go on, now. Don't you be late on my account. I'll tidy up the kitchen."

She put her cup in the sink and turned to go. Her voice echoed from the hallway. "We can talk tonight."

I found the trolley schedule in the kitchen and decided I was going to make my way down to the bay. It wasn't as sunny as the day before, but having spent the last two months inside a hospital, I craved the out-of-doors. Besides, I'd go stir crazy in Aunt Hat's house, which looked like a refuge for ugly knick-knacks.

Until I saw the ocean, I thought the whole world laid between the mountains of Coal Valley—not because I didn't *know* there were places like this; I'd studied geography in school. I knew there were plains, Rocky Mountains, and oceans, but when you've never been anywhere but one little corner of the world, you can't truly imagine the rest of it. And when that corner of the world is Coal Valley, the Pacific Ocean may as well be the moon.

Blue flowed from heaven and spilled to the bottom of the world. I took a deep breath and smelled the morning. Salt and fish tickled my nose. If only I could throw my troubles into that blue water and watch them sink deeper and deeper until they disappeared forever.

"It's beautiful, isn't it?"

I turned. A woman with a black shawl drawn across her shoulders stood to my right.

"Yes," I agreed. "It is beautiful."

"My name is Isabel," she said, her speech heavy with a German accent.

"Hello, Isabel. I'm Sylvia."

"Hello, Sylvia."

We stood for a while in silence. The sun skipped across the top of the water, leaving footprints of light.

"I never get tired of looking at it," Isabel said. She took a step, bringing her closer to my side.

"I've never been here before," I said. "I mean, I just got here yesterday. I'm visiting my aunt."

"My mother and I came here at the start of the war. I come here to remember those we left behind. The water—it gives me peace."

"Then I've come to the right place."

That night, I was ready for Aunt Hat's talk. I convinced her to give me two or three weeks to rest before I made the long trip home—and I convinced myself I would be strong enough by then to tell her about Sassy.

The next morning, I returned to the bay. It was cool and cloudy, and no one was around. I walked along the water's edge, exploring the area. Off shore, a huge ship patrolled. I sat down on a rock and lit a cigarette.

"Hello, Sylvia." It was Isabel. She had the same shawl wrapped tightly around her. "May I sit with you?"

I scooted over and she sat down. For a while, neither of us spoke; instead, we looked out at the water. I noticed her hands. They reminded me of my Mama's hands—rough and chapped from a life of endless work.

"How are you today?" Isabel asked.

An hour later, we parted ways, and I returned to the trolley stop. I realized that for the first time since the accident, I had thought of someone besides myself. We met the next day and walked for miles. We tested our voices, and like caged birds released, discovered our wings still worked. We soared high above the clouds.

Aunt Hat never asked what I did with my days, and I never told her about Isabel. By the end of my first week, I fell into a routine. I caught the trolley as soon as Aunt Hat went to work and returned before she got home. Isabel would meet me on the waterfront and spend the morning with me. We discovered a café where we could drink coffee and escape the rain showers that were more prevalent than the sunshine. There, we shared our pain. There, I began to heal.

Like working a puzzle, we placed the pieces of our lives out on the table. As we talked, the pieces fell into place. At one time, Isabel's family had been successful and wealthy. Her father and husband were watchmakers and silversmiths. But they were Jews, and when the Nazis rose to power, they lost everything. Her father managed to get her and her mother out of the country, but the rest of her family was left behind. She didn't know what happened to them, but she feared they were all dead. Her mother died last winter—of a broken heart, Isabel said—and she was alone. She lived in a rooming house downtown, where she cooked and cleaned for room and board.

I aired my life before Isabel like last winter's quilts hung outside in the spring air. I told her about Gaines and how he died—our lost dreams and plans. I told her about Fancy and the accident. Finally, I poured my heart out about Sassy.

Then I listened.

Isabel spoke of what it was like to live under a strict curfew and not be allowed to buy food or enter restricted buildings. She told me what it felt like to be spit on because she was a Jew. She explained how one by one, Jewish families disappeared in the Nazi raids. Her fear was still stark and raw, like a gushing wound. She described so vividly how her family huddled together at night and waited for the Nazis to come for them that I couldn't sleep at night for imagining it.

She wept for her family—those who had everything taken away from them. She told me what it was like to leave her husband and father behind and immigrate to America. For the first time, I understood there were things in this world so hideous and terrifying I could not even imagine them.

Isabel had lost everything and everyone, but she had survived. Here I was, a woman who had lost her parents and husband—but in exchange was given a child. My flesh and blood—the only remnant of Gaines I had left—and I gave her away.

Madge

It was raining. That's why I went on home. It had been almost a week since I got the mail, but Buster would be home that night, and I had my mind on making a pot of vegetable soup. Lord, I still can't believe I up and married that man, but I admit it—it's good to have somebody to come home to at night. I been lost since Sylvia took Sassy and run off. If I can just keep him away from the drink, maybe we can make a go of it.

It was Buster who brought me the letter. The night before, I told him I hadn't got the mail in a week, so when I was closing up the shop, he showed up with it. We were going over to the diner for supper, so I was hurrying to get the floor swept. When he came through the door, I never even looked up. "Buster," I said, "take that trash out back, and I'm ready to go."

He said, "You might ought to read this first."

I grabbed the envelope and tore it open. I was surprised it was from Hattie Mae and not Sylvia. "God, I hope nothing's wrong with Sylvia or the baby."

Buster picked up the trash and disappeared through the curtains that led to the back door.

When he came back, I was sitting in the chair at my station with the letter laying in my lap. "What's a-matter?" he asked.

"I told you something was not right!" I stood up and shook the letter in Buster's face. "I told you Sylvie would never go to Hattie Mae's unless something was bad wrong."

"What's wrong?"
"I'll tell what's wrong."

Dear Madge,

I know Sylvia's accident has placed the burden of Sarah Jane's care on you, so I have enclosed a check to help with the expenses. Sylvia is gaining strength every day and should be home by summer's end. I know she misses the baby, but takes comfort knowing she is in your care. If you could write Sylvia a letter telling her how the baby is growing, I'm sure it would cheer her up. If Sarah Jane needs anything, please let me know.

Sincerely,
Hattie Mae Mason

I waved a check for fifty dollars in Buster's face. "Buster," I said, "we're going to Seattle."

Sylvia

It was Sunday afternoon, and Aunt Hat and I had just set down on the front porch with a pitcher of iced tea. I had a bad headache, made worse from not sleeping the night before because I decided I was going to tell Aunt Hat about Sassy. The past two weeks with Isabel had given me the strength to get on with my life. I didn't want to hide anymore.

"Did I tell you a new shipment of cloth and sewing notions arrived this week? Before you leave, you must come to the store and have a look around," Aunt Hat said. "By this time next summer, I will have things arranged so I can come and spend a month with you and my grandniece. I will make that a yearly tradition."

"I was thinking about going home next week," I said.

Aunt Hat sat up straight in her chair. "Are you well enough? I know you're anxious to get home to the baby, but you still look like a strong puff of wind will blow you away."

"That's what I want to talk to you about."

"I told you and told you, you need to go and see my doctor! He can give you a tonic that'll put some meat on your bones, and that's the God's truth."

I sighed and closed my eyes. Aunt Hat had completely misunderstood me. She was off on a tangent, talking about doctors and tonics. I must have dozed off, because I didn't hear her stand up. When her glass of tea hit the porch and broke, it startled me awake. I opened my eyes, and for a second, I thought I was still asleep and dreaming, because Madge and Buster Dawson were coming up the walk.

My hand flew to my throat. I stood just as they reached the steps to the porch.

"Where the hell is Sarah Jane?" Madge said.

Aunt Hat gasped and swung around. Everything went black.

I woke up in a dark room with a cold, wet rag on my head. My head pounded, and when I tried to sit up, the room started spinning. Madge gently pushed me back down on the bed. "Lay still, Sylvie."

She took the rag off my head, dipped it in a pan of water, and wrung it out. She placed it on my forehead before speaking again. "Sylvia, you've got to tell us what's going on. Where's the baby?"

I took the rag off my head and grabbed Madge's hand. "I had to do it. You don't understand. I had to."

"Do what? Sylvie, honey, where's the baby?"

"I gave her away." The relief was immediate. It rose up off my chest and disappeared through the ceiling like the morning mist in the sun. The tears I wanted to cry for so long finally came.

I watched Madge's face turn to stone. "Tell me everything," she said.

Madge

Mercy Hospital gave me the creeps—how many crosses on the walls and Mary statues does a person need? It doesn't seem to bother Hattie Mae. She didn't waste any time going straight to the head of the hospital. I about wore a hole in the rug outside his office door while Hattie Mae and Sylvia was in there. When they finally come out, Hattie Mae was huffing and puffing, and Sylvia was pale as a ghost.

"He says he will investigate," Hattie Mae said. She threw her big pocketbook down on the bench and set down. It was clear she wasn't going anywhere.

"I'm going outside to smoke," Sylvia said. She disappeared out the door.

"Stay with Hattie Mae," I said to Buster. "I'm going with Sylvia."

I found her smoking just outside the main entrance. She held up her hand with her palm out and turned her back on me. I stepped in front of her and grabbed her arm, forcing her to look at me. "What happened?"

She threw her cigarette down and flung herself into my arms. I let her cry and patted her on the back. "It's going to be all right," I said over and over.

"She's gone, Madge. They're not going to tell me where she is."

For two days, we set in that hospital and waited while Hattie Mae went in and out of the office with the word *Administrator* emblazoned across the door. The whole time, Sylvia smoked and paced. That evening, I talked her into taking a walk with me. We left the hospital and strolled down the street. Sylvie blinked in the sunlight like she'd been in the dark so long her eyes wouldn't adjust to the light. It was hot and humid, and the air was stale, like summer had gone on too long. As we walked, I could feel the sweat run down my back.

"I've made a mess out of my life," Sylvia said. "I lost my husband, and Fancy, and then I gave my baby away. What kind of woman gives her baby away?"

"Sylvia, I don't blame you for what happened. And you can't blame yourself."

Sylvia stopped and looked at me. "How can you say that? This is all my fault."

"I know you, Sylvie, and what you've had to go through is enough to kill a strong person. I believe all of this was caused by what my mommy called baby birthing blues. Mommy says, when some women have a baby, they feel like they fall in a hole and they can't get out. You're not alone, Sylvie, but you think you are, because it's something women just don't talk about. And Sylvia, I know you've not been right since you had Sassy—and you know it too. None of this is your fault."

Sylvia started to cry. Then she turned back toward the hospital and took off running.

Sylvia

I didn't stop running until I found the part of the hospital where I spent two months of my life. I had to find Sister Marie. She was my only hope.

I went down the hall, looking into each room. The familiar smell of alcohol and sickness triggered memories I had tried to run away from. I found her in a patient's room. She was sitting by the bed of an old woman who was asleep. She was reading from the prayer book that was as familiar to me as the Bible my mama had kept on her bedside table. When she saw me, she rose and came to the door.

She took my hand like she had been expecting me. "Follow me, and I will find a place where we can talk."

She led me to a small room that had nothing in it but a table, two chairs, and a large cross on the wall that dwarfed the furniture. She placed the chairs so they were facing each other and motioned for me to sit down.

"I have prayed for you, Sylvia," she said. "I prayed for God to give you peace."

I nodded and closed my eyes, searching for the right words. Sister Marie sat with her hands folded in her lap. I blurted out, "I want my baby back."

"Have you spoken to the hospital's overseer?"

"For three days, I've talked to anybody who will listen to me! My aunt is here, and she's talked to them too, and they keep giving us the run around and saying they have to investigate the matter! They keep waving the papers I signed in front of my face and saying everything was done legal."

Sister Marie nodded. She laid her hand on top of mine and looked into my eyes. "Child, you know where your daughter is."

I couldn't have been more shocked if Sister Marie had reached out and slapped me. I jumped to my feet. "No, I don't! I just told you I was trying to get her back."

"Listen to me," Sister Marie said. She grabbed my hands and pulled me back down in my chair. Her grip tightened. "Search your heart. You will know where she is."

My mind raced. I said, "If I knew where she was, I wouldn't be here. I told you—they won't tell me who has her."

Sister Marie lifted the rosary that hung from her belt and ran her fingers over it. When she spoke, her words were as soft as the down on a baby duck. "Ask yourself this—who would have wanted her?"

In my mind's eye, I saw my mama bent over the fireplace, laying a fire. I saw her strike the match and lay it on top of the carefully arranged sticks of kindling and paper. I saw the flame flicker, then catch, and then blaze. And I knew. I knew it had to be Fancy's mother.

I said, "But Sister Marie, I told her the *truth*. I told her Fancy was not Sassy's father."

"Child, when you lose someone you love, you have to grieve. Some people turn to God; some turn against God—but they all seek comfort. Fancy's mother believed your daughter was her son's child, and this gave her comfort—it made him live on through the child. It was easier for her to keep believing this—even though you told her it was not true—than believe he was gone forever."

The veil lifted, and I saw it all clearly. I bolted from my chair. "Do you think I can get her back?"

Sister Marie stood. "God answers prayers. You are here, are you not?"

I hugged her, and she patted my back. When I pulled away, she was smiling. She said, "Go with God, child."

I talked Aunt Hat into letting me go see Fancy's mother alone. When the taxi dropped me off, I stood and stared up at the huge brick house with its flower gardens and manicured lawn. Fancy had been very matter-of-fact about his family's money—his education, his car, the things Buster had told me about his daddy being in the steel industry. All these things pointed to more money than I'd ever seen—but this was more money than I could even imagine.

I knocked on the door, and it was opened by an honest-to-God Negro maid in a starched gray uniform. She let me inside and went to fetch Mrs. Howard. In just a minute, the maid was back. She led me into a living room full of expensive furniture. Everything was in different shades of blue. I wandered over to the fireplace and looked at the family photos displayed on the polished mahogany mantle. I stared at Fancy's. It must have been taken four or five years ago, but that shock of blonde hair falling into his eyes was unmistakably Fancy.

"Hello, Mrs. Richardson."

I wheeled around, and there stood Fancy's mother. She was dressed in a slim gray skirt and pink blouse. A delicate gold cross rested on a chain around her neck. Like Sister Marie, she looked like she was expecting me. She gestured toward the flowered sofa. "Please, sit down."

I had laid awake all night, planning what I was going to say. I was prepared to do anything—beg and plead, if I had to—to get my daughter back. Before I could launch into my speech, Mrs. Howard said, "I knew you would come."

All I could do was nod.

She looked down at her hands. "When I saw you at the hospital, I knew you were suffering. I knew the day would come when you would be able to take care of your daughter, and I knew you would want her back."

She raised her eyes to my face. Her right hand stroked the gold cross at her throat.

"Fancy would never have fallen in love with a woman who would have cast off her child."

"Mrs. Howard, I told you the truth. Sassy is not Fancy's daughter."

Tears glazed her eyes. "Yes, I know, but he loved her—and that was reason enough."

I came back the next day, and like she promised, Sassy was there. She had been living with Fancy's sister, Beatrice, who had a daughter Sassy's age. I took Aunt Hat, Madge, and Buster with me. Buster stood with his hands in his pockets, like he was afraid to touch anything. Aunt Hat talked to Fancy's mother and Beatrice, working out the details, while I got reacquainted with my daughter, who had grown from a baby to a toddler and was walking all over the place. She was dressed in a little pink dress and sturdy white walking shoes. Around her neck, she wore a tiny gold cross. It had a delicate, scrolled design etched on it. I tried to give it back to them, but they insisted she keep it—that and three suitcases of clothes and toys.

When at last we drove away, I said, "Sister Marie was right. God does answer prayers."

Winter, 1955–1956

Sassy

"To-day we love what to-morrow we hate; to-day we seek what to-morrow we shun; to-day we desire what to-morrow we fear. "Daniel Defoe, *Robinson Crusoe*

The mist clung to the mountain tops like a giant spider web spun across the silver morning. I inhaled a draught of morning and smiled. Christmas was just a week away, and I decided I was going to find the picture-perfect pine tree, chop it down, and decorate it myself. Aunt Hat may have ruined my Thanksgiving, but she dern sure wasn't going to ruin my Christmas.

I walked past the school to the old logging road that led up the mountain. The familiar perfume of coming snow drifted past me. Like the record Mama kept playing over and over, I was dreaming of a white Christmas.

As promised, Kitty was waiting for me. I couldn't understand why she was so excited. Her house had a magnificent Christmas tree—seven feet tall and decorated with red, gold, and silver glass balls and strands of colored lights. And the star—it lighted the top of the tree like it had been freshly plucked from the heavens. Never had I seen a Christmas tree like that—for that matter, never had I seen a house like Kitty's. She had everything, yet she couldn't wait to go with me into the woods to chop down a little pine tree. That was Kitty. She was big on doing things like this—the way *she* thought they were supposed to be done. Aunt Hat called it being opinionated.

When I got the tree decorated, I was going to wrap the gifts I bought the day before. Madge had taken Mama and me over to Princeton to celebrate Mama's birthday and do Christmas shopping. We were scared to death Aunt Hat was going to go, but she said she didn't feel like running all over creation for no good reason.

We had a grand time! After shopping, we took Mama out to dinner at a Chinese restaurant. It was Madge's idea. She knew I had never eaten Chinese food before, and I was excited until I saw the menu. It was confusing—how do you roll an egg?

Madge loved the fried rice. She said that just proved you could fry anything and it would taste good. Since me and Mama didn't know what to get, Madge ordered for us. I figured it didn't matter anyway; our waiter barely spoke English, so it was hard to tell what we'd get. No matter what Madge said, he bobbed his head up and down and scribbled on his notepad.

When he brought our food, he gave us two little sticks called chopsticks, which looked like flat pencils. We laughed ourselves silly trying to eat with them. Madge said she hoped they served breakfast because if we didn't start eating with our forks, we'd still be there for breakfast. After the meal, they gave us something called a fortune cookie. I broke mine open, pulled out the little piece of paper, and read my fortune: "You will have a long and prosperous life." Mama and I laughed at Madge's fortune. It said, "You are kind and courteous."

Madge said, "Lord, young'uns, I'm going to put that up on the mirror in my shop and make every old biddy that complains read it."

I laughed. Mama looked at her fortune and handed it to me. I read, "Your beauty outshines the morning sun."

Madge said, "Hey! That's supposed to be my fortune. This one here is yours." She threw her fortune down and grabbed for Mama's. We were still laughing when we left the restaurant.

I couldn't wait to give Kitty her Christmas present. It was a silver ID bracelet with *Kitty* on it in fancy script. Since she and her family were leaving the next day to spend Christmas with her grandparents, we were going to exchange gifts that night. I was going to sleep over at her house—my very first sleep-over ever—and I decided I was going to tell Kitty about Aunt Hat and Mama *and* boarding school.

Kitty and I hadn't gone far up the mountain when she said, "That's it! It's perfect!"

A little pine tree stood all alone amongst the bare hardwoods. Its branches were full, but it wasn't very tall. It looked like someone had put a splash of green in the middle of the barren trees so next spring, they'd remember what green leaves looked like.

We took turns with the ax, and soon the little tree was felled; then we half-dragged, half-carried it back down the road to the school. We stopped to rest, laughing at how our hands, covered with pine tar, stuck to everything we touched.

"I'm sorry you got that all over your hands."

"Are you nuts? This is incredible!" Kitty cupped her hands in front of her nose and took a deep breath. "I love this! It smells like—like Christmas!"

She broke into "Jingle Bells." I joined in, and we were off down Maple Street, half-hidden by the tree. We got several waves and honks from cars, and a few people rolled down their windows and yelled, "Merry Christmas!" By the time we got the tree up the stairs to the apartment, we were exhausted.

I had already moved the furniture around so the tree could set in the front room window, which was perfect, because that was the only wall that had a place to plug in the strand of lights. We put the tree into a bucket of sand I had ready, careful to pack it tightly around the base of the tree. Then we poured water on the sand to weigh it down and keep the tree from drying out. Last, we stood back and admired the little tree. Already, its scent had swept through the apartment, leaving a trail of peace on earth and good will to men in its wake.

We scrubbed our hands until they were free of the sticky tar, but not the stains. Then I got the box of decorations from the hall closet. I admit I was a bit ashamed of our meager decorations, but when I opened the box of mostly handmade ornaments, Kitty gasped.

"Where did you get these?" She reached in and lightly traced her fingers over them. "They're beautiful. Did your mother make them?"

I laughed outright. "My mama!" *Not hardly.* "Her mother made them—my grandmother Smith. She died when Mama was only sixteen."

Kitty picked up a crocheted angel. To me, it looked homemade and yellowed with age. To Kitty, it looked like *her* idea of what Christmas decorations should be.

"How did she make this?"

"Mama said she crocheted them with cotton thread and then starched them until they were stiff."

"But how did she make this look like an angel?" She put the angel back in the box and pulled out a candy cane and snowman. "Or like this?" She held up a delicate snowflake and spun it around. "This looks like it's going to melt any minute."

These ornaments had been on every Christmas tree I could remember. I thought they couldn't compare to the shiny glass balls on Kitty's Christmas tree, but I tried to see them through her eyes. To Kitty, they looked like they were right out of Christmas in the book *Little Women;* to me, they just looked old.

"Where's the popcorn?" Kitty said.

"Popcorn?"

"You *have* to make garlands of popcorn for the tree," Kitty said. She put her hands on her hips and looked around.

"Mama has some tinsel in the box."

"Tinsel! You can't put tinsel on that tree."

"Why not?"

"Because it's a *real* Christmas tree, and *real* Christmas trees have popcorn strands and homemade ornaments."

I smiled. "Well, in that case, I better make some popcorn."

By the time Mama got home, the tree was decorated, and the mess was cleaned up. It was almost 6:00, and Kitty's dad was coming to pick us up, so Kitty and I were in my room, packing my overnight bag. I thought I heard a car horn, so I went into the front room to look out the window to see if it was Kitty's dad. It was dark outside, so I had left the tree lights plugged in and the front room lights off. At first, I didn't see Mama. I set my bag down on the couch and went over to the tree so I could peer around it to see out the window. Kitty's dad's car wasn't there, so I turned around to go back to my room and almost stepped on Mama. She was lying under the Christmas tree, her feet barely visible.

"Mama! What in the world are you doing!"

"Sassy, come down here."

"What?"

"I said, come down here. Get under the tree with me."

I laughed. "You want me to crawl under the tree with you?"

"Yes, you got to see this."

"Okay." I sat down on the floor, stretched out flat on my back, and inched my way under the tree until I was next to Mama.

"Now, close your eyes and count to ten before you open them," Mama said.

I did as I was told, and when I opened my eyes, I felt like I was floating on a cloud inside of a rainbow.

"Oh, this is beautiful," I whispered.

"It surely is."

We lay still, admiring the tree. Kitty came out of my room and called, "Sassy? Where'd you go?"

"I'm under here," I called.

She walked into the front room. I could see her feet over by the couch. "Under where?"

"Under the Christmas tree."

Kitty crouched down and looked under the tree. She squealed, flopped down on her back, and scooted under the tree.

Mama said, "Now close your eyes and count to ten before you open them."

Kitty obeyed. When she opened her eyes, a puff of air escaped her lips, followed by a huge sigh.

Kitty, who Mama said could talk the hind leg off a dog, had nothing to say. We lay there and listened to each other breathe while admiring the halo of lights. Mama slid her hand into mine, and I slipped mine into Kitty's.

"Merry Christmas, girls," Mama said.

I paused before the house and drank it all in. I wanted to remember how it looked so maybe I would dream about it, and in the dream, it would be my house. The windows were draped with pine boughs that were tied with big red velvet bows, and a giant wreath made of pine branches hung on the door. Through the window, I could see the lights of the Christmas tree, beckoning us inside.

Kitty grabbed my arm. "Come on! Mother's got dinner ready."

I was still awed by Kitty's house. It belonged to Valley Consolidated Coal Co. and had been empty since the previous summer, when the company's president had moved to Bluefield. Mama said the company kept it for their bigwigs to live in. When I told Kitty what Mama had said, she just laughed.

I didn't tell Kitty that my whole life, I had imagined a handsome but shy boy lived there. He had private teachers and didn't go to school, so everyone made up stories about him—he had a hump on his back and was hideously ugly; he was insane and had to be kept locked up or he would kill people—but I knew the truth. I knew he was handsome but sensitive and shy, and one day, we'd meet and fall in love. He and I would have an exquisite wedding in that house and invite everyone in town. I'd walk down the magnificent staircase, which would be decorated with yellow roses and ribbons, and he'd be waiting for me.

Once inside, I had to pause and look up at that beautiful staircase. Even now, I couldn't believe I was friends with someone who actually lived there. Heck, I still couldn't believe I had a friend.

We ate dinner in an honest-to-goodness dining room. The table was so big, it had twelve chairs. In the center of the table was an arrangement of what Mama and me called Christmas flowers, but Mrs. Martin called them poinsettias. On either side of the flowers set silver candle holders with tall red candles. When Kitty's mama lit the candles, I almost swooned. I always wanted to eat dinner by candlelight.

I said, "You have a beautiful house, Mrs. Martin."

"Why, thank you, Sarah. After dinner, why don't you get Kitty to show you around?"

When dinner was over, Mr. Martin took his newspaper and coffee and went to the family room. I offered to help with the dishes, but Mrs. Martin waved me off. She said, "Kitty, why don't you show Sarah around?"

I looked at Kitty and bobbed my head up and down. She laughed and said, "Come on."

We bounded up the stairs, which were covered in a rich green carpet. I let my hand trail across the polished banister. I'd never seen a staircase in a house that was as wide as a room. Kitty said, "I'll show you my room first."

When we reached the second-floor hallway, I stopped and stared. The wall was covered in fancy framed photographs of all different shapes and sizes. There were pictures of people, animals, landscapes, houses, and even cars. Kitty poked her head out of her room and called, "Sassy, where are you?"

"I'm looking at these pictures."

Kitty drifted back down the hall. "Those are my mother's."

"Where'd she get them?"

"She took them. She's a photographer."

I repeated, "She's a photographer."

Kitty laughed. "Yeah, that's one of the reasons she agreed to move here. She wanted to take pictures of everything."

"Do you think she'd show me how to take pictures?"

"I'm sure she'd love to. She has a studio on the third floor with a darkroom. She tries to show me stuff all the time, but it's just not my thing. Now, come on."

Kitty took my hand and started pulling me toward her room. I laughed, stumbling behind her. Her room was painted the color of summer sunshine. A big bed with a white iron headboard welcomed from the center of the room. It was covered with pillows and stuffed animals of all different sizes, shapes, and colors. I ran and jumped right in the middle of Kitty's bed. She squealed and jumped in right next to me. I grabbed a white stuffed cat and held it up so I could see it. I said, "I feel like I'm inside one of my books."

Kitty stopped laughing. She turned on her side and raised herself up on her elbow so she could look at me. "Sassy, that's how I felt today. When we chopped down that pine tree all by ourselves and decorated it with your grandmother's ornaments, I felt like I was celebrating Christmas like it was meant to be."

She sat up and drew her knees up to her chest, wrapping her arms around them. She continued, "And when I crawled under the tree to look at the lights with you and your mother, I felt so special—like someone had given me an amazing gift. Sassy, my mother would *never* do anything like that! You don't know how lucky you are."

"Yeah, lucky," I mumbled. I sat up arranging my legs Indian fashion.

Just then, Kitty's mother appeared in the doorway, carrying a tray. "Sorry, I can't knock, but my hands are full." She came in and set the tray on Kitty's desk. "I just made some gingerbread and thought you girls might like some while it's still warm."

I jumped off the bed and went to her. I said, "Thank you, Mrs. Martin. I love gingerbread!"

She smiled. "Oh, good. Does your mother make gingerbread? We'll have to compare recipes."

I laughed. "My mama? No, she doesn't make anything, but my Aunt Hat does."

Mrs. Martin glanced at Kitty, who said nothing. "Well," she said, "I'll leave you two alone."

She turned away, and I jumped after her. "Mrs. Martin, I love your pictures."

She turned around, and her smile lit up the room. Her hair was blonde like Kitty's, and even though there was a definite resemblance, Kitty looked more like her father. She wore a slim gray skirt and a dark green sweater that made her green eyes sparkle. Around her neck was a simple gold cross. "Why, thank you, dear. Are you interested in photography?"

"Oh, yes."

"Would you like to see my studio?"

"Mother!" Kitty's voice made us both wheel around.

"Not now, dear," Mrs. Martin said to Kitty. "I mean another time, when you two aren't visiting." She smiled at me. "I look forward to it. Now, I'll leave you two alone." She went out, closing the door.

"Let's dance!" Kitty said. She got out her record player and started stacking records. For the next hour, we laughed and danced, ate gingerbread, and danced some more.

We talked about everything and nothing. I wanted to tell Kitty about Aunt Hat and boarding school, but I just couldn't. Around 11:00, we put on our pajamas, turned off the lights, and got into bed. The darkness gave me courage. I said, "Kitty, do you ever wish you could go to another school?"

Kitty giggled. "I *am* going to another school, silly. I used to go to Foxcroft Academy."

"Oh, yeah," I laughed.

"Why did you ask me that?" Kitty said.

"I guess I wonder what it would be like to go to another school. Last summer, my Aunt Hat brought me information about a boarding school in Tacoma, Washington. She wanted me to go to school there—she still does. She says she'll pay for it."

"Really? How come you never mentioned it before?"

"The only reason I ever thought about going was because skipping seventh grade and going to high school was kinda hard—not like work hard—just, well . . . I didn't have any friends—that is, until you."

Kitty sat up and turned on the bedside lamp. She twirled a strand of hair around her forefinger, let it go, and did it again. Finally, she said, "You know, I'm supposed to be in the seventh grade, too. But when I enrolled in school here, they said I'd already had all of the seventh-grade classes, so they decided to put me in high school. My mother hates me going to school here, anyway. She thinks the school's not good enough."

I sat up and tucked my legs under me. I said, "Mama found the stuff about the Tacoma Academy."

"What do you mean, she found it?"

"I had it hidden under my bed, so when she found it, she thought I wanted to go to school there. But I really don't want to go to Tacoma to school, and I sure don't want to go anywhere that's close to Aunt Hat. That's why she's here for Christmas. She came because she thinks she's taking me to this school in January."

Kitty sat still, frowning in concentration. She twirled her hair around and around her finger. I asked, "What am I going to do?"

Kitty sat up straight and grabbed my arm. I asked, "What?"

She smiled. "Well, there's just one thing to do—go to boarding school together."

A *woosh* of air escaped my lungs. "What? You'll go to Tacoma with me?"

"No, silly." Kitty laughed and tossed her head. Her blond hair swished across her shoulders. "Your aunt says she'll pay for you to go to boarding school, right?"

"Yeah."

"So you'll go to boarding school. Foxcroft Academy is a boarding school."

"You mean you went to a boarding school?"

"Yeah, and my mother would love it if I went back."

I had so many questions running through my head, I didn't know what to ask first.

Kitty said, "I'm glad that's settled," and reached to turn off the lamp.

"Wait a minute! Where is this place?"

"Foxcroft? It's in Middleburg, Virginia. Close to Washington, D.C."

My heart started racing as my future hovered in front of me—a bright red ribbon floating in the breeze. All I had to do was reach out and grab it, and it would be mine. I lay down and pulled the covers up to my chin. Kitty turned off the lamp and plopped down on her back.

"Don't worry," she said, "my mother will take care of everything."

And she did.

It was everything I hoped for—and nothing I expected.

This place did not look like home. The land wasn't exactly flat—there were rolling hills, but I could look off in any direction and see for miles. At Foxcroft, I could understand why people once believed if you went too far, you'd simply drop off the earth. If I stood in front of the enormous red brick academic building and looked to the right, there was a forest and a lake. If I looked to the left, there were rolling hills dotted with trees and buildings. And there was always a breeze. I never felt so exposed in my life.

The first time it snowed, I couldn't believe my eyes. It looked like it was snowing sideways. In Coal Valley, you stayed inside when it snowed, unless you had to go out. Here, everything went on as usual. People just put on their boots, bundled up, and went on through the snow. The school was also big on what they called winter sports. If anyone had told me I would be ice skating on a frozen pond, I'd have called him crazy—but in no time, I took to it like a pig to slop.

Kitty and I shared a room on the second floor. We lived in what they called a suite, which had a room with a couch and chairs so it was like a living room and four bedrooms. That meant we shared a bathroom with four other girls—that made Kitty mad, but it don't bother me. Our bedroom was bigger than our living room at home. It was painted a pale yellow with white trim. We each had a bed with a bedside table, a dresser, a desk and chair, and our own closet.

The first week, I felt so strange, I couldn't sleep at night. By the end of the second week, I couldn't remember what coal dust laying on top of snow looked like. But it was the smell of home that I yearned for the most. The scent of coal dust, as metallic and damp as the inside of the earth, had seeped into my pores, the way coal gets under the skin of the miners. Until I came to Foxcroft, that odor was part of my daily life, and I missed it. I missed the way it whispered secrets from the time before people walked the earth. I know that no matter where I went, I would miss that smell.

When Mama's first letter came, I waited to read it until I was alone in the library.

January 20, 1955

12 Maple Street
Coal Valley, VA

Dear Sassy,

I am so happy to be writing to my daughter at her fancy new school. I want to know about all of your new friends and your teachers, too. I hope they are feeding you good. I doubt you'll get any chicken and dumplings or fried baloney up there.

The girls at the shop ask about you, and send their love. Me and Madge laughed yesterday at poor old Miss Chaney. She must be near ninety. Her daughter brought her in to get a permanent. For some reason she kept asking me, "Now who did Sassy marry?" I kept telling her you were just thirteen and had gone off to school, but she thought I was saying you was out of school. In her mind, if a girl was out of school, she was supposed to be married.

Sassy, I'm so proud of you and the way you stood up to Aunt Hat. You know I would've never wrote to her and told her to come and get you, if I hadn't found those papers you had on that school in Tacoma. I should've known it was all Aunt Hat's doings.

I knew going to high school was going to be hard, but you acted like everything was just fine. And then I saw those letters from that girl in Washington and I realized how unhappy you were. I know I should of talked to you before I jumped the gun and sent for Aunt Hat, but all I wanted was for you to be happy. And how look at you in that fancy girls school with Kitty and all of your new friends! We'll just forget that misunderstanding about Aunt Hat and school. It's water under the bridge now.

I'm happy you found a friend like Kitty. Give her my best. I hope you make lots of new friends. Sassy, you know I'm not one for preaching about things. But there's one thing I want to tell you. You are as good as any girl at that school.

Just because you're from the mountains and don't have any money, don't let them make you feel like they're better than you. They're not. Money don't make you a better person. Sometimes it makes you a bad person.

Madge says to tell you to behave yourself and study hard. We are so proud of you and I'm sure your daddy would be proud of you too. This is a golden opportunity, Sassy. Grab hold of it and enjoy every minute of every day.

Write to me soon and tell me all about your new school.

Love,

Mama

I closed my eyes. I could smell the beauty shop—permanent wave solution, shampoo, and cigarette smoke. I could hear the tinkle of the bell over the shop door. There stood Mama at her station, combing Myrtle Stiltner's hair. And Madge, with a cigarette dangling from her lips, came in from the back room, carrying a stack of towels.

I opened my eyes, and the Cut and Curl Beauty Shop floated away like the sun disappearing behind a cloud. I sighed and walked down the path to music class, planning my letter to Mama. I wanted to tell her about Elizabeth, who had hair the color of carrots and freckles all over her face, and Maria, the most beautiful girl there, who had curly black hair and green eyes that flashed like lightening bugs. I pictured her smile when I described eating foods that until a month ago, I'd never even seen. I knew she would laugh when I described my algebra teacher, whose glasses were so thick that her eyes looked like they were floating underwater. And I could hear her bragging loud and long about her daughter, who was going to a fancy boarding school on the other side of Virginia.

There were some things I wouldn't tell her—like how for the first week I hardly spoke for fear the girls would make fun of the way I talked. Then Kitty sat me down and gave me some pointers on what I was saying wrong, like how the creek that ran through the woods was called a brook, that supper was called dinner, and Coca-Cola and Pepsi were called soda, not pop. She told me to watch my verb tense—that sometimes I slipped and said "I seen" and "I done." She also told me not to say words like "atall," "over yonder," and "I reckon." I knew if

I told this to Mama, she'd get her back up, which is another thing I'm not supposed to say. I know that Kitty just wants to help me fit in.

I *would* tell her about my music class and how the teacher said I had a beautiful voice. I was shy at first, but I loved to sing, and before I knew it, I was singing my heart out. Then the teacher asked me to stay after class, and I thought she was going to throw me out, but she said I had talent! I started taking private voice lessons. Every time I thought about how Mama said my daddy liked to sing, I got a lump in my throat. I hoped that up there in heaven, he could hear me sing.

Winter, 1955–1956

Sylvia

"We should regret our mistakes and learn from them, but never carry them forward into the future with us." ~Lucy Maude Montgomery, *Anne of Avonlea*

No books laying around. No saddle oxfords to polish. No poodle skirts to wash. No one to take care of. No one to ask questions. And no one to check up on me.

I dreaded the walk to work in the nasty slush left from the thaw the day before. It had frozen back overnight and looked like pools of leftover gravy. At least it was Saturday and I only had to work a half day. Tony was picking me up at 3:00.

When I got to the shop, Madge was already there. I could tell right away she was in a foul mood, so I decided not to mention Tony. Madge hated him.

"Good morning, Madge," I said, trying the "I think everything's just peachy" approach.

"Where the hell is my blue comb? I've looked all over for it and I can't find it."

I walked over to her station and picked it up. "Is this what you're looking for?" I held it up.

"It wasn't there a minute ago."

I put the comb back and went into the back room to get a cup of coffee. I picked up the pot, and it was almost empty. *Surely Madge hasn't drunk a whole pot of coffee.* It had to be worse than just a bad mood. When I went back out front, Madge was standing at the window, staring outside. "It sure is ugly out there," I said. She didn't say a word. "Maybe it'll warm up enough to melt most of this mess." Still not a word. I started to walk away, but something told me not to. Instead, I laid my hand on her shoulder. "Madge?"

She stayed still, but reached across her chest so she could pat my hand. Her hand was cold and coarse; a million heads of hair had been washed with those hands. I couldn't count the times they'd wiped away my tears over the years. "What's the matter?"

"I hate this time of year. Winter won't turn loose, and it feels like spring won't never come."

I waited. I'd known Madge for half my life, so I knew when she got like this, it was best not to push her. Finally, she turned and faced me. "It's Buster. He's bad off."

"Oh, Madge, I'm sorry. What happened?"

"Heart attack. The truth is, he drank his self near to death."

She set down at one of the hairdryers and fished her cigarettes out of her pocket. I pulled a stool over and set down in front of her. "You know, after thirteen years, I still can't believe you married him."

Madge snorted. "Well, that makes two of us."

"That was a summer we both won't ever forget."

We set for a minute in silence. I sipped coffee, and Madge smoked. I watched my past float past me, riding on Madge's cigarette smoke—gray and dirty.

Madge looked at me with tears in her eyes. "I said no so many times that one day, I said, yes." She paused. The ashes from her cigarette fell unchecked on the floor. "It was different times, Sylvie. The world was at war, and we didn't know from one day to the next if Hitler might drop a bomb on us. You know how the preachers tell you to live each day like it's your last; well, in those days, we did."

I nodded my head. My heart was too full to speak. I knew that I'd wear the scars from WWII for the rest of my life.

Madge continued. "Buster was working and earning good money. He'd quit drinking. And I believed him when he said he wouldn't drink no more. You and Sassy was gone, and I was lonely. And I wanted a chance to *live*. My whole life was nothing but hard work, and by God, I wanted a chance to live a little before I died."

She picked up an ashtray from the table next to her and stubbed out her cigarette. She stood up and walked past me to her station. I trailed after her like a puppy. She started arranging the bottles she used to work her magic.

"So one Saturday afternoon, I was closing up when he come through that door." She pointed to the front door, staring at ghosts. "He was dressed up and had a fresh shave and haircut. And Lord-a-mercy, he smelled so good." She closed her eyes. "So when he said, 'Madge, what you say you and me go get married?' I said, 'Okay, let's go.'"

She opened her eyes and turned to me. "He took me home to change clothes, and we drove over to Bluefield and got married by the justice of the peace. We didn't even have wedding bands." She looked down at her left hand. With her right thumb, she rubbed the place where her wedding band would have been. "I tried, Sylvie. God knows I tried. But Buster just couldn't leave the drink alone. Mommy says he has the Irish curse. All those Dawsons are red-headed Irish, and can't none of them leave the bottle alone. But I tried to make a go of it. God in heaven knows I tried."

"I know you did, Madge. Hell, everybody in this town knows you did. You put up with him longer than any other woman would've."

The bell over the shop jingled, and Lanta Looney popped through the door like a jack-in-the-box. She no more got inside when Iris Albans paraded in, wearing a ratty old coat with fox tails hanging from the collar. Our day had begun.

Anthony Marino was the perfect gentleman. I met him at a party in Bluefield. He was Italian and spoke English with a thick accent that charmed me right down to my toes. That night, his eyes had followed me all around the room. I knew he was watching me, but I pretended like I hadn't noticed him. Then he introduced himself with a "How do you do? I am Tony Marino." Then—honest to God—he kissed my hand. That was all it took for me to ditch Roy, my date, and let Tony drive me home. Since then, we went out every weekend.

Madge hated him. I knew she would. At first she called him "that Mexican" until I convinced her he was Italian—or Eye-talian, as she said it. Then she said you couldn't trust Eye-talians—they had bad tempers and knew how to give you the evil eye. Since then, Tony picked me up at the apartment, but Madge knew I was still seeing him.

I was sweeping up the hair from around my station when Madge closed the door on the last customer. She said, "Want to grab a bite at the diner?"

I steeled myself for what was coming. "I'm going out."

"That damn Eye-talian? When are you going to learn he's bad news?" I kept sweeping, but I could feel her gaze on my neck. "Sylvia, listen to me. I don't like the way he looks at you."

I wheeled around. "Looks at me—you don't like how he looks at me? What's that supposed to mean?"

"It means just what it says—he looks at you wrong."

"Wrong how?"

"Like you're something that belongs to him."

"Madge, I promise you. Tony is a perfect gentleman."

Madge stared at me, and our eyes met. "Mark my words. There's something not right about that man."

The party was in full swing when we got there. The room was crowded with people dancing to "Rock Around the Clock." I stood there, snapping my fingers, while Tony went to get us a beer. Tony wasn't much for dancing, but Lord knows I loved to kick up my heels, and I had on my red high heels, too—my favorite dancing shoes.

Tony came back with our beer, and we found a table. We drank and watched the people dancing. When they played "Earth Angel," Tony asked me to dance. He held me close, and I inhaled his cologne. It smelled high-class and expensive, like his clothes. I'd never dated a man who was always impeccably dressed and perfectly groomed. I let my fingers whisper across his neck, touching his curly black hair. He drew back and stared into my eyes. I shivered. His irises were so black, I couldn't see the pupils. His eyes glinted like a piece of polished coal. Tony thought I was trembling from his touch, so he drew me tight against him.

When we got back to our table, a man walked over, leaned down, and said something in Tony's ear. The man left, and Tony said he had to go talk to some men about business. He'd be back soon. I watched him disappear in the midst of the dancing bodies and cigarette smoke.

I finished my beer and turned around to find a man standing there with a fresh one held out to me. He was bound to be where the phrase *tall, dark, and handsome* came from. I smiled and took the beer. He said, "You looked thirsty."

"Thank you," I said.

"May I?" He pointed to the chair left empty by Tony.

I smiled and took a drink of the beer. Pat Boone was crooning "Ain't That a Shame," and I swayed to the music.

"What's a beautiful woman like you doing here all alone?"

"I'm waiting for my date to return."

"He must not be too smart a fellow if he goes off and leaves a beautiful woman like you. I'm Max."

"Hello, Max. I'm Sylvia."

"Hello, Sylvia, would you like to dance?"

I glanced around, and Tony was nowhere to be seen. "Max, I'd love to." By the time we finished our third dance, I was ready for another beer. While Max got us a beer, I slipped outside to smoke. I was fumbling for a lighter when Tony said, "Allow me."

He struck a match and lit my cigarette. His black eyes glittered in the flash of light. I took a step back, like an invisible hand had pushed me away from danger. "Thanks. Got your business finished?"

"Yes. I am sorry to neglect you like that." He paused and watched me smoke. I threw my cigarette on the ground and stepped on it to make sure it was out. Tony said, "You know, you really should not smoke. It is not good for you."

I was too surprised to reply. Tony took my elbow and guided me back inside to our table. He sat me down and went off to get fresh drinks. I saw Max standing across the room, leaning against the wall with his ankles crossed. He raised his beer to me and smiled. I waved.

On the way home, Tony was quiet. My head was buzzing like flies were circling my ears. I rubbed my eyes. I had drunk too much and was afraid one of my headaches was coming on. I leaned my head back against the seat and closed my eyes. I woke with a start when Tony pulled against the curb in front of my apartment. I sat straight up in my seat. "Sorry, I fell asleep," I said, "It's been a long week."

"You are very beautiful when you are asleep."

When Tony said things like that, I always flashed him my biggest smile with some demure comeback like "you're just the sweetest man" in my best Scarlett O'Hara imitation. But something was different that night. I said nothing. I wanted a cigarette, but after what he said at the party, I didn't want to smoke in front of him. He got out of the car and came around to open my door. The cold came rushing in, and I gathered my coat and got out. Tony, always the gentleman, took my coat and held it while I slipped my arms into the sleeves. He walked with me to the door and waited while I fished my key out of my purse. I asked, "Do you want to come up?"

"No, it is late, and you are tired. It must have been all that dancing."

I turned around to face him. "What dancing?"

"The dancing you did with the man you picked up as soon as I left the room."

His voice was light and unconcerned, but the message was unmistakable. Hot anger surged through me. I said, "What did you just say to me?"

He grabbed my arms and pinned me against the door quicker than a trap slams down on a rat. He put his face an inch from mine. His smell—liquor and cologne and something I was afraid of but couldn't describe—made me turn my head away. This time, his voice made shivers go up my spine. "I saw you dancing with that man."

I struggled to get out of his grasp. "Let go of me!"

"Did you think I would not see you?" He pressed his body hard against me. "Did you think you could make me look like a fool and get away with it?"

I stopped struggling, and he let me go. "Get the hell away from me," I said.

I saw his fist coming like it was in slow motion. When it connected with my jaw, my head jerked back and crashed into the door. A burst of white light exploded into a million spikes. I struggled to keep standing. His voice returned to the calm, unconcerned tone it had been a moment ago. "When you are with me, you will do what I say. Simple, yes?"

With one hand, I rubbed my jaw, and with the other, I tried to push him away. I winced when I opened my mouth, but I managed to say, "You bastard. Get away from me." This time, when he hit me, I didn't see it coming. This time, when the light exploded in my head, I couldn't stay on my feet. The last thing I remember was his laughter.

I woke up on my couch, a blanket thrown over me. My purse and key were lying in the center of the coffee table, and my shoes were placed just under the table, side by side, like whoever put them there was concerned I might stumble over them. It was daylight. I sat up, and pain shot through my head. I ran my fingers across my face. It hurt like hell, and I knew it would look worse. I stumbled to the bathroom and looked in the mirror. "That bastard."

I swallowed one of the pain pills Doc gave me for my headaches and filled the bathtub. I washed the makeup from my face so I could see how bad it was. My left eye was swollen and looked like someone had drawn a thick black circle around it. My right jaw was a pale shade of violet. I opened my mouth and worked my jaw back and forth. It hurt so bad, it brought tears to my eyes.

I eased into the hot water and let it punish my skin. I looked down, and that's when I saw the bracelet of bruises on my wrist. In that moment, I saw Sassy's face. It was the morning she was leaving for boarding school. She was getting in the Martins' car when she jumped out and ran back to me. She hurled herself into my arms and hugged me like she'd never see me again. When she finally let me go, I laughed and said, "What was that for?"

"Mama, who's going to take care of you?"

I laughed and said, "Me? Why, Sassy, I can take care of myself." Her look had searched my face like she didn't believe me. Then she smiled, hugged me again—only that time, it was a brief squeeze—and got back in the car.

The tears came then, scalding my sore face. My sobs echoed off the bathtub, filling the tiny bathroom. I cried until I was exhausted, and still, tears leaked from my eyes. Not one tear was shed for Tony Marino. They were all for Sassy.

When the knock sounded at my door, I knew it was her. I never once thought it was Tony. I knew I would never see him again. I also knew Madge had been to the hospital in Princeton, West Virginia to see about Buster, and she was stopping by on her way home to tell me how he was doing.

I thought about not answering, but I knew when I didn't show up for work in the morning, she'd be back—no use putting it off. I swung open the door and stepped back. Madge blew by me, cussing so hard I could see the words bounce off the walls. I sat down on the couch and lit a cigarette. Madge kept pacing and cussing, shedding her coat and purse as she walked. Finally, she rounded on me and stopped. She dropped down on the couch and put her arms around me. I fell against her shoulder and let her pat me on the back and cluck like an old mother hen. Then she pushed me back and scowled. "Let me see how bad it is."

I sat still and let her check me out. She took a hold of my chin and turned my head from side to side. Then she felt all over my face. "Don't look like nothing's broke. Bend down here and let me feel your head."

With the fingers of her right hand, she burrowed under my hair and started rubbing the back of my head in small circles. I jerked away when she found the knot on the back of my head.

She got up and disappeared into the kitchen. I could hear her muttering and banging around in my cabinets. She came out carrying a dish rag filled with ice and a bowl. I didn't have to ask what was in it. I could smell it—vinegar. She set it down on the table and handed me the ice. "Put this on that pop knot." Then she disappeared again, this time in the bathroom. She came out with a handful of cotton balls that she dropped next to the bowl. "Lay down," she commanded, dipping a cotton ball in the vinegar.

"You're not putting that stinking stuff on my face." I pushed myself back into the pillow.

"It's what my mommy does for bruises, and it works. It makes them fade fast. Now lay still."

I lay down and let her dab vinegar all over my face. "*Shew,* God, this is taking my breath!"

"It ought to! What did I tell you about that damn Eye-talian?" She put the cotton ball down. "Now we'll do this again in an hour." She stared at me like she was going to say something else, then stood up and went back in the kitchen. I heard her banging around again, and when she came out, she had a bowl of chicken noodle soup and a Coke. She said, "Set up and eat this. I know you ain't eat nothing today."

I ate, and Madge smoked. I could see the wheels turning in her mind. Sure enough, when she finished her cigarette, she stubbed it out in the ashtray and said, "Now here's what we're going to do. Tomorrow, I'm going to work and tell everybody you slipped on the ice and fell. That you're bruised up and sore but you're alright. Then I'm going to pay Sheriff Frank a visit."

I set my bowl down. "No! Madge, don't do that."

"That man beat the hell out of you, and you're not going to tell the law? Why? Did he threaten you? You ain't told me what happened."

So I told her—all of it. I learned long ago it was better to tell Madge all of it the first time. When I finished, she stood. "Lock this door behind me. I'm going home to get my stuff. If Mr. Eye-talian big shot comes back, I'll have a little surprise for him."

By Wednesday, the swelling was down and my bruises were fading, so I went back to work. I still smelled like vinegar, but I had to admit, Madge's remedy worked. Every customer had a story to tell about falling on ice, and by closing time on Saturday, I had told my lie so many times, I was starting to believe it.

Thanks to Darcy Skeens, nobody was giving my bruised face a second thought. The talk of the shop was how she up and left her husband, Mitchell. They married last spring, and everybody thought they were happy. They lived just out of the coal camp in a little blue house her daddy gave them. She came to the shop from time to time. Alice was the last one to cut her hair, so everybody was asking her what happened, but she didn't have any idea.

I was combing Minnie Calhoun's hair and only listening with half an ear. She said, "Mitchell ain't a drinking man."

"He's a hardworking man. I can tell you that," Frieda Mays added. "His mommy was a cousin to me on my daddy's side. All them Skeens is hard workers and easygoing, too. Wonder what in the world happened?"

"Darcy is a pretty little thing, so I don't see Mitchell looking at another woman. She was good to keep house, and there wasn't nothing said about her leaving for another man, was there?" Minnie asked.

"She never had eyes for nobody but Mitchell, but I always thought they weren't suited for each other," Madge said.

"How so?" Frieda asked.

"Mitchell was a Skeens. He never had much to say, and Darcy was like a bird—always chirping about something."

For a minute, the only sound in the shop was the hum of the hairdryer. Then Myrtle Stiltner spoke up. "Mr. Stiltner said it was that tree they used for firewood."

I stopped teasing Minnie's hair and turned around so I could get a good look at Myrtle. Maryetta quit combing Frieda's hair and listened. Knowing she was the center of attention, Myrtle sat up straight and leaned forward like she was about to reveal a deep, dark secret. "You all remember that big storm we had back in the August? The one that broke dog days?"

That got my full attention. I thought she was going to bring up the woman who showed up in the middle of that storm and accused me of stealing her husband. I looked at Madge, but she was looking at Myrtle. "Well, Mr. Stiltner said all that week that a big storm was coming. He's good at predicting—"

Madge interrupted her before she got off on what a good weather prophet her husband was. "What about the tree?"

"Oh, well, Mr. Stiltner said he told Mitchell not to burn the wood from that tree."

"What tree?" Madge interrupted again. "Myrtle, you ain't making no sense."

"I'm talking about that big oak tree that was on the Skeens' land. It was struck by lightning during that big storm last August—split it right down the middle. Mitchell told Mr. Stiltner how he sawed it up to use for stove wood in the winter, and Mr. Stiltner told him he better not, cause you know what happens when you burn wood from a tree that's been struck by lightning."

She paused, and we all stared at her. Madge was the first one to speak. "No, what?"

"Why, Madge, don't you know if you use wood from a tree struck by lightning, it will cause you trouble? Mr. Stiltner says you shouldn't even bring it in your house. But burning it in your stove—then you're just asking for it. I thought ever body knew that." She sat back in her chair and added a sniff like a big exclamation point.

We all looked at Myrtle, then looked at Madge, and then went back to what we were doing. Frieda was the first to offer her estimation on the subject. "You know, ever thing was fine with those two last summer. It weren't till cool weather set in that they started having troubles—right about the time ever body fired up their woodstoves. I remember the talk when she got churched."

I didn't have to ask what getting churched meant. As a child, I'd been to the Old Regular Baptist Church enough to know. They voted you out for such transgressions as playing cards, dancing, or—heaven forbid—going to the circus.

Madge said, "What *sin* did they put her out of church for?" I smiled, knowing that Madge was being a smart ass, but it was lost on the rest of the women.

"She spoke out in church one time too many," Frieda said.

"What do you mean, 'spoke out'?" I asked.

"I mean, she was bad to give her opinion during Bible study and not let her husband speak for her. But what got her churched was arguing with the preacher."

"Well," I said, "that certainly explains it."

Madge winked at me over Minnie's head.

Myrtle said, "See what I mean. Mr. Stilther said that was the kind of troubles you could count on if you burned wood from a tree struck by lightning."

I could tell Minnnie was thinking it over, so I wasn't surprised when she said, "I guess I've heard of things a whole lot stranger than that." I thought if Aunt Hat was here, this was the place where she'd declare, "That's the God's truth."

I was glad to see the last customer leave, because Madge and me was going over to the diner for a bite and then to the Lynwood to see *Seven Year Itch* with Marilyn Monroe and Tom Ewell. Madge was sweeping the floor, so I went in the back room to put up the bottles of new hair color. I didn't hear the bell ring when the door opened.

I parted the curtains, and there was the sheriff, talking to Madge. He was one of the biggest men I had ever seen. Well over six foot tall, he was a solid wall of muscle. His presence filled the room. I didn't know Frank Compton personally, but Madge did, and she'd done exactly what I begged her not to do.

I took a deep breath and walked into the room. Sheriff Compton nodded at me, and Madge turned around. "Sylvia," she said, "you know Sheriff Frank."

"Hello, Sheriff."

Madge said, "Sheriff Frank has some news for you."

He nodded—more like a slight tilting of the head than a nod. If he had had on a hat, I was sure he would've tipped it at me. "Mrs. Richardson," he said, "I'm sorry to hear about your troubles."

This time I was the one to nod. Then I looked at Madge with the hatefullest look I could muster. The sheriff pulled a piece of paper out of his pocket and unfolded it. He handed it to me and asked, "Is this the man who called himself Anthony Marino?"

"What do you mean, *called himself* Anthony Marino?" He didn't answer me, but stood waiting for me to look at the picture. It was grainy and looked like it was taken from far away, but it was definitely Tony. "That's him."

He took the paper from me and put it back in his pocket. He said, "The man in that picture was Lorenzo Benedetto. He was wanted in Chicago for questioning about a murder."

I felt my knees buckle. Sheriff Frank grabbed my arm, or I would've hit the floor. Madge said, "Let's set down over there."

She led us to the table in the corner. Sheriff Frank kept his hand on my elbow like he was afraid I'd fall if he didn't hold on to me, and the way I felt right then, he was probably right. When we all set down, he continued. "When Madge told me an Italian named Marino had assaulted you, I remembered the police were looking for an Italian named Benedetto. The description Madge gave me of Marino fit the description for Benedetto. I contacted the state police, and they went to pick him up."

He paused. I looked at him and nodded my head for him to continue. "When the officers showed up, he tried to sneak out the back door, where he had a car waiting. When they went after him—" He hesitated and eyed Madge, who nodded. Sheriff Frank said, "He pulled a gun on the officers and shot at them."

This time, when he paused, I blurted out, "What happened?"

"The officers returned fire." He looked in my eyes, and I saw true kindness. He dropped his voice to barely above a whisper. He said, "He's dead."

Spring, 1956

Sassy

"'Shall we never, never get rid of this Past?' cried he, keeping up the earnest tone of his preceding conversation. 'It lies upon the Present like a giant's dead body.'" Nathaniel Hawthorne, *The House of the Seven Gables*

Spring was different at Foxcroft. It came in with a big bang. It didn't sneak up on you like it does in the mountains. One day, I walked outside and the sun was brighter, the grass was green, and the trees looked like they'd woke up and put on green underclothes. There were birds in the trees and bugs in the air, and I was homesick. I kept hearing that old Hank Williams song Mama liked, "I'm So Lonesome I Could Cry."

I wanted the mountains. I wanted to watch their colors change from a soft lime to a deep emerald. I wanted to see the ladies come to town in their spring dresses like flowers blooming on the sidewalk. I missed the shop with an ache deep down inside of me—the voices, the smells, the women who came in looking all sad and careworn and left all duded up and smiling—but most of all, I missed Mama. I missed how she threw back her head and laughed with everything in her. I missed the click of her heels on the stairs. I missed watching her when was concentrating on a haircut, her cigarette burning in the ashtray next to her, the butt circled with her bright red lipstick.

I did the one thing I could think of to keep from crying. I went outside to the big weeping willow tree that was down near the creek (that I was supposed to call a brook, but never could). Overnight, the tree had turned into a big green umbrella. I sat down under it, leaned my back against the trunk, and closed my eyes. I pretended I was home. I let my fingers trail across the grass, seeing spring with my fingertips. When that wasn't enough, I took my shoes and socks off and wiggled my toes in the soft, spongy grass. I smiled. It was a good thing Aunt Hat couldn't see me; I had my shoes off before the tenth of May.

A voice wafted under the tree. "What in the world are you doing?"

It was Kitty. "I'm remembering," I said.

"Remembering what?"

"Home."

"Oh." Kitty crawled under the tree and plopped down next to me. "How do I do it?"

"Lean back against the tree trunk and get comfortable."

Kitty scooted back and wiggled her shoulders like she was molding her back to the tree. She stretched her legs straight out in front of her and put her hands on her knees. "Now what?"

"Well, you just feel."

Kitty closed her eyes, and I leaned back against the tree. I inhaled the wondrous smells of dank earth, seasoned wood, and the tang of new grass. Kitty interrupted my thoughts. "When does it happen?"

I opened my eyes and found Kitty staring at me. I said, "Don't you feel anything?"

"Yeah, my butt hurts, and this tree is scratching my back." She stopped. "But that's not what you mean, is it?"

I shook my head.

"Do you think it would help if I took off my shoes?"

"Probably not."

"Yeah, I don't think so either."

Kitty waited while I put my socks and shoes back on so we could walk to dinner (which I still called supper) together. When we sat down, she put her hand in the pocket of her skirt and pulled out a letter. "I almost forget," she said. "My mother wrote you a letter."

"Me?" She handed me a cream-colored envelope. "Why would your mother write me a letter?"

"Read it, silly, and find out."

Woodland Park
Allen Town, Pennsylvania
May 5, 1956

Dear Sarah,

I hope this letter finds you in good health and good spirits. I know you and Katherine are looking forward to a break from your studies and are getting anxious for summer vacation. Her father and I are looking forward to Katherine joining us when school is out.

I am writing to invite you to come for a visit. If you'd like to come home with Katherine, I will be picking her up on June 1st and going to our home in Allentown, Pennsylvania. We will be returning to Coal Valley at the end of June and you could return with us.

If you are still interested, I will be happy to show you my photography studio and dark room. I know you are anxious to see your mother, but we'd love to have you visit us. Let me know if you'd like to come, and if your mother agrees to the visit. Then I will contact the school and alert them that you will be leaving with Katherine at the end of the term.

Kind Regards,
Bea Martin

I looked up at Kitty, who was waiting for me to finish reading the letter. I said, "Your mother invited me to come to your house in Pennsylvania. She wants me to come home with you and says she'll take me back to Coal Valley at the end of June."

Kitty whistled a low puff of air out of her mouth. "That's super fantastic!" she said. I just stared at the letter I was still holding in my hand. The words "I know you are anxious to see your mother" leaped up at me like water splashing in my eyes.

"What's wrong? You want to come, don't you?"

"Of course I want to come."

"Your mother will let you come, won't she?"

"Yeah, I think so."

Just then, Lila and Margaret sat down at our table. "What's up?" Margaret asked, flipping her long auburn hair over her shoulders.

Kitty said, "We're just making plans for the summer."

"Ooooo, I can't wait to get out of here," Lila complained.

I thought Lila was the cutest thing. Her skin was the color of fresh cream, and her big blue eyes were fringed with long black eyelashes. She was short and plump, which just added to her resemblance to a porcelain doll.

"We're spending most of the summer at our beach house in Maine," Margaret said.

Lila reached for the basket of rolls on the table and took one. She broke it apart and took a bite. I folded the letter from Mrs. Martin and slipped it under my thigh. "So, where do you spend the summer, Sarah?"

I glanced at Kitty. "I'm going home—I guess."

"And where's home?" Lila asked, taking another bite of her roll.

I glanced at Kitty again. She spoke up. "Sarah lives in this quaint little town in the mountains. My parents have a house there, too. She's visiting me in Pennsylvania for a month, and then we'll go to our summer home."

Margaret said, "You actually live year-round in the hinterlands?"

I looked at Kitty and saw color flush her cheeks. I said, "Well, I—"

My pause made Margaret assume I didn't understand. She said, "Hinterlands means a remote—"

"I know what it means! And yes, I live there year-round." My chest heaved, and I felt the blood rush to my head. "And on top of that, where I live, people mine coal and live on farms with pigs and cows. And they have creeks instead of brooks, and they eat supper when you eat dinner."

Margaret stared at me like I'd just grown another head. The color that had rushed into Kitty's face a moment ago drained away. Lila, however, finished her roll, picked up her napkin, and daintily wiped the corners of her mouth. She said, "Kitty, why don't you and Sarah come up to New York this summer? We could all go shopping and see a play."

Kitty said, "That sounds like fun, doesn't it, Sarah?"

Just like that, it was back to *dinner* as usual. Margaret picked up her spoon and started eating her soup. Kitty grabbed a roll out of the basket. I nodded my head, not trusting myself to speak. I'd just announced I was from so far back in the mountains that people kept pigs and cows—and it felt good! I took a deep breath. The words from the first letter Mama wrote scrolled across my mind: "You are as good as any girl at that school. Just because you're from the mountains and don't have any money, don't let them make you feel like they're better than you. They're not."

Lila said, "I'll be spending June with my father in New York and July with my mother in Connecticut, so plan to come to New York before July."

States were dancing around in my head—Pennsylvania, New York, Connecticut—I still wasn't used to being at Foxcroft. Could I really get to go to any—or all—of these places? I figured I would go home to Mama and Coal Valley as soon as school was out and spend my summer reading books and helping out at the shop.

I looked at Lila, who was buttering her third roll. "Why do your parents live in different places?"

Kitty hauled off and kicked me under the table. Margaret set her glass of milk down with a thud. I looked at Kitty, who was glaring at me. I gave her a "what did I do now?" look.

Lila laughed. "My parents are divorced." She pointed to my roll. "Are you going to eat that?"

The day we left for Kitty's house in Allentown, the clouds danced cheek to cheek across a brilliant blue sky. Kitty dozed on the seat next to me, but I was wide awake. I wanted to see every mile. I told Mrs. Martin that I'd never been to Pennsylvania—or anywhere else, for that matter. Until I came to Foxcroft Academy, I'd never ventured from home.

Mrs. Martin brought her camera. It was a Leica and looked incredibly expensive. Before we left, she took pictures of me and Kitty in front of the school. She insisted we stop at the *Welcome to Pennsylvania* sign and take pictures of me standing in front of it. She showed me how to hold the camera, snap the picture, and push the lever twice to advance the film, and then she let me take some pictures of Kitty. I was afraid to touch it, but she laughed and said, "It's just a camera." She also said she'd show me how to develop the pictures in her dark room.

The mountains in Pennsylvania weren't much compared to those in Coal Valley, but the city was amazing. It had a massive concrete bridge that Mrs. Martin called the 8th Street Bridge. She said it was built because the Little Lehigh Creek kept flooding the roads. I said, "Well, hallelujah, you do have creeks here." Mrs. Martin threw me a puzzled look, and Kitty laughed.

The city had so many buildings, they looked stacked one in front of another like books on a shelf. I asked, "Do we get to go downtown while I'm here?"

"I'm glad you asked," Mrs. Martin said. "I thought we'd go to a concert at Symphony Hall, explore the rose garden and the museum. Sarah, did you know the Liberty Bell was hidden here from the British during the Revolutionary War?"

"No, ma'am."

"It was. We can visit the place and do some shopping. What do you say, girls? Does that sound like fun?"

I smiled at Kitty. She gave me a half smile and turned to stare out of the window. "Yes, it sounds great," I said. Kitty didn't say anything. I saw Mrs. Martin glance at her in the rearview mirror.

Their house was outside the city in what Mrs. Martin called the suburbs, but I thought it should be called the fancy part of town. All of the houses were brick with emerald green lawns quilted with bright splotches of flowers winking in the sun. The further we drove, the bigger the houses got, and the more land there was between them. The Martins' house was at the end of a long driveway that circled in front of the two-story brick house. It had a wide front porch supported by four enormous white columns. A flood of roses ran the length of the porch, splashing red, pink, and white in all the right places.

"Is this your house?" I asked. I knew it was a stupid question, but I couldn't stop myself.

Kitty laughed. "You're so silly! Come on!"

She jumped out of the car and started up the steps. I got out of the car, took a step, and hesitated. Kitty called over her shoulder, "Are you going to stand there all day? Come on!"

"Don't we need to get our luggage?"

Mrs. Martin came up behind me. "Donald will take care of your luggage. Go ahead, dear."

"Donald?" Like I'd conjured him, a man appeared and started unloading the car. I ran up the steps after Kitty.

"Come on, I'll show you my room."

We stepped into a marble entry hall. It was deliciously cool after the hot drive. On the wall to my left was an oval mirror. I looked around at the front hall, my eyes coming to rest on my face in the mirror. My face was flushed, my hair mussed, and my eyes were bright. I looked almost . . . almost pretty.

"Miss Katherine, it's good to have you home," said a heavyset Negro woman. She came through a doorway, wiping her hands on her apron.

"Draxie!" Kitty grabbed the woman around the waist.

"And who do we have here?" Draxie asked, enveloping me in her smile, which crinkled the skin at the edges of her big brown eyes. Her round face was the color of black coffee.

"This is my friend, Sassy."

Draxie chuckled. "Well, Miss Sassy, I do like your name."

I smiled. "I'm Sarah Jane Richardson, but my friends call me Sassy."

"Well Miss Sarah, when you and Miss Katherine get settled, I have a snack ready for you in the kitchen."

We climbed the massive staircase to the second floor, our feet sinking into the burgundy carpet. Kitty's room was painted robin's egg blue and was twice the size of her room in the house at Coal Valley. It had sapphire blue drapes tied back with thick gold cords and matching sapphire carpet. I asked, "Why didn't you tell me you had servants?"

"Who? Draxie and Donald?"

"Yeah, and whoever else you've got."

"I don't know. It's not something you talk about—'Hey, Sassy, Draxie is our cook, and Donald is our gardener. And, oh yeah, Sue cleans house twice a week, too.'"

I laughed and plopped down on Kitty's bed. It had a pale blue bedspread with tiny yellow and white flowers on it. "Okay, I see what you mean. I just wasn't expecting you to live in a house with servants."

"Sassy, when are you going to learn those things don't mean anything to me? I don't want people to like me—or not like me—because of what I have or don't have. I want people to like me for *me*, just like I like you for *you*."

I nodded. But I couldn't help but wonder if Kitty would feel that way if I was the one living in this house with servants and she was the one living in Coal Valley in a tiny apartment.

Mrs. Martin's darkroom was amazing. Kitty couldn't understand my fascination with it. She even told me I didn't have to *pretend* to be interested in her mother's photography just to be nice. I laughed and said she didn't have to crawl under the Christmas tree with Mama or eat fried baloney sandwiches to be nice, either. When she protested that she loved both, I said, "See, that's the way I feel about your mother and her photography."

By the end of the week, I developed my first picture. I actually watched my face appear on the paper floating in the tray of chemicals. It was like magic. In the amber glow of the safelight, I hung my picture on the clothesline next to Mrs. Martin's pictures. She said, "I'll frame it for you so you can take it home."

I grabbed her around the waist and hugged her. I said, "I can't wait to show Mama." Mrs. Martin let her fingers trail over my hair before releasing me. She said, "I have some books on photography, if you want to look at them."

"Yes, please."

She took me into the room next to the darkroom. It was filled with shelves of books, photo albums, framed pictures, cameras, and camera equipment. I stared, trying to take it all in. "Where did you get all this stuff?"

Mrs. Martin laughed. "I've been studying photography for many years. I went to the Academy of Art University in San Francisco."

"In California?"

Mrs. Martin laughed again. "Yes."

"I didn't know you could go to college and study photography. I thought it was like . . . a hobby."

"Sarah, you can study just about anything you can imagine at college. And yes, photography is a profession and a hobby. How about tomorrow afternoon we go out in the country and take some pictures?"

"Yes, please!"

Mrs. Martin smiled and walked across the room. She stopped in the doorway and turned around. "Feel free to explore my studio. It's hard to tell what you might unearth in here."

The next day, I tried to get Kitty to go with us, but she insisted photography wasn't her thing. She said she would wait for me beside the pool.

Mrs. Martin and I drove off. She said to tell her when I saw something interesting, and she'd stop so I could photograph it. I asked, "Like what exactly?"

"Like what *you* think is interesting."

I mulled this over. "But I think lots of things are interesting."

"That's good. Just shout out when you see something."

"But what if it's not really interesting? What if you don't think it's interesting?"

Mrs. Martin laughed. "Sarah, it doesn't matter what I think. These will be your pictures."

"Then stop right here."

When we got back, Draxie had lemonade and shortbread waiting for us. Kitty hurried me into my bathing suit so we could go swimming. I still couldn't believe they had a swimming pool—but more than that, I couldn't believe I was there and learning to swim. Kitty was determined to make me a swimmer, and I'd already mastered floating on my back. We were splashing around when her mother appeared. "Girls, I have a question. Katherine's grandmother has invited us to visit her this weekend. Would you like to go?"

"Gran lives in Pittsburg," Kitty said. "It pretty much takes all day to get there."

"She wants us to stay a few days," Mrs. Martin said.

I smiled at Kitty and nodded my head. "Sounds like fun," she said, splashing me.

"Mrs. Martin?"

"Yes, Sarah."

"Will we have time to develop the pictures I took before we go?"

Mrs. Martin laughed. "We'll work on them after dinner."

That night, when Kitty and I were getting ready for bed, I asked, "Is your dad going with us to your grandmother's?"

"Dad? No, Gran is my mother's mother. Why?"

"I just wondered."

Kitty sat down on the bed next to me. "Why did you ask if Dad was going?"

"I guess I'm just curious about having a dad." I felt myself blush.

"Oh, I didn't think about that."

Kitty frowned. "You don't remember your father?"

"No, he died in Italy in World War II. I was just a baby."

"What about your grandfather or uncles?"

"My grandparents died when my mama was sixteen. I just have one great-aunt."

"Oh, yeah, I remember your aunt."

For a moment, neither of us spoke. Then Kitty looked at me and said, "My dad is a good father." She paused, concentrating on what to say next. She looked down at her hands. "He works hard—too hard—which is why he never goes anywhere with us. But when he's not working, he's fun to be around. He has a great sense of humor and is a really smart man." She paused.

I nodded. Kitty put her arm around my shoulder and laid her face next to mine. I could feel her kindness enveloping me like a warm blanket on a cold night. She whispered against my cheek, "I'm sorry."

This is where I knew I should make a joke and lighten the moment, but I couldn't think of one. Instead, I laid my head on Kitty's shoulder and began to cry. She wrapped her arms around me and let me cry until I could cry no more. Then she went into the bathroom and came back with a cold, wet washcloth and a glass of water. She pulled the pillows out from under the bedspread and propped them up against the headboard. "Here, get into bed."

I climbed into bed and sat back against the pillows. Kitty settled down Indian fashion in the center of the bed facing me. I said, "I'm sorry to act like such a crybaby."

"Oh, Sassy, I'm your best friend. You can tell me anything."

"I know. Kitty, I don't mean to act like the poor little orphan girl. It's not like I don't have a Mama and a home, it's just—" I stopped, afraid I'd start crying again. Kitty waited, twirling a lock of hair around her finger. She was looking at me with such concern—such love—that I told her something I never told anyone. "When I was little, I used to dream about my father. It was always the same dream."

Kitty went still. I continued. "I dreamed he wasn't really killed in the war. He was just injured and lost his memory. That's why he never came home. Then one day, he woke up and remembered everything! And he came home to us. And we moved into this big house on a hill where Mama cooked supper every night and we sat around the table after supper and talked and laughed. Then we'd go into the living room and sit together and read and talk about books. Then Mama would bring us gingerbread and milk before bedtime."

I closed my eyes. The spicy smell of gingerbread filled my nostrils. I breathed in and out and opened my eyes. "After we ate, Daddy would say, 'Off to bed, Sassy girl,' and I'd go to kiss him goodnight, but before I could touch him, I always woke up."

I looked at Kitty. She said, "Sassy, you've no idea how amazing you are."

"What?"

"You are so smart, and talented, and strong."

I shook my head. "I'm none of those things."

"Yes, you are! You are so incredibly strong. Look at how you left Coal Valley and went to Foxcroft. And I'm not saying anything's wrong with Coal Valley, but the way you were able to pick up Foxcroft classes in the middle of the year *and* make all As, is pretty amazing. On top of that, you wowed everybody with your voice, and by the way, you never told me you could sing like that."

"But Kitty, I feel like I'm living in the inside of one of my books. Like none of this is real."

"Of course it's real! You're sitting right here in front of me. We just got out of school for the summer, and in the fall, we'll be back at Foxcroft together."

"I'm not like those girls. I'm not like you—I'm just pretending."

"Stop saying that—you are just like me! And of course you're not like the girls at Foxcroft; you're better than they are."

I pushed back the covers and scooted over so I could grab Kitty's hand. "Listen to me. I can never be like you. Don't you see? I'll always be Sassy—that girl from the mountains. I don't belong here. I don't belong at Foxcroft. And now that I've left Coal Valley, I won't belong there either."

"How can you say that?"

"Because when you leave Coal Valley and get a better education than the people there, you're getting above your raising."

I could see Kitty turning this over in her mind. "Are you saying they don't want you to get an education?"

"No, it's not that. Lord, how do I explain this?" I hopped off the bed and started pacing back and forth. How did I get Kitty to understand something I wasn't sure I understood myself? I just knew that this was the way of the mountain people—my people—where family, home, and our *place* were things to be preserved and protected.

I said, "It's okay to get an education, but you're supposed to get it *there*. When I went off to Foxcroft, a lot of people took that to mean I was saying Coal Valley wasn't good enough for me. That I was forsaking my people—my roots."

"But how can they look down on you for getting an education?"

"First of all, I'm a girl. My place is to get married, have babies, and have them in church every Sunday."

"Your Mama's not like that."

I sighed. "No, she's not. She may not believe that way, but she's tried to live that way."

"What do you mean?"

I sat back down on the edge of the bed. "Mama once told me that she and my daddy never intended to stay in Coal Valley—they planned to go where they could have a better life. But the war took all that away from them. And that left Mama with two choices—go to Seattle with Aunt Hat or stay in Coal Valley."

"I've met your Aunt Hat. I can see why she didn't want to live with her."

"Mama is too independent for that."

"But that's a good thing!" Kitty sprang up and stood facing me. "Your mother is independent and—and a free spirit. She's not like other women. And she sure isn't like my mother. My mother smoothers me." She started thumping herself with her hand. "She doesn't let me do anything on my own. She plans out every inch of my life. She never asks me what *I* want to do."

I stared at Kitty. Her mother wasn't like that. She was kind and gentle—sophisticated. She *always* let Kitty do what she wanted. "But your mother always asks you what you want to do."

Kitty pushed a big sniff of air out of her nose and put her hands on her hips.

I insisted. "She does. Like when she asked if you wanted to go to your grandmother's house."

Kitty plopped down on the bed next to me. "Oh, Sassy, don't you see? That's what she does. She wasn't really asking my opinion. She wasn't asking you or me if we wanted to go to the symphony. She wasn't asking if we wanted to go sightseeing downtown. She was *telling* us we were going. Pretending to ask is her way of telling me we're going somewhere or doing something. And she does it to my dad too. He never says no to her either."

I tried to see Mrs. Martin as the woman Kitty described, but all I saw was her kind face bent over the developer in the darkroom. Then Kitty's voice drifted in front of me like a dark shadow falling on my path. "You don't know how many times I've wished my mother was like your mother."

I felt my stomach lurch. How could I tell Kitty that my mother was *not* the person she thought she was? How could I tell her about Mama's boyfriends—about the women who accused her of trying to steal their husbands?

"Hey, Sassy, are you listening to me?"

"Yeah, I heard you."

"I can't imagine having a mother like yours. She's so beautiful. She looks just like Grace Kelly. Did you see the movie *Dial M for Murder?*"

I shook my head, and Kitty launched into a description of the movie. How could I explain to her that I loved my Mama with the fierceness of a mountain lion, but God in heaven, it was hard being her daughter. Being Mama's daughter was like standing in line to ride the Ferris wheel. You watch everybody laugh and squeal as they go around and around. The music plays and the lights dance. You've saved the Ferris wheel for last because it's your favorite ride, and just when you get up to the window to buy your ticket, the carnival barker shouts, "No more rides tonight."

I could feel the sweat pooling in the bend of my knees and running down the backs of my legs. Kitty raised her arm to push the hair from her face, and I could see the sweat ring under her arm.

"We're almost there, girls," Mrs. Martin said.

All the windows were down in the car, but the air rushing over us was muggy—soupy, Mama called it. I was as exhausted as if I'd been running for miles.

"How about we stop for a Coca-Cola?" Mrs. Martin turned off the road in front of a tiny building that had a sign almost as big as the structure. It said *Dotson's Drive-In.*

"Want to stretch your legs?" Mrs. Martin opened the door and walked toward the building. It had a window in the center of it and a white board forming a window ledge that ran the width of the building. All around the window were signs advertising hamburgers, French fries, banana splits, and milkshakes.

Five minutes later, we were back on the road with giant cups full of ice and Coke. Mrs. Martin switched on the radio, and Chuck Berry's "Maybellene" filled the car. By the time we turned down the road with houses like the one Kitty lived in, we were singing along with Elvis Presley, "You ain't-a nuthin' but a hound dog, cuh-crying all the time."

The driveway to Kitty's grandmother's house was lined with massive trees that shared their shade with the road. I felt my sweat dry in the noticeably cooler air. Up ahead, I spied the dark red brick house rising up out of the trees. It was about the same size of the Martins' house, but it was much more ornate. White shutters trimmed the rows of windows, and it had something I'd never seen before—a balcony with white balustrade. I pictured myself there in a long white gown, gazing at the stars, reciting, "Romeo, Romeo! Wherefore art thou, Romeo?"

The same white balustrade adorned the wide porch, which not only was as long as the house, but also turned and ran down both sides. White wicker furniture and wooden rocking chairs paraded up and down the porch, their bright red cushions complementing the pots of geraniums setting amongst the furniture. The only thing missing was me curled up on one of those chairs with a book.

Mrs. Martin led the way up to the door that was opened by a Negro maid. She even had on an honest-to-goodness maid's uniform—gray dress with white apron. Mrs. Martin hugged the woman, who had the biggest bosom and skinniest legs I'd ever seen. I swear she looked like she was walking on two match sticks. Mrs. Martin said, "How are you, Aunt Ella?"

My head whipped around, and I took a closer look at the maid. I punched Kitty. "Did she say—"

Kitty gave me a "hush up" look and stepped up to hug her. "Aunt" Ella said, "You all must be wore out. Come on in the living room. I've got sandwiches, my special ladyfingers, and mint ice tea set up in there. Mrs. Howard is on her way in. She's been out in that rose garden, as hot as it is. I done told her she needs to stay out of this heat."

She ushered us into an enormous room done in different shades of blue. The furniture looked so heavy, I wondered how they ever got it in the room. Kitty shouted, "Gran!"

A lady stood in the doorway. *Lady*—not *woman*, not *grandmother*—was the perfect word to describe her. She was of average height and slim, with gray hair swept up in a fashionable do. She wore a sleeveless yellow dress and white sandals. Her only jewelry was a small gold cross at her neck. She hugged Kitty and Mrs. Martin and turned to me.

"Hello, Sarah. I've heard so much about you."

I stepped forward and held out my hand. She took it and held it in both of hers. Her hands felt cool and sturdy. I looked down at them. They were blue-veined and freckled, with short manicured nails. A grandmother's hands—something I'd never known.

"It's nice to meet you," I said. "Thank you for having me."

Kitty and I stayed long enough to eat and chat so we wouldn't seem rude, then Kitty took me off to explore the house. The rooms were large and airy, with polished windows washed in sunlight. I was fascinated by two things—the music room that had a grand piano and the family room that had the biggest television I'd ever seen. It was twice the size of the one the Martins had. Kitty said, "Gran never misses *I Love Lucy.*"

The upstairs hallway had a menagerie of framed photographs on the wall. Kitty said her mother had taken most of them. The largest picture was of Kitty's grandparents. They were sitting in chairs, and standing around them, I counted eight people. I recognized Kitty's mother, who I realized resembled her father. There were also pictures of children at various ages—some posed around the Christmas tree or outside with Easter baskets; others were candid pictures of kids playing with a puppy or eating watermelon. I picked Kitty out in many of them.

An ache I could not understand settled in my chest. At that moment, I would have given anything to be in those pictures—to have a family.

Kitty gave me a strange look. "Come on," she said, grabbing my arm and pulling me down the hall.

"I was looking at that picture of your grandparents. I didn't know you had such a big family. And by the way, I don't see Aunt Ella in there."

Kitty laughed. "Oh, yeah, I grew up calling her Aunt Ella. It's just something the family's always done—like an endearment, I guess. I asked Mama once, and she said Aunt Ella is from Alabama, and when she came to work here, she told them to call her Aunt, so they did. And I do have a big family; you should be here at Thanksgiving and Christmas when they all show up."

She opened the door to our bedroom. The room was sunshine yellow with more of the heavy furniture that seemed to dominate the house. But the bed—it was enormous and had a canopy. All my life, I wanted to sleep in a bed like that. An "Oh!" escaped my lips.

Kitty grinned. "I know. It's something, isn't it?"

"I've always wanted a canopy bed. Can I lay down on it?"

"Sure, silly."

She took my hand, and together we ran and hopped on the bed. I looked up at the pale blue canopy and felt like I'd reached up and pulled the sky down over my head.

"I am going to sleep so good in this bed," I said.

At dinner that night, I met Kitty's grandfather, who she called Granddad. The first thing he did was to pull a quarter from behind my ear, which he dropped into my hand. He did the same thing to Kitty when she hugged him. When dinner was over, Kitty kissed her grandparents, and we started to leave the room. Her granddad said, "I hope you ladies will be joining us for mass in the morning."

I wasn't sure, but I thought mass had something to do with church. I smiled. Kitty said, "Mother, did we bring dresses?"

"Of course."

The next morning, I put on a green sleeveless dress and white shoes that belonged to Kitty. She wore a similar blue dress. I stood in front of the mirror, admiring my outfit. I tamed my hair into a low ponytail, and Kitty tied a matching ribbon around it. She opened a drawer and pulled out what looked like two lace handkerchiefs and handed me one.

"Uh, thanks," I said.

Kitty moved to stand beside me at the mirror. With bobby pins, she pinned the handkerchief over her hair. "Here, let me pin yours on." I handed it to her and bent down so she could pin it on my hair. "We cover our hair when we go to mass."

I nodded like I understood.

On the way to church, Kitty's gran asked me where my family worshipped. I swear, I almost laughed out loud. I pictured Mama with one of these lace handkerchiefs on her head and a Lucky Strike cigarette in her mouth. A giggle escaped, and I slapped my hand over my mouth. Kitty gave me a "what are you doing?" look. I took a deep breath and said, "We're Old Regular Baptists."

Kitty's grandfather glanced at her grandmother. "How nice," she said.

When we got there, people were already going into the church. It was a mammoth gray stone building with a tall steeple sprouting in the center of it like a milkweed in a flowerbed. A sign out front said *St. Peter's Catholic Church.* I stared up at the stained glass windows. The colors vibrated in the sunlight. I felt a shiver run down my spine. I'd never been in a church like this. The only stone church I ever saw was the Methodist church in Coal Valley, but you could set that church down in the corner of this one and not even notice it.

Kitty smiled at me and hooked her arm through mine. We followed the adults up the steps and through a massive wooden door. She said, "Just do what I do."

It took a minute for my eyes to adjust to the dimness. It was cool, like the inside of a cave. I looked around and thought about a book I'd read about King Henry VIII and his break with the Catholic church. Halfway up the aisle, I sneezed. Kitty looked at me. "What's that smell?" I whispered, holding my hand over my mouth.

"Incense."

We sat down on a pew that had purple cushions. I thought of the hard pews I set on in Aunt Hat's church. I looked around. In the front of the sanctuary, there were several layers of platforms, each one higher than the last one. On one platform was a pulpit and on another was a table with candles, but what caught my eye was the enormous statue of Jesus on the cross that covered the wall from ceiling to floor. Aunt Hat's church would have loved to have had that, but they wouldn't have thought much about the statue of the Virgin Mary that stood on a stone pillar.

All of a sudden, organ music started coming out of the ceiling. Everybody stood. A few men and some little boys wearing robes came walking up the aisle chanting something that was a song, but at the same time wasn't. One man carried a big book covered in red velvet. Another carried a huge gold cross. Others carried candles, and one guy had a little gold pot on a string that he swung back and forth. The same smell that had made me sneeze was coming out of it, and I sneezed again.

The service was the strangest thing I ever saw. It started with the priest saying, "In the name of the Father, and of the Son, and of the Holy Spirit." Then the people said, "Amen." I thought, *well, they'd have lost Aunt Hat right there*. It was called the Holy Ghost—not Holy Spirit—in any church I ever attended with her, as if the word ghost would evoke stronger divine images.

I kept waiting for the preaching, but other than a few Scriptures, it was just a bunch of talking by the priest and a bunch of answering by the congregation. Since I didn't know what to say, I kept quiet. Then a man went up to the altar, spread a cloth on it, and set a big gold cup and a plate on it. The next thing I knew, everybody stood up, and the priest spoke again; then he hushed, and the congregation talked. Then we all kneeled, which explained the funny little cushions on the floor in front of us. Then we stood up again. Kitty whispered, "Stay here." Then she and her family joined the people who were leaving the pews and walking to the front of the church where the priest stood. For a minute, I thought they were lining up to shake hands with the priest and leave, and then I realized a man stood next to the priest holding the plate. He was giving everybody a cracker, and the priest was giving them a drink out of the cup. Finally, something I recognized—the Lord's Supper. But it sure was a strange way to do it.

On the way home, Kitty's grandmother said, "Well, Sarah, what did you think of our service?"

"It was very nice."

"Was it like your church service?"

"Oh, no, ma'am. Baptists are a lot louder than Catholics. When Brother Thomas gets fired up, he has to shout and dance a little. Some of the people in the congregation do too, and there's always a few people who speak in tongues. Sister Eula Faye does it every Sunday."

"I see. How nice."

Kitty's grandfather glanced at her again, and Kitty's grandmother started coughing and had to cover her mouth with a handkerchief.

Summer, 1956

Sassy

"There is nothing like looking, if you want to find something . . . . You certainly usually find something if you look, but it is not always quite the something you were after." J. R. R. Tolkien, *The Hobbit*

I couldn't believe in three days, I'd be back in Coal Valley. Mrs. Martin took us downtown shopping, and even though I protested, she bought me a white sundress with a blue sailboat on the front. I don't know how much of it was the excitement of being in a big city or how much of it was the heat, but by the time we got home, I had a headache. I was pretty sure part of it was the heat radiating from the sidewalks, and part of it was that I couldn't stop craning my neck to look up at the tall buildings. When we got home, Kitty wanted to go swimming, but I begged off and went upstairs.

I wandered into Mrs. Martin's studio and started pulling books off the shelves. I realized I wouldn't get another chance to look through her photography collection if I didn't do it in the next couple of days. I looked through about a dozen books before I found one about photographing wildlife. I sat down in the floor and leaned back against a shelf, and soon I was lost in the story and photographs of an African safari.

When I closed the book, I looked at the wall of shelves behind me. There were photo albums on the bottom shelf. I pulled one out and found it was full of old sepia photographs of people standing or sitting ramrod straight with somber faces. They were labeled with names and dates. I discovered photos of Kitty's great-grandparents and other family members. Most were dated at the turn of the century, but there were some from the late 1800s. The next album was full of more old photos—some sepia and some black and white. I was fascinated by the ones of dead people in coffins—some were children.

By the time I'd gone through that whole shelf, I was finding pictures of Kitty's mother and her brothers and sisters when they were children. That's when Kitty popped into the room.

"There you are," she said. "What in the world are you doing?"

She dropped down on the floor next to me and started to laugh. "Check out the clothes they wore." She grabbed the album. "Look at this picture of Gran—her dress is down to her ankles."

We laughed and made fun of the pictures, imagining what they were doing or where they were going. Then Kitty said, "Want to see pictures of me when I was little?"

"Sure!"

Kitty jumped up and went over to the other side of the room. She pulled photo albums off the self and stacked them on the floor. She laid her hand on top of the tall stack. "You can tell these are when Mom got into photography."

Together, we pored over the pictures. Kitty turned the pages while I watched her life flash by – family dinners, picnics, vacations, parties, even snowball fights. People were laughing, dancing, hugging, and making silly faces. A life rolled past my eyes that I had only read about in books. Kitty picked up one album that had her name on the cover. "Check this out," she said.

First, there were pages of pictures showing Kitty cradled in her parent's arms. These were followed with pictures of Kitty's first tooth, first Thanksgiving, and first Christmas. In the Christmas pictures, a four month old Kitty was propped up next to a tricycle. Then there were pictures of Kitty bundled up in a snowsuit. Her father stood in front of the house, holding her. There was so much snow it looked like the house had been set down in the middle of a snow drift.

While I looked at this album, Kitty pulled out about a dozen more. I couldn't believe these photo albums were full of pictures of Kitty. Mama might be able to scrape together two dozen pictures of me.

"Want to see a picture of my sister?"

At first, I thought I misunderstood her—sister? I said, "You have a sister?"

"I had a sister—actually, two—a twin sister who died right after she was born and an adopted sister. See, here's her picture."

Kitty handed me the album, and there was a picture of Kitty and another little girl. They had on matching dresses and were sitting next to each other on a rug. Under the picture it said, *Katherine and Helena.*

The strangest feeling washed over me, making my stomach lurch and a tingling travel down my spine at the exact same time. Aunt Hat called that feeling "somebody walking on your grave." I asked. "What happened to her?"

I turned the page, and there were more pictures of Helena. One was of her standing, and under it was written, *Helena's first steps.*

Kitty leaned over the album and peered at the pictures. "I don't know."

I turned and stared at her. "What do you mean, you don't know?"

"The only thing I know is that she only lived with us a couple of months before she went back to live with her mother. My parents were supposed to adopt her, but her mother changed her mind."

"Changed her mind?"

"Yeah, she took her back."

"Why?"

"I don't know. My mother won't talk about it. She says it's too painful."

I turned the page, and there was a full page picture of Helena. I suppose it was what used to be called a color picture—but the colors looked like they'd been added after the picture was developed. Other than a muddy brown background, her dress was white, and her cheeks had pink spots like rouge. What caused my heart to start racing was the gold cross necklace she wore. I knew I'd seen it before. I turned the page, but there were no more pictures of Helena.

"Hey," said Kitty, "she looks sort of like you—I mean, you as a bald-headed baby. And she looks sort of like me too. See? We really do look alike—both bald-headed—but her eyes were darker." She examined the picture closer. "Brown, I think." She handed me the album and stood up. "Let's go get something to eat. I'm starving."

I turned back the page to the picture of Helena and stared at it. Kitty had already stood up and was shoving books back on the shelf. "Kitty," I said, "you and Helena have on matching necklaces."

"Yeah." She kept putting books back on the shelf. "In case you haven't noticed, Catholics are big on crosses."

"Do you still have the necklace—the one you wore in this picture?"

Kitty finished shelving the books and came over to give me a hand getting up. "Yeah, it's in my jewelry box." She looked at me curiously. "Why?"

I stood, still holding the album. "Can I see it?"

Kitty led the way to her room. She rummaged around in a little white box that was lined with blue velvet. She pulled out a small black box. She opened the box, looked at what was inside, and handed it to me. "Can we go eat now?"

I stared at the necklace. I murmured, "You go ahead. I'm not hungry."

"Okay. Suit yourself." Kitty walked to the door of her room and turned back to look at me. "Sassy, are you sure you're okay?"

"Yeah, I still have this headache."

"Do you want me to tell my mom?"

"No!"

She narrowed her eyes. "Are you *sure* you're okay?"

"I think I'll go to lie down for a few minutes, but first I'm going to take this photo album back."

"Okay, I'll be downstairs."

I waited to make sure Kitty was downstairs before I went back to Mrs. Martin's studio. I sat down on the floor and pored over the pictures of Helena and Kitty. I opened the box that held the necklace and traced my finger over it. The gold cross had a delicate scrollwork design that made me think of ancient castles and knights in shining armor. Carefully, I removed the picture of Helena wearing the gold cross—the one that said *first steps*. I held it and the necklace side by side and examined them. This necklace was definitely identical to the ones both girls wore in the picture. I turned the picture over, and written on the back were the words, *Helena's first steps. 10 months old. July 30, 1943.*

I went back to Kitty's room, slipped off my shoes, and crawled into the bed. I closed my eyes, but I saw the cross. I remembered how warm it felt in my palm and how the scrollwork felt under my fingertip.

There was something so familiar about that necklace. I had the strangest feeling I'd seen it before.

I woke early the next morning with my stomach complaining for my lack of dinner the evening before. Kitty slept, her long blond hair splayed over the pillow. I stared at her face. Her pale brown eyebrows were perfectly shaped, and her skin was tanned a golden color. I picked up a strand of my limp hair and studied it. It was roughly the color of straw, and I didn't have to look in the mirror to see my scraggly dark brown eyebrows. No matter how much sun I got, my skin just got red. When the redness went away, it turned back to white—not a trace of tan. I whispered, "I'm not like you, Kitty. No matter what you say. I'll never be like you."

In the kitchen, I found Draxie at work on breakfast. "Why, looky here who's up with the chickens," she said.

I smiled. "Morning, Miss Draxie."

"I reckon you going to get all you can out of your last day here. Set down." She pointed to a stool at the counter.

I climbed up, and she handed me a glass of fresh-squeezed orange juice. "Somebody didn't eat no dinner last night. How come?"

I took a drink of juice. "I was looking at some old pictures and fell asleep."

Draxie busied herself at the stove. When she turned around, she held a plate heaped with bacon, eggs, and toast.

"Dig in." She smiled and stood for a minute watching me like she was making sure I was going to eat. "I'm sure going to miss you, child."

I set down my fork and hopped off the stool. I grabbed Draxie around the waist and hugged her. Her scent—Dove soap and peppermint— enveloped me. She laughed and hugged me back.

I got back on my stool and went back to my breakfast. Draxie opened the refrigerator and poured me a glass of milk. I asked, "How long have you worked here?"

"Law, let me see. I come here when the Martins got married. That's been more 'n twenty years ago."

"Do you remember when Kitty was born?"

Draxie chuckled. "Miss Katherine was the littlest baby I ever seen, but she sure was a fighter. It's a shame about her twin. 'Bout broke Miz Martin's heart."

She started running water in the sink to wash dishes. I waited until she shut it off. My heart started pounding. I asked, "Do you remember Helena?" I hurried to add, "Kitty told me about her."

Draxie answered, her back to me. "I surely do. Now that really did break Miz Martin's heart. I was so afraid that was goin' to happen. That little child was the saddest thing—she didn't hardly smile."

"Where did she come from?"

Draxie grabbed the frying pan off the stove and plunged it into the dishwater. "The church was the one that give her to Miz Howard."

"Kitty's grandmother?"

"She was the one who come here with the child. Mr. and Miz Martin took her in, and from the first day, they treated that baby like their own. With little Helena, Miz Martin come around to herself. She took care of them babies and wouldn't hardly let me or nobody else do a thing for them. Then that woman showed up."

"What woman?"

"The one that was the child's mother. She come crying and carrying on about how she made a mistake and wanted her baby back. I tell you right now, I wouldn't of give that baby back to that red-headed Jezebel. No, sir. But the Martins did, even if it did almost kill Miz Martin." Draxie turned around. "Hand me that plate."

I looked down at my empty plate, surprised to see my breakfast gone. I handed it to Draxie and slid off my stool. "Thank you for that delicious breakfast."

"You're welcome, Miss Sassy."

"Draxie?"

"Um-hum?"

"Did you say the woman that took Helena had red hair?"

"Sure did. I seen her myself."

"Was she pretty?"

"Humph." Draxie snorted and turned back to the sink. "Oh, yeah, she was a looker."

I went to the living room and found the book of poems I was reading—*North of Boston,* by Robert Frost. I curled up in the blue velvet chair in front of the window. The sun lay across it like a wide yellow ribbon, and I pressed my back into its warmth. I looked around the room—the flowered sofa, the glass-top coffee table, the wide fireplace with a mantle filled with family pictures. I watched the dust moats pirouette in front of the window. I was going to miss this room. I looked down at the poem *The Woodpile* and read, "So as to say for certain I was here/Or somewhere else: I was just far from home."

When Kitty got up, she hurried through breakfast and sent me to get into my bathing suit. My last day at Kitty's had begun. She wanted to make sure I was swimming well before I went home, so we spent most of the day in the pool. That evening, we got all dressed up for dinner. Draxie fixed me a going home dinner—roast beef and gravy, mashed potatoes, macaroni and cheese, bowls of vegetables, plates of yeast rolls, and her special chocolate cake for dessert. Mrs. Martin lit candles and used the china dishes from the glass front cabinet in the dining room. Mr. Martin hugged me and told me I was welcome to come back anytime.

I barely made it out of the car before Mama burst through the apartment door. She must have been looking out of the window and saw the car pull up.

She yelled, "Sassy girl!"

"Mama!"

We hugged and laughed, then hugged and cried a little. Mrs. Martin and Kitty stood by, laughing with us. Finally, we settled down and started unloading the car. It took us about five trips to get all of my stuff up to the apartment. Then Kitty and Mrs. Martin drove off, and it was just me and Mama.

I stood in the center of my tiny room and stretched out my arms. "I'm home."

Mama came up behind me and slid her arms around my waist. "Is everything just like you remember it?"

"Yeah."

"Are you hungry? I can fix you a sandwich."

"No, thanks. I'm tired. I think I'll just go to bed."

"Good night, Sassy. It's good to have you home."

Mama closed the door behind her. I picked up my smallest suitcase. That's where I hid it. Before I unpacked anything else, I took the picture out of the bottom of my suitcase and sat down on the bed. I ran my index finger over the cross. Why did I get this queasy feeling in the pit of my stomach every time I looked at this picture? I turned it over and read for the hundredth time: *Helena's first steps. 10 months old. July 30, 1943.* I slid it back in the bottom of my suitcase and took out the black jeweler's box. "I'm sorry, Kitty. I'll give it back. I promise."

The next morning, I was woke up by somebody pounding on my door. I opened my eyes and tried to focus on my surroundings. I spied the pink bedspread bunched up at the bottom of my bed and realized I was in my own room, in my own bed.

"Sassy, you goin' to sleep all day?"

Madge! I jumped out of bed and yanked open the door. And there she stood, with her arms held out. "Madge, I've missed you!" I grabbed her, almost knocking her off her feet. Her smell—cigarettes and hairspray—was as familiar to me as wood smoke in the fall. She pressed her cheek to mine and whispered, "Sure glad you're home."

"Me too." I couldn't help but notice that when my face pressed against her hair, it didn't budge. She held my hands, stretched out my arms, and took a step back.

"Let me have a look at you. I got to see if you look any smarter."

I laughed and hugged her again. She let go of me and said, "I do believe your boobs have growed a little."

"Miss Madge!"

Mama laughed. "Come on in the kitchen. I fixed you some fried baloney and eggs."

For the next hour, Mama and Madge smoked and drank coffee while I talked about school. I told them all about my suite mates and my classes. I described how my history teacher would lean back in his chair and doze off and one of the girls would drop her book just to see him jump. I explained how the library looked with its massive stone pillars and polished marble floors, and how the books filled the room from ceiling to floor. They laughed when I described the food—how none of the vegetables were ever cooked until they were done, and the meat was never fried. And there was way too much seafood in that place.

I saved the music for last. I told them how I was chosen to be in the chorus and how much my teacher liked my singing. This tickled Mama, who said I got it from my daddy, because she couldn't carry a tune in a bucket.

Madge said, "Well, I say you get ready, and we'll hop on over to the diner and have one of Shelby and Brenda's Sunday specials. I hear it's fried chicken."

Walking down Maple Street, I inhaled the acrid smell of coal dust. Since it was Sunday, there were no coal trucks on the road but their diesel still flavored the air, and their trail of left-behind dust was in every nook and cranny of the buildings and sidewalks. No matter where I went in the world, I would know that smell—the scent of home.

"Have you told her yet?" Madge asked.

"Told me what?"

Mama laughed. "Thanks, Madge."

"Told me what?"

"Hattie Mae's coming Wednesday," Madge said.

I groaned.

"Welcome home," Mama said.

Walking through the diner, I got about a dozen hugs. It took us ten minutes to get to a table, because I had to stop and answer questions about school. Brenda Sue came and took our order, and Madge told her to make sure my chicken was good and fried since I hadn't had anything fried since January.

I was sitting with my back to the room, so I didn't see the Stiltners heading for us, but Madge did. "Here comes big-mouth Myrtle and *Mr.* Stiltner."

"Sassy, is that *you?*"

I shifted slightly in my seat and looked at the Stiltners. "Hello, Mr. and Mrs. Stiltner."

Mrs. Stiltner said, "I told Mr. Stiltner that was you. Didn't I?"

Mr. Stiltner nodded his head, his bowtie sliding up and down his neck. "You certainly did."

"When did you get home?"

"Last night."

"It's awful late for school to be getting out." She pursued her lips and waited. I looked at Madge, who raised her penciled on eyebrows and tilted her head as if to say, *you're on your own.* Mama lit a cigarette and stared off into space.

I said, "School closed two weeks ago. I went to Pennsylvania with Katherine Martin for a visit."

"Would that be the Martins that live in the big house?"

"Yes, ma'am."

"I heard they was from Pittsburg. Didn't you hear that, Mr. Stiltner?" He nodded.

"Actually, they live in Allentown, but Kitty's grandparents live in Pittsburgh. We visited them while I was there."

Mama dropped her cigarette, and it rolled across the table, landing on Madge's napkin. Mama scrambled to catch the cigarette, while Madge grabbed the napkin before it caught on fire. I looked at Mama. All of the color had drained from her face. When she picked up the cigarette, her hands were shaking.

"Whoa, be careful there," Mr. Stiltner said.

Mrs. Stiltner never missed a beat. "So, did you get enough of that school? I told Mr. Stiltner I bet you'd be ready to stay in Coal Valley now."

I glanced at Mama, who was taking a long draw off her rescued cigarette. Madge spoke up. "Where Sassy goes to school is up to her. Move over, Myrtle. Here comes our food."

They stepped back and let Brenda Sue put our plates on the table. Then she asked us if we wanted anything else, but the Stiltners still stood there. I realized Mrs. Stiltner was waiting for me to say whether or not I was going back to Foxcroft, and Mr. Stiltner was waiting for permission to go.

I said, "I loved school, and right now, I plan on going back."

"Well, Mr. Stiltner and I will let you enjoy your dinner." After a last hard look, Mrs. Stiltner turned and headed back through the diner with Mr. Stiltner close behind her.

Madge muttered, "Damn busy-body."

I glanced at Mama, who was concentrating on buttering a biscuit. She hadn't said a word.

"You all right, Mama?"

"Yeah, that Myrtle Stiltner gets on my last nerve."

It turned out to be a pretty somber lunch. Mama didn't say or eat much. Madge tried to keep the conversation going, but she ended up giving a monologue about the shop. On the walk home, the sun was high in a cloudless blue sky. The humidity was down, and a cool breeze curled around us. This was my favorite part of summer—before it got unbearably hot, which always seemed to set in after the fourth of July.

303

We passed the courthouse when the clock struck two. Madge said, "It's a right nice day. How about I get the car and we go for a ride?"

"You two go ahead," I said. "I need to unpack."

Madge tried again. "How 'bout we go to the movies? *Dial M for Murder* is playing over to the Alamo."

I stumbled, and if Madge hadn't grabbed my arm, I would have fallen.

"You all right?" Mama asked.

"Yeah. Thanks, Madge. Why don't you and Mama go on without me? I'm still worn out."

"Well, we don't have to go tonight. It'll be showing all week."

When we got back to the apartment, I disappeared into my room. I got out the shoebox and took out Helena's picture. I sat down and stared at it. I could hear Mama and Madge talking in the living room. I leaned back against the headboard, sliding my pillow under my head and stretching my legs out in front of me. I touched the cross with my finger, then brought it to my throat, where the cross would rest if I was wearing it. The cross . . . I opened the box that held Kitty's necklace. I stared at it. Where had I seen it? Did I really want to know? Part of me wanted to throw the picture away, sneak the cross back into Kitty's jewelry box, and forget about it, but a bigger part of me knew this cross was important. But how?

I put the necklace and picture back in the shoebox. At that moment, I decided I was going to search for answers. I had to know why looking at that picture and that cross made feel like I was on a Ferris wheel that had stopped with me on the main tip-top.

I wandered into the kitchen and found Mama sitting at the table, smoking a cigarette. I took a Pepsi out of the refrigerator and rummaged around in the drawer under the sink for the opener.

"You coming down to the shop tomorrow?"

"Do you want me to?" I pulled out a chair and sat down.

"I thought you'd want to see everybody. And you could use a haircut. Just a trim to get the split ends."

Mama ground out her cigarette and stood. She walked behind me and pulled my hair into her hands like she was fashioning a ponytail. "It's growed a lot. Got thicker too."

I closed my eyes and concentrated on the feel of her fingers running through my hair. "Mama?"

"Yes-um."

"Do you have any baby pictures of me?"

"Why, sure I do."

"Can I see them?"

"I don't know, right off, where they are." She kept finger-combing my hair.

"Mama? Tell me what I was like when I was a baby."

Mama laughed. "What a funny question."

"Was I a good baby? Did I cry a lot?"

"Why, you were good-natured like your daddy."

"What was my first word?"

Mama's fingers stilled. "*Ball.* You said ball because you had this big red ball you loved."

"When did I start walking?"

Mama dropped my hair and stepped back. She laughed, but it sounded forced. "Lord, Sassy, I guess you were about a year old. Why all these questions?"

I turned sideways in my chair so I could see her. "No reason. Just wondering."

When I woke the next morning, Mama was gone to work. I checked the kitchen table to see if she'd left me a note or a list of chores, but there was none, so I wandered around the apartment like a stranger. I stood outside of her bedroom door, willing myself to go in. I'd never invaded Mama's privacy before.

I eased into the room and let my eyes adjust to the dimness. Mama had left the shades pulled against the heat of the day. On her dresser set the little cedar chest that held the letters my daddy had written to her during the war.

I rested my hand on it. I remembered asking Mama, when I was about eight years old, what was in it. She had opened it and showed me the letters. She said they were all she had left of my daddy. I had never wanted to read them. I knew that the day would come when I'd feel differently, but when I thought of my daddy, I didn't want to think of the war.

I went to her closet and opened the door. A string hung from the single bare light bulb in the ceiling. I clicked it on. Shoeboxes lined the floor and were stacked on the overhead shelf. I pushed her clothes to one side and got down on my knees in the doorway. I started against the wall and opened each box, peering in. Shoes. High-heeled shoes. I had no idea Mama had that many pairs of high heels. She must have kept every pair she'd ever owned. When I looked in the last box, I stood and surveyed the boxes over my head. I went to the kitchen and got a chair, climbed up, got a stack of boxes, and got down. I looked through them before getting back on the chair for another stack.

The ceiling sloped, so the shelf wasn't very wide. The boxes were only stacked two wide and six high. When I pulled out the third stack, a hatbox appeared like a sudden drop of rain on a sunny day. I had to remove the next stack of shoeboxes before I could get to it. Carefully, I slid it toward me. The octagon-shaped box had once been blue, but was faded to a sad lavender. I got down off the chair and took it to the kitchen, where I found a rag to dust it off. Then I took it to my room.

I set it on my bed and ran back to Mama's room. I put everything back in her closet the way I found it, then stood back to survey my work. With the shoes put back, you'd never know the hatbox was missing. Satisfied, I dragged the chair back to the kitchen.

I stood in the doorway and stared at the box. It was Mama's property and I had no business with it. But there was no going back now – I picked up the box and pried off the lid. The past drifted out and curled around me like a wreath of smoke. On top was yellowed wax paper folded to make an envelope. It was full of dried flowers pressed flat. I laid it beside me on my bed and lifted out a stack of pictures, cards, valentines, and scraps of ribbon. In the bottom lay a pair of white gloves—elbow-length and made of satin.

I forgot about everything except the gloves. I pressed them to my face, and a trace of some exotic perfume lingered in the folds. I inhaled its scent. Images of Mama in a ball gown dancing with a tall, handsome man in a tuxedo flitted across my imagination. I slipped my hand into one and pulled it up to my elbow. I admired it, turning my arm back and forth. I put on the other one and stretched out my arms. I stood and twirled around the room like I was dancing with Prince Charming. I waltzed out into the living room, my arms poised in a mock embrace. Around and around I went until I fell on the couch laughing.

I took off the gloves, and the spell was broken. I went back to my room and sat down next to the box. I folded the gloves and placed them in the bottom. I sorted through the stack of keepsakes until I had all the pictures in a separate pile. I spread them out on the bed. There was one of me as a baby, lying on my stomach. I had a blanket draped over me so that my face was the only thing showing. At least I was smiling. On the back it said, *Sassy, three months.* There were two faded snapshots of me propped up in front of a tiny Christmas tree. On the back was written *Sassy's first Christmas.* The last picture of me when I was a baby was dated January 21, 1943. I was sitting on Mama's lap. I studied how she was holding me. Her back was ramrod straight, and her elbows were spread away from her body. Instead of cuddling me against her, her hands gripped my arms so that I sat perched on the edge of her lap. Neither of us was smiling.

The next picture of me had *Easter 1945* written on the back, which meant I was about two and a half. I was sitting in a little rocking chair, staring at the camera, as solemn as a judge. I looked through the rest of the pictures, putting them in order by the ages on the back. There were two of me that said *Thanksgiving 1945,* two that said *Christmas 1945,* and one of me standing next to a fake picket fence that said *Sassy age three.* There was one of me holding a stuffed bunny that I vaguely remembered. On the back it said *age four and a half.* There was at least one of me at Christmas dated from 1946 to 1949, and several of me standing outside at some place I couldn't identify. There was nothing written on the backs, but I looked about four. Then there was a school picture for every year.

I looked through the rest of the pictures. Mama had showed me the only two pictures she had of her parents. One showed a stoic-faced old man and woman. They were standing in front of a log house. On the back of the picture was scrawled *Noah and Mary Jane Smith 1940.* There was another picture of them much younger, still stone-faced.

This time, they were sitting in what looked like straight-backed chairs. It was dated 1922.

There was one of Mama as a little girl, her hair was long and curled with a big bow on the side of her head. She wore a dress fashioned like a sailor suit. She was smiling, her head slightly tilted. On the back it said, *Sylvia age four.* There were some pictures of her in elementary school, but the one that fascinated me was of her standing next to a flowerbed. Even in a black and white photograph, the flowers were beautiful. On the back, it said *1937.* I realized that Mama was thirteen in that picture—the same age I was—and she was already beautiful, her smile dazzling. Compared with her, I looked drab and ordinary. But worse than that, put side by side with Mama, I looked like a little girl.

The only picture I'd never seen before was of Mama standing in front of a car. A tall, handsome man was standing next to her. He had one arm casually draped across her shoulders, and she was leaning against him. She had on a dress that was cinched at the waist with a wide belt. She looked so thin—so frail—that she'd surely fall if he wasn't supporting her. I turned it over, searching for a name or a date, but the back was blank.

I started to put the picture down when it hit me—I'd seen this man before. There was a shadow across his face, but I was sure I'd seen him before. I studied him. The photo was black and white, and it was taken far enough away that the car and the mountain could be seen in the background, so they weren't close enough to get a clear picture of their faces. I laid it aside and looked through the cards and other keepsakes, but there was nothing that had anything to do with me.

I picked up the pictures of me again, putting them in order from youngest to oldest. The pictures ranged most of my life—with one exception. There was not one picture of me between ages four months and two and a half years.

I went to my closet and pulled out the shoebox. I took out Helena's picture and laid it in the middle of the pictures of me. I stared at them. My heart fluttered in my chest. If I didn't know better, I'd think Helena was me.

I got the hatbox and put everything in it, adding the pictures on top of the pile. I closed the lid and picked up Helena's picture. My finger traced over the cross necklace. Besides Kitty, I didn't even know anybody who had a cross necklace, so why was it so familiar?

I put Helena's picture back in my shoebox, and then put it and the hatbox in my closet. When I turned around, there on my bed laid the wax paper envelope of dried flowers. I got the hatbox back out of the closet and picked up the envelope. I tried to hold it and take the lid off the box at the same time. When the lid came off, the envelope went flying out of my hand. I tried to catch it, but instead I managed to pull it open, and the flowers flew out of the packet, landing all over my floor. There in their midst something glittered. It was the cross necklace.

When I left the apartment, I had no destination in mind. I just wanted to get out of there so I could think. I followed the river out of town, my feet leading me back to a place I'd been once before—the day my childhood ended, the day a strange woman busted into the beauty shop and accused Mama of stealing her husband. I'd found comfort there then, but now I was seeking more. I needed answers.

It was the edge of dark when I climbed the hill to the little white church. The door creaked open, and I slipped inside. The stillness swaddled me. I made my way to the front of the church. In the muted light, it looked the same as it had a year ago. I sat down in the first pew and stared at the cross on the front of the pulpit. I opened my hand. In my palm lay the cross necklace.

I thought of the Catholic church I'd gone to with Kitty's family. It had been a beautiful, ornate church, but this little sanctuary with its bare wood floors and severe emptiness was just as lovely. There were no candles—no incense. Instead, I breathed in the scent of beeswax and lemon. This little church was taken care of with the love you'd shower on a child—a child you wanted—a child you loved.

The tears ran unchecked down my face. I bowed my head and prayed. "Can you hear me, God? I need your help. I don't know what to do. Please, Lord, tell me what to do."

I sobbed so hard I couldn't sit up. I lay down in the pew and listened to my heart breaking. The church had grown dark by the time I was able to stop. I had tried to wash away the truth with my tears, but I couldn't. Helena and I were one and the same, and for some reason I could never fathom, that meant Mama had given me away. There was no other explanation why she had the necklace that was identical to Kitty's. I had lived with Mr. and Mrs. Martin as their daughter – a daughter they had taken pictures of wearing the heart necklace. *Oh God*, I thought, *that's why Mama didn't know when I took my first steps.*

As long as I could remember, I'd dreamed of living in a big house with a big family. I had imagined what it would be like to have brothers and sisters—a father. It had always been just me and Mama, and there were times I longed for a different, less solitary life. But never in my wildest imaginings did I dream that all of those things had at one time been mine.

There was no other explanation. It all added up. Mama had no pictures of me when I was a year old, nor did she ever talk about what I was like when I was a toddler. She had the necklace, and the crosses were identical. The question was—why? Why had she given me away?

According to Draxie, the Catholic Church had given me to Kitty's grandmother, and she had given me to Kitty's parents. So Mama must have given me to the Catholic Church. Somehow, I ended up in Pennsylvania. But why? How? What would happen to make my mother give me away? And why, then, did she come and take me back?

I walked home in the gloaming with the crickets serenading me. The mist on the mountain tops stole downward toward the valley, leaving behind an ethereal trail. The humidity of late summer was setting in, and with it came unpredictable storms and unbearable heat. But the heat couldn't compete with the unbearable hurt in my heart. It lay there, black and heavy. I'd left Coal Valley in January as Sarah Jane Richardson. I'd come back in June with no idea who I was or who I was supposed to be. Worse than that, I had no idea who the woman was who called herself my mother.

Summer, 1956

Sylvia

"Among many morals which press upon us from the poor minister's miserable experience, we put only this into a sentence—Be true! Be true! Be true!" Nathaniel Hawthorne, *The Scarlet Letter*

"Why ain't Sassy come 'round?" Madge asked.

I was getting everything ready for Lanta Looney's permanent wave. She was the first customer on my appointment book. "She says it's because she's been reading some books she's supposed to have read by the time school starts back. But I swear, Madge, I don't know what's got into her. She's been as sullen as an old maid."

"Ah, Sylvia, don't you remember what you was like at that age? Sassy's almost fourteen—she's a growing up. Teenagers ain't supposed to like adults." Madge opened the drawer at her station and got out a fresh pack of Pall Malls. She tapped it against the heel of her hand before opening it and offering me one.

"Thanks." I took one and waited for Madge to hand me the lighter. We smoked for a while in silence. "I swear, Madge, I ain't done a thing to make her mad at me. The only date I've been on was dinner with Frank, and he's the sheriff, for God's sake."

"By the way, how'd that go?"

"It went fine, thank you very much."

"Why, Sylvia Richardson, I do believe you're blushing."

"I am not!"

"Don't tell me you're sweet on the town sheriff."

"I ain't sweet on nobody. Besides, I thought we was talking about Sassy."

"We are. Want me to talk to her?"

"No, she'll come around."

"What's Hattie Mae saying about it?"

"Oh, she talks to Aunt Hat all right. It just seems to be me she don't want nothing to do with."

The bell rang over the shop, and Aunt Hat trudged in. Madge muttered. "Speak of the devil."

"Sylvia." Her voice reached out to me like a slap in the face.

"Aunt Hat, what a surprise! I didn't know you—"

Aunt Hat barreled on like I'd never said a word. "Where's Sarah Jane?"

"What do you mean, where's Sassy?"

"I just left your apartment, and no one's home."

Madge gave me a look that said *I don't have a dog in this fight* and made a hasty retreat to the back room.

"Sometimes she goes out for a walk." My words sounded lame, even to me.

"Is she over at the Martins' big fancy house?"

I ignored her sarcasm. "No, they've gone back to Pennsylvania for a spell."

She dropped her enormous pocketbook on one chair and her body in another. I thought, *surely she's not going to just sit here.*

"Don't you have anything to drink in this place? I'm parched."

I went to the back room and came back with a glass of water. "Here you go."

I caught a glimpse of Lanta in the window. The door opened, and she breezed in, calling, "Hello everyone." I'd never been so happy to see her in my life.

I hurried her into my chair and started combing her hair. "Do you want me to cut it some?"

She said, "Lordy mercy, yes, it's plumb shaggy."

The bell jingled again, and Alice and Maryetta came in. They took their things to the back room just as Madge came through the curtains. She went over to Aunt Hat and sat down in the chair next to her. "Hattie Mae, can I get you a cup of coffee?"

I watched them out of the corner of my eye. Aunt Hat was all smiles, talking away with Madge. When Frieda Mays came in, Madge got up, and so did Aunt Hat. Without a word to me, she left.

When I saw Madge go into the back room, I followed her. She was rummaging around on the shelf that held the bottles of hair color.

"What did Aunt Hat say?"

"About what?"

"About Sassy."

Madge turned around with a bottle of Loving Care for brunettes. "She said the same thing I did. Something's bothering Sassy."

"What? I don't remember you saying that."

"Well, I'm a saying it now."

She breezed through the curtains, leaving me standing there.

The day had started with Aunt Hat and it ended with crazy Agnes Singleton. Madge warned us she was coming and bringing her daughter. That poor girl was almost as crazy as her mother.

The first thing Agnes did was pull out her pictures. She spread them out on the table and started pointing out to Madge what was wrong with her hair. I know it was morbid, but I couldn't help myself, I had to look. I walked over and peered over Madge's shoulder. There laid Agnes in her coffin—arms crossed, eyes closed.

She said, "There ain't enough curls up here in the front." She patted the front of her hair above her forehead. I looked at Madge, who was studying the pictures of Agnes laid out in her coffin with the same expression she'd have if she was looking at birthday party pictures. I shuddered and went back to my station. I set down in my chair and watched Madge go to work on Agnes's hair.

The shop had gotten unusually quiet. Everybody was talking in low voices, no doubt about crazy Agnes. She started this stuff about a year ago—ordered her coffin with a special light blue lining so she'd know what it looked like. The fact that she was as healthy as a horse didn't stop her from planning her funeral.

After she saw the coffin, she set out to find the right dress to match its lining. She showed up at the shop with a dress she was going to have her picture taken in—inside the coffin—so she was sure it matched the blue lining. Her poor daughter was the one who had to take the pictures. Madge asked her how she was going to tell if the dress matched by looking at a black and white picture, but Agnes just went right on like she didn't hear her.

We heard from Myrtle Stiltner that the funeral director, Old Joe Stacy, just shook his head when he saw Agnes coming. She said he told

Mr. Stiltner that he took her to the basement where he kept the coffins and let her crawl in it and have her picture taken.

When Crazy Agnes was satisfied with the dress, she started coming 'round to get her hair done the way she wanted it to look at her laying out. This was the third time she'd come back to get Madge to tease it higher and put more curls in the front, because as she pointed out, nobody was going to see the back.

That evening, I went home and found Sassy holed up in her room. I changed my clothes, got a beer, and set down on the couch in front of the fan. I lit a cigarette and took a sip of beer. I stared at Sassy's door, wondering for the hundredth time what was wrong with her. I figured it had something to do with the Martins. I should've never let her go off to Allentown with them. I had no idea they had any family in Pittsburgh or that they'd take Sassy there. But what was the chance that the Martins would know Fancy's people? It was Fancy's mother that got Sassy from the nuns, and she was a Howard. She took her to Pittsburgh, because that's where she was when I got her back. And Madge was right; Pittsburgh is a hell of a big place. What was the chance that the Martins would know anybody in Pittsburgh who knew anything about me or Sassy?

I finished my beer, and Sassy still hadn't come out of her room. I hollered through the door, "You alive in there?"

"I'm reading." I could barely hear her flat reply.

"Well, come on out here a minute."

I set down at the kitchen table and waited. I told myself I wasn't going to lose my temper, no matter what she said. She finally come dragging in the kitchen. I couldn't tell if she looked down in the mouth or just hateful. "Set down and talk to me a minute. I don't feel like I've talked to you in a week or more."

Sassy made no movement to set down; instead, she stood behind a chair. "What is it?"

"Where were you this morning?"

Sassy frowned and blinked her eyes slow, like she didn't know what I was talking about. So I spoke to her like she was a four-year-old. "This morning—when your Aunt Hat come knocking on the door."

"Oh, that." She looked over my head and out the kitchen window.

"Well?"

She let her eyes drop from the window to my face. "I didn't feel like talking to her, so I didn't answer the door."

I stared at her. If someone had told me that Sassy would do something like that, I'd laugh at them. But then, that was the Sassy I knew before she went off to a fancy school and started hanging around with Kitty Martin. This Sassy acted like she had every right to ignore her Aunt's knock because she didn't feel like talking.

I took a deep breath. "Let me get this right—you didn't answer the door because you didn't *feel* like it?" Sassy stood mute, with no expression. I stared at her. She didn't look defiant, but what else could I call it? "Would you set down and stop staring at me like that? I'm trying to talk to you. I'm trying to figure out why you would do that to Aunt Hat."

Then she did something she'd never done before. She walked away—went into her room—and shut the door.

I forgot all about my promise to stay calm and not lose my temper. With a "Shit fire!" I stormed out of the kitchen and threw open her bedroom door. Sassy was laying on her bed with her back to me. She was curled on her side with her knees drawn up. At first, I thought she was reading a book like nothing had happened. But when I grabbed her by the shoulder, I saw that she was crying.

She jerked away from me like I just stuck a hot match to her. All of the starch went out of my sails, and I sank down on the bed. Sassy scooted as far away from me as she could get. She was up against the wall and sobbing like her heart would break. I froze. *Lord, God,* I thought, *what's the matter with her?*

I sat still and waited. My head started pounding. The last thing I needed was a headache. When the sobs subsided into snubbing, I said, "Sassy, can't you tell me what's wrong?"

She sprang up and went down on her hands and knees like a lion. She put her face an inch from mine and shouted, "Why did you give me away?"

I jumped back and almost feel off the bed. I grabbed the night stand and righted myself. All the mistakes I'd made—all the lies I'd told—rolled out in front of me. We stared at each other. Sassy was the first one to move. She drew herself up on her knees in the middle of the bed and pointed her finger at me. "Don't try to deny it. I have proof."

She reached under her pillow, grabbed something, and hopped off the bed. She stood facing me and extended her arm straight in front of her, her hand in a fist. At first, I thought she was going to punch me. Then she opened her fist and let a necklace dangle from her fingers. On the end of the chain was a little gold cross.

Pain shot through my head, and I grabbed my forehead with my hand. "Where did you get that?"

"No, Mama. The question is, where did *you* get it?"

"I . . . I . . ." I sank back down on the edge of the bed and covered my eyes with the palm of my hand, trying to make the pain stop before it blinded me. I wrapped my other arm across my stomach like I was going to ward off a blow. When I looked up, Sassy was gone.

I stumbled out of her room calling, "Sassy."

I found her seated at the kitchen table, her hands clasped in front of her on top of the table. She said, "Sit down, *Mama.* You wanted to talk. Let's talk."

The day I'd dreaded for almost thirteen years had finally come. It was time to pay for my sins. "Sassy, I don't know what you *think* you know..." I paused, but she just stared at me with such pain in her eyes, I faltered. "But . . . but a lot of things happened in a short time and I—I just lost control of my life."

"So you just up and gave me away?"

"It wasn't like that."

"So what was it like? Explain it to me."

"Like I said, I don't know how much you know, but—"

Sassy sprang up and left the room. She was back before I could get out of my chair. She dropped two pictures and a black jeweler's box in front of me. My hands shaking, I picked up the first picture. It was Sassy at that age when she wasn't a baby anymore but not yet a toddler.

She was standing all on her own, wearing a dress with a big collar, and lying across it was the necklace.

Sassy said, "Look on the back."

I turned it over, and written on the back in neat handwriting were the words *Helena's first steps. 10 months old. July 30, 1943.* Carefully, I laid it face-up on the table. *Helena.* I remembered hearing Fancy's mother call her that.

Sassy pushed the second picture in front of me. She said, "It took me a while, but I finally figured out where I'd seen that man." She pointed to Fancy. "I knew I'd seen him somewhere. Then the other night, I realized where it was. It was in another picture—one I saw at Kitty's house. The one of Mrs. Martin's brother that Kitty called Uncle Fancy. He was killed in a car accident not long after she was born."

Tears filled my eyes. I was trying hard to stay calm, but the picture of me and Fancy was just too much. I had used him as my ticket out of Coal Valley, and he died because of me.

"Now open the box."

I did as I was told. Inside the box was a cross necklace identical to Sassy's. There was no mistaking the scrollwork on the cross. I looked up at Sassy. She laid the cross necklace she held alongside the one in the box.

"What you didn't know was that the Martins bought their *daughters* matching necklaces. The one in the box is Kitty's. The other one was Helena's—or should I say *mine.*"

Sassy sat back down at the table and stared at me. I wiped the tears from my eyes and pressed my hand against my forehead. I began. "Fancy had to go to Pittsburgh for work, and since his parents lived there, he was going to see them. He asked me to go, so I was in the car with Fancy when the accident happened. You were too. Thank the Lord, you weren't hurt. I was thrown from the car and had a concussion. The headaches I get—they're from the head injury. I spent almost two months in the hospital in Somerset, Pennsylvania—where the accident happened."

"So you gave me away because you were hurt and couldn't take care of me? What about Aunt Hat? What about Madge? Wouldn't they have taken care of me until you got better?"

"It wasn't like that." I paused and rubbed my eyes.

"Then how was it? Explain it to me."

I searched her face to see if there was any chance I could make her understand. I had no choice. I had to try. I began again. "You know your daddy was gone to war when you were born. I had a really hard time. I was—I was lost."

"Lost?"

"I mean, I was lost at what to do. I didn't know how to take care of you. I'd never even held a baby before you. And I was worrying about your daddy—after he got leave to come home and see you, they sent him overseas. And I was alone. It was like I was wandering around in the dark."

I looked down at my hands. They were red from the permanent wave solution I used that day. I rubbed them together and kept my eyes on them. I took a deep breath and said, "I couldn't love you. I tried. But there was something wrong with me—the doctors called it melancholia; women call it baby blues. It's supposed to go away, but mine didn't. It got worse. Aunt Hat couldn't stay with us because Uncle Danny Ray died, and she went back to Seattle. Madge did help. She did. But I—I was just so lost. And when I got the telegram that your daddy was dead, it got worse."

Sassy said, "If you were so upset that my daddy died, then why were you going to Pittsburgh with Kitty's uncle?"

I whispered. "I don't know."

"You don't know! You don't know!" Sassy stood up and started pacing back and forth in the tiny kitchen.

I was afraid she was going to run away again, and I knew I had to get it out or I'd never have a hope of making her understand. I set up straight, grabbed a dishrag off the sink top, and wiped my face with it. It was cold and smelled faintly soured, like old milk.

"After I got the telegram about your daddy, the army sent me a letter telling me what happened as best they knew and that Gaines was buried

in Italy. It was winter and so cold I couldn't take you out, so I was—"
I started to say *trapped,* but I caught myself. "I was stuck inside with
you. Madge was staying the nights with us, and then she got sick. She
didn't want to give it to you, so I was left alone with you. And I started
imagining things—like if I laid you down, you'd die, so I was afraid to
go to sleep. Then I got another letter. This one was from a soldier that
was a friend of Gaines and had been with him when he died. He said
he was sorry—that your daddy was a fine man and soldier, and that he
promised Gaines he'd write to me and tell me that his last words were
how much he loved us."

The tears were running down my face. I wiped them away and
continued. "He also sent me a letter your daddy had wrote but never
got to mail. And when I read that letter, it was like Gaines died all over
again."

I looked up, and Sassy was standing in the window with her back
to me. I stood and gripped the table top. "I ended up in the hospital."
I faltered. I couldn't tell my daughter that her mother was in the crazy
hospital. I could say I gave her away, but God in heaven, I couldn't say
I was put in the crazy hospital.

"When I got out, Fancy Howard was such a good friend to me." I
emphasized the word *friend.* "He asked me to go to Pittsburgh with him,
and we had the accident. The hospital they took me to was a Catholic
hospital. I gave you to the nuns who ran the hospital because I wanted
you to have a family who would love you and give you a good life. When
I got out of the hospital, I began to realize what I'd done, so I started
trying to find you. And when I did, I was able to get you back."

Sassy wheeled around with fire blazing in her eyes. "That's it?" Her
voice rose to a shriek. "That's the best you can do?"

"Sassy, please, try to understand. I was sick. I thought you'd be
better off without me."

"So you just gave me away!" She pounded her fists on the table.
"How could you do that?"

Like an echo, someone pounded on the door to our apartment.
We'd been so involved in our argument we hadn't heard anyone coming
up the stairs. Sassy wheeled around and put her hands on her hips. "So!

You got Madge to come and try to smooth this over—just like you always do."

She strode to the door and jerked it open while yelling at me over her shoulder. "Well, you can just forget it."

"Forget what?" Aunt Hat pushed past Sassy and entered the room. "What is all this yelling about?"

I froze and looked at Sassy. She stood stock still, eyes wide. Aunt Hat marched over to the couch and set down, parking her giant pocketbook on the floor in front of her. She pointed at first me and then Sassy. "You two come here and set down."

We obeyed like whipped dogs. I set down on the far end of the couch, away from Aunt Hat, and Sassy set on the edge of the chair that set catty-corner to the couch.

Aunt Hat said, "Now, that's better. Does this yelling have anything to do with Sarah Jane not answering the door this morning?"

I looked at Sassy, who dropped her head. Just having Aunt Hat in the room had taken the starch out of her.

Aunt Hat fixed her gaze on Sassy. "Oh, yes, Sarah Jane. I know you were here. What I want to know is what is so bad that you are hiding in here?"

Sassy raised her face and stared at me. Her voice trembled. "I found out that Mama gave me away when I was a baby."

"Is that so?" Aunt Hat asked.

For a moment, I thought Aunt Hat was going to pretend she didn't know anything about it. Then she said, "Yes, she did."

My heart skipped a beat. I thought, *That's it. It's all over.* Aunt Hat was finally getting the chance to tell Sassy what a miserable excuse for a mother I was. Hell, she'd probably tell her what a miserable excuse for a human being I was too.

Aunt Hat twisted in her seat so she could look Sassy square in the face. "Sarah Jane, you are almost fourteen years old, and even though that's not grown up, it's old enough to know what happened."

"I already know," Sassy said.

"And what *exactly* do you think you know?"

I spoke up. "I told her I had a hard time when she was born and that it got worse when Gaines died. I told her I was in the hospital." I threw a pointed glance at Aunt Hat when I said *hospital*. "I told her that Madge tried to help me, but I got worse. I told her that I was going to Pittsburgh with Fancy Howard when the accident happened. I stayed in a Catholic hospital in Pennsylvania for a month, and that's when I gave her to the nuns."

Silence filled the room. Aunt Hat had her eyes fixed on Sassy. She waited to give her a chance to respond. "Now, let me tell you some things that happened that you don't know."

I started to get up, but Aunt Hat held her hand out like she'd grab me if I tried to escape. "Sit still, Sylvia. I want you to hear what I have to say."

I closed my eyes and braced myself.

Aunt Hat said, "Sarah Jane, when you were born, your mama was only eighteen years old. The world was at war, and her husband was in the middle of it. If anyone is to blame for what happened, it is me."

My eyes flew open, and I jerked my head in Aunt Hat's direction. "When you were born," she continued, "I came to stay with Sylvia. I was here when your father got leave from the Army and came home for the last time. I saw with my own eyes what it did to your mother when he left for overseas. I planned to stay with her as long as she needed me, because I know what the winters can be like in Coal Valley, and even though I never had a child of my own, I've helped raise plenty - and I know what a woman who has the birthing blues looks like. I also know what can happen when a new mother has no one to help her get over the melancholia."

I stared at Aunt Hat in total bewilderment. I glanced at Sassy and saw that her face had softened and that she was listening.

Aunt Hat continued, "Then my brother died back in Seattle. For many years, I'd lived with him, and before the war, we started a dry goods store. My mistake was in leaving Sylvia to go bury Danny Ray. He was beyond my help, and she was in need of it. But I cared more for that store than I did my own flesh and blood." She paused and shifted in her seat so she could look at me. I felt tears well up in my eyes. She said, "The Lord knows I will answer for that someday. When I tried to get back here, the weather and the war made it impossible. By the time I could get here, Sylvia had left for Pittsburg, so I stayed in Seattle."

I had never in my life seen Aunt Hat cry. If you'd asked me, I would've sworn she was incapable of such an emotion, but her eyes filled with tears. She said, "Sylvia was so bad off that yes, she did allow the nuns to find a home for you."

For the first time, Sassy looked at me. A tear escaped and trickled down her cheek. Aunt Hat shifted again in her seat and looked at Sassy. "Sylvia was not in her right mind when she did that. She was suffering from severe melancholia. She'd seen doctors and been in the hospital, but they weren't able to help her. One of the problems was the doctors were men, and men can't understand what a woman goes through when she has a baby. And you can't either, Sarah Jane."

Aunt Hat locked eyes with Sassy until Sassy dropped her head. Love for Aunt Hat bloomed in my heart like a wildflower. I had never noticed before how much she looked like my mama. She continued, "When Sylvia left the hospital and come to me in Seattle, she started to come back to herself. She told me what she'd done, and I went with her to the hospital where she had given you to the nuns. Your mother told them she wanted her baby back, and after many days of talking and searching, she discovered they gave you to Francis Howard's mother. And to make a long story short, we went to Pittsburgh to the Howards, and Sylvia got you back."

Aunt Hat sighed and leaned back against the couch like she was exhausted. Sassy looked down at her hands, and I sat still, listening to my heart pound in my chest. Aunt Hat heaved herself off the couch and picked up her pocketbook. She looked first at me and then at Sassy. "Sarah Jane, your mother loves you, and since the day she got you back, she's tried to do right by you. Lord knows I haven't agreed with everything she's done, but I know she's tried to make up for what happened. The rest is up to you now. I've said all I'm going to say on the subject."

And with that, she walked out the door and left us alone.

"Live all you can; it's a mistake not to. It doesn't so much matter what you do in particular, so long as you have your life. If you haven't had that what *have* you had?" Henry James, *The Ambassadors*

1960
Sylvia

I opened the closet door and hung my wedding dress next to the dress I worn to Sassy's graduation only a month before. The silk swished like a whisper on the wind. On the floor under my dress set a pair of matching high heels. I slipped them on and walked around, admiring my new house—no, my new home. Everything was in place. I brought the last of my things over from the apartment that morning. My mama's old log cabin quilt looked right at home on our bed. I ran my hand across its softness. *Mama, I wish you and daddy were here.*

I went over to the hi-fi Frank bought me for a wedding present and turned it on. Johnny Cash's voice filled the room. When the song got to my favorite part, I sang along. "I love you because my heart is lighter/ Every time I'm walking by your side/I love you because the future's brighter/The door to happiness you've opened wide."

"Sylvia, would you do me the honor of being the sheriff's wife?"

That's how Frank Compton proposed to me. I'd been a widow for twenty years, and I thought my chance for happiness died with Gaines, but Sassy taught me that I was not the worst person in the world. She taught me that a mistake—no matter how big—can only ruin your life if you let it. So I looked into Frank's eyes and said, "Only if I get a badge."

I enjoyed the tap of my high heels on the new hardwood floors as I walked to the front room window and looked out at my yard. A silver maple waved its icy fingers in the breeze. Frank had laughed at me when

I asked for a white picket fence, but there it was—a backdrop for the flowers I brought from the old home place. They took right off, too, next to the rosebushes Frank was so proud of. Who would of thought that I'd marry a sheriff—hell, who would of thought I'd marry a man who loved roses!

I had a blessed few minutes to myself before Sassy got back from the bus station with Aunt Hat. Aunt Hat was coming in on the noon bus, and she and Madge were throwing me a "surprise" bridal shower that night at the diner. The wedding was set for Friday afternoon at the Methodist church. Frank was taking me to Nashville for our honeymoon. I was finally going to see Hank Snow at the Grand Ole Opry.

When we get back, it will be time to get Sassy off to the University of Virginia—the first person in the family ever to go to college. We are all proud of her, and I know her daddy would be too. It's just like he said the last time he held her, "She's a smart one, Sylvia. You just wait and see."

Made in the USA
Columbia, SC
16 November 2020

24719993R00205